JOHN LE…

CHUM OF

SERVED T… 15 DO

IN 1964 IN ADEN AND BOTH HAD A FEW BATTLES WITH OR AGAINST THE ARABS IN AND AMONST THE RADFAN.

PATTIE (MY WIFE) BOUGHT THIS BOOK FOR MY 80th BIRTHDAY PRESSY X. THANK'S PATTIE.

John W Lees was born in Farnworth, Lancashire, England, on the 23rd of September 1938, the son of Joe and Amelia Lees. He attended the Plodder Lane Primary School. At the age of 11, he moved over to Harper Green Secondary Modern School. Though not a brilliant scholar, he constantly improved until at 15, he secured an Apprenticeship in Sheet Metal Work, a trade that his father and his grandfather had made their occupation and living from. John wanted to join the Royal Marines at the tender age of 18; however, his father, Joe, persuaded him to complete his apprenticeship, first to gain the much-prized City & Guilds of London Diploma and with it, the Tradesman's status. John did exactly as his father had requested. (Later on in life, he would value this advice.)

At the age of 21, he carried out his boyhood dream and joined the Royal Marines in 1960. Tough training would be encountered during his 11-month basic training, but John took to it like a duck to water. He would journey halfway around the world, serving in places such as East Africa, Muscat, Aden, Yemen, Karachi, Kuwait, Bahrain, Southeast Asia, Malaya, Singapore, Hong Kong, Perth, Normandy, Norway, Narvik and Budo. He was in 42 Commando RM to stop a war between Iraq and Kuwait during 1961-62. He travelled up the spine of Malaya ending at Grik on the Thai border in pursuit of the remaining communist terrorists. He was in 45 Cdo RM during the dissident uprising in Aden Protectorate during 1964-65, mainly in the Radfan Mountains near the Yemen Border.

John was married in 1963 in a whirlwind romance to Phyllis Wigston, formerly from Belfast, Northern Ireland. They have now been married for 55 years and have six children. John, Phyllis and family migrated to Australia in 1979. Having the qualifications as a tradesman, he quickly found work at de-Havilland constructing All Aluminum Coastal vessels for the Burmese Navy. Unfortunately in 2011, they lost Rachael to cancer, it was a great shock to Phyllis, who loved her so much. She also loves each and every one of her children. John has tried to tell his story in this book in an adventurous spirit and with love and passion.

"We'll see you on the Beaches."

Dedicated to the Royal Marines who died in the Indonesian Confrontation, 1962–1966.

Chappell	R.	RM15686	Cpl. 42 Cdo RM	L. Company	20 February 1964
Clark	I.C.Lt		42 Cdo RM	L. Company	16 March 1966
Collins	T.J.		42 Cdo RM	L. Company	16 March 1966
Davidson	P.F.	RM17455	Sgt. 42 Cdo RM	L. Company	11 February 1965
Dannells	P.J.G.	RM19528	Cpl. 40 Cdo RM	B. Company	4 November 1965
Deering	M.A.	RM20642	Mne. 40 Cdo RM	A. Company	30 October 1964
Formoy	R.D.	RM16883	Mne. 40 Cdo RM	L. Company	12 December 1962
Foster	C.W.	RM10369	Sgt. 42 Cdo RM		13 March 1966
Gillingham	G.J.	RM20270	Mne. 42 Cdo RM	L. Company	24 December 1962
Hind	J.T.O.	RM20875	Cpl. 40 Cdo RM	K. Company	13 April 1964
Jennings	R.	RM19233	Mne. 42 Cdo RM	L. Company	12 December 1962
Kierans	G.	RM16941	Mne. 42 Cdo RM	L. Company	12 December 1962
McFarlane	W.G.	CH4743	Sgt. 42 Cdo RM	L. Company	12 December 1962
Marriott	M.	RM17999	Cpl. 40 Cdo RM	B. Company	1 January 1964
McRea	E.	RM17368	Mne. 42 Cdo RM	K. Company	13 April 1964
Powel	F.S.	RM21017	Mne. 42 Cdo RM	L. Company	12 December 1962
Rolld	G.Lt.		42 Cdo RM	L. Company	1 August 1963

Later, some Marines who died of their injuries were buried at Kranji Military Cemetery in Singapore.

Tom lies buried in the Roman Catholic Church at Crownhill in Plymouth, Devon, England…
R.I.P. TOM…

From RM19461 Mne. John W Lees.

– RM16201 SGT JIM PAUL –

CALIBRÈ 2

by

John W Lees

AUSTIN MACAULEY PUBLISHERS™
LONDON • CAMBRIDGE • NEW YORK • SHARJAH

A CIP catalogue record for this title is available from the British Library.

ISBN 9781528910729 (Paperback)
ISBN 9781528910736 (Hardback)
ISBN 9781528910743 (Kindle e-book)
ISBN 9781528959636 (ePub e-book)

www.austinmacauley.com

First Published (2019)
Austin Macauley Publishers Ltd
25 Canada Square
Canary Wharf
London
E14 5LQ

Acknowledgements

RM.12623. Corps Bugle/Major. John M. Satchwell. RM
RM.19457. Lieutenant. Jack French. RM.
Sgt/Major. Gordon Norton. 'B' Coy. 40 Commando RM.
National Museum Royal Navy Portsmouth. For photographs.
RM.18026. Gil Warden. Corporal. RM.
P.O.19773L. Cpl Pete Pearson RM
Lorraine Tiller (Curators Dept) N.M.R.N. Portsmouth.
Robert Shergold. One of my sons.
Alison Firth NMRN. Portsmouth.
Tiarne (Vandine). Driscoll. Financial adviser.
Tamsin Stares RMA. HQ. Org. Portsmouth.
Special mention to all RM. Assn Secretaries. Thank you!

In Memorium

Marine Dave Young, sadly missed. 42. 43 Cdo's RM. R.I.P
L/Cpl. Tom Magee. HW 3. 42. 43. 45. 40. Cdo's RM. R.I.P
L/Cpl. Johnny Colclough. 43. 42 Cdo's RM. R.I.P
Marine. RM18965. Eugene Bryson 42. 41. 45. Cdo's RM. R.I.P
Marine Dave Addison. HW3. 45. 43 Cdo's RM. R.I.P

We all meet interesting people in our lives and this story encompasses some of the young boys I have come into contact within the Royal Marines.

For instance: On joining the Royal Marine Corps in 1960, we were given a pamphlet entitled *Men of Pride*. In it was a certain paragraph which has stayed in my mind ever since:

"On joining the Corps, you will meet boys and young men from all parts of the United Kingdom, even some from abroad. You will not make friends with them all, but the ones you do make friends with will be your friends to the end of your days."

It is a large family unit that encompasses time and the world. Now scattered like hayseeds in far-off countries.

Chapter 1
Plymouth Division

High above Plymouth sound, the entrance to Plymouth's Naval Dockyard, are the castellated battlements of the Royal Marines Stonehouse Barracks, one time, a prison for French prisoners of war, whose handwriting can still be seen in some of the bowels of this forbidding place.

Tom stared out to sea, which was shrouded in mist, the Eddystone Lighthouse blinked its warning eye and belched out its ominous sound to mariners foolish enough or unfortunate to be out at sea in these treacherous conditions.

Tom had been on duty for almost forty hours watch-keeping, two on four off, every minute the rain had not eased; his black foul weather gear glistened with wetness and the spray as he strode amongst the cannons, which had guarded Plymouth well in the days of sail.

As far as the records of the Royal Marines could attest, there had always been a member of the Martial family in the Corps, a remarkable achievement. Tom was no exception, a first-class marine in every sense of the word, professional and dependable.

Tom stood a little over 6 feet tall, broad and muscular without an inch of fat, as though it had all been burned off his body by the succession of the rigorous demands of the Marine Corps. A handsome man with a square jaw, a straight nose which flared slightly at the nostrils, a deep cleft in the chin, blue eyes and a steady gaze. His hair was dark brown and all swept back, just the hint of a natural parting on the left side. His hands and wrists, heavy, large. Not many men tangled with Tom, he had an aura of both fear and respect around him. He was attractive of limb, form and face. Women of all ages found him a compelling man.

In the support of a commando unit, Tom was a 'heavy'. The greater the calibre, the better he liked it. More power to his arm, he said…

The little A40 transmitter crackled into life, "How do you read me. This is zero two for zero one, over!"

Tom picked up the tiny mouthpiece and responded in the *affirmative* to his *oppo* on the other side of the castle, "Zero one for zero two, receiving you loud and clear, over!" Tom spaced out his words evenly.

"Zero two. I am on top of the boatshed; bandits are approaching my position from seaward in Gemini's. Inform guard commander and turn out the guard RV at my position immediately. Use caution on approach… Out!"

Tom quickly radioed the guardroom explaining the situation to the guard commander.

Leaving the A40 and his black foul weather gear behind, Tom stole into the darkness his camouflaged denizen smock making him almost invisible. Like a cat, Tom found his old friend Johnny Lees who had been following the progress of the incursionists.

"Looks like they're IRA," Johnny whispered. Tom nodded gravely.

"Then we're in for a rough one," Tom responded, gravel-throated.

After sizing up the situation, Tom retorted quietly, "I'm going higher up onto the ramparts to your right. That's where they'll finish their climb."

Johnny nodded in agreement.

"They're probably heading for the armoury and ammo store," Johnny whispered.

Silently, Tom made his way along the outer wall to begin his climb to the higher ramparts. He lost no time and effortlessly gained the vantage point he sought.

One false move would have meant certain death on the rocks and the waves below.

Far below, he could see the rubber assault craft and a dark figure of a man at the stern but as for the hooded invaders, nothing! Tom glanced around in all directions, even upwards; as he did so, he just caught sight of three blimps rising pretty rapidly into the cloud mass.

At the same time, a muffled eruption below on his side of the wall in the vicinity of the armoury and another in quick succession was heard. Tom launched himself to the roof below.

He hit with both feet; para-rolled over the edge of the building and dropped onto one of the hooded 'bandits', killing him instantly.

Smoke and fumes were engulfing the area after the demolition charges had blown the locks off the armoury and the ammo store. The air was alive to the crack and thump and whine of the bullets as they passed close by to Tom and ricocheted off the stone walls. Tom saw a black shape of a man behind the blaze of a sub machine gun.

The hooded shape pitched forward as if hit by an express train, still firing, his bullets arching into the air, until he hit the ground, and lay very still.

Johnny Lees raised his pick helve in mock salute to Tom and flashed a toothy smile. Tom let out a sigh of relief and picked up the first dead man's weapon.

Overhead, three rolling explosions rent the air, showering down chunks of metal fragments like hailstones.

"What's the drill, Tom?"

"We'll keep up a steady fire at them," growled Tom.

Quickly they went about their task.

"Grab the other dead guy's gun," Tom urged.

They used the dead men's bodies as protection and lay down to wait for the suspected IRA bandits to make their move.

"The guard commander can't be long now!" Johnny muttered.

Tom nodded in agreement.

Seconds ticked away, the rain was still sheeting down as Tom and Johnny faced the big doors of the armoury/ammo store.

A screech of brakes and the smell of burnt rubber tyres told them both that the guard had finally got to their position.

Whispered passwords and the sergeant of the guard had crawled his way to Tom's side.

"What's going on, Martial?"

Tom opened his mouth to tell him and was engulfed in a ball of fire and debris as another explosion blew outwards. The bandits inside burst through the smoke and haze in a star-shell attempt to get away in all directions, it nearly succeeded but for Tom yelling out "Fire!".

The marine guards fired over the heads of Tom and his party and literally slammed the IRA bandits against the walls with the force of their firepower.

It was all over. Tom lay there exhausted, the sound of fire trucks and ambulances filling the air as the mop up operation began. Tom looked down and was beginning to talk to the young sergeant of the guard and trailed off knowing that he was looking death in the face.

Tom woke up to the sound of reveille and the twittering of the birds in the trees outside of his open window.

"Martial!"

"Oh no," groaned Tom.

The sergeant major was mounting the stairs with the heavy tread of his authority.

Tom swung his leaden legs over towards the floor as the sergeant major wrenched the door open.

"Ah, there you are, Martial!"

"You are to report to the CO at precisely 0730 hrs. Do you understand?"

"Yes, Sergeant Major!" Tom answered blankly.

"Give Lees a shake and tell him he's on CO's too! Incidentally, you put on a good show last night. Well done, lad!"

Half a smile and a wink of his blue/green eyes, the sergeant major retreated noisily. Tom had a grudging respect for old 'Danny Boy', he was of the old school from World War II. Would be due for pension soon, Tom mused.

The RSM eyed them up as Tom and Johnny entered the orderly room. They stood stiffly to attention in front of the RSM's desk.

The dress of the day being battle dress, black belt, puttees, SV boots and Green Beret.

"Sir, Marine Martial and Marine Lees reporting for duty as ordered, sir!" Tom said his face a mask of strength and innocence.

"That tie, Martial, is not regulation. You've been bleaching it, haven't you, eh?" The RSM's face inches away from Tom's.

"Begging your pardon, sir, but it's the same colour as yours, sir," Tom replied.

"Be quiet! Did I give you permission to speak?"

"No, sir," both Marines spoke at once in unison.

The RSM glanced at them both, nodding his head in mock disbelief.

"Turn to the right in single file. Right, turnah!" The RSM preceded them into the CO's office.

Standing near the door (in a quieter voice now).

"Quick, march. Halt. Salute! Marines Martial and Lees reporting, sir."

"Sit down, Martial. Lees, you sit there."

The CO sat facing them in the office.

"The reason I've asked you here this morning is to shed some light on the events of last night. Now, tell me, in your own time, what did happen last night?"

Both marines told their story of events and the de-brief lasted well into the day.

"Well, I think that about wraps it up. Have you any questions?" the CO asked both marines.

“Yes, sir, I’ve got one! The three blimps I saw, what were they?”

“As far as we can make out, they used those to scale the walls very quickly. They hung to them as far as the ramparts releasing them on arrival. Quite ingenious, really. They then had some kind of altimeter which, when it reached a certain height, detonated to cause a diversion and damage, of course. The balloons were filled with helium gas.”

Chapter 2
The Longroom

"Marine Martial!"

"Yes, Sergeant Major," Tom replied gruffly.

"Step into my office, will you!"

QMS Danny sat back in his chair rifling through a mound of papers on his desk occasionally looking up at Tom.

A half smile playing around his eyes.

"We're finally getting rid of you, Martial. You've been drafted!"

"Is that right, Sergeant Major? Where to?"

"We're sending you to the farthest place possible, my lad. You're going to Borneo! See if you can play around with some of those head hunter women!" he said with a chuckle and his lips cheesed down. "Now, get out of my office and report back here at 0730 hrs tomorrow, when I'll give you your orders."

Apart from the London Bar down Union Street, the nearest pub was the Admiral Nelson, most of the marines called in on a regular basis.

"You look a bit sick Tom, what's up?" It was Jimmy Young.

Tom had known him for about 8 years; Jimmy used to be in his detachment, but had opted for the heavy weapons store man.

"You'll have to find a new DC. I've been drafted!"

"Do you want another wet?" Pete asked.

"Yeah, why not. I'll have a bitter!"

Tom's eyes travelled along the bar past Pete taking in all the sea of faces which over the months had etched themselves into his mind. There was an eye and half a face, black lustrous hair. A familiar gesture with her hand. The eyes, a beautiful emerald green.

Tom remembered her, through the mists of time, came a picture of her when he had been in training near Exmouth.

The squad had gone ashore that night to sample the local brew and see the bright lights.

In Tom's heart, that night was hard to forget.

The squad had wandered into a local village hall, where a barn dance was in progress.

Scrumpy cider and home brew beer was served in a makeshift bar at the far corner of the hall. Tom and the rest of the squad headed, descending on it like locusts.

Looking around, Tom spotted a young girl in a yellow dress. Tom caught her gaze and held it.

The villagers were glad the marines had dropped in, for things were beginning to liven up.

The marines in their dress, blues of navy, white and gold contrasted with the homespun yarns of the Devonshire dales.

Tom and the boys danced, fooling around, laughing and joking with the high spiritedness of youth.

Tom mused. He didn't know whether he was drunk or just happy from the atmosphere that pervaded the tiny hall.

At any rate, it was a nice satisfying feeling they all had.

Tom and Linda had been drawn together as only the creator had intended and as they walked slowly along the pathway which led to one of Devon's most beautiful beaches, Tom slid his arm around Linda's slender waist.

Linda took her shoes off and walked barefoot in the sand.

The sound of the surf hitting the shore, the moon shedding its pale glow. The balmy night air engulfed them; Tom took her in his arms, slowly and deliberately kissed her long and passionately, her unzipped dress floated to the ground along with the rest of her finery.

Tom undressed quickly and together they ran along the wet sand and plunged into the cool waters of the sea.

A huge wave carried them back towards the beach so they body-surfed until the wave receded and lost its power and they were left high on the sandy shore. Slowly, Tom made love to her, gasping and out of control, making love with the pent-up passion of youth. For Linda it was the first time, not so for Tom, he had been making love to women since his first erection and had mastered the art of seduction. Clinging together naked, gasping, as wave after wave of ecstasy swept over them in a cascading fountain of pleasure.

"Here's your beer, Tom!" yelled Pete, slamming it down in front of him, startling him out of his reverie.

"Jesus Christ, you scared the shit out of me," Tom responded.

"Do you know that 'party' at the end of the bar?" Jimmy whispered, "You've been staring at her long enough!"

"I knew her once a long time ago," Tom replied.

"Hey! Look up. She's coming over here," said Pete.

"Hello, Tom," her sensuous voice captivated the marines in the bar. "I haven't seen you for a long time. How have you been?"

"You look fine, Linda. Sit down," Tom said a little huskily.

"Pete, bring another bar stool."

"Sure, Tom."

There was no doubt about it. Linda was a beautiful woman.

The six years taking nothing away from her, but adding more allure and sophistication in the way she walked and talked.

"What brings you to Plymouth then?" Tom asked, as he gently guided her onto the barstool.

"It's a long story, Tom, but I'm here to take over my uncle's antique business. He died recently and left me the shop—bless him. What about you?" Linda asked. "I want to know all about you." She gently touched his face brushing a lock of hair off his forehead.

"You're looking a little bit older, but it suits you—more mature and so handsome!" Linda purred on. She gazed around beaming at Jimmy and Pete, who were absolutely wrapped in her and just seemed lost for words.

Tom gestured to Pete for a round of drinks.

"What're you having to drink, Linda?" stammered Pete.

"She'll have a brandy and ginger," Tom interjected.

"You remembered then, Tom," Tom nodded, half smiling at her.

Jimmy had picked up his guitar and was quietly picking out a few chords and caressing a tune out to her. He sang the ballad with that certain feeling of warmth and tenderness that only comes with men that share trials and tribulation with the possibility of death together.

Everyone in the pub joined in the singing, some good, some bad and some just plain forgot they couldn't sing, but sang anyway.

Linda and Tom gazed at each other, the firelight flickering across her face made her aglow, desirable, soft and warm. They were happy together in that moment of time.

A precious intangible link between a man and a woman. The desire for her was overpoweringly strong. They laughed and told stories, sang and drank, and the night was good and full of good cheer.

Jimmy knew that Tom and Linda would leave soon, so as a parting song, he sang *'The Forty Shades of Green'*.

They left quietly with the songs and the music filling their ears. Linda linked her arm in his and snuggled into his shoulder. They didn't talk much, just drank in the night air and walked until they came onto the 'Hoe'.

It was a lovely summer's night. The moonlight shimmered over the water in Plymouth sound.

They found a seat carved out of the white Plymouth Rock.

Tom's arm went around her and she snuggled gently into his chest. She began to speak and quietly unfolded the years since he had seen her last.

She had waited and hoped and prayed that he would walk back into her life, but after a year had gone by she had given up hope of ever seeing him again.

She had met and married a young lieutenant in the marines. His name was Christopher Davenport. They had made a good life together; he had taken her to the West Indies where he had served as an aide-de-camp in the British Embassy. They had been very happy together, but Christopher had yearned to taste some real action and had volunteered for chopper training. Chris had done well on the helicopter course and had come out with a very high score. The draft board had then posted him to 40 Commando RM. Far East Command.

40 Commando was engaged in operations against the Indonesians in Brunei, Sarawak and North Borneo.

He'd written almost daily to her and seemed in good spirits. Then suddenly his letters had stopped.

The admiralty had informed her that Lieutenant Davenport was 'Missing in Action!' [MIA]

She had gone frantic with worry, writing, making phone calls to various heads of departments, MPs, anyone who would listen. Her own father had worked tirelessly, finally getting a search party authorized, which returned empty handed.

Lieutenant Davenport and his special forces team had just simply 'disappeared'. The jungle had opened up and swallowed them whole.

All the time Linda refused to believe that he was dead.

After she poured out her heart to Tom, she said, "Tom, will you help me to find him, when you go out there? You're the only one who can help me now!"

"I will do all I can, if it will make you happy," Tom said consolingly.

He felt a little awkward not knowing what words to use.

She relaxed then, all of the tension and frustration of the past few months melted off her.

Tom lit a cigarette and handed it to her.

"It's been a lovely evening, Tom." She cupped his face and kissed him gently. Then she was on her feet, pulling Tom after her and embraced him firmly.

"Let's walk down to the 'Barbican' and pick up my car. Do you fancy a nice thick steak?" Linda inquired.

Her mood had changed again, possibly for Tom's benefit, not wanting to spoil the magic of the night for him.

Young couples drifted past, oblivious of everyone except themselves. A few 'jolly jacks' were staggering around hurling good-natured abuse at everyone after a boozy night on the town.

"Here we are. Do you want to drive?" Linda asked, throwing him the keys.

It was a gold Triumph Stag. Tom eyed it appraisingly.

"Where are we going?" Tom growled.

"We'll go to the chapel," Linda chortled.

"The where?" Tom asked incredulously. "You've got to be joking!"

She laughed tossing her black hair back, her eyes twinkling in the moonlight.

"I'll tell you where to go; just drive!" she urged.

"Head out towards Devonport through Union Street onto Cumberland Road, then we need Chapel Street. I'll tell you when to turn, okay."

It was indeed a chapel from all outward appearances, but the sounds were hardly reverent, more congregational perhaps.

The interior was plainly furnished with an L-shaped bar along the far side near the altar. The pulpit still clinging to the wall. High beams and open space overhead lit by a series of giant wagon wheels suspended from the exposed beams along the rims of the wheels, lights were fixed in abundance. What struck Tom was the highly polished finish of the wood, a deep red lustrous colour.

Red and white checked centre cloths and small table lamps giving a cosy intimate feel to the place.

Tom and Linda headed over to the bar. "What would you like to drink, Tom?" Linda asked.

"Well, seeing as I'm in the marines…" Tom winked.

"Okay," she chuckled, "one large rum, coming up."

"George! Could we have some service down here?" Linda shouted.

The bartender's eyes lit up when he saw Linda. "Way hi, Linda, me darlin! You've nae bin ta see me, lass. Where've ya been?"

"I want you to meet someone, George. This is Tom Martial, a very dear friend of mine, and he's in the Royal Marines."

George eyed him with caution. "Well, I can see I'll have ta watch ma tung. I'm reet pleased ta meet ya, Tom," he said in his thick Geordie accent, offering his hand in friendship.

Tom's large hand closed on George's in a firm grip.

"Good to meet you too, George." Tom's blue eyes gazed at him steadily. A slight tremor ran through George and he decided there and then that Tom was not a man to trifle with.

"What's ya pleasure, Linda? What'll ya have, eh?"

"We'd like to try a couple of those delicious steak suppers, George, like you made for me before." Linda winked at him. "And we'll have brandy and a very large rum for Tom whilst we're waiting. Okay, George? Include a bottle of your best wine with the steaks!"

"Aye, leave it ta me. I'll prepare it myself."

Tom and Linda sat down in a cosy corner near the bar and just talked.

"Do you know the story of how this place got its name and became a pub?" Linda asked.

Tom shook his head.

"There was a rich family who once owned most of this part of town, including this chapel. The father grew old and died. To each of his children, he left something he thought would benefit them. One of his sons was an out-and-out drunk—a waster. So the old man, in his wisdom, left him this chapel, thinking that he would mend his ways and have some use one day of spiritual blessings. After inheriting the chapel, the son, after some very soul-searching thought, turned it into a pub which gave him a handsome income, and, of course, he could do what was closest to his heart and carry on drinking in comfort."

"Sounds like a pretty switched-on character to me," Tom grinned.

"Ah, here's the steaks."

"George, you're beautiful," she said as she lightly kissed him softly on thc cheek.

"You're a canny lass," George said appreciatively.

Tom drove back to Linda's apartment, after the best steak he had tasted in years. She cradled her head on his arm as they drove. "You will stay with me tonight, won't you, Tom?"

"Isn't there a saying about wild horses or something," Tom said grinning.

Linda's apartment was a bizarre collection of antiques, old and modern, every foot and wall space littered with bric-a-brac, paintings, carvings, bronze busts, most of it old and valuable, silverware, candelabra, vases, clocks, an old marine drum as a coffee table. The bed very feminine and overstuffed.

Linda had left the bedroom door open, she had a weakness for mirrors, for they were hung on every available space which gave a depth of feeling beyond the dimensions of the room. Tom was able to watch Linda undress with comparative ease.

She really was the most well-proportioned and beautiful woman, her black hair cascaded around her ivory shoulders.

The valleys and the undulations of her body glowed in the soft lamplight. Large pink nipples jutted out from her ample breasts with a fierce desire.

Nothing else mattered now, Tom unbuckled his belt slowly and purposely, and advanced towards the bedroom, throwing his shirt off as he went. Linda's lips parted slightly as Tom pulled her towards him in a passionate embrace, his lips crushing into hers.

Linda slid slowly down his body kissing him all the way. She was on her knees now and unzipping his trousers, which fell to the floor to reveal his massive throbbing penis. Tom was well endowed. Linda played with it for a while, gently pulling back the foreskin to reveal the vital head, pink and moist. Linda's eyes shone as she placed her mouth over his manhood and sucked greedily in a frenzy of passion.

Tom stepped out of his trousers and stood over her, he dominated her, he always had, but she didn't care, she had always loved him in her heart and now they were together at last, stealing time.

They made love as if there was no tomorrow, his massive member thrusting into her black forest, making her come, in wave after wave of ecstasy, her fluid cascading over Tom's throbbing organ, then slowly it ran down her long beautiful legs.

The lights were dimmed and they slept soundly in the overstuffed bed occasionally awakening to make love again.

Until, at last, finally satisfied and spent, they slept in each other's arms until the coming of the morn.

Chapter 3
Princeton

After receiving his 'orders' to proceed to 40 Commando Royal Marines in the Far East, with all the necessary documentation, jabs, passport, tickets rail and plane etc.

Tom was given ten days' embarkation leave which were the most fulfilling and enchanting days of his life. Sharing with Linda every hour and moment, breathing into one another life and laughter.

During the day, they were seen sailing in and around the many tiny inlets along the coast. Late afternoon and they were speeding along the country roads towards her cottage at Princetown on the edge of Dartmoor to saddle up the ponies which she kept there. They would have a fast canter through the woods and onto the Torrs.

The views were spectacular from there, and both drank in the beauty of their surroundings.

Tom had often been to Dartmoor, he was no stranger to it; this was where the Royal Marines were trained. Spent endless days and nights traversing its treacherous bogs and frozen streams. During the winters with its snow and sleet and biting winds, swirling the snow into your eyes so that you thought you might never see again.

Yet now, as he looked at the same landscape, it was as if he was seeing it for the first time.

Dartmoor! The very name sending shivers into the hearts of all that hear it and the legends surrounding this mist-shrouded place.

Tom knew of all this folklore but was not afraid, this raw beauty he understood, and this was his heritage, his England.

They dismounted and lingered for a while staring over the landscape, no need for words here.

Linda laughing, bounded into the saddle, "I'll beat you to the cottage."

Tom half-smiling cantered after her.

Linda prided herself on her culinary and cooking skills and with delight she would concoct the most delicious meals Tom had ever tasted.

The evenings were spent by the fireside or down at the local pub, a one-time place of ill repute, known as 'The Jamaica Inn'.

Travellers knew no ill until they spent a night at The Jamaica Inn, robbery, violence and murder were the fate of unsuspecting gentry.

But now in the 1960s, the pub was alive with life and gaiety.

Everyone knew Linda; she spent lots of time just talking to the old timers, old men her uncle before her had known.

Always there was the warmth of the log fires at night.

Especially at the cottage and it would be in front of this particular fireside that Tom and Linda would make love. It was here that they came to know love and to share love.

"I think I've made you happy, haven't I, Tom?" Linda asked.

Tom looked down at her and read the mixture of emotions in her face.

"Yes, you have, but you've made finding Christopher a hell of a problem," Tom murmured.

Her brow furrowed thoughtfully. "I just know you'll find him for me, no matter what..." she trailed off not wanting to add anything further.

Chapter 4
Jetstream

The roar of the jet engines built up to maximum revs, until like a huge bird it catapulted itself into the air. Almost standing on its tail, it climbed to a height of 30,000 feet, where it levelled out and headed in a south-easterly direction, on the first stage of the journey to Singapore.

"Excuse me, please. May I get you something to drink?"

The stewardess leaned over attentively, cool and crisp in her sarong kebaya. Brown oval eyes stared into Tom's clear blue eyes.

There was a momentary stilling of time, each aware that they desired one another desperately, they could feel it in their necks and throats, so great was their animal attraction.

She moved on to the next passengers, but cast shy glances back at Tom.

Tom knew instinctively that he must have her, but how?

They flew on over France, the great city of Paris far below them, and the River Seine twinkling in the sunshine.

There is a special delight and excitement when you're flying high over the earth, how anyone could be afraid of travelling by air baffled Tom. It was so beautiful.

Her perfume, delicate and exotic, brought Tom back from his musing.

"Very sorry to be so long. Please, excuse me."

She placed a small silver tray before Tom which contained tiny bottles of spirits. A tall lager beer stood on a mat in the centre invitingly.

Brilliant whiteness filled the cabin, Tom took hold of her cool hands and together they gazed out of the portal at the majesty of the Swiss Alps. The captain of the BOAC VC10 was highlighting the many interesting features along this route.

Beautiful cities, high mountain ranges and vast arid deserts slipped by as they flew on and into the greatness of the star-spangled night.

Tom was woken with a cool hand upon his cheek, he couldn't remember but he must have fallen asleep.

"Salamat pagi tuan. That means 'good morning' in my language," she smiled down at him, her face lighting up her exquisite Asian features, truly she was a delicate flower of the east.

A small hot towel was placed in his hands and he gratefully wiped his sleepiness away. A breakfast tray followed and a much-needed cup of coffee. Life was beautiful after all.

She swayed down the aisle attending to the other passengers. Tom's gaze followed her hungrily.

They were now in the South China Seas rapidly approaching Kai-Tek Airport near Hong-Kong. This would be the last stop before Singapore. Tom's chances were diminishing fast.

It was raining heavily outside, lightning flashes lit up the cabin as the aircraft battled its way through to the landing strip down below, bucking and rolling with the turbulence of the monsoon rains.

The other passengers were looking around now, a little uneasily.

The stewardesses moving easily amongst the passengers, calming and reassuring them in a gentle and professional manner.

Tom got up and moved aft, both to stretch his legs and to use the Heads. He revelled in the danger of the moment, his countenance exuded the excitement and the exhilaration he felt, which transmitted itself to the passengers who saw him and gave them added confidence.

Suddenly the plane dropped into an air canyon, the pilot could not see it or avoid it, it was just there. The plane bucked and rolled sending Tom and the lovely Asian stewardess into a cargo hold, which opened and closed as they tumbled in.

Tom was on his feet first and groped around in the dark for the hatchway. His hand brushed against the girl's breasts, he felt a growing desire for her. His lips were upon hers and caressing her neck, he unbuttoned her blouse. Her nipples were erect and her whole body quivered with a desire she had never known. Her sarong was being parted and Tom's large member was searching for her sweetness, she gasped as his large throbbing penis entered her vagina, a searing pain shot through her followed by the most exquisite feeling she had ever had in her life.

She wanted more of it, gasping and clawing at Tom in a fever of excitement and pleasure. For fifteen minutes, he laid it into her, she made Tom ejaculate by a final climax which sent shivers of ecstasy down to their toes.

The plane landed at Kai-Tek Airport in Hong-Kong for a refuelling stop and to change crew. Tom bade farewell to his China girl, with tears in her eyes and heart she said goodbye. She gave him a photograph of herself with a small inscription on the back: "Hope you like it; keep it safe. May it live in part of your heart forever. Shirley 'Dimple' Wong."

The journey to Singapore was completed without mishap and the plane touched down at Pe'er-Lebah Airport.

It was dark but the tropical heat still clung to the island like a wet blanket.

Tom grinned in the darkness; truly he was back in 'Singers'.

The aroma was all around him, unmistakable, a curious mixture of charcoal burners, incense, cooking food and the open sewer system, fondly referred to as 'Sweet water canals'. Even if he were blindfolded, he would have known this part of the globe.

A Royal Marine Sergeant and a driver led Tom to a waiting Land Rover, which lost no time in threading its way through the teeming masses of Singapore Chinese.

Weird sounds of oriental street music, the clashing of symbols, the cries of the traders as they ply their trade.

A city which never seems to sleep.

The Land Rover sped on, blaring its horn angrily, hens, chickens, ducks, dogs, rickshaws, trishaws all scattered from its path. Then before long, they were crossing the Causeway, which joins Malaya to Singapore. Through the customs post, lights flashing ominously and onto the black treacherous roads of Malaya.

It's only seventeen miles from Johore Bahru to Ulu Terim.

A twisting, torturous route, especially at night.

The cambers of the road are formed in the opposite direction to the normal, ending in disaster for the unwary.

Legend has it that British and Australian prisoners of war purposely constructed them that way in order to foul up the Japanese convoys.

Tom lay awake in the tropical night. Perspiration trickling down his body, no effort was required to sweat, it just kept oozing out.

Tom lit a thin cigar musing over the day's events.

Tom's sleep was shattered by the blaring bugle call of reveille. The bastards had piped it in on the PA system.

Tom rose from his sweat-soaked bed and shook himself awake.

A thin mist swirled closely to the ground; beads of water glistened off every blade of grass and shone like tiny diamonds.

The whole camp was deserted except for a very small rear party, it all seemed weird to Tom being used to the hustle and bustle in the Plymouth based Commando.

Tom donned his shorts and running shoes. A run would do him good.

A huge English style breakfast followed ham, egg, kippers, beans, fried bread, sauté kidneys, grilled tomatoes, poached or scrambled eggs. The list was endless.

"Hiya, Tom! Gawd, you're a sight for sore eyes, mate. Just arrived, have we?" a big rawboned chef shouted across the main galley servery.

Tom grinned, as the lanky chef straddled a chair facing Tom and proffered a spade like hand.

"Haven't seen you since '59. Werve ya bin, eh?"

Nutty Edward's London born and bred, witty and profane, a rum rat and bar fly. Dark features and hairy, with a big hooknose, noticeably striking blue grey eyes, his one redeeming feature.

"Big spread for a rear party, Nutty. What's the drill?"

"Atts and Dets, mate. Yanks mainly learnin arr to foight in't friggin jongle, cor blimey. Next door at jongle flamin warfare. I wus glad I dun mi time over in bornayo. Too many crawlez, mate. Vats apart from the ones wif stripes on."

Nutty gave a wheezing laugh at his own joke.

"Edwards, what do you think you're doing? Get over here at once!"

An irate-coloured sergeant had appeared all bluster and fluster.

"Awrite colours keep yar blaady hur on mite," he winked at Tom. "I fink he's lonely."

Nutty turned back as he was about to leave.

"Hear, Tom, wats anuver word for London, mite?"

"Smoke?" queried Tom.

"I don't mauned if hoy do."

Tom produced a slim panatella from his breast pocket. Grinning, he handed it over to nutty.

"Cheers, mate." Nutty headed off to the galley smelling the richness of the tobacco as he went.

"You will be ready to move out at 1800 hrs to board flight number 143 to Kuching. It's an RAF flight so it's going to be a little bumpy. You will report back here at that time, is that clear, Martial?"

"Yes, sir," Tom growled.

"I suggest in the meantime, you keep fit and feel free to use the swimming facilities in the jungle warfare school, next door."

"Yes, sir. Very good, sir."

Tom swam lazily around the pool, his strong powerful strokes propelling him effortlessly.

"Tom, Tom, youeeee."

A young woman in a red spotted bikini was waving wildly at the other end of the pool. She was in the centre of a group of young American servicemen, over from Vietnam no doubt.

"Hello, Tom! Remember me?"

"Of course I do, Cecilia. Who could forget you!"

She beamed at Tom. "Let me introduce you. Boys, this is Tom Martial of the Royal Marines."

"Hi there! Sure am glad to meet you, sir!"

Each one of them shook his hand with genuine respect. Tom felt strangely older somehow.

"Now, if you'll excuse us boys," Cecilia interrupted, "I'd like a word with Tom."

"Right on! We'll see you tomorrow, Cecilia."

Tom and Cecilia lay on banana loungers and talked of home and Plymouth.

Tom glanced at his Rolex. "Is there anywhere around here we can get a drink?"

She nodded her head, "I'll take you to a nice place, you'll enjoy it there," she grinned.

She drove down the twisting Malay roads with the confidence of a good driver knowing exactly what she was doing. Tom stretched back in the seat enjoying the ride.

"Does Ray know you're entertaining the American army?" Tom said with a grin.

"Well, we're both mature adults," she said, winking at him.

She drove the car into an arched carport and cut the engine. A strange quietness engulfed them; large mature trees gave a tranquil atmosphere to the old colonial house.

A young Malay amah girl appeared, resplendent in her sarong kebaya.

"Salamat pagi mem," she bowed to them both.

"Would ma'am and Tuan like a cold drink?"

"Yes please Sitti, make one of your special rum punches and then, please, don't disturb us until I ring for you."

Sitti lowered her eyes submissively.

It was a fine old colonial, cool and shady, wide steps ran up to the second floor, which emerged onto the verandah that encircled the entire house. Here, the breeze could be caught and wafted through the slatted wooden windows.

The verandah was covered with bulnosed corrugated iron.

Exquisite wrought ironwork like filigree lace adorned the outside edges.

A positive oasis from the heat of the tropics.

At the far end of the room, which they had entered was a magnificently carved bar in dark lustrous wood.

With elegant red upholstered bar stools complimenting it.

Sitti entered and delicately placed a silver tray on the opium table near the rattan settee. Crystal glasses surrounded a huge pineapple, which had been scooped out to accommodate a delicious rum punch, the bouquet of which permeated the tropical sultry air.

"Nice place you've got here." Tom glanced around the room idly.

It was a beautiful mixture of colours, Chinese and Malay artefacts adorned the room.

Cecilia came and propped herself at the bar, where Tom was standing. Her breasts poked him provocatively and her eyes shone mischievously.

Tom took hold of the pineapple and quaffed off half of the contents handing it to Cecilia. Holding the pineapple in both hands, she began to drink slowly, she wasn't very successful as the weight of the pineapple was proving too much and the drink was running down her throat and onto her breasts.

Tom slid his arm around her and released her bikini top letting her breasts spill out. Tom bent down and gently fondled and kissed her large protruding nipples, Cecilia kept on drinking at the end of which she was laughing and embracing Tom.

Hungrily, she pressed her lips to his, making little moaning noises. Tom's hands slipped the rest of her bikini off. Tom led her to the large rattan settee, she lay there breathing heavily, her breasts rising and falling, a trickle of rum punch ran between those lovely mounds. Tom bent down and caressed each nipple with his lips.

She had a beautiful body, large firm breasts tapering down to a trim waist, her hips flaring to merge into nice rounded, long legs. Her skin lightly tanned except where her bikini had been leaving ivory white skin in contrast.

Her nipples were huge and protruding. She was a very desirable and beautiful woman.

Tom stood over her, discarding his shorts as he did so, to reveal his throbbing member. Cecilia's eyes widened as she huskily whispered, "Tom it's been such a long time, too long."

She took hold of it with both hands and softly slid her mouth over it sucking gently.

She could stand it no more, she slid his wet member down her body and guided it into her tunnel of love, arching her body to engulf it all. Her breath came in gasps and moans of ecstasy as they violently made love.

Cecilia came many times, each orgasm greater than the last, until gasping and spent Tom ejaculated inside her with a force she had not known before.

They lay there for some time, the fan whirling around like the blades of a helicopter, it reminded Tom of a promise he had made and why he was here.

"Come with me," Tom whispered. He explored and found the bathroom dragging Cecilia in with him.

The shower felt good on them and revived them. Tom gently soaped her down lingering over her ample breasts.

Presently they emerged from the shower dressed in bathrobes and sank heavily into the armchairs; they each cradled a cold beer can to their heads.

It was Cecilia who spoke first, "Tom have you eaten today?"

The meal was absolutely superb, created by Sitti who constantly flitted by with a tastier dish.

Cecilia drove Tom back to the camp in her Riley Kestrel, Tom sank back in the leather bucket seats, smoked a cigar and relaxed, idly chatting as she drove.

They reached the gates of Burma Camp and were halted by the marine guards. Their inquiring attitude soon turned to smiles when they realised who they were.

"Tom, good to see ya, haven't seen you since Lympstone!"

"Knocker White, long time no see, last time I saw you, you were only nine stone wet through, must've been eating your weeties eh?"

Knocker White glanced at Cecilia and winked.

She beamed a smile back at him.

"Raise the gate Jan!" Knocker ordered. He waved them through.

"See you later Tom, we'll have a beer!" shouted Knocker.

Tom waved as they sped up the drive.

After a long lingering kiss, she bade Tom farewell, and with tears in her eyes, she nosed the black Riley down the long driveway to the guard post and the road home.

Tom watched her from the hill as she gunned the heavy motor along the snaking road. A couple of blasts on the horn, a wave and she was gone.

Chapter 5
Borneo

Tom donned his jungle greens, picked up his kit and reported to movements for his flight to Borneo.

The Hastings touched down at a small military airfield just outside of Kuching, Sarawak, Borneo. This was militarily termed, the first division.

An armed convoy awaited the new arrivals near the command centre and after lengthy checks of stores and personnel were finally cleared for the long trek into the interior.

"Now then my lucky lads, I want you to pick up these weapons as you are allocated them, prove them, inspect them and load up your magazines with the ammunition provided. Is that clear!"

"Yes, Sergeant Major!" everyone shouted in chorus, before breaking into a good-natured laugh.

The journey took six hours along rough jungle roads. When a vehicle got bogged down, it had to be towed out by the vehicle in front of it, the marines de-bussing automatically to push it back onto the hard core they were travelling on. Often the road disappeared due to the heavy monsoon rains.

Apart from some sporadic firing by the Mk2 ferret scout cars, the journey passed without major incident.

Borneo is a continent of jungle as far as the eye can see, the green is all around you, every shade of green. The temperature is ninety degrees (F) and the humidity is ninety percent, ideal for plant life but hard for humans.

The inhabitants are 'Ibans', 'Sea Dayaks', 'Chinese', 'Malay' and 'Indian'.

The southern states (Kalimantan) are populated by what are commonly known as the Indonesians led by President Sukarno, and it was to these latter ones that Tom would be fighting. The marines had nicknamed them 'the Chokies'.

The Indonesians calling themselves 'The North Kalimantan National Army' had seized key points in Sabah, Brunei, (British

North Borneo) and Sarawak. The sultan of Brunei had requested British military aid and troops.

The objective of the Indonesians had been the oil-rich northern states and to smash the recently formed 'Malaysia'.

That in a 'nutshell' was what the confrontation was all about.

Hostilities had started in 1962 and would last until 1967 as far as the Royal Marines were concerned.

Mopping up operations would continue but that's another story.

The armed convoy clanked to a halt, tailboards banged down, spewing out their jungle green cargo.

"All right you men line out. Unload, for inspection, port arms!"

The weapons were duly inspected and the order ease springs was given.

"Welcome to G5. I'm QMS Scones. When your name has been called, fall out and report to the QM's store for your G1098 equipment. Answer your names. Marines! Archibald, Bryson, Buchanan, Carter, French, Martial, McEwan, McHenry, Pearson, Sherwin, Slade, Smith A.J, Turnbull, Walker, Warden, Wood, Young…"

"Where's the nearest water hole, Tom, my throat's as dry as a gorilla's armpit."

"I don't know, let's do a recce and find out!"

"We'll have four glasses of beer, down here, right now!" Jack's vibrant voice boomed out, amidst the cackle and clatter of the Naffi Bar. Heads swivelled 'round like the Marines turret on the Quarterdeck.

"That's Jack, there's only one Bootneck with a set of lungs like that! Glad to have you with us Jack!"

The little Chinese barman, shakily gunning the tiger beer into the tall glasses as fast as he could.

Tom and Jack stood side by side, hands resting lightly on the bar.

Now the chanting started, "Down, down, down, down, down."

"Steady, steady go!"

Down, down, down, down, down, neck and neck on the first pint, the second one. The chanting is reaching fever pitch now! Finally Jack throws his glass into the gash bin, which shatters into a thousand pieces… Tom is still downing his. "Jack wins!" chorus half the marines.

"Bullshit!" comes back the reply.

It was a great night. The bawdy songs, sods opera's, Fluffy Farrell on the old piano, the stories more colourful as the amber fluid flowed.

The atmosphere of being amongst the marines in a fighting unit, once more.

"Up and at 'em…you lazy bastards. Hands off cocks and on with socks… Wakey… Wakey… Wakey… rise and shine!"

Light was just filtering through the canopy of trees. The early morning jungle noises heralding the dawn…the tree frogs. The sequoias' and the little tree monkeys, joining in a cacophony of sound.

Tom half-rose and fell out of his camp bed onto the earthen floor, head pounding and groggy he staggered off to the heads for a very necessary morning George.

Amidst the noises and oaths of last night's revellers, one of the marines was trying to light a cigarette but couldn't focus enough to light the end of it.

The sergeant major surveyed the sorry sight before him, a company of marines fully booted and spurred armed to the teeth, ready but not willing, waving around like a field of corn. "I hope you've all had your weeties this morning because we're all going for a little stroll. (There was a low groan from all the assembled ranks) and God help any of you that falls by the wayside. If you can't take it in the morning, you shouldn't take it at night! Martial!"

"Sergeant Major," Tom replied gravelly.

"Take the point; you're lead scout; lead off!"

The march to the company group G3 was a grueller. The climate, the oppressive heat, the flies, the mossies, the leeches, sucked the energy out of the marines. Everything that could bite, suck or feed did so.

Tom hadn't seen such bad bush since that operation in Malaya chasing the CTs to the Thai border at Grik.

This was much worse.

Jack caught up with Tom to relieve him for a spell. "What do you reckon, Tom?" whispered Jack.

"I reckon it's going to be another cunt-of-a-day," Tom grinningly whispered back.

Jack stifled a laugh.

They travelled all that day, keeping to the high ground as much as possible, hacking their way through in the deep clefts and ravines, fording the rivers and streams.

Tom remembered the stories of the Chindits and the death marches of the Burma railway prisoners under the Japanese. He gritted his teeth with a new resolve.

It's not as bad as they had it.

He knew the spirit of them, he felt at one with his British predecessors. His right arm gained a new strength, like a runner gains his second wind. So Tom was shrugging off the tiredness and putting on a new mantle.

He was becoming a fitter, fighting, marine, machine.

A snapping of the fingers brought Tom out of his reverie.

Jack was using the silent jungle signs, O group. OC patrol group. Immediate!

Tom and Jack sped down the track towards Captain Moorelands.

In whispered and hushed tones, Captain Moorelands issued his orders. Compass bearing, map references, likely enemy ambush positions and routes. Final destination.

A sealed map lay on the jungle floor with coded messages written on it. "For reasons of security together with my instructions from the colonel, I have kept these orders sealed. I can now tell you what our mission is. We have been charged with the responsibility of rescuing the British Resident Commissioner together with his wife, family and staff from this former police station, which lies in the centre of this new Indonesian Camp." This lies on the Limchang River. The captain took out the aerial shots of the camp and proffered them around the 'O' Group meeting. Explaining all the details of the rescue plan which the troop commanders and their SNCOs wrote and absorbed with a new determination and grit.

"Any questions?" The captain's suave manner penetrated the group.

"Yes sir, harbour position for tonight?"

"Here at this fork in the river."

"Yes, French."

"Sir, if we're bumped by the Chokies, where's the RV point?"

"Good point. Make it to this point here on the Brunei road where it crosses the Limchang River!"

"Martial."

"Sir."

"You are to get us to this harbour position before 1530 hrs. Is that clear?"

"Yes, sir."

Tom consulted his own map, wrote down the compass bearings and the relevant details and timings, shouldered his pack, hefted his weapon easily and made his way back to the point detail.

Chapter 6
Limchang

The prismatic compass swung lazily around the sea of graticules, finally settling on the designated course.

For a moment, a large blue eye looked through the prism, plotted the direction, surveyed the jungle, raised the machete and started to hack the way to Limchang.

The image of Linda swam before him and he imagined he was with her again in Plymouth. Her dark eyes shimmered like black corals, beckoning, urging, mocking, her provocative lips parting to whisper, Tom, please Tom, find him for me, be my love, be my love, sweet, sweet, love.

Drenched in sweat, Tom shivered. A cold wind had started to blow. Yes, from afar like an express train getting stronger. Tropical rain, huge gusts of wind, driving the rain in torrential downpour. Black now with lightening streaking overhead and a tumultuous roaring and noise.

No need for stealth anymore.

Pretty soon, the ravines would be swollen. Tom signalled and roared back. "Make for the high ground!"

The noise of the monsoon rains lashing down in blinding torrents of water. The marines flanked over to the high ground clawing there way upwards. The wind whipping their voices of command away. Survival gritted their teeth as they clawed their way ever upward.

Tom and Jack reached the top first. Here, it was safe. They ripped their packs from their backs. Seconds were important now. Big Jack, a giant of a man, deftly uncoiled the nylon rope he always carried.

Some of the marines were now in serious trouble, water was up to their chests and mud was sucking them down.

Securing the rope to a large tree, Jack hurled himself back down the slope. The sheer physical strength of the man, bellowing and bullying, lifting men from the sucking mud was a sight to behold.

Captain Mooreland was the last to be rudely grasped by Jack and hauled to safety, gasping and coughing, he dragged himself to the safety zone.

The wind and the rain continued unabated for the rest of the day, the streams now swollen rivers.

The marines spread themselves around the hill like a necklace. Lightning flashes and thunder rolled on into the night.

After a brief respite, a roll call was taken, to satisfy the Captain no one was missing. Fresh orders were given, no movement before first light. A watch would be kept.

Camouflaged mushrooms sprouted on the hill that night, the marines staving off the cold and the rain by stringing out their simple Bashas.

The whisper "stand to" awoke Tom from his fitful night's sleep. Bleary eyes gazed out onto a steamy jungle.

It was a grey greenish morning, not yet light but not dark. The secquiadas (cicadas) tree frogs and the monkeys, as always heralding the dawn.

The marines always stand-to at dawn and at dusk. Waiting for an attack that might never come but if it did, the marines would be waiting and ready.

Stand down!

Mud spattered, rain soaked figures, steaming with their own body heat emerged from their temporary homes. Cramped limbs stretched, glad to be moving.

With practiced ease, they set about the morning's routine. Sentries out. Weapons cleaned and oiled.

Hexamine stoves were lit and a welcome wet of tea brewed.

"Hey up," Jack whispered to Tom, "have a cuppa cha."

Tom grinned and took it gratefully, gulping down the scalding liquid.

"Jack, did you hear the one about the gunfighter?"

Jack shook his head slowly.

"This gunfighter rode into a small Texas town and entered the local saloon bar. A poker game is in progress and a cowboy is smoking a big cigar. Standing at the bar, the gunfighter whips out his pistol and shoots the cigar out of the cowboy's mouth. The cowboy doesn't say anything, just carries on playing poker.

'Say stranger!' the barman, says, 'Could I take a look at your *piece*!'

'Sure,' says the gunfighter, handing over his pearl handled colt.

'Mighty fine looking pistol, mister, mighty fine. You see this foresight here sticking up? File it off, make it nice and smooth. This trigger guard here? Cut it off and make it real smooth.'

'Now why should I do that?' drawled the gunfighter.

'You see, the guy you shot the cigar out of his mouth?'

The gunfighter nodded.

'Well, thet's Pecos Pete, and when he gets through playing his game of poker, he's going to *shove thet pistol right up your arse!*'"

Jack was curled up laughing quietly, tears rolling down his cheeks.

Still laughing to himself, Jack returned to his position and quickly stowed his gear.

"Saddle up," was the whispered command. "We're moving out."

Captain Moorelands stretched out his arm in the axis of advance, Tom quickly took up his position as lead scout.

Checking his compass regularly to keep on course to G.3.

Tom kept to the high ground as much as possible, here the jungle was less dense. The streams were now swollen and wide, ropes were used to cross over.

A gruelling pace was kept and the miles were swallowed up.

The jungle seemed to be thinning slightly and presently Tom came upon a faint track leading in the general direction that they were going.

Tom sent word back to take extra caution. Silently, they padded along the faint trail. Tom's keen eyes missing nothing, likely ambushes, booby traps and pits. Anything that was not part of the jungle was perused and evaluated and then passed over.

Tom froze, fist clenched in the air (the sign for enemy front, halt!). The sign was relayed down the length of the patrol. Automatically, the marines melted into the jungle into defensive positions.

Jack slithered over to Tom in crocodile fashion. "What's up Tom?"

"Something's wrong," whispered Tom. "I can feel it."

Jack surveyed the area with a practised eye. "The base of that large rain forest tree, they've probably dug into it, using it for an OP."

"Nip back to the captain and report what we've found, Jack. I'll scout around here."

Jack gave the thumbs up and departed.

The captain surveyed his maps upon receipt of the information and decided he couldn't go around it. That the OP would have to be silenced.

"The keyword is 'stealth', French, do you understand?"

"Yes sir, leave it to me sir. I used to be a poacher back home. With your permission, I'll borrow your handgun and silencer."

"By all means, French, good luck!"

Tom had done a recce of the area and was observing the enemy OP through his binoculars when Jack slid alongside him.

In whispered tones Tom outlined the plan of action, the position of the trip wires and the booby-trapped areas.

During the OC's brief, Jack had stripped, cleaned and oiled the handgun taking no chances as to whether it would work or not.

Total surprise was the keynote here. Jack would have to use all of his field craft skills, if he was to succeed in silencing this forward OP.

Jack stripped off all unnecessary kit and equipment and began to camouflage himself to break up the body outline.

In place of the bush hat he donned his Green Beret, now he was ready, for what would be a very dangerous stalk.

With thumbs up and a cheesy grin, Jack began the long arduous crawl.

Before he'd gone very far, Tom grabbed him by the foot.

"You'll need these!" Tom whispered. Holding out spare grenade pins. "Have you got your knife?"

"Never leave home without it!" Jack jokingly retorted.

The minutes ticked by slowly, the jungle was hot and humid. Ants went about their busy life unperturbed by the life and death struggle that would soon erupt in their part of existence. The jungle was always alive pulsing with sounds of thousands of species of insects.

The marines remained quiet where they were as the jungle grew around them and went about its daily business. Half an hour dragged past, then an hour. Tom kept up his vigil of observation, sweat running down his brow and into his eyes as the tension built up.

Where was Jack, had he been taken? Tom wiped his eyes of the sweat and replaced the binoculars, searching the jungle floor for even the slightest movement. A slight sound behind Tom made him look back.

A young marine crouched at Tom's feet, sweat pouring off him, a slightly built lad of eighteen, with sea green eyes and a freckled sandy face, gazed at Tom with awe and respect.

Tom grinned at him amiably, which seemed to relax the boy and gave him a little more confidence when he spoke.

Tom guessed he was the sergeant major's runner, sent up for the latest 'info'.

The boy's thick lips mouthed out the only words necessary, "Sitrep OC." Tom nodded, took out his notepad and hastily scribbled a message to Captain Moorelands urging the utmost patience at this time, giving a rough map of the obstacles faced before the OP. Could be taken. With a friendly wink, he dispatched the boy back to the main group.

Meanwhile, Jack was diffusing a trip wire on the end of which was a white-phos grenade. With almost loving care, he was following the taut thin wire back to where the grenade would be anchored, any wrong moves now would mean a slow and agonizing death. White-phos burns into the flesh and keeps burning through, unless you immerse it in water, as soon as it meets the air again then it continues to burn. You virtually have to cut it out from the flesh.

He inserted one of the pins Tom had given him making sure there were no other surprises attached to the other end and crawled under it.

He continued on his course keeping the rain forest tree as his axis of advance. In his mind, he knew there would be other obstacles to neutralize but where were they?

Jack put himself in the mind of the enemy. *Where would I put them?* he thought. Slowly, he was inching his way toward the enemy OP.

Knowing full well that the position would be guarded with numerous trip wires, attached to these would be anti-personnel or fragment grenades.

Jack was now covered in green slime off the jungle floor and resembled some kind of marine creature, slithering along. Another trip-wire, this one running at an angle of forty-five degrees. Very cunning, once you were in the apex of it, three simultaneous explosions hit the soldier from front and side.

Ever so carefully, Jack traced it back to the live side and again inserted another pin, making it safe. Two more to immobilise. Jack followed the slim taut trip wires and completed each task trying not to think of the consequences of a mistake. The task completed so far, he moved on to his target.

Another hour passed slowly, not a sign, just the normal jungle sounds, vision very limited in the jungle. A never-ending labyrinth of trees and vines. Tom at the moment was keeping watch for Jack, should any firing break out, then Tom would direct fire onto the enemy's position.

Each man to his own, thought Tom, Jack was the best man for this kind of action, the long complicated stalk of the hunter and the hunted. Even so, Tom was worried about him.

Two low coughs penetrated the oppressive, fetid, stillness of the jungle.

Tom cocked his head to one side listening, as two birds fluttered upwards, winging their way out of the clearing.

Tom watched intently in the direction of the enemy OP.

There was a movement of some sort, yes! There it was again,

From near the tree, a huge mound was rising in the air, some kind of beast covered in mud and slime.

It was coming in their direction.

Tom rose to meet the challenge adopting the kneeling position, safety catch off. Ready to fire.

A serious doubt crossed Tom's mind, a sixth sense, stopped him squeezing off the trigger. *What if?* At that same moment, an arm raised in mock salute to Tom and a white toothy grin appeared in that mass of shit and slime.

Tom exhaled with relief, it was Jack.

Then he was serious again. Fist clenched pulling down vigorously, followed by arms crossed in front of the body. Jungle signs which conveyed a vital message to Tom:

'Stop, observe, be alert, be ready, obstacle in line of advance.'

Tom sank slowly to the deck, slithering backwards to a whispered message to the waiting marines (OC.) Captain Moorelands to report to leading scouts.

Thereafter by a series of jungle signs, the message was relayed to the OC.

Three fingers on shoulder, making an 'O'. Hand on head and a wanking motion with the hand to convey urgency.

Tom was in the firing position when Captain Moorelands slid alongside.

Stealth would win the day not force of arms, not yet.

"What's the situation Martial?" whispered the captain.

Tom filled him in on the detail so far.

"What's your order sir?" Tom whispered in the captain's ear. "We hold fast here for the moment, till French returns. That's all."

Tom signalled back to the rest of the patrol.

Tom worked much better when he had control of his own detachment in the heavy weapons role, whether it was machine guns, mortars or mobats, it was more independent, although a damn sight heavier going.

The captain read the look on Tom's face and smiled understandingly.

Jack was now clearly visible across the clearing, crouching, searching the ground, as he warily retraced his marine crawl through the obstacles.

Finally, his chest heaving and straining, still covered in the green slime jack squatted down Indian style in the little 'O' group.

Captain Moorelands and Tom appraised Jack with a professional eye. "Well done, French," murmured the captain.

"Your blood's worth bottling." Tom added with a grin. Jack cheesed down in silent mirth. Even the captain found it mildly amusing.

"Better have some water French, you're looking a little dehydrated to me."

Jack gratefully accepted the proffered water bottle, pouring half of the contents down his throat in one gulp.

Casually, he wiped his mouth with the back of his huge hand.

"Now sir this is the situation…"

Jack informed the captain that there would be ten booby traps out front including a huge dugout animal pit with sharpened stakes at the bottom. Around the inner perimeter, they had arranged rows of panjees.

"You needn't worry about the Chokies on duty, they're dead."

"We'll need to diffuse the rest of the trip wires sir," added Jack.

"I take your point French," the captain concurred.

"Martial, make your way to the rear and inform the sergeant major we need the assault engineer up here."

"Very good, sir."

With that Tom made his way aft, glad to be moving again.

The enigmatic 'McHenry' (AE) arrived on the scene, small, wiry, darkly handsome, a face used to smiling a lot.

'Mac' as he was affectionately known, came from a small fishing village in the south west of Ireland called 'Balydavid', a quiet unassuming man who took life's problems in his stride.

Jack, Tom and the captain quietly filled Mac in on the present situation and observed the relative positions of the booby-trapped areas to their front.

"Do you think you can find and mark a direct path, from here to that large rainforest tree, over there?" the captain asked quietly.

Mac only grinned, "Yes sir, leave it to me, I just happen to have the very thing with me."

With that, he unwrapped his waterproof bag and carefully took out a lightweight metal mine detector. With a practised ease, he assembled it. Then he discarded any unnecessary equipment. Placing the earphones on his head, he was ready.

The captain looked at him incredulously. "Where did you get this from, McHenry?"

"Well sir, I just happened to be walking through the QM's store in Kuching, minding my own business sir, and it occurred to me that this little beauty would be better off with me than sitting on a shelf doing absolutely nothing," McHenry grinned broadly, pleased with himself.

The captain smiled, clapped him on the shoulder, "You'd better get on with it then, McHenry."

Very carefully and professionally, McHenry swept the area on a direct path to the enemy OP which was now silent due to Jack's efforts several hours before.

Finally, McHenry came back. Tom and Jack hauled him in over the small bank to where they were, sweat pissing out of him but the everlasting grin still on his face.

"Pathway clear sir, just walk between the white tapes, don't go to the left or right, but straight between the tapes or you're gone!" He made a cutting motion with his hand across the throat to emphasise the point.

By hand signals and clicking of the fingers, the rest of the marines were alerted to move out.

Tom again took up lead scout and lost no time in covering the ground to the OP.

After a quick appraisal of the situation there, he motioned for the rest of the patrol to follow, keeping careful observation of possible enemy locations.

The captain arriving there first, then Jack. The captain noted the two Indons lying like rag dolls in the bottom of the observation post gun pit.

Heavily armed and well camouflaged, each one had a third eye now in the centre of his forehead, a red horrible sticky mess trailed out of the back of each head, blood had sprayed all the inside of the OP. Flies already clustering on the bodies.

The captain took out a small miniature camera and quickly took pictures for the report he would have to make later.

In small groups, the marines traversed the clearing to the OP position. Being careful to step only where the marine in front of him had stepped. The captain positioned his men further along the faint trail, ready for the next stage of the advance.

Jack handed the captain's sidearm back to him, silently he advised that two rounds were missing as he swung open the chamber of the 38 Smith and Wesson. The captain nodded and reloaded.

'O' group! SNCOs to captain in ten minutes (jungle signs only) now were used. The thumb and index finger forming the 'O'. Three straight fingers on sleeve, followed by three fingers on shoulder… in ten minutes! Spread fingers flashing twice.

Automatically, JNCOs would take charge of their respective sections two JNCOs per platoon (sometimes an extra L/Cpl). As each section came over their own LMG Group (light machine gun) supported them.

Troop HQ bringing up the rear.

As each one came in, the captain would direct them to a defensive position and would thus be accounted for.

Meanwhile, Tom and Jack were scouting ahead, in the secure knowledge that they would soon see an Indon border post.

The trail was much wider now the pale blue sky visible above their heads as the canopy of trees was thinning out. There was nothing to impede their progress and swiftly and silently they sped along the open trail.

A lone green scorpion scuttled along, its claws held out in front and tail provocatively swinging in the hot fetid air. Tom gave it a wide berth and signalled to Jack, who, just grinned and when he came up to it crushed it with the butt of his rifle. Tom shivered a little, he really didn't like creepy crawlies especially ones that could kill you.

Presently, they came into more open country with the green Lalang spreading out below them very lush and inviting.

At the bottom of the valley lay a fairly wide river and beyond that in the rising ground on the other side of the river stood a brand new Indon camp with prepared gun positions, artillery and mortar pits.

Tom faded into the nearest cover and urgently signalled Jack with a clenched fist. In turn, Jack transmitted the same signal to the rest of the patrol, who in turn faded into the jungle.

Together they peered out over the crest of the hill they were on. Tom using the binoculars made rough sketches of the various positions and recorded them in his notebook, for his report to the captain.

The camp was a hive of activity and could not have been there very long, maybe a month or two at the most. At a guess, the camp could hold about two hundred soldiers, with neatly laid out 'Bashas' along one side. Stores and HQ on the other. Native labour could be seen digging extensive slit trenches and firing points. Tom and Jack took all this information down ready for their report to the 'O' group. Gingerly, they withdrew to the comparative safety of the jungle canopy, and sped swiftly back to the main body.

The marines had fanned out in all-round defensive positions, something like the old idea of the British hollow square of the 1800s. Not all were on watch, whilst one marine stood guard or rather lay on watch, his 'oppo' would be making tea and 'nosh'.

Tom and Jack quickly found the captain and huddled down in a tight little 'O' group with the lieutenants and SNCOs squatting, eagerly listening to the lead scouts and the captain's orders.

Both Tom and Jack shrugged off their packs and squatted down.

The sergeant major's runner thrust two steaming mugs of tea into their hands. The young marine with the freckles and the sandy hair, eager to please.

"Shit! You're a good flip to the front, cheers," Tom said, as he gratefully and carefully sipped at the welcome wet of tea.

"Is it okay to smoke sir?" Tom inquired.

"Yes, I think so, consider the smoking lamp lit!" The light banter of the captain smoothing away any wrinkles that might have cropped up during the exhaustive trek of the past few days.

"Okay Martial, what did you find on your recce?" The captain asked.

"About a mile away there's an Indon camp," Tom began. He pulled his notebook out and with a rough model, which he constructed with loose earth and twigs, he conveyed to the circle of NCOs and the captain what lay ahead and possible attack approaches and layout.

Tom related everything that he had seen and observed in detail. He had taken bearings and distances to all the gun pits and the positions of Sangers, magazines, ammo dumps, tunnel entrances, new diggings, accommodations, galley, mess tents, and observation towers.

Tom left nothing out, filling in detail as he was asked.

After he finished, there was a moment's pause.

"Anything to add French?" asked the Captain.

"Yes sir," growled Jack. "If we positioned a man on this forward slope here (pointing to the ground model) properly dug in and camouflaged, he could pick off quite a lot of the key personnel in that camp sir!"

"Like a sniper you mean, French," retorted the captain.

"Yes sir!" growled Jack.

The captain contemplated the information and for a while was silent. Making brief notes from time to time. Each man eyeing each other, weighing up the task ahead.

"Right then!" exclaimed the captain. The suddenness dragging everyone out of their reverie.

"Here are your orders."

"Sergeant Major, you will detach Corporal Hartley and two marines to go back to the enemy OP. We've just come through. They are to be the grave detail. Inform them to take the bottom half of the dead Indons ID discs off and keep them safely, until we reach our objective at G3. Instruct Corporal Hartley to operate the enemy radio set should the need arise, using his newly acquired linguistic skills in Malay, I believe! I want that done immediately. Your next task is to get to this position here with the rest of your troop (he pointed to a position well beyond the Indon camp at a bend in the river). You will act as the cut-off troop, anyone who escapes the initial assault and proceeds in your direction you will stop. Clear, Sergeant Major?"

"Yes sir, any prisoners sir?" the sergeant major inquired.

"We abide by the rules of war. We could do with one of their senior members for interrogation, but that's really hoping for too much at this stage, however I'll leave the final decision to you Sergeant Major!

"Lieutenant Walters and Sergeant Pickford of number one troop, you will ford the river at this point and make your way to this lightly wooded area here to the left of the objective. Lining out at an angle from the river to the camp. Making only shellscrapes. Your support group to the high ground, here! You are to engage the enemy at first light on my signal of a red Vereys flare. Radio silence will be observed until this time.

"Lieutenant Davis and Sergeant Smith of number two troop will take up position to the right of the Indon camp in this jungle area here. On my signal, will open fire on the enemy positions.

"Colour Sergeant McFarlane and myself will do a frontal attack in the line of advance. We will of course have to be across the river by first light and be waiting for your initial covering fire.

"Marine French! As you have suggested we need a sniper at this point overlooking the camp, so I suggest after this 'O' group that you make your way to this point here, dig in during the dark hours, camouflage your position and as suitable targets present themselves engage them. Okay French?"

"Yes sir!" growled Jack rather pleased with himself.

"Marines McHenry and Martial," the captain went on smoothly, "your detail will be hardest and most dangerous. You are to take the claymore mines we acquired this morning, courtesy of the Indonesian army (a little light laughter from the group), and you are to place them underneath the Indon longhouses here, here, and here." He pointed to positions on the location model.

Tom whistled lightly through his teeth. McHenry's face cracked into a toothy grin and with the banter only Irishmen can get away with said, "You'll have to crawl through a mile of broken glass and pigshit to get to it." Everyone grinned at the remark.

"Pay attention, McHenry, we don't want any mistakes! You are to place the claymores under the Bashas linking them up to a central point assisted by Marine Martial, make your way towards Lieutenant Davis' position and await my signal! On my signal, you are to detonate the mines, is that clear?"

"Yes sir, perfectly clear sir," grinned McHenry.

"Okay that's the end of the 'O' group, good luck!"

With that, the group went about its various tasks and duties. Each leader passing on the vital information to their own troops who had been waiting and making ready for the coming battle.

Night-time comes swiftly in the Borneo jungle, but before it smothered the entire land, shadowy figures moved out to take up their allotted tasks. The marines would spend an uncomfortable night after crossing the river. A river which would hold a variety of hazards, such as snakes, reptiles, leeches not to mention sand flies and the 'mossies' which made life unbearable especially at night.

Tom and McHenry shouldered the heavy packs of claymores and silently made their way to a point in the river, which they considered a fair crossing could be made. Tom was first to go shrugging off the heavy pack and taking the length of rope, which every marine carries. The darkness was almost complete when he started across paying out the rope as he went, it was not an easy crossing, twice he got caught up in underwater branches and had to extricate himself. The current was pretty swift and the thought of some lurking reptile and the gathering darkness lent itself to weird thoughts of losing his wedding tackle. But he struggled on to reach the opposite bank on which lay the enemy. Tom tied off the rope on a solid tree trunk and made his way back to McHenry. It was now inky black and very difficult to see but he followed the line of the rope and found McHenry and together they brought their equipment over and flung themselves onto the higher reaches of the bank fairly exhausted by the effort. Tom used the time to rummage around in his pack for a 'mars bar' and gave half to his oppo McHenry. They rose and cautiously made their way up the steep bank coming out into very tall Lalang (elephant grass). No longer were they in total darkness, and the moon cast a pale glow over this natural clearing made even lighter by the construction of the Indon camp. At the edge of the Lalang, Tom dropped to one knee to get his bearings and spy out a good hideout for what remained of the night. The camp was not an easy target, double cyclone fenced with towers on Four Corners and a command post in the centre, it looked formidable. Tom scanned the area with his binoculars, which weren't night vision but at least they increased the survey area greatly. Tom nudged Mac and pointing to a clump of bushes which jutted out of the jungle about three hundred yards from the fence line, that would be the best he could find. By a series of leopard crawls, they traversed the open ground; each one covering the other as they made their way to their objective.

The night was hot and humid, perspiration soaked them through, cautiously they crawled under the protection of the dark canopy, the earth was colder to the touch and thankfully they rested for a while.

Tom took stock of the position and made mental notes on possible attack approaches to the camp. Having only the moonlight, it was not an easy task.

It would be six hours before they would make their move into the Indon camp; Tom whispered he would take first watch telling Mac to get his head down and get some much needed sleep.

At 0400 hrs, Mac gently shook Tom awake to start the dawn attack on the camp that lay before them which was now shrouded in a low ground mist, the moon was bright but now on the wain.

"It's perfect," whispered Tom. Mac nodded in agreement.

"Better break out the iron rations," whispered Tom. Mac had already anticipated his request and thrust an open can of beans and frankfurters into his hand, grinning broadly in the murky gloom. They both ate hungrily although it was a cold meal, wasting nothing.

"Don't forget your paladin!" Tom whispered, as he pushed a pill into Mac's mouth. Mac nearly gagged on it, but accepted the joke with good humour.

It was time for them to move out and penetrate the outer defences of the camp. Quietly and quickly, they made sure that they had not left anything behind. Tom led the way sliding along in the grass like a snake. He had noticed a small gully that might just be big enough for them to crawl through; even so he would approach with caution. It was the longest crawl he had ever done especially towing behind a backpack of explosives. Finally, they reached the gully which was small but just about big enough to crawl through. It was also evil smelling like a runoff from a cesspit. They both inspected the approach, Mac pulling on Tom's sleeve to warn him back. He was panning the area very slowly with a little stick and a length of fishing line, which he had made part of his kit and on the end he had fastened a 25 ore Norwegian coin made of silver. In the centre of which was a small hole as produced by the bank of Norway. Slowly and cautiously, he advanced up the gully and then he stopped frozen. The line had contacted an obstacle running horizontally and Mac could feel the very slight tug on his fishing line and like a good fisherman he knew he had a bite on the end. Mac slowly and gently followed the line to its end where a stake driven into the bank held a lethal cocktail of white-phos and high explosives. Mac would have to make it safe mainly by touch and memory of this particular set-up. Sweat poured from his forehead and ran into his eyes stinging him with its salty mixture. Long minutes ticked by and the cover of this murky fog and darkness would be lost. After passing the lethal bundle back to Tom for later usage, he advanced further into the stinking morass. Painstakingly measuring every inch of the way as he slowly and thoroughly swept the area ahead of him as gentle as a mama-san practicing Tai-Chei in Tienamin Square Beijing. He was through the first wire and Tom followed warily behind him dragging an even bigger load now. Mac thought that there wouldn't be any more trip wires on the inside of the compound and indeed this proved to be a correct assessment. They were now inside and quickly they made the comparative safety of the longhouses that had been built to house the Indonesian army. The longhouses were built on stilts in the traditional manner of the Ibans and afforded Mac and Tom a great amount of cover. They lost no time in placing their explosive devices in the best possible locations, Mac was of course the man of the moment directing Tom and giving him what he thought would be on the job training. Working with Mac was a joy. He never lost sight of his mission and the ever-present smile on his face was always there. The first rays of sunlight were stabbing through and the night symphony was giving way to the dawn chorus. The jungle and its inhabitants were beginning to stir. Swiftly and deftly with a practised ease, McHenry anchored the wires to a central point from which he would run out the main detonation wire system. Mac grinned at Tom that all was ready and casually sauntered off to a safe position underneath the administration building paying out the wire as he went. Tom was a little nervous feeling very vulnerable and naked; however, he panned his observation in all directions as he and Mac got to a position that would afford them the best possible protection from the explosion and also the firefight, which would soon follow. The final connection was made; Mac glanced at his watch and began counting down the seconds on his fingers in front of Tom grinning broadly as he did so. Zero! There was a *pop* and a *whoosh* as the red signal flare arched its way through the early morning light. All hell broke loose as massive amounts of firepower rained down into the Indon stronghold. Mac had pressed the buttons at the instant the flare appeared and this now exploded the mines in sequence, which caused sympathetic explosions within the buildings and towers resulting in massive fires breaking out amongst the sleeping Indon soldiers, some of whom were like live torches staggering blindly around. Their part of the assault was done and both of them dived for cover behind a pile of logs, under one of the HQ buildings. Unfortunately, they had dived into a pile of pigshit which was stinking.

Mac grinned at Tom and whispered, "What did I tell you!" For what seemed like hours, the attack continued, the Indon camp now a fiery, smoking, gutted place. Bodies sprawled in grotesque postures, smoking and on fire, jerking sporadically as the rounds hit them again and again. At last, the firing ceased abruptly, a weird silence permeated throughout the camp. Tom and Mac covered in foul smelling pigshit with ears ringing from the explosions and rocket fire, gingerly looked over their hasty defence position. The rest of the marine patrol was approaching the main gates of the camp in arrowhead formation led by the enigmatic Captain Moorelands. Gates proving no problem as they were blown away with the rocket launchers and they were in, searching for pockets of resistance or live enemy.

Tom and Mac withdrew to the shadows of the buildings making their way cautiously to the centre of the camp where the former police station lay. As they neared the stronghold, they were singing a popular Western cowboy song, which was easily recognisable by the Marines and pinpointed the location of the high commissionaire and his wife in the local police prison cells.

Mac grinned at Tom, and in his Irish brogue said, "Well, we know for sure where they are now." Tom had gone and was up the station steps like a mountain goat, blasting the door open with his weapon and boots. One Indonesian soldier made to fire his weapon and was blown away for his trouble. The others put their hands in the air in surrender. Mac was close on Tom's heels and together they sought out the prison cells, after securing the soldiers with the ancient handcuffs plainly on display.

Tom motioned McHenry into silence and pointed upwards to the ceiling. He had heard a faint rustling from above. So, he cautiously removed his heavy rifle and webbing letting it fall silently to the floor. McHenry knew the drill cupping his hands together into a makeshift stirrup bending down low to give the maximum lift as Tom ran and sprang onto his cupped hands. With sheer strength and agility often practised in training, he was catapulted through the flimsy canopy of the ceiling. Tom always carried his sidearm with him and this was now drawn as he straddled the beams above. There in the gloom was a figure, which had a familiar headdress; Tom exercised caution not to shoot 'if' you had a shadow of doubt as to friend or foe. The shadow spoke shakily in broken English and was prostrating himself as he said, "Police Tuan; NO SHOOT!"

Tom called down to the rest of the troop led by Captain Moorelands, "We got a native policeman up here!"

Chapter 7
Final Phase

The cells were unlocked to release the Resident High Commissioner, Dick and Dolly Norris; Captain Moorelands taking the care and attention to make sure they were in good health. However, the situation had to be resolved and the remainder of the rebel forces rounded up or killed. He dispatched the other troops of marines in a search and destroy configuration, which proved very successful in the end but alas five marines had been killed in the final stages of the rescue operation. Some of whom were borne, under fire, on the shoulders of, Platoon Commander Sgt Johnny Pickford to the makeshift hospital where Dolly and the Royal Naval SBA were caring for the wounded.

Captain Moorelands realised he had some junior officers who had just recently been drafted into the unit and as such he doubted that they could carry out the onerous task of 'House clearing', obviously a daunting task even to experienced marines. He, therefore, gave them a rough guide as he conducted a very fast 'TEWT'. Dividing his group into manageable 'section' configurations. Ammo, water, grenades and Nutty bars were replenished before the teams set out on their various tasks. He gathered the officers, SNCOs and JNCOs around him and drew a rough sketch in the dirt of the local market area which also had some accommodation above and behind the shopping area, called the Suqh. At this juncture, the signaller handed Captain Moorelands an important message from GHQ 'Sunray'. Captain Moorelands had at last got in contact with the signallers base in Kuching where he corresponded briefly with the CO Colonel Briggs and gave him a rundown on the situation at Limbang (Sitrep).

In closing, the CO informed him to get Marine Tom Martial and four other handpicked marines of Tom's choosing as they had been contacted by the admiralty in London to instigate another search for Lt Chris Davenport and his special forces group. A helicopter was being dispatched immediately to pick them up.

"Get onto 1, 2, 3 sections and send this message that Marine Tom Martial report to my position immediately." He delayed the push forward through the village until this matter had been dealt with. The marines adopted all 'round defence and waited, occasionally popping off a shot as targets became visible and some incoming rounds spattered near their positions. The captain waited anxiously for Marine Martial and was studying the surrounding area and orientating it with the map. Marine Martial appeared and sank down beside the captain. Giving a brief detail of the message he had received, he handed the signaller's message over to Tom; he ended with the information that the chopper would be at this position in fifteen minutes so he had better get a move on. Tom weighed up the situation quickly and gave the signaller the names of four marines that he wanted on this mission. However, he also stipulated to GHQ 'Sunray' that he also would require a Naval SBA available to accompany the rescue party on its mission. These were the names: Marines; McHenry (AE), D. Young (GD), G. Warden (GD), J. French (PW).

The chopper arrived and with his team intact, Tom gave the pilot from 'stick leader' the message that all were aboard and belted up. The Wessex lifted up vertically and at a slight angle, they could see the mass of leafy jungle passing away, as they headed off to base camp and GHQ.

"Get yourselves cleaned up, the CO wants to see you all in thirty minutes; Okay! Get a move on boys," roared the RSM, trying to compete with the noise and the wind of the helicopter downdraught.

Tom and his team just grinned looking at one another. "ROGER THAT!" they replied in unison.

"You know the drill! Weapons first, cleaned, to the store. Shit, shave, shower and shampoo. See you at the CO's office!" The CO's 'office' was a wooden hut built on brick pillars to be above any flood water levels. These huts had been made for the plantation workers, but had been commandeered due to the Indonesian confrontation. A covered verandah walkway was in the front of the building; again it too was made of wood.

Standing outside the office was the RSM. Resplendent in tailored jungle green shirt and shorts, his Sam Browne highly polished, almost the colour of dark oxblood. SV Boots, puttees, Green Beret one inch over the left eye solid silver and gold split globe and laurel cap badge glittering in the dappled sunlight; garter tabs in the unit's colour, campaign ribbons absolutely horizontal to the ground, his RSM's gold wire insignia worn on his right wrist,

G10 watch on the left. With both hands grasping his ebony cane topped with a silver mount. Barrel chested, bull-like neck, large bushy moustache, piercing blue eyes that seemed to bore through you. RSM Jock Chisel was a man one didn't argue with at all!

"All right get fell in," he yelled. He slowly inspected the line, taking in the dishevelled but fairly clean marines on CO's. "You all are a disgrace! Have you been sleeping in this gear?"

"Yes sir!" they all chorused (with intoned humour in their reply). A hint of a smile on his lips, he turned and opened the door to the CO's office "Are you ready, sir?"

"Yes RSM march them in."

"Attention! Quick march, halt, right turn, salute! Sir! The special ops section for your briefing!"

"Right then RSM, have them stand at ease. RSM! Would you pull down the map and all of you gather round here so you can see the terrain that you will have to cover."

The very detailed map covered the entire wall, like looking down from about 200 feet. "Tomorrow you will be flown to this point here! This is your starting point known as Simmangang. From then on, it will be a hard slog into this higher range. You will each be given a waterproof map of this area in case you get separated. Look at this area here which is very swampy due to the recent monsoon downpour. We think the helicopter may be down in this area, there is no other explanation; however, our patrols have been unable to locate any debris or even a sign of the missing chopper. I cannot emphasize the urgency of your mission; it is vital you find whatever is left and especially the Pilot, Lt Davenport and his special forces he was transporting. Time is running out gentlemen. You can see here on the map a sheer rise in the terrain, once you've followed this winding river course, I suggest you get *Jin Tin* your Iban tracker to locate one of the native craft in order to get to the base of this prominent feature here!" (The marines had nicknamed him Jin Tin as they couldn't pronounce his Iban name). The colonel pointing on the map highlighting the difficult dense jungle clad search area. "RSM! Would you bring in the diplomatic bag?" (Tom took out his notebook from his map pocket taking all the info down; as it would be valuable to refer to in the days ahead.)

"Now this piece of kit is rather special, it is still only in the experimental stage, although it has been tested out by our chief Boffin Francis Chichester (Later to become Sir Francis Chichester). He gave it a thorough testing but with certain modifications which have been incorporated into this particular model. It comes in a very light waterproof case and as you can see here when you switch it on and point it towards a heat source, it gives off a red glow. This is due to body heat which this machine picks up as a heat frequency. It also doubles as a transceiver by thumbing on this switch on the left. When you send your final request for 'case vac' to our control here in Brigade HQ, the call sign will be 'Anchorman'. You can see if I point it at you French, the screen is then illuminated with a ruddy glow. It will also pick up any electrical energy fields however faint or hidden. I have arranged the armourer and the QM PW to instruct you on all the special equipment you will be issued with. Remember you are a on a search and rescue mission, I must 'emphasize' that you are not to engage the enemy, you are not a fighting patrol; however, you will defend yourselves if you are bumped. Avoid contact with enemy patrols; stealth is the keyword on this mission. There is only one more thing to say to you, and that is 'good luck' and may you be successful, our hopes are resting on your shoulders." Surprisingly, he shook their hands as they made their way outside.

"Better look lively boys, the RSM's got his eyes on us!" Tom growled.

"Martial! Come here!" The RSM's finger beckoning threateningly at Tom. *Now what have I done!* thought Tom.

"Yes sir!" The RSM seemed to relax; his eyes fixed Tom in a man-to-man manner.

"I want you to take this compass with you." He produced it from his side trouser pocket which was attached by a green thin lanyard. "It was my father's compass which he had in the Second World War and he passed it onto me when I joined the Royal Marines. I want you to use it on your expedition, it will never let you down, it is strong and much lighter than the G1098 Prismatic compass that usually is issued. Also, it is made in Scotland, need I say anymore?"

Tom was taken unawares by this kind gesture and just mumbled, "Yes sir, very good sir, Er! Do you want me to return it you sir?"

The RSM made no comment, just looked at Tom and said, "Good luck, Martial." Turned on his heel and marched away with his usual swagger; hefty cane of office under his left armpit.

Chapter 8
Simmangang

"Stick leader to pilot all secure and ready for take-off."

"Roger that. Stick leader, standby." The Wessex helicopter rose steeply and with the jet turbines increased speed rapidly and they were soon skimming over the jungles of Sarawak. Looking down, it looked like a green lush carpet; however, the marines knew it contained some dangerous creatures: swamps, leeches, venomous snakes, not to mention the high temperature and the oppressive humidity of about 90% and 90°F. Still, it looked lush, green and inviting to the eye.

It was only a short trip from Commando HQ to Safe Base G2 at Simmangang. Located on a prominent hilltop, it gave a good field of fire and was well dug in. Below, the ground was an intricate series of tunnels which the marines manned at night whilst in base camp. Platoons taking it in turn to be out on seven and nine-day patrols.

"All right, you men look lively; make your way to the QM's briefing Basha!" Laid out were their new equipment and specially modified weapons that the armourer had been working on for their unique search and rescue operation.

The armourer spoke, "First of all, we have camouflaged aluminium ladder racks which have been modified to carry your equipment. Here, you will see that on the top has been added a small retractable extension. Should you need a stretcher, simply slide this section out and it will click onto the base of another, and so on until you have the length you require for any wounded men you may find. We are supplying you all with 44 pattern back packs, two per person; one is for your Asian ration packs, the other is for bandoliers of ammo and fully loaded magazines, smoke grenades. Iron rations and nutty bars. Instead of the usual machete, we are issuing you all with a native Iban Parang; these were obtained courtesy of Jin Tin's village Kampong. Weapons! You will all carry a 9mm browning automatic side arm. We have acquired three AR15 Armalite assault rifles, 5.62mm with underslung grenade launchers from the US Marines in Viet-Nam. This is a comparatively light weapon. See me afterwards for instruction on the use of the grenade launcher for those that have never used it before, okay? FRENCH! You will carry this Australian modified .303 single bolt action rifle, everything has been cut down to absolute minimum including the length of the barrel, and it also comes with a telescopic sight for sniper-effective shooting. Also from Australia is a beefed up (in the breech) SLR which has been modified to fire fully automatic and has a bipod attached for sustained fire role. Marine Warden! You will carry this weapon. The GP boots are also Australian; they have a thin metal ss plate inserted in the sole. This is to protect the wearer from treading on something unpleasant. The rest of you will carry the AR15 Armalite! Martial! You will also be issued with this stainless steel multi-function tool get to know all of its uses especially as a wire cutter."

Screeching to a shuddering halt, a dust and mud splattered Ferret Mk 2 (armoured car) ground to a halt outside the QM's Basha. "Thanks mate." Into the gloom of the long hut strode leading seamen 'Bungy' Williams, a rather dishevelled, unshaven SBA (Naval Sick Berth attendant). Roaring with delight on recognising the 'boys' grinning impishly, he hugged Tom then Jack and slapping everyone on the back, still grinning he asked McHenry for a roll (self-rolled cigarette).

The Sgt Major roared, eyes bulging. "Do you MIND, Williams! We are conducting a briefing here, SO BE QUIET!" Bungy still grinning, licked the cigarette paper and lit up.

"Keep your hair on Sgt Major, only just got 'ere!"

"WHILST I'VE GOT YOUR UNDIVIDED ATTENTION, WILLIAMS! YOUR MEDICAL KIT IS OVER THERE, ready to go. We have provided every kind of first aid equipment that we possess. You will also carry the silk helicopter landing panels, and one smoke grenade, for if you are to be airlifted out of the Ulu. Incidentally! All of you will carry two ampoules of morphine; it goes in the usual place in the pockets around your bush hat along with a single edged razor blade; UNDERSTOOD? Now, due to the fact that you have dissimilar CALIBREs, you as a group will have to decide how much ammunition you will need for each weapon, not to mention the load you will all have to carry. This includes water, food, ammunition, grenades various. You will not carry a bayonet; instead, we are supplying you with survival sheath knife which has compass, wire saw blade, fishing line, split rings and a small blow gun with arrows. Unscrew the cap and it is nicely packed inside. Martial and French will each carry a silencer for the browning sidearm. McHENRY! Your AE (assault engineer) backpack is over here, it has all the necessary PE (plastic explosive): cortex, detonators, timing and priming devices that we think you will need." Smiling, he said, "Take a tin of Tiger Balm each, good for insect bites! Right now! Go down to the planters' huts and get all your fighting order equipment together, return here and in this store take whatever you think you might need to use on your search. It only remains for me and the armourer to say good hunting; good luck and come back safe!" He handed Tom a water bottle, "Remember, only a capful per night (it contained Neat Pussers Rum). Oh and if you find any wreckage, attach this to it and it will beep out a constant signal to our control tower which will pinpoint its exact location. One twist of this catch here will turn it on, active!"

The marines set to work and with the practised ease of a poacher; assembled the necessary vital equipment they would need. The new boots were a bit of a problem; however, Jack suggested they have one size slightly larger and put in an insole to cushion the feet. (As issued in cold wets boots for arctic warfare.)

"'Ere, don't I have a weapon?" chirped in Bungy Williams. "For self-defence like!" Tom and Jack stared at him in disbelief.

"Now, you know Bungy you're not supposed to be armed!"

"I know," he whispered, "but I fought I'd like to be a roughie-toughie like you guys."

Tom and the boys cheesed down a grin, "Okay, but keep this browning out of site till we leave camp."

Grinning, Bungy selected a gleaming blued metal sidearm and a box of 9 mm ammo.

Slowly and methodically, each marine began packing his kit for the search and rescue, each carrying enough of what they thought they would need and to work as a well drilled team. "I'm not taking this modified SLR. I have never fired it and I don't know how it will react in the Ulu." It was Gil Warden that had spoken and of course Gil was pretty switched-on with all military weaponry except this one. "I'm carrying the Bren gun. I know it's heavier, but, at least, I am conversant with what it can do!"

Tom looked thoughtful and nodded in agreement with Gil. "Well, you would be more comfortable with the weight if you thread this helicopter strop through the sling, that way it will cushion it on your shoulder; okay Gil?"

"Fair enough, Tom!" Jack took stock of the automatic beefed up 7.62mm SLR, hefting it in his big hands, being a PW (Platoon

Weapons), he sized it up and declared to Tom, "I'll carry it, see how it performs in combat situations!"

"But that means you're carrying a double load," Tom remarked.

Jack just grinned. "Just leave it to me Tom, the other weapon is a single shot, this one is supposed to be fully automatic which if we are up against a bigger force, we will need everything we've got to throw at them. Savvy?"

"Sure Jack, you know the score!" Packing of the essential gear continued. Night rig would be a zoot suit, which was an early design 42 Commando Marines had made up from bottle green parachute material and were exceptionally light to carry. Nylon sleeping bag inner would be all that was needed for fetid hot nights in the jungle; these were also very light to carry. Black elastic rubber soled gym shoes. Rope and toggle carried by every marine, plus a new alloy karabiner, very light and super strong. Jack would carry the long length of nylon mountaineering rope and alloy folding grappling hook. All would carry hexamine stove and blocks, 1 aluminium mess tin and mug, large waterproof bag and filter canvas sock plus tablets for water purification. Paladin tablets. 1 stun grenade, 2 thunder flashes, black masking tape, 50 ft x 3mm nylon parachute cord, camouflage cream, small insect repellent. Canadian Police, plastic torch very light and waterproof. G1098 omega wrist watch. No operation is complete without sound planning and preparation (P&P). Jack nipped out to the MMG section, coming back with 20 rounds of 303 tracer ammo and a large piece of green hessian. This, he placed on the dirt floor, reading from the map the contour heights and river flows complete with obstacles which included the dreaded swamps they had to either bye-pass or raft over. Using rocks to signify the hills, silver paper to show rivers and swamps, made quite a good impact on the marines. In other words, Jack had made a mock-up of the terrain that they would be searching. "Okay, listen up! This is the base camp here, where we are, and over here is the extent of the jungle land mass we have to cover." Jack looked around at all faces intent on driving home the massive task in front of them.

Finally all was ready. "Okay, saddle up, we're moving out," ordered Tom. The marines hefting their heavy packs. Tom inspecting their loads just to make sure it was all ship shape with nothing loose dangling or jangling. Noise has to be obliterated in the jungle. The marines have to advance in silence, using only jungle hand signals.

In a well-spaced single file, they started off on their long journey, their faces streaked in green and black camouflage. The marines who were still on guard and camp duties watched silently with a certain sense of great pride at this spectacle of their most mature marines filing past and out of the gate, the sentries saluting them in tribute and respect. One of the guards peeled off and approached Tom with a written signal that had just come in and that was the list of casualties at the raid on Limchang. Tom was saddened to see the deaths of two of his friends, Marines Dick Jennings and Sandy Powell. Dick was pleasant, always smiling, a good soccer player. Sandy was always cheerful and kept up a good patter with his friend Nutty Edwards, Tom was aware that Nutty would miss Sandy a lot. So with a heavy heart, Tom said a silent farewell to his oppos.

Outside the gate, all weapons went up in the air and were fully loaded, safety catches on. They made their way down a rough based road that the Australian field engineers had laid recently. Half a mile on and they entered the comparative cool of the jungle canopy where everything is green, even their faces had a green hue to it. The jungle is alive with the never-ending cacophony of sounds from its creatures, both great and small.

It took several hours to reach Jin Tin's kampong crossing over a narrow stream where the native Iban girls were busy doing the washing of clothes. Standing bare-breasted and with their infectious smile and white teeth contrasting with their chocolate brown skin glinting in the dappled sunlight. The marines gave them a friendly wave as they passed through to the village.

Jin Tin was waiting at the tiny wharf which had served the Kampongs for many years. It looked a bit rickety but surprisingly supported the heavily laden rescue party. They had all worked with Jin Tin before on their patrols and so they held him in high esteem and noisily greeted him. He was slightly built standing not more than 5 feet tall, heavily tattooed and regarded by his people as a warrior, which was distinguished by the snake tattoo which was engraved on his throat and just under the jaw. He also had one of his earlobes enlarged which contained magic potions to ward off evil spirits. Dressed only in his leather sirat (loincloth), and his baju gagong (tough animal skin shirt), carrying his native parang in a sheath suspended from a leather ornamental belt. His blowpipe was his favourite weapon, silent and deadly. The darts which were poisonous fitted neatly in a bandolier across his chest which also held at the bottom a pouch which contained his meagre food supply.

An ancient animal skin served as a water carrier the top bound with leather thongs around a simple mouthpiece complete with hard wooden stopper. Lying alongside the jetty were three 10-feet-long native Perau (longboats) power being supplied on each boat by an outboard motor with a very long drive shaft to the screw propeller. (This protected the screw propeller from damage if they drove across a submerged log.)

Jin Tin had negotiated that the Iban owners would carry them upstream to a position near the foot of the high escarpment that they would have to climb in order to reach their destination against the enemy Kalimantan Army.

It was precarious loading of all their equipment in the shallow water vessels, and not without its trepidations and near fatal capsizing as each boat was gingerly loaded. Tom handed Jin Tin the negotiated payments to the boat owners and presently they set off on the first leg of their search and rescue operation. All weapons were in all round defence, once settled on the boats. It was an exhilarating trip as the Ibans gunned the outboard motors mercilessly up the river not wanting to be in potential enemy territory after dark and especially carrying British Marines.

Tom had noticed that Dave Younger was very quiet and subdued, not at all like his normally cheerful personality.

He decided that he would have a word with Dave when they got to their debarkation point at the foot of the jungle-clad escarpment. A vigilant observation of the river and the potential ambush points were kept by all the marines, whilst also observing the wildlife they encountered. Rounding a bend in the river, they noted a large snake of immense size entering the water and heading straight for the boats, this specimen was similar to the anaconda found in the South American Amazon jungles. Large head and jaws, full body especially in the middle and about 75 feet long. Needless to say, the boats put on extra speed to keep ahead of the reptile. The marines just grinned and gave a sigh of relief.

Two and a half hours later and they were nearing their destination, looking for a possible dry landing in the marshy banks. However, the Ibans knew their territory and selected what was once a peaceful collection of kampongs that they had known and traded with before it had been overrun and gutted by the Kalimantan Army. Their lives and community lost in a desperate attempt to capture the whole of Northern Borneo, Sarawak, Brunei.

After unloading on the rather flimsy jetty, Tom and Jack consulted the map, oriented it and took the compass bearing to the feature they had mapped out previously.

Before they man-packed out, Tom took Dave aside to find out what was upsetting him. His normal handsome features were truly lined with an inner torment. "What is bothering you, Dave? I've noticed an inner conflict and as leader, I must tell you now to level with me as to what it is that has caused this change in you, it's not normal. I've known you for years and it really upsets me to see you like this. Come on, Dave, tell me!"

Dave's eyes filled up a bit and slowly he revealed that Jean, his wife, was expecting their first baby and she had some complications during her pregnancy. Because Dave could not be by her side in Singapore to help and comfort her, it had slowly built up in his brain that maybe she could lose the baby.

Tom put his arm around the boy and just said, "I know what you must be thinking and how it gnaws at your guts, she will have the best of surgeons and nurses at BMH Singapore, please do not worry unnecessarily. When we eventually finish this rescue mission, and we come out alive, I will do everything I can to get you to Singapore on compassionate leave. Trust me!" Dave nodded dumbly and, at least, he knew he had a friend in Tom that he could turn to and trust.

A mental picture of Linda came into his mind's eye, smiling and happy and hopeful he would find Christopher somewhere out there in pain and terrible agony. Tom shook his head, *Let's get on with it!*

Quietly Tom intoned, "Saddle up, we're moving out, make sure you've got all your gear!"

After leaving the derelict Kampongs, the jungle closed around them as they hacked their way through, the going got tougher, sweat just saturated them as if they had swam ashore. Ahead was Jin Tin; being a lot lighter clad, he had not as much trouble as the marines. Point man at this stage was Gil Warden, he had been with Tom and Jack in the Malayan jungles and all knew the routine by heart. They travelled in silence, each man lost in his own thoughts, nevertheless having an all-round surveillance of anything out of the ordinary. Coordination of mind and limbs were essential if they were to survive. Tom glanced back at McHenry who as always was grinning back. Tail end Charlie was Bungy Williams brandishing his new toy the browning automatic, poking it in every bush and levelling at everything at an angle of 180°, Tom hoped he had got the safety catch on and grinned about the SBA's antics. *Roughie-toughie, eh?* he thought, *We'll see!* At least he's quiet.

Unlike the sounds emanating from the jungle around them, the whooping of the tree monkeys and ever-present beating wings of the cicadas, belching of the green tree frogs as they tried to attract their female counterparts. Black and red bull ants, one inch long, with a fierce bite if they got on your skin. They had been making steady, reasonable, progress since leaving the comparative cultivated section by the river the ground was rising up slightly from the valley floor and Tom expected they would leave the thickened primary jungle behind. Two hours had passed and so Tom signalled the party for a rest period fanning out in all round defence, weapons facing outboard. Half would make a brew of tea and the remainder would be on guard. It was an automatic drill within the marines' combat training and always worked well should they be attacked at any time day or night.

"You're being watched," whispered Jack to Tom.

"I know; saw them a few minutes ago." In the trees high above them were two Orang-U-Tangs, unmistakeable rust red hair and blackened faces, jowls hanging slackly from their faces. "That tells me that there is no enemy around here," whispered Tom. Jack nodded in agreement. They were a family, the male very big, and his mate with a little light coloured baby primate. After a while, their curiosity of the humans fulfilled, they swung off into the trees in an effortless show of strength.

Tea for the marines on guard was stealthily carried forward and drank gratefully, which was hot and sweet.

Tom studied his map and took a compass bearing being careful of the fluctuation due to the metal weaponry they were carrying. Satisfied, he signalled the group to saddle up and move out in a well-spaced single file, and so the hazardous journey continued. This time the ground although well covered by the high overhead canopy was rising quite steeply. The steady silent slashing of the parangs as they hacked their way through this continent of jungle.

After what seemed like hours of physical stress and strain; eyes bulging with fatigue, they reached the base of the expected escarpment which rose from the jungle floor thousands of feet above them.

Tom gave the hand signal 'all round defence' and slowly and gratefully they sank down shucking the weight off their shoulders as they splayed out on the jungle floor. Jin Tin was sitting on a rock a little above them seemingly at ease in his environment but always alert with one ear cocked for any kind of unfamiliar noise.

They rested awhile, contemplating the more rigorous task ahead, the ascent of the massive feature in front of them.

Tom clicked his fingers twice, placed his hand on his head and made an O with index finger and thumb, signalling an order's group (O group). One by one, they slid over to him. Tom pointed up towards the escarpment. "We have to be at least halfway up this cliff face today as it is getting late and we have to harbour up by 1600 hrs, understood? Jin Tin will take the rope up and secure it. Jack will go up minus heavy equipment and be able to haul everything we have one by one. On reaching a suitable site, start preparing your area. Okay?

"Gil you will be second, Dave you will go up third, McHenry you are fourth, Doc is fifth. I will be sixth."

Jack unslung the climbing rope and signalled to *Jin Tin* to take it up to an anchor point he had picked out from below. On the cliff face were large roots that had been growing for centuries in search of water and sustenance similar to the Angkor Wat Temple in Cambodia. Jin Tin was climbing with the agility of a monkey, grinning to the marines below as he climbed. He selected a good level platform and secured the rope. Jack took hold of the rope tested it with all his strength then started the climb with rigorous drive. One by one the, man packs were drawn up interspliced with the marines and soon they were located in their new position.

Tom looked around but was not happy about the position and pointed upward. "We have to go higher," he whispered. The marines nodded in agreement and so they set to, Jin Tin again going first with the rope. The cliff face was now leaning slightly outwards; however, with the large roots for hand and foot holds would be a distinct advantage. Slowly and laboriously they climbed; sweat dripping from their faces in the intense heat and humidity. As each got to the end of the rope, Jack hauled them up the last section with his tremendous strength. Again, Tom surveyed this location and decided that although it wasn't the half-way point, it would be a splendid place to harbour up. It, having an overhang similar to a cave entrance which would be ideal for cover. Tom whispered, "Okay break out the iron rations and harbour up." Smiles creased the faces of the group. No fires, no smoking after dark. The watch roster is in the same order of ascent, use the toggle ropes to attach to your wrists no movement, no noise, after dark.

Tom remembered the sgt major's quiet instruction, "Only a capful at last light."

Chapter 9
The Summit

Tom had been on the last watch of the night and so was able to see and hear the jungle coming alive, the night sounds giving way to the incessant hiss and the vibrant sounds of the cicadas, whooping of the monkeys as they foraged for their incessant need for food. The burping of the bull frogs in the streams and swamps covering the land. It was time to start again on their rescue mission, but first all preparations must be done. Tugging on the toggle ropes was begun and as each marine awoke, he instinctively reached for his 'iron maiden', as he fondly referred to his weapon. Stretching aching limbs a few press-ups to get the circulation going and the dreaded task of changing from dry night gear to their daytime wet gear. However, a nice mug of tea was a welcome 'Wet' (brew). All weapons were to be cleaned in rotation and not all together so that half were in defence should they be attacked. Which was unlikely in their present position; however, 'never put all your eggs in one basket' was a favourite slogan in recruit training, a long time ago. Tom made eye contact with all his men and judged them to be in good spirits. McHenry as always was busy brewing up and rolling a cigarette at the same time with his cheesy grin, nothing seemed to worry him at all. Gil Warden, the quiet achiever, complete and confident. Dave Younger was on his first commission, quiet unassuming though resourceful, he would do well. Big Jack French, strong, absolutely reliable with an incredible knowledge of most weapons, field craft and tactical planning, the marines had taught him well. Bungy Williams the SBA, surprisingly seemed to be enjoying his trip with them; however, he looked very untidy, with his wispy thin beard he had just a few weeks ago started to grow. Jin Tin had taken up post on a ledge overlooking the marines, some 20 feet below. He had taken up the rope which was dangling ready for the final assault.

And so the climb began with fresh energy and the will to succeed. Jin Tin once again at a higher point and at each stage belaying the rope down to Jack who would then hike up to Jin Tin, then haul up the heavy man packs. Each marine with his weapon slung over, and around the shoulder and neck. They had now left far behind the tree canopy and were feeling the fierce heat of the sun. What was it that the old Chinese philosopher had said? 'The longest journey starts with the first step!' How very true; however, in this case, the first hand hold and the first toe hold. Luckily, they had selected good leather boots to accomplish this arduous task.

Onward and upward they climbed, seemingly it would never end. Now, they had come to a very wide ledge which had some vegetation and when all were together, they stared up in wonder. The climb would get harder, staring at them were huge boulders 60 feet in diameter piled as high as the eye could see. Dave murmured, "The devil's marbles." Tom and the group thought, *My God, he's right,* but just nodded at the epitaph. Let's hope it wouldn't be used on their tombstone.

This phase would see them climbing over and around the inside of this phenomenal force of nature probably caused by a gigantic volcanic eruption thousands of years ago, spewing out such large chunks of lava which had developed into solid rock. The marines although very tired and exhausted, likened it to the old black and white film. *Tarzan and the Lost Continent.*

After eight gruelling hours, they finally made it to the top and exhausted lay in strategic all round defence positions. They rested awhile, each man with his own thoughts and hopes.

Spread out before them was a carpet of jungle, so far below. From this vantage point, all the vista was visible and good planning and observation would triumph for the rescue party. Tom gestured and indicated that this would be their harbour up position for the night and so preparations began to settle down in this quite exhilarating high position. The marines unpacked whatever they would require for the night, it was now middle of the afternoon and so it was indeed time for a brew and some nosh.

Tom wasted no time as he was brewing up, he also unpacked the waterproof bag containing the thermal imager. This was new kit to him and he carefully inspected it. Very much like a large pair of binoculars, eyepieces an off switch and dials. The base was like a Rolex watch, it had a bezel that could rotate 360°. A small tripod at the base, which could be elongated to accommodate the difference in the height of ground. He selected a perfect position overlooking the entire valley beneath them. *Here goes,* he thought, switched on and peered through the eyepieces. *WOW!* He recoiled at the clarity of this new invention, slowly he went back to focus on the picture he was witnessing. Jack had been watching Tom and slithered over to see what had been disturbing him. Tom moved over to let Jack take a peek through the eyepieces of the Thermal imager. "WOW!" Jack said softly; immediately, he grasped the absolute use of this new kit. Jack whispered in Tom's ear, "This will revolutionise future engagements in the marine corps and any other military conflict." Looking through the lenses, all warm blooded animals, humans that gave off heat were easily identifiable, even as they moved deep into the jungle, it was possible to see to a distance of 20 miles thereabouts. Tom and Jack kept looking and plotting any human activity transferring the information and co-ordinates onto their maps. In the meantime, Gil Warden and Dave Younger had been on a recce of the immediate area, just to make sure they were not in for any surprises. On the highest point of this mountain was a 'Trig Point' which they, after returning, informed Tom and Jack. "That's interesting; it gives us our exact position on this map. It will also help the pilots when they start the case-vac operation. That's if we are still in one piece by then and have found any survivors from the Lynx crash! Keep on looking for anything out of the ordinary, we must have a plan!"

Meanwhile, Jin Tin and McHenry after they had selected their personal harbour position, had been off scouting for a way down from this high mountain position. The reverse side of this high plateau was a more gradual gradient sloping down to the jungle floor thousands of feet below. They had also found a submerged underground pool of fresh water which of course they had tested, Jin Tin gesticulating that it was 'bagus, baik lah!' To McHenry's ears, this sounded good especially with the wide smile of *Jin Tin* as evidence. Even so, the marines would sieve it through and use the purification tablets. However, it was a good discovery as their water supply was at a low level. McHenry deduced that this water which was totally fresh was constantly being renewed on a more or less daily basis. He had been in Borneo and knew of the temperamental weather patterns. His training as an AE (Assault Engineer) was typical of his thoughts. "We have to use our ponchos for overhead cover and maybe catch some into our water bags and bottles," he murmured to himself. "Better get back and spread the word."

Tom and Jack, meanwhile, had been observing all movement to the front and had collated quite a bit of evidence of enemy activity on a prominent feature in the middle distance. Where they had concluded that was the location of an Indon Camp. They had noticed that patrols were regularly employed and of platoon strength maybe slightly larger than any marine patrols, which generally were only at section level. Tom had, on looking into the thermal imager for long periods noticed a split second red dot in the middle of the large lagoon separating the position of the enemy and their position. Tom had dismissed it as he thought, *I'm getting eyestrain*. However, he mentioned it to Jack who would keep a weather eye open for any more millisecond flashes, when he took over the task of observer, whilst Tom got his nosh and mug of tea. He collected some strong straight branches and erected his Basha for the night, McHenry had passed on the info that heavy low cloud would all probability bring in exceptional amounts of water droplets known as 'Dew point' where the two temperatures meet and the result is a thorough soaking wet ground surface but not raining.

Jack grunted, which caught Tom's attention, "Yeah, you were right; there is a faint red dot right in the centre of the lagoon, here." He pointed and marked the spot on his map. "It is not natural, so must be from some electrical piece of equipment. It's got to be our missing Lynx!"

"XMPTL.13 was the number of the chopper, wasn't it?" Both gazed over the edge at the massive valley below and particularly at the lagoon and possible routes of approach. "Tomorrah! We go along this ridge until we reach this point here on the map and there seems a way down which is more gradual than this side has been, we have a compass bearing to the Lagoon so will just keep pressing on until we hit the water! Okay, Jack?"

"Roger that."

"Listen Jack, the number on that chopper sounds to me like it was an experimental job to test the chopper in this theatre of war out here in tropical conditions!"

Jack lay on his back looking up at the tall tree canopy. "I've been noticing that, that tree there is missing a few branches right on the very topmost tips."

"So! What are you getting at?" mused Tom.

"Well, just supposin our Lynx comes thrashing over here early mornin when it's really cloudy and just nicks that low branch on his tail rotor which sends him into a spin and he clues up, down there in the drink, what da ya fink eh?"

Tom churned this info over in his mind and just nodded at Jack. "You might just be right Jack."

Tom gesticulated by hand signals for an 'O' group to his position. Quietly, he told of the latest findings that he and Jack had collated and the evidence that 'maybe' the helicopter was in the middle of the lagoon. He looked around at the faces of the marines to see if they had understood. "At first light, we must be ready to move out all weapons checked and oiled, all equipment packed and stowed." He showed the group the destination looking down over the vast expanse of jungle and lalang.

They retired to their respective holes in the ground and began their night vigil two hours on, four hours off. It was true what the QM had told them the tiger balm did keep off the mossies! He also remembered the QM's last words, "One capful per night!"

It was not a good night as McHenry had informed them it was very cold and wet with the heavy cloud. However, they had collected enough water to sustain them for a day or two. They had also sampled this water which was straight from the heavens and therefore not contaminated, washing down their Paladin tablet, it tasted good.

First light saw them fully booted and spurred, *Jin Tin* shivering and eager to get going down to the jungle floor where for him it would be very warm. Jack would be lead scout after Jin Tin. So in single, spread out file, they crossed part of the ridge to descend on a very rough track, probably animal, that zig zagged a torturous route to the confines of the huge cavernous rain forest thousands of feet below. At certain points, Jack payed out the rope in order for the men to get a safety line, to hold onto.

It was heavy going with their loads and soon they were wishing they were still at the top in comparative coolness, although damp.

Everything was going all right, thought Tom as they lowered themselves down a fairly steep incline of the mountain. Tom's thoughts had strayed to Linda again and although his eyes were focused on his surroundings, his mind had the ability of total recall of events back home in Plymouth with Linda's beauty, her black hair and expressive green eyes, and a smile to light up the room.

He froze, *What was that!* He heard a muffled, faint cry and a thud. All the marines had also heard it and were in the on guard position, kneeling. Tom looked forward and rear, making sure everyone was accounted for. He noticed at the rear Dave Younger was missing. Today he was the rear end Charlie and he wasn't there. Tom motioned everyone to stay where they were and he trekked back to the rear to see what could have happened to Dave. The undergrowth was quite thick, difficult to locate what had taken place. He stood stock still ears and senses alert to any sound alien to the jungle and its constant vibratory noises. Minutes passed, as he crept forward and upward, he heard it again and made his way to the source of the sound. His fingers had found a ledge and he gingerly lifted himself onto it. There in the middle was a hole in the ground no bigger than a man, from which he assumed Dave had fallen. Now, everyone had passed over that area with safety except for Dave which had suddenly caved in due to the passage of time, weather and heavy loads of the marines. Tom shucked off his equipment, found his torch and shone it down into the abyss. Dave was trapped on a ledge about 20 feet down. Tom whispered, "We're coming down for you, hold on." Feebly, Dave nodded.

McHenry came up alongside, "I'm going down."

However, Bungy Williams had also come alongside and declared to all and sundry, "I'm going down! I'm the doc on this mission!"

There was no answer to that and so the rope was passed from Jack up forward to the rear. Bungy tied a suitable fireman's chair knot and was gone through the hole like a jack rabbit. He grinned up at them as he descended and whispered, "Roughie toughies, eh!" Tom just grinned at him and McHenry. The rope had been secured round a suitable tree branch above them and together McHenry and Tom Belayed Bungy to where Dave would be on the ledge.

Meanwhile, Jack had loped back through the line of advance; on the way he put Gil as lead scout with *Jin Tin.* "Keep a sharp lookout," he whispered. "Just take cover and keep your eyes peeled." Gil nodded, he knew the drill. Cautiously, he crept to the group around the hole. "What's up, Tom?" Tom gave him a brief rundown on the present situation. Jack nodded understandingly.

Bungy was making steady progress down into this yawning abyss. "Bit creepy down here," he muttered. Using his torch, he slowly and surely approached Dave's position on the ledge. "Better have a look where we are in this hole." He swung his torch around. "Bloody hell!" he gasped. "Can you hear me, Dave? Whatever you do, don't move!" His torch had shown him the vast extent of the cathedral like cavernous hole they were in, stalagmites and stalactites abounded in this enormous cave. Bushy found he was suspended high up in this nightmarish place. "Right Dave, how are you feeling? Any broken bones?"

Dave slowly shook his head and just mumbled, "I don't think so, but my head hurts and my knuckles, my knee feels bad."

Bungy said, "Okay pal! Lie very still, I'm going to give you an injection and I am going to put a dressing on your face and head. After that, I'll signal the guys to pull you up to safety."

Bungy took off his harness he had made and gently slipped it on to Dave. Gingerly, he stepped onto the ledge expecting any minute that he would plunge down into the depths below. It held, and so Bungy tugged twice on the rope to indicate the need for evacuation of Dave.

Up above; Tom, Jack and McHenry took the strain and began the delicate task of hauling Dave to safety. Meanwhile, Gil Warden and *Jin Tin* were farther along the track keeping their eyes peeled for any enemy patrols, *Jin Tin* as usual sitting high up in a tree perfectly camouflaged having a greater view of the surrounding area. You must remember these trees are rain forest trees and have a height of around 80ft. Most have vines running down their entire length which makes for easier climbing but to be careful of the snakes which abound in these tropical jungles. *Jin Tin* loved snakes and found them tasty, chopping them into snake steaks when the team would harbour up for the night, the skin he carefully peeled back and cleaned off any fatty tissue deposits and rolled it into a suitable flexible green leaf, tying some lalang grass around like a postal package. The skin he would sell to the Chinese, as they would fashion it into various items of merchandise for sale.

Dave had been successfully hauled inch by inch through the hole he had crashed through. The 'Doc' had done a pretty good job down there in that dark ominous looking cave; however, to Tom, Jack and McHenry, he still looked a bloody mess with blood oozing out from the 'first field dressing'. Tom spoke first, "This is going to be a problem for us!" Jack and McH both nodded.

The 'Doc' poked his head through the hole he had managed to shin up the rope on his own steam. "Well, gimme a pull up, will ya! I'm hanging in mid-air!"

Tom and Jack grinned at him, hauling him out to safety. "What do ya think, Doc?" Jack growled.

"Well he's young and he's very healthy, maybe after a good night's sleep and I give him a painkilling injection, he'll be able to make it for a day or so then his recuperation system will have kicked in and he will be all right, that's my diagnosis of his condition; I'll keep looking after him don't you worry."

"There is one thing we have to do!" McH whispered.

"Well, what is that?" Tom inquired.

"His kit and weapon are down that hole," responded McH.

"Are you volunteering to go down?" Tom said with a grin.

"Well, I didn't say that! Did I? However, I'll be going down if you insist!" His disarming Irish brogue and his cheery grin making the situation light hearted. "I'll need some dead sticks and take some PE down with me." McH prepared himself; all unnecessary heavy gear was offloaded.

Securing the nylon climbing rope to the overhead branch, he threw the rest of it into the gaping hole. "Wish me luck," as he stepped lightly to the hole.

McH turned to face them and said, "Here, what's the name of that fucken Injun!"

Tom and Jack both spoke in unison, "Geronimo!!" With a grin, McH launched himself, abseiling down the hole.

It was dark, ominous and threatening. McH used his torch, he had reached a point where he could let go with one hand and use his torch to get his bearings and try and locate Dave's gear and weapon. Sure, there was a something down there far below. "How much rope have I got left?" he muttered. "I think I'll have to take the chance and just get down below." He slid slowly down and thought, *At any minute, I'm going to run out of rope.* However, by keeping the rope wrapped around one leg and the other in his left hand which would signal the end of it he made his way down. "Yeah, that's better," he muttered. His feet had touched 'Terra Firma', *The more firma the less terror,* he thought. He unpacked his sticks using the torch to get a look at his new surroundings. He lit the sticks and had a little fire going, it lit up the massive cavern he was in; next he put a small stick of PE on the fire, and this gave extraordinary light to the rest of the massive complex. Wasting no time, he connected Dave's gear and weapon to the rope and gave it two tugs to signal for the lift to begin.

Looking around at all this natural phenomenon, McH likened it to a cathedral with intense colours and water flowing through the bottom of it. It was stunning and suddenly he was not afraid; instead he was filled with an appreciation of God's creativity. *Dark stirring shadows clung high up in this vaulted ceilings seemed to move*, he thought.

The rope came snaking down for his ascent. He gave a final look around, hoisted his 44 pattern backpack and looked at a possible way up. Using the rope, he would be able to reach certain levels and ledges, he didn't put the blazing fire out as it gave him tremendous light to plan his way up and out. Marines are trained in rope work particularly hand over hand climbing, with McH being quite light and fit, he swung himself up to every conceivable ledge and gantry using the rope when coming on, any way unpassable. He finally reached the fairly large ledge that David had landed on, which he judged to be about 20 feet from the surface and the hole. "Just a little bit further to go," he muttered; spitting on his hands more for luck than anything, he swung out and started the hand over hand technique, legs and feet gripping the rope as he jack-knifed his way to the top.

Grinning as always, he emerged from the hole, and Tom and Jack lifted his body out of it. As he came out, there was a whoosh of air, everyone ducked for cover. Out of the hole came hundreds of bats streaming out in a giant wave of dark flying creatures emitting little cries and tweets.

Everyone hit the deck not knowing at that precise moment what was going on. The danger over, heads bobbed up, startled looks on all faces, then grins, "You certainly stirred up a hornets' nest there, McH," Tom whispered hoarsely.

"Saddle up Jack! We're going forward to see how Gil and *Jin Tin* are getting on and what the situation is." Tom took out the light compass that RSM Chisel had given him and took a bearing for the forward push. "Mac, you and the doc stay here with Dave, we'll have to harbour up here for the night; Jack and I will return ASAP! In the meantime brew up and keep a watch, look after Dave, we can't go anywhere at the moment, we'll hope he's okay and fit to travel tomorrow!"

With that, he took a few strides forward and recalibrated his bearing so that he wasn't among weaponry that would distort his reading. Signalling Jack to keep well to the rear as he advanced forward.

Fully alert to every sound and likely ambush positions, they silently crept through the jungle, fully loaded with one round up the spout; safety catch on.

Tom was very aware now that his team was disjointed and very vulnerable to attack; he had to get them back into shape to continue the search.

Meanwhile, Bungy had been cleaning Dave's head, hands and knee wounds and had painted them with iodine. Which Dave found damned painful but gritted his teeth to shut off the scream he really wanted to do. McH had also brewed up and prepared some stewed beef with curried rice, this he was going to get Dave to eat when the doc had finished the dressings.

One hour later, Tom had found Gil in a rough hide he had made at the base of one of the heavily buttressed rain forest trees. The Bren gun hidden by foliage ready to fire in the fully supported position. Tom nearly missed finding him, he was that well concealed. Gil had selected a good high vantage point rising to about 20 feet above the rim of the swampy lagoon. They both gazed out onto the lagoon that previously they had spotted from their summit lookout, yesterday.

"Seen any 'Chokies' out front," Tom whispered.

"Not on your life Tom, only the ducks as you can see," Gil replied, grinning broadly.

Jack had finally caught up and took cover to the right of Gil. "You've got a good position here boy," Jack observed as he cast his expert eye around.

Chapter 10
The Lagoon

The jungle kept up its incessant animal and insect noises, especially now near the water's edge the bullfrogs with their deep throated croaking, mosquitoes were in abundance near this grand oasis of jungle slime. Tom handed his insect repellent around to Gil and Jack, "Gotta fight 'em off," Tom whispered.

Tom addressed Gil, "You and *Jin Tin* will have to stay here; Jack and I will go back to assist Dave. It'll be dark in about two hours; we've just about got time to go back to see everything is okay for tomorrah! We will see you at approx. 0700 hrs. Okay to that?" Gil nodded in agreement.

With that Tom and Jack peeled off and made their way to the remainder of the group at the 'Hole'.

Tom had noticed a very valuable source of transportation across this expanse of first swampy conditions then deepening into a large lagoon of some depth and size. Tomorrow they would return and the use this native resource. *Utilisation of resources and materials,* echoed through Tom's brain.

McH and Bungy had been busy setting up the harbour position; also, they had a brew going which was indeed a welcome sight for Tom and Jack.

"How're you feeling now, Dave?" both inquired.

"Not too bad, but my knee is giving me 'heaps', I hope it is going to let me get mobile tomorrow," Bungy interrupted in the conversation telling Tom that he would give him a painkiller injection; tomorrow he would give him some 'special tablets', he said with a wink to Tom and Jack.

That sorted, the team set about preparing for tomorrow's early start for the 'Lagoon'. Dave's load would be halved, sharing out the heavier equipment with the remainder of the party.

The darkness soon enveloped the jungle, there is no twilight, all sight of anything is lost, even your own hand is not visible in front of your face. The night sounds take over, cicada's wings beating incessantly to a pulsating rhythm and the ever present croaking of the bull frogs.

The use of the tiger balm ointment was liberally applied to face and hands, it tends to deaden the skin to any sand flies and mosquitoes, all took their paladin tablets to ward off the risk of contracting malaria. *"Remember only a capful at night,"* Tom remembered QM's last words.

The usual dawn chorus of the whooping monkeys woke the marines who had managed to get a few hours' sleep, after their watch; bleary-eyed, they began to break camp, testing their cramped muscles to get moving. They had a deadline with Gil at 0700 hrs and no matter what, Tom was determined to fulfil his pledge. Dave was getting treatment from Bungy the SBA and to all appearances he seemed a little better this morning. Taking the little compass that RSM Chisel had given him, Tom stepped out in front a fair distance and took a bearing which they would march on this misty, dripping, morning.

Tom signalled McH to take the lead and off they all trekked, Dave in the centre with the doc. Jack bringing up the rear, as tail end Charlie.

Two gruelling hours later they arrived at Gil's 'hide'.

"Not bad timing Tom, only fifteen minutes out from what you reckoned yesterday; how's Dave getting on?" asked Gil.

"He's done well, considering his fall the other day," Tom replied.

Tom walked down the line talking in a quiet manner to his patrol, "Drop your gear; all round defence and one by one get a brew going and some nosh!" He looked Dave over and noticed he was heavily bandaged around his head and part of his face; however, he had made it this far but the pink flush he wanted to know about.

So he approached Bungy, "What did you give Dave this morning?"

Bungy winked and said "Benzedrine." Tom pursed his lips, but said nothing.

Quietly, Gil told the boys about his vigil at the Lagoon, "I have never seen such a beautiful spectacle of creatures in the wild who came to the water's edge to drink and feed, such a scene that I will treasure for the rest of my life."

Tom took out his slim notepad from his map pocket and sketched a raft made entirely of bamboo which he had noticed was growing in a great cluster nearby. Bamboo is a peculiar type of weed which lies underground for many years then in the space of one year it will grow to heights of sometimes 80ft tall. It is also used by the Asians in all manner of household items, cups, mugs, chairs, lounges, screens, fences; but Tom wanted it today for a raft with an outrigger fitted for stability. The vast amount of hollow sections in the bamboo would float easily. Having finished his sketch he passed it round to the team to show exactly what he wanted them to make. A picture speaks a thousand words.

The raft would be 10ft long and 4ft wide, the outriggers a further 3ft from the sides, this he thought would give greater stability on the lagoon.

Tom signalled to *Jin Tin* who was perched high up in the biggest rain forest tree to come down and join them. He showed him the sketch and *Jin Tin* smiled broad and said, "Bagus Lah!" which Tom interpreted as being very good? Tom showed *Jin Tin* the Parra cord he had, and gesticulated for him to think of what else could he find to bind the raft together. *Jin Tin* just grinned and disappeared into the jungle labyrinth on his special task.

After a very welcome brew and nosh, the team stripped off all unnecessary equipment and set to the task of preparing the bamboo into 10ft lengths. Pretty soon a start was made on lashing them together. The outrigger lengths would be at 90° to the base of the raft, thus the main body would be lashed to these. *Jin Tin* had indeed found some useful lengths of strong vine no thicker than the normal Parra cord. Half the day was spent on making this raft and outriggers; but finally it was finished. *Jin Tin* had also made himself a native craft which of course was much smaller but highly manoeuvrable and light. He would search the far bank Tom planned, for anything out of the ordinary.

"Okay," Tom addressed his team. "Fit the equipment on an even pattern. When we get it afloat, we will have to wade through this swampy area until we get to the water. Keep your weapon and attach it to your wrist. Jack! Get the grappling hook attached to the climbing rope we're going fishing," he said with a grin. He cut a thin stave from a young sapling.

"Dave, you will stay here in this hide I am swopping your Armalite for the SLR LMG. It will be okay for you in this position. Remember only 3 taps at a time. Okay?" Dave nodded, "We will be back tomorrah, if everything goes to plan, InshaAllah!" Tom shook his hand and was down to the rest of the team, patiently waiting and a silent wave to Dave as they pushed the raft out sliding and squelching in the slimy mass of the Lagoon.

Dave watched them go with a sinking feeling in the pit of his stomach. "Hope they make it," he said to himself, as if in a silent prayer.

With their packs and equipment lashed aboard the raft, they paddled alongside and were presently in clear deeper water. "Hope there's no sharks," Jack quietly joked to the crew.

"Nah, the crocodiles have eaten them," McH retorted with his usual Irish wit.

After travelling half way into the Lagoon, Tom hoisted himself aboard the raft and took hold of the rope and grappling hook swinging it outward to land in the area he thought of looking where he had seen the little red dot on the thermal imager. They swam the raft in various directions with Tom swinging the lead has he put it, similar to a sailor on the old sailing ships, where seeking the depth was important to a ships safety.

"I got something," he quietly said to the men. "Here, Jack get aboard and secure it for me, I'm going down the line to see what we've got on the end." Tom took out his survival knife and bound it to the stave, making a rough lance, just in case there was anything down there of a ferocious nature. His weapon, he lashed to the raft and quietly he slipped into the water and followed the line down to what he hoped would be the crashed Lynx helicopter. The water was an eerie green but was reasonably navigable; he just kept following the line. A dark shape loomed up out of the darker depths and yes it was indeed the Lynx. He just had time to give a quick inspection before he really had to surface for air. He clawed his way back up the line and coughing and spluttering, crawled onto the raft.

Jin Tin had finished his raft which was more like a surfboard measuring just 6ft long and about 18 inches wide; he lay on it and virtually paddled or swam, propelling it forward with each stroke, it was quite fast. He approached the main raft and standing, he used sign language, two fingers to his eyes and a sweeping gesture with his arms to tell Tom and Jack that he was going for a 'look see' across the Lagoon. They both watched him go and smiled at the little brown figure on a raft. "Looks like a tadpole," Tom remarked, grinning. "I'd better get some air in my lungs." He also rummaged through his 44 back packs and found the homing device he had been supplied with. Taking great gulps of air and then compressing his body to his toes, he did this for a few times taking in as much air as possible then exhaling it, finally one last intake and clutching his spear and the homing device he lowered himself over the edge and was gone, following the line of rope.

This time he made a closer inspection of the helicopter which lay on its side, unfortunately on the side (Starboard side) which had the access door, entry and exit for any personnel it would be carrying. Anyone in there could not have got out. He looked at the cockpit, it had only the co-pilot navigator still strapped in but the shield was badly damaged, the co-pilot or rather what was left of him, dead.

Tom was now running out of air so he managed to attach the homing device which he peeled and stuck; pressing the red button. He made a quick exit for the surface following the rope ever upward. He reached up out of the water, gasping for air and said to Jack, "Hack off a piece of bamboo; I'm going to tie the rope to it for recognition."

In the signals hut at Brigade HQ, the marine signal operator passed on to the signals officer, "Sir, we have a homing signal emanating from the Lagoon in the first division Sarawak." The signals officer looked at the screen and immediately took and recorded the grid location information, he promptly went in to see the colonel, the CO of marine operations in Sarawak.

The colonel on seeing this responded very quickly and told the young lieutenant, "Get this information out to all our contacts especially HMS Bulwark and HMS Fearless, tell them this is urgent and to stand by for my orders as to ultimate procedure!"

"Yes sir!" The young lieutenant went about his task, presently there was cautionary activity aboard both ships.

The ships were lying off shore occasionally making forays up the coast and also supplying and replenishing store and equipment ashore. (On HMS FEARLESS this announcement.)

"Do you hear now? This is the Captain speaking, we have just received an urgent signal that we hoped we might be hearing, it is a homing signal from the Search and Rescue team sent out 3 days ago. We advise that the following personnel will be required; SBS divers, hovercraft drivers and fleet protection group, MMG section to man the port and starboard mounts. All ammunition equipment for loading to be done immediately, more information will be at your disposal later. That's all… OUT."

A frenzy of activity on board both ships took place each man knowing what was required of him in their own professional manner, sailors and marines pulling together. On board, HMS BULWARK, 848 squadron were placed on full alert with the information (O group) at hand in the briefing room on the central control island, amidships, starboard. During the briefing which was quite extensive, only a few of the chopper pilots would be required. Amongst them would be Lt Nick Wise. Who because of his daily flights over this vast area had a better knowledge of the Terrain? The code word for the scrambling of helicopters and pilots was '***ANCHORMAN***'.

Meanwhile at the Lagoon, *Jin Tin* had made it to the other side of the water. Paddling ashore and keeping a low profile he hid the little raft and proceeded ashore having spotted a broken branch after a long probing search. He was a good tracker and could read the jungle like his back hand. There were tell-tale marks of the passage of at least a platoon with scuffs of soil and overturned leaves which he had observed with some interest. He padded along the trail of these marks and soon he was enveloped in the dense jungle canopy.

Back on board, HMS Fearless in the operations and briefing room the assembled crew were given the details of the position ashore and the co-ordinates. "Your mission is to proceed up the Limchang River to this position here." The intelligence officer pointed to the map with his stick. "Then as it will undoubtedly be getting dark, lay up somewhere here, in this rather scrubby area. At first light, on command, proceed over to the lagoon and despatch the SBS Divers who will, under the command of Cpl Polli SBS, investigate the position of the homing device and if it turns out to be the downed Lynx, secure lines ready for its airlift. At all times you will observe any enemy movement and respond accordingly. The code word for all out action is '***ANCHORMAN'!*** That's it gentlemen and may I say good luck on your special mission!"

Half an hour later the massive rear end of HMS Fearless opened up and the hovercraft powered out to sea with Lt Waters at the helm of his MOA and second in command Marine Owen, all marine personnel fully kitted out, aboard. Marine Owen had served aboard HMS Striker and knew everything about landing craft and the new Hovercraft which he had recently taken a course on in Portsmouth, A jovial likeable person was Owen.

At Brigade HQ, Lt Colonel's Bob Loden and Robin Briggs were being transferred to HMS Bulwark for an executive meeting with all Captains and heads of depts. This was to co-ordinate all avenues of approach in order to enable a smooth running rescue operation. Captain Wiltshire spoke next.

"Now you've all heard the briefings, is there any more information that maybe we have missed or overlooked?" The signaller Marine Wilson hoisted his hand tentatively. "Yes Wilson, what do you have to offer?"

“Well sir, I was thinking that we could contact the USS Kitty Hawk which I have been in contact for the past few days, she is in our waters and is passing on her way to Viet Nam, well sir she has aboard the new Rotodine Helicopter, which they call the Chinook! I could contact the captain, with your permission sir! And make a request to them for the use of this helicopter which has a massive lifting capacity, ideal for the winching in of the Lynx.”

There was a moment of silence whilst this idea was digested and assimilated, finally Captain Wiltshire answered, “You know gentlemen, that is a cracking idea, well thought out Wilson, of course you have my permission, get on to it right away, when you do reach the captain I wish to speak to him myself!”

“Yes sir. Roger that!”

The USS Kitty Hawk was meanwhile cruising gently through the South China Sea practising her take-off and landing drills. This carrier was well equipped with all manner of Aircraft, sleek modern Bombers, fighter jet aircraft, light helicopters (Bell 47s), UH-1 Iroquois (Huey). Nimrods and of course the mighty Chinook Rotodine.

The signal came in from HMS Bulwark and was transferred to the captain in the flight control centre tower.

“It’s Captain Wiltshire of the British combined operations Commando carrier RO8. HMS Bulwark wishes to speak with you sir!”

“Okay Lieutenant, put him on the speaker.”

“This is Captain Lee Schrader of the USS Kitty Hawk, how can we be of service to you sir!”

Captain Wiltshire outlined his request for the use of one of their Chinooks for a special search and rescue operation in progress in the jungles of Borneo.

Chapter 11
Semper Fidelis

The skipper of the USS Kitty Hawk turned to his executive officer and said, "Bob will you get Colonel Beaurhanse to report to me here."

On meeting, the colonel gave the captain a very casual salute and sat down beside the captain. "Okay Marvin what's the score?"

"Well, Mike we've been asked by the Captain of the British Ship HMS Bulwark to help out with a dust off in some godforsaken place in Borneo. What d'ya say about that eh? We've been given the coordinates, should be simple in and out, I know the British could eventually get the goddamn bird outa the water but we've got the muscle at the moment!"

"Who's leading this mission Marvin?" Mike inquired

"Well, from what I've been told two marines with a special handpicked bunch of guys, name of the guy in the lead is Tom Martial and I think they said Jack French! Would ya believe that! In our Marine Corps they'd be the equivalent of P/Fcs." (Private 1st class.)

Mike spoke next, "I know these guys, I served with them for a short time in 42 Commando in '61. Great bunch of marines I shit you not! I say GO!"

"Just between you and me and that Bulkhead we have to be careful about our involvement in this latest confrontation, we don't want to cause any embarrassment in Washington or cause an international incident, on the other hand we feel obliged to help our brothers in arms. What you've gotta do is this, blank out any insignia of marines, or designated aircraft numbers. Blank 'em out, okay!"

"Yes sir, okay. Roger that! I'm right on to it." With that, he saluted and strode off to contact his team in the aircraft hangars.

Meanwhile back at the lagoon; *Jin Tin* had been padding through the jungle on his own quest, following the faint trail he had seen. It was a long trek that he was undertaking for he knew the jungle well; however, caution was always in his nature. Not only had he expert knowledge of his local environment, but the marines had trained him at the jungle warfare school in Ulu Terram, Johore, Malaysia. That was to sharpen him up to the latest techniques, especially the military ordnance that was being used by both sides of the conflict.

On and on, he padded, climbing steadily; twice he had to take cover as a Kalimantan patrol passed close by. That signalled to him that he was in close proximity of the Indon firebase.

He climbed one of the big rain forest trees and reached the very topmost branches where he had a great view of the surrounding area and of course now he could see and assess the situation. He looked at the firebase for quite a long time taking in every detail which he would have to convey to the team when he returned from his foray. He especially took mental note of what he judged to be a bamboo prison with two guards outside. The front was open and the interior was carved into the rock of the hill. Inside, he could make out the shape of a rough native platform style bed and on it lay an injured man. He was not an Indon Soldier as far as he could make out, so he figured it might be the pilot of the chopper they were seeking. Satisfied he had observed enough information, he shinned down the tree and made his way back to the search and rescue team at the Lagoon.

It was now late afternoon when he reached the edge of the lagoon finding the team already on the bank and in cover the raft partially hidden in the overhanging foliage. He was excited and a stream of Pidgin English and odd Malay words together with gestures pointing in the direction he had been trying to inform Tom and the crew what he had seen. One of the words that he used was 'Orang Puteh', Tom scratched his stubbly jaw and thought it sounded familiar, 'Orang' meant something like 'old man' or 'man of the forest' and indeed it was the first word of 'Orang u Tang' which could mean 'man'. The word 'Puteh' sounded like 'white'! Maybe Jin Tin was trying to say that a white man was up there in the Kalimantan base camp.

He turned to Jack and said, "I think he's found our missing pilot, Chris Davenport."

"I hope so," growled Jack.

Tom turned to the team and quietly said, "Saddle up, we're moving out. Gil, you're lead scout; McH follow him; Doc, you stay with Jack and me, nice and easy and quiet, keep your eyes peeled okay? Let's go." Jin Tin as always way out in front of the team.

In a single file well-spaced out, the team made their way on the compass bearing that Tom had taken when they landed on the marshy bank of the lagoon. Hours of continual trekking through this tough bush was exhausting in the tropical heat and humidity, ever alert and mindful of trip wires or medieval booby traps that was the custom of these Asian races.

Tom reckoned they must be approaching the outer perimeters of the Indon Camp as they were progressively climbing steadily through the thick jungle scrub, sweat was pouring out of every pore drenching them but also doing what it was intended, and that was to keep the body relatively cool. Tom motioned a halt to the team who gratefully sank into the familiar all round defence positions. Tom shrugged off his heavy ladder rack and packs looking around at the giant rain forest trees. He took out the thermal imager and the telescopic sight from Jacks sniper ·303 rifle, motioning to Jack and the boys he headed for a suitable large tree to climb. He wanted a bird's eye view of the 'Chokies' camp and the layout, to plan his next move before it got too dark as it was now late afternoon and soon it would all be in total darkness.

It was a painful journey to the topmost branches, this is what the marines trained for when climbing those thick hemp ropes in the middle of winter hand over hand slowly making it to the top. At last, he was able to rest on a branch like the eagles nest. He took the thermal imager from his pack and turned it on pointing it at the Indon firebase. He could see quite clearly the figures and the complete system of the camp, he also noted the two guards which were posted outside a bamboo stockade and lying recumbent on a makeshift native bed was a figure shrouded in white. He deduced that this was the Pilot that the team was searching for. He focused on the figure with the sniper sight and he could see plainly that it was indeed a European (he was fair-haired) and not an Indonesian; he adjusted the sight very carefully hoping to really verify that he was injured, alive, and not dead. It was now getting darker and he shinned down to join the team and give all of the marines a full-on report of what he had observed.

Jin Tin, sat in on the O group but was not able to grasp all that was being said, the only part of the orders group he understood was when Tom gave a mime and gestures to what the plan that the team was to do at first light, especially for *Jin Tin's* role he had to play.

Quickly, they cleaned and inspected their weapons; nothing must go wrong with their fighting ability. No fires, no smoking, no movement, no talking, only dry rations, to be eaten. From left to right each man would take turns on watch throughout the night, woken by their toggle ropes stretched one to another. Tom remembered the QM's final words, "Only one capful per night."

He smiled at the recollection; the QM was a colourful character and had been in the corps *forever.*

Chapter 12
Dawn Mission

A grey/green mist hung over the landscape; the marines' cramped limbs complained as they slowly stood upright making sure everything was secure and ready to go. *Jin Tin* was nowhere to be seen, he had melted into the jungle on his mission, which Tom had conveyed to him.

Tom gathered the team around him telling the doc and Jack to take their 44 packs off the ladder racks and to reverse the backpacks one to the front secured by the web straps that had secured them to the ladder racks the rear pack going on their backs, ammo pack to the front. These three ladder racks would be used after getting to their destination and slotting them together to form a stretcher. "Doc! You will quickly attend to the pilot and see to it he is not in pain! Okay? We'll use a sleeping bag inner to cover him making sure he's well strapped on, give him a 'shot' Doc to knock him out!"

"Gil, you go up forward with McH you are his protection. McH, do your stuff with the trip wires and the PE when we're on the move fell a few trees that might hold me up a bit!" McH his usual toothy grin gazed at his friend in understanding of the orders.

Well before dawn, *Jin Tin* had moved out following his trail he had made before which was the upturned leaves which had a fluorescent quality to them in the dark. As dawn broke, he was high in the jungle canopy and looking down on the Kalimantan basecamp and more importantly observing the two guards in front of the Bamboo prison. He had a personal score to settle with the Indonesian Army, who he classed as rebels and invaders of his precious land, they had razed one of his relatives Kampong on the river they had arrived at earlier. He could remember some of the villagers who were like kinfolk to him and his family. Inwardly, he had sworn revenge on all invaders who had practiced murder, rape and fire. His sister had been raped and murdered by the rebels who were attached to the Kalimantan Army as Islamic fundamentalists.

Slowly he took his blowpipe and fitted a poison arrow, this would be an almost impossible shot at the range he had chosen, but he was confident he could kill both of these 'Chokies', without a sound they would be dead within seconds.

His father had shown him how to make and shoot this blowpipe and to collect the jungles deadliest poisons, what plants and what snakes to milk their venom.

It was now approaching the first glimpses of dawn as he took careful aim, drew a deep breath and shot the arrow silently; it sped to the guard nearest and hit him in the base of the neck just below the skull severing his spinal cord and any communication of intelligence to the brain. He dropped silently to the ground as the other sentry looked around to see his friend on the dirt track, he looked up at the trees which was the last thing he ever saw as the arrow penetrated his eye and then into the brain.

It would not be long before the marines got to the basecamp and could have free passage to the Bamboo prison. However, *Jin Tin* had his own agenda which fitted in nicely with the overall planning of this rescue mission. He cut a young sapling tree shoot which was strong and very resilient about 18ft long. Silently, he made his way to the outer perimeter wire trotting at first then breaking into a very fast run with his sapling horizontally gripped like a pole vaulter. Being very light of weight and stature, he thrust the pole very near the barbed wire fence and sailed high into the air landing on his feet very lightly making for the largest of the watchtowers which he guessed quite rightly that it would contain the Captain of the Indon Kalimantan forces in this sector.

The wandering sentries inside the compound he despatched with his native double-edged skinning dagger to the base of the skull approaching them from behind. He climbed the tower's ladder effortlessly, just in time; he hid behind some woven native baskets as the captain emerged from his cabin.

He had only just awoken from sleep and as was his usual custom was enjoying his mug of black coffee laced with a measure of Chinese five stars brandy. A small noise behind him, like a rustle caused him to look around and as he did so, *Jin Tin's* parang swung high in the air and severed the captain's head clean off, where it tumbled sickeningly onto the decking, bleeding profusely with his eyes glazing over in sudden death. His body jerked in the nervous twitches as the heart still pumping, shot his life blood out in violent spurts of red.

Jin Tin picked up the head triumphantly placing it in a thin canvas bag and attached it to his belt.

The marines had reached the barbed wire fence and saw that the guards were laying in their death positions, so wasted no time in cutting through the barbed wire with the multi-purpose tool which now came in handy. Tom motioned to stand back as the barbed wire would on being cut spring back retracting rapidly. Next obstacle would be the panjis (slivers of sharpened bamboo) lying in the long grass, usually smeared in human excrement to inflict blood poisoning in the actual wound once the unwary had been pierced by them. They used the ladder racks positioned low in front of their line of advance and swept all of the panjis away from them.

Tom, Doc (Bungy) and Jack carrying the ladder racks to the Bamboo stockade slashed open the bamboo doors. Entering to see to Lt Davenport, who was in bad shape. He had lost considerable weight, his face was a pulpy mess and so was one of his legs which were a festering mess. The doc looked very concerned at his condition stroking his head and muttering some encouraging words. "What's up me duck!" as he stuck the needle into his shoulder to ease the pain. Chris would know that indeed he was in safe hands with the doc's accent. A faint smile tugged at his lips and a glimmer of hope lit his eyes for a second or two.

He quickly got a few dressings on head and legs and together they snapped the ladder racks together and eased Chris Davenport into the sleeping bag inner. Rapidly, they strapped him in for the journey back to the lagoon and hopefully to be picked up by the support backup crews.

Meanwhile, Gil Warden and McH had formed a rearguard, Gil lying on the fringes of the jungle with his trusty Bren gun and McH laying trip wires and PE around possible tracking routes.

Tom and Jack hoisted the stretcher onto their shoulders and made their way silently to the outer wire where they had come in; it was getting very light now and soon the base camp would be coming alive with activity.

A drop of blood dropped onto a guard who had been posted as sentry to the captain's watchtower, he had dozed off; he rubbed the blood off thinking it was a fly or mossies; he blinked and looked at the red blood which he couldn't understand where it came from. He looked up and caught another spot of blood which he perceived came from the decking high above him. He decided to investigate and find out what on earth was going on.

McH and Gil were in the meantime laying their PE to the giant rainforest trees. They were specializing in the two that faced the main gate standing 80ft high they were ideal from Mac's point of view. He was working flat out attaching an explosive necklace around their bases. With the new PE(Z) that had caught his attention at the Simmangang briefing. First of all, it wasn't dangerous neither was the ordinary PE until it had a detonator attached to it and most important a delayed action fuse. Mac had up till now wired up four trees and put down the metal skewers for the trip wires which when Gil and he were ready to withdraw on their rearguard action behind Tom, doc and Jack, it was risky business, timing was crucial.

Dave Younger at the Lagoon had not had a comfortable night, he had managed to walk a little way and relieve himself, but he was still not feeling very well the pain was still a problem constantly throbbing, that forced him to swallow the tablets that Bungy had left for him. Not knowing what was happening was his constant nagging doubt.

Tom and big Jack were now going through the panji patch, which now were no problem as they faced outward away from them, the Australian boots proving their worth now. The doc following close behind ever watchful for his patient and quick glances to the rear.

They were through and heading straight for the cover of the jungle canopy which soon enveloped them, it was a downhill controlled dash.

Behind them in the Indon firebase, a bell was ringing frantically accompanied by clamour of whistles and military activity. They had at last discovered the dead soldiers and the absence of their wounded prisoner.

The stretcher bearers, Tom and Jack, passed close by Mac and Gil. "Keep us covered for as long as possible," Jack growled.

Mac put his thumb up and grinned, "Roger that Jack!"

The firebase was manned by about a company, numbering some 120 soldiers with attached ranks; it would prove to be a formidable task getting back to the lagoon and maybe some form of backup that's if it came on time which was Tom's greatest hope at the moment.

Mac could see a platoon of 'Chokie' soldiers heading for the main gate of the compound soon they would be out in pursuit of the rescue team. Gil looked over to Mac nervously weighing up the exact time that Mac would blow the first trees. Sweat trickled down his face as he tried to focus on the targets. Now they were out and were only fifty yards from the trees when Mac twisted the firing switch. The first explosive charge went off which sliced through the trunk like a hot knife through butter, the second explosion which was greater virtually lifted the tree and knocked it forward. Both explosions went off at the same time and both huge trees fell with an earth-shattering noise branches breaking off in all directions amongst the platoon heading out of the gate. Gil opened up with his Bren gun and gave several long bursts before getting up and making for another fire position. Mac who had the AR15 with underslung grenade launcher popped two grenades well to the rear of the platoon landing inside the camp.

"That'll slow 'em down a bit," he smiled his toothy grin at Gil, who took heart from this pleasant southern Irishman. Both made their way in a rearguard action to cover the withdrawal of the stretcher party.

Tom turned his head to Jack and said, "Let the stretcher down, we're not going to make it at this speed."

"Put this stretcher on my back, we'll make a better pace, Jack you go in front and clear the way, Doc you stay behind the patient and make sure he is not in any difficulty and he is still unconscious, Okay lift it on, make sure the lashings are firm!" Jack said, "Sure you'll be all right with that weight."

"Sure I will; remember we heavy weapons carry this weight most of the time. You can spell me if you like?" Jack just cheesed down at this remark. They set off making much better speed now, although Tom found it rough going in a semi crouching position; he wasn't going to admit it. Doc was keeping his eyes on his patient with increasing anxiety for him; let's hope we make it he thought.

Jin Tin had silently crept away from the captain's observation deck and stole past the dozing sentry, taking up his long pole he had vaulted back over the barbed wire barricade and made his way independently to where he thought the escape route that Tom and Jack would eventually take. He climbed a tree and just waited and watched for any movement in the jungle canopy below; knowing and hoping that his tracking skills were absolutely correct.

Back at Brigade HQ as well as on HMS Bulwark, the signallers had pinpointed the exact location of the homing device that Tom had placed on the submerged Lynx helicopter and were transmitting this information to the American Aircraft Carrier USS Kittyhawk as well as the crew of the hovercraft which had been dispatched the day before and lay in waiting on the River Limchang under cover; just waiting for the code word to be sent… '*Anchorman'*.

The SBS underwater team had suited up and were waiting patiently having their first mug of hot steaming tea. A section element of the Fleet Protection Group supported by the MMG (·303

Vickers) section were kitted up, the Medium Machine Guns had been mounted up and checked, loaded, and ready to go. Appropriately named; Cpl Nick Vickers was in charge of the two gun crews.

"How long do you think it'll take to get back to the lagoon Tom?" Bungy queried. He was getting concerned about His patient Chris Davenport.

In between gasps for air, Tom replied, "Well, I would say at least an hour at the pace we're going!"

Just at that moment, *Jin Tin* swung down from his lookout in the tree, frightening the shit out of Bungy, he nearly went for his Browning but just arrested his arm in time. "Fucking hell, Jin Tin, you scared the shit out of me!" Bungy was sweating profusely. "Fucking jungle bunnies," he muttered.

Tom and Jack just grinned. "It's all right for you roughie toughies you're used to all this shit, I should be back on board ship taking a shower and having a cup of tea!"

Jin Tin pointed with his parang and gesticulated to Tom a different route through the jungle which would be quicker. Tom grasped his meaning, 'Follow Jin Tin, Jack!' so off they went to get back to the lagoon and hopefully to some kind of safety, but nothing would be safe until they had got the hell out of this dense jungle.

Mac and Gil were active in their rearguard action just enough to quell the onslaught of the Kalimantan Army group, many had been killed or seriously injured in the blasting of the two rainforest trees. Mac nodded to Gil as they both took up a firing position. Mac twisted the firing switch and yet another massive explosion followed by a secondary blast that nearly blew their eardrums out, two more massive trees fell with sickening thuds and cries from the second platoon sent out. Gil once more gave a few bursts from the Bren gun and changed his magazine, before legging it in pursuit of little Mac who was laying more trip wires in likely lines of advance; then hot on the trail of Tom and Jack. They couldn't be far in front, could they?

Gil was the first to realise the stretcher party had changed direction he was a veteran of the Malayan jungles and could read the signs of where the leaders had gone. He was mindful that the 'Chokies' weren't too far behind. "Mac, you go and catch up with the main party, I'll stay here and keep them at bay."

Mac with his cheeky grin said, "Not on your life, I wouldn't miss this for quids." With that, they both took up fire positions and waited for the inevitable whatever that would be. Casually, Mac took out his plastic Tobacco pouch a slowly rolled a cigarette. Gil looked at him, shaking his head in disbelief. "May as well die happy," Mac said and grinned.

The stretcher party had made better progress, although Tom was feeling the pangs of fatigue but pressed on the marine phrase running through his mind, *No pain, no gain!* Jack was beating a path through this dense jungle with *Jin Tin* way out in front leading the way. Three quarters of an hour later, they were standing on the edge of the lagoon which was swampy and treacherous. Jack and Bungy eased the stretcher off carefully and slowly lowered it. The lieutenant was not breathing; if he was, it was very shallow. Bungy was now very concerned and quickly brought out of his bag a resuscitation appliance, ripped open the plastic bag and gently inserted it into his mouth and throat. Bungy began to blow into the instrument very gently and after a few anxious minutes they all were glad to see he was breathing on his own. He took out another needle and inserted this in the shoulder; it was another shot of morphine.

Jack drew Tom away and said, "Make the call, Tom!" Tom unwrapped the thermal imager and switched it on a few lights lit up and a few tiny beeps sounded, it was working he sighed with relief. Looking at it, he decided that yes that switch there would be the transceiver. He turned the switch to 'ON', there was a lot of mush and then it levelled out to a quiet hum.

"Hello Sunray, this is Sierra/Romeo, how do you read me, over!"

"Sierra Romeo, we read you loud and clear, what is your position over."

"Sunray, we are at the designated lift-off position. Verify on our homing signal. We have bandits in close pursuit. Code word *Anchorman, Anchorman, Anchorman!"*

"This is Sunray; message understood, wilco! Over and out."

The code word was flashed to the various transmitter/receivers on the net. A klaxon sounded aboard USS Kittyhawk. "Now hear this! This is the Captain speaking, all detailed personnel to action stations, Chinook crews close up ready for take-off; may I say good luck you 'Gyrenes'."

This and similar messages were being given on HMS Bulwark and the Hovercraft Bosun with the SBS divers on board. The hovercraft fired up noisily inflating her huge rubber floatation skirt and within a few minutes was breaking cover, gaining speed, she sped along the river Limchang making her way to the downed chopper and more importantly the rapid extraction of the search and rescue party. However, the main task of the SBS divers was the location and hook up for the mighty US Chinook helicopter to winch to safety. The winch man in this case would be absolutely important.

Colonel Bob Loden had stayed on board HMS Bulwark whilst Colonel Briggs had elected to return to Brigade HQ. This would be an ideal platform for both of them in controlling whatever forces or issues which would probably eventuate over the next day or so.

Colonel Loden was with Captain Wiltshire discussing the overall strategy of this mission.

"What do you think so far Bob, anything to add?"

"I was thinking Bill; we could do with an escort for the Chinook possibly use a very small light aircraft to overfly the extraction process!"

Captain Wiltshire clasped his hands together with the two index fingers touching his lips in deep thought. Finally he answered, "Well, we do have HMS Eagle within striking distance from here and she does have at least three Douglas A4 Sky hawks, they're originally American aircraft; however, they have been specially adapted for our use in the Fleet Air Arm. They are light and highly manoeuvrable, Pratt and Whitney turbojets, twin 20mm cannons aboard her and I think they would be ideal for this operation! Range about 700 hundred miles." He wrote out a message for the captain of HMS Eagle and gave it to his Executive officer Lt Commander Herbert Thistlethwaites to transmit it. "Also alert RM Lt Nick Wise 848 squadron to standby for case-vac of the injured pilot. Flying instructions will be on my orders."

"Very good, sir."

"Where is HMS Eagle now, Bill?" Colonel Loden asked.

"Well, according to our last communication, she should be about 250 nautical miles away in the south china sea. The Sky Hawks at an average speed of 695 MPH, they could be here within thirty minutes or so."

"We could think of contacting USS Kitty Hawk for refuelling should it be necessary!"

Lt Waters, Bosun of the hovercraft were making good progress and was now reaching the swamp area where the river overflowed into the lagoon, his trusty offsider Mne Owen scanning the screen for the telltale blimp that was the homing signal, which Tom had attached to the downed Lynx chopper.

"Action stations! SBS divers stand by for de-bussing."

The hovercraft was sweeping around the Lagoon in a wide circle and as the homing signal became more intense in sound they knew it was absolutely close. Lt Waters could now make out the bamboo pole floating in the water and what appeared to be a rope attached. "Okay all SBS DIVE NOW!" Each diver, two on each side with their underwater lights flopped backwards, making for the depths of the Lagoon, following Cpl Giovanni Carlos Pollii who had found the rope and was travelling down its length to where he hoped the Lynx would be.

Meanwhile, Mac and Gil were still half an hour away from the stretcher party and by using fire and movement techniques were doing a great job holding back the pursuing Indonesian platoons. Mac had run out of PE and was now using the grenade launcher to hit the rear of the platoons, which he hoped would unnerve them and possibly slow them down. Gil would fire a few taps, then take off for another position to the rear of Mac, who then would leg it beyond Gil's position.

The divers were at the wreck now and were positioning the strops that would haul the Lynx up. One by one, they bobbed to the surface holding the main lifting ring which would be fitted to the giant Chinook.

Colonel Mike Beaurhanse was at the controls of the Chinook which was fast approaching the centre of the Lagoon. "Say we seem to be on course that the hovercraft down below, stand by all personnel we're going down to meet the 'Bootnecks'!" With that, and a giant thrust, he slowly lowered the Chinook into a lift-off position. "It's up to you now winch man do your stuff!"

The hovercraft had moved out of the way of the downwind and was standing by to pick up the SBS Divers after hook up.

Slowly, the Chinook lowered down to the divers who were getting buffeted by the turbulence as they were wearing protective head gear with their breathing apparatus they were able to withstand this massive downward force. After successfully hooking up, the SBS Team dived and swam away to the comparative safety of the hovercraft.

Mac and Gil had now joined up with Tom. Jack and the doc still using covering fire as full firepower was being rained down in both directions. The crack and thump of rounds passing close by overhead as the projectiles went through the sound barrier.

The Chinook was now taking hits passing through the large bulk of the Helicopter. "Hell, I didn't think it would be this hot! Give 'em a blast with the Mini Mo! Gunny!" Colonel Beaurhanse barked into the radio net.

Just then the scream of the first of the Sky Hawks hurtled through, firing their 20mm cannons at the enemy positions which they judged to be on the higher ground overlooking the Lagoon.

"Shit that was close!!" Jack, Tom and the doc had their backs to the oncoming jets and were not aware they would be air supported at all. Colonel Beaurhanse grinned from ear to ear.

"Goddam limeys," he said, still grinning. He gave the two rotors more power and slowly the Lynx was being hauled up out of the water there would be tremendous weight of water inside the body of the downed helicopter. The tail rotor of the Lynx appeared first, then the body with water pouring out of her, as gravity will control all loose elements. Finally, she was free and travelling higher into the air to her destination aboard HMS Bulwark where the grim task of opening and moving the remains and the corpses of the special forces had remained for several weeks. Not a job for the faint hearted or squeamish.

Chapter 13
The Extraction

On board HMS Bulwark Captain Wiltshire announced over the SRE that the Chinook carrying the Lynx would be arriving in the next twenty minutes and all detailed personnel are to be on deck for its arrival. Lt Wise close up for take-off on the forward section that is all out!

Lt Waters was busy on the aft section of the hovercraft and was picking up the SBS divers who had completed their mission of recovery. The hovercraft was circling the area where the divers were getting hauled aboard by a simple round rubber ring catching it as they came alongside which with the speed of the vessel took them clean out of the water. Marine Owen was at the helm. Overhead, the crack and crackle of the incoming rounds was unnerving; however, the MMGs were returning fire with their steady chug, chug aiming at the rifle and AK47 (Kalashnikov) flashes, Nick Vickers had instructed the crews to 'hose' them down starting from the middle of the hill and moving laterally side to side, that, meant a ·303 bullet would land at 4inch intervals. Lt Waters had just got the last frogman aboard when he took a shot to his leg, he staggered around in acute pain until the SBA (sick berth attendant RN) arrived rendering him first aid and giving him a shot of morphine, dipping his finger in the blood and marking his forehead with the letter 'M'. Also returning fire on the flashes was the small section of the Fleet Protection Group.

On the opposite bank of the Lagoon, Marine Dave Younger had set his backsight to the maximum and was firing steady bursts at the enemies' flashes using the automatic Australian SLR on its bipod using his one good eye to squint down the sites.

The Chinook was making good time and was being escorted by two Sky Hawks from HMS Eagle. Colonel Mike Beaurhanse was feeling mighty comfortable with this arrangement and was having animated conversations with the two fleet air arm pilots. "Wish you guys were coming with us to Vietnam, we could use your talents there boy!" In a clipped English voice, one of the pilots responded.

"It's not our show Colonel but thanks for the compliment. ETA to Bulwark should be ten minutes we'll be with you all the way. Zero Victor 1 out."

Lt Nick Wise was approaching the Lagoon in his Bell 47 with two wire framed baskets for casualty evacuation. The artificers and engineers had fitted the helicopter with floats and so he could land on water or swampy areas. He could see the amount of action going on down below and so made a direct path to what he thought would be the pickup point. The coloured panel had been roughly placed on the patient, Lt Davenport on the improvised ladder rack stretcher. At great risk he ignored the amount of incoming rounds and glided down to a cushioned landing on the edge of swamp which was the side of the lagoon.

Tom, Jack and the doc carried Lt Davenport waist deep in water and slush to lift him into the basket on the port side of the Bell 47, the crackle of incoming fire was still very near and dangerously close. They strapped him firmly onto the basket, Tom motioned to chopper pilot Nick Wise indicating by pointing across the water, "We have to pick up another marine!" Tom clutched on to the starboard struts as the Bell 47 rose turned and headed for the farthest bank where Dave Younger was. The chopper glided effortlessly over the water ducking under the canopy of the trees. Tom leapt out in waist deep water making his way to Dave's position. Tom grabbed all the gear and with Dave limping and Tom supporting, led him to the Starboard basket where he strapped him in with his weapon and gear on top. The Bell 47 left with both patients leaving Tom alone as he saluted them, "Godspeed," he murmured.

Marine Owen was now at the helm roaring towards the rescue team's position which was becoming very 'hot' and would possibly be untenable soon. The MMG crews were giving the 'Chokies' some serious exchange ordnance.

Jack had been using the modified ·303 Lee Enfield bolt action with the ammo he had purloined from the MMG section at Simmangang. They were tracers and has he had the thermal imager which he peered through occasionally and then popped off with the Lee Enfield finding a target nearly every time. Watch my tracer was a training technique and so more concentrated fire was directed by the marines aboard the hovercraft onto the point of impact.

One by one, they withdrew from the swamp each marine being covered by the fleet protection group backed up by MMG section who were pouring fire at the opposition like there was no tomorrow, giving 'em shit as one marine exclaimed. Once all aboard, Marine

Owen gave the hovercraft full throttle raising a misty spray so great it became almost impossible to see the vessel as it sped for the river Limchang and comparative safety. Out of range now, the incessant crackle of shots diminished to nothing; only the roar of the Rolls Royce engines could be heard. Mac rolled a cigarette and offered it to Lt Waters who had sustained a shot to his leg. Mac grinned down at him, “Top of the mornin to you sir, how’s it goin?”

The Lt grinned back and drew on the ‘tailor-made’. “It’s getting better now you’re all aboard,” he answered.

The remaining sky hawk swooped down on the remaining Kalimantan Army group and rebels firing his twin 20mm cannons, then rocketing skywards in a near vertical climb turning his nimble craft around he headed after the wake of the hovercraft after what appeared to be a successful search and rescue mission. He swooped down once more passing over the hovercraft and performing a victory roll as he passed over on his way back to HMS Eagle.

On board HMS Bulwark, the Chinook had been relieved of its underslung air freight load and the gruesome task of removing the corpses of the special forces it once contained.

Presently, a tiny dot appeared of the Bell 47 carrying the rescued Lynx pilot and Marine Dave Younger. Those that were required on the flight deck were waiting with great expectation of seeing their Royal Marine pilot Lt Chris Davenport who had been a popular marine officer amongst all of the crew that he came into contact with. On the covered hatchway at the foot of the air control Island, stood Colonel Bob Loden he wanted to see firsthand the young Chris Davenport and to see for himself his physical condition.

On the bridge with Captain Wiltshire was Colonel Mike Beaurhanse having an informal chat with the captain thanking the colonel for his part in the rescue mission. Alongside them were the crew of the Chinook. Pleased and relieved that everything had gone A-OK. Tea was being served by one of the stewards. The Gunny sergeant looking crestfallen. “TEA!” he muttered with a grin to his fellow US Marines.

Joining the group was Lt Commander Herbert Thistlethwaites. “Bert, I want you to send a signal to the lords of the Admiralty in London and Portsmouth, when Lt Wise arrives with Lt Chris Davenport aboard; to say that the search and rescue mission was a success; however, please convey our concerns about his condition and that we will do all in our power to see he makes a full recovery. Take a look at him first to make your report concise.”

"OH! And make a special mention to Rear Admiral Henry Cunningham so that he may inform his daughter who is married to Chris Davenport."

"Very good sir, I'm on my way." The commander shook hands with the US Marine air crew and departed on his mission.

The message was received by the Lords of the Admiralty about the success of the rescue mission and the subsequent retrieval of the downed helicopter. They then called for a press conference with the media. All leading newspapers were given the absolute good news and the safe withdrawal of the search and rescue mission; although not without its casualties and the bad news of the death of the special forces that the Lynx had been transporting. The headlines in the newspapers the following morning read, "Missing Lynx found in Borneo".

A Royal Marine Search and Rescue Team have been successful in locating the missing Lynx helicopter which went missing in the dense jungles of Borneo. Lt Chris Davenport RM has been found alive but in critical condition. The Special Forces he was transporting are reported dead. Next of kin will shortly be informed.

***

The hovercraft had entered the great river Limchang and was now out of range of enemy fire, so Marine Owen throttled her down to a lower speed, mindful of the flimsy native craft that used this river to earn their livelihood.

"Here, what's he carryin in that sack Jack?" one of the FPG Marine rifleman inquired. He was pointing at the bloody sack that *Jin Tin* had attached to his belt.

"Don't ask! It's a trophy from the Chokies camp." Jack gave him a steady look to emphasize the remark.

"Oh, you don't say!" Still looking a bit puzzled, lit up a cigarette and puffed away, still in thought.

The SBA was making Lt Waters as comfortable as possible taking his temperature and redressing the gunshot wound to his leg. Next stop would be at *Jin Tin's Longhouse* which lay on the river his family would indeed be very pleased to see him home alive and well. An hour and a half later, they arrived at the Longhouse. Tom took out a self-seal plastic bag which had been given to him for any emergencies or payments. He shook Jin Tin's hand and clapped him on the shoulders and said, "Terima Kaseh Banyak! Baik Lah?" The bag contained $1000 (Ringgit) Malay dollars. *Jin Tin's* eyes bulged and sparkled, he put his hands together as if in prayer.

"All hands to the starboard side for leaving dock routine," was the pipe aboard from the coxswain. Doc produced his Bosons whistle and piped Jin Tin onto the flimsy pier decking.

The last thing they saw of him was he had taken out the severed captain's head holding it aloft for all his family members to see. A great shout and the whole village knelt muttering their animistic prayers. The village leaders had taken up their ancient staffs of office and were dancing around the upper decking; chanting and striking the deck with the clacking staves made of iron wood, to drive out any evil spirits.

Today, for Jin Tin would be a most important celebration as the next leader of the head-hunters of Borneo. He waved goodbye for now, to his new found friends of the Royal Marines.

The hovercraft swept down river which widened out to the open sea waves crashing over her as she hit the incoming swell, a salty tang pervaded the cabin, seemed to have a calming effect on the marines. An hour later, they were approaching the familiar sight of the Amphibious Assault Groups Ship. HMS Fearless she also had a sister ship HMS Intrepid but she was on another mission. The stern end of the ship started to open massive doors that allowed the sea to become a floating dock. Marine Owen edged the bulky hovercraft through the open doors to arrive safely at the farthest end of the dock. The doors were closing and the motors were being shut down as she settled slowly down with the rapid ejection of the sea water.

The difficult task of getting Lt Waters through the ship to the aft flight deck was done by constantly changing the carriers of the wounded Lt who had elected to use the firemen's lift technique instead of battling their way through with a weighty and unwieldy stretcher through the twisting maze of ladders and companion ways. Tom, Jack and the boys wondered why they didn't design amphibious ships to allow marines in full combat gear and heavily laden, through to their debarkation and lift-off points.

They were now awaiting the Wessex helicopter from HMS Bulwark which would convey them to the Commando Carrier R08. The Bulwark had a reasonably well equipped Sick Bay Berth (hospital style wards). Unusual but this ship had taken on an RM medic and also a QARRNS nurse (Queen Alexandria Royal Naval Nursing Service), this was to be an experiment in the presence of these two for specialist care.

When the Bell47 had landed and the patients had been stretchered to the sick bay via the central liftwell which seemed the best and easier passage to the Sick Bay. The ship's surgeon and his two specialist nurses had set about looking after Lt Chris Davenport and Marine Dave Younger. Chris was in very bad shape and so they set about taking away the dishevelled clothing he had worn for weeks. Especially the empathy of the female navy nurse, taking loving care of this once handsome young flyer. Stroking his blond hair and murmuring encouraging words to him even though at this time he was only half conscious of what was happening. The ship's surgeon was talking into his small tape recorder as he set about identifying the wounds on the body. "Very serious lower leg wound, this man needs specialist treatment at BMH Singapore and will have to be transported ASAP, as I am very much afraid he has onset of gangrene setting in!" The nurses looked at the surgeon and slowly nodded their heads in agreement. Solemnly, they dressed his leg and his head wound and gave him a sedative to make him more comfortable.

The message previously of the safe arrival of the rescue mission personnel and the pilot had been flashed to Colonel Briggs in Brigade HQ. Who had breathed a sigh of relief that the mission had been successful although not without its dangerous consequences? As a courtesy, he had passed this message on to the British High Commissioner Dick Norris, who was also relieved to hear that 'his' rescuers had also come out unscathed. From the high commissioner's office, he sent the message to the young sultan of Brunei who on hearing about this successful mission and the condition of the young pilot and the marine. Responded with the question, "Can I be of assistance in any way?" Dick Norris mulled this over for a few minutes then decided he had to pass this vital information back to Brigade HQ with a special footnote to be passed onto the ship's captains.

Captain Wiltshire was handed the message and decided to visit the Sick bay and talk to the ship's doctor, Surgeon Lt Harry Beasley. He saw and heard the gravity of the situation and decided there and then that affirmative action was required to save this young pilots life. Back on the bridge he sent a message to the British High Commissioner's office that indeed they would appreciate any help from the Sultan, as the patients had to be transported to BMH Singapore ASAP.

This message was transferred to the sultan's office, without hesitation the sultan replied. "I will send my personal jet to Kuching

Airport to await the transportation of any of your wounded personnel."

- ❖ The message from HMS Bulwark was received in London and Portsmouth of the rescue mission's success and was greeted with much appreciation and immediately dispatched to Rear Admiral Sir Henry Cunningham. KCB, DSC. Also to the media newsgroups. The Rear Admiral immediately telephoned his daughter, Linda, with the good news, "Get yourself packed with a few necessities; I am booking you on the next VC10 flight to Singapore. I have also took the opportunity and booked you into the RAFFLES Hotel. I will let you know what time and where to report to."

Within a few hours, the Admiral had arranged transportation on Vickers V10 OF 101 Squadron RAF based at Brize Norton. It was due out at 0830 hrs the following morning on one of its first long flights carrying mainly service personnel of varying ranks on a normal service exchange rate. "You will be driven from Plymouth to Brize Norton by the chauffeur of the commanding officer of 43 Commando RM Stonehouse barracks. Be ready for an early call. At Paya Leba Airport Singapore, you will be picked up by the driver of Admiral Mark Donovan. Good Luck and a safe journey! Mable and I pray for you. We send all our love to you and Chris." Linda put down the phone and although relieved and excited at the good news; was concerned that Chris was in a bad way being so long in captivity.

"Maybe tomorrow will be better than it has been for me." Tearfully, she started packing.

Chapter 14
Lion City

The doorbell rang shrilly at her shop and flat on Union Street Plymouth at 0130 hrs, making Linda jump a little, although she realised immediately who it ought to be. The door was the usual wood and glass and she could plainly see a tall uniformed man standing in the doorway.

"Morning, Mrs Davenport. I am to take you to Plymouth airport near Roborough. Have you got your luggage?"

"Why yes! Plymouth Airport?" she questioned.

"Well, yes it's not a big airport but was once used by the Royal Navy. The navy are sending a helicopter from RNAS Culdrose for you."

Outside stood the CO's personal car, which was a Bentley gleaming in the street lights.

"I thought we were going to Brize Norton?" Linda said.

"I am afraid it's all been changed, your new destination is Stansted Airport; all personnel are now to take the British Airways New VC10 which is more comfortable and it will be its first inaugural flight for British Airways to Singapore. The passengers have all been notified of the change in plans, have you read the newspaper headlines?"

She opened the Daily Mail to read, "Missing Lynx found in Borneo." She sighed as she closed her eyes in a silent prayer.

The Bentley purred along highway A374 on to Alma Road, Outland Road, crossing over the A38 onto Tavistock Road going nearly to Southway but turning right onto the B3432 Finally turning into the road which led to the grassy airport, near Roborough and not far from the Royal Marines Camp at Bickleigh.

Standing near a lighted hangar was the Westland Sea Scout (Later renamed the Wasp). The Bentley drove near the chopper and parked up, opening the door for Linda Davenport.

The two fleet air arm pilots exchanged appreciative glances at one another as Linda came into view. "Morning, ma'am. This is Bill Dunham and I am Roger Lane. Glad to have you aboard!

Incidentally, we knew your husband Chris, as we did our flight training together."

"Allow me to get your luggage. After you, Mrs Davenport."

Linda always looked beautiful even at this early hour with her black luxuriant hair and flashing green eyes and voluptuous figure (like the modern day Nigella Lawson).

Once aboard, the Sea Scout coughed into life and slowly the rotors began to circle in ever increasing speed, lifting the little helicopter airborne nose drooping down to get as much thrust as possible. The marine driver saluted them as they swept past.

Linda had never been in a helicopter before so it was quite exhilarating for her. The co-pilot motioned to her to put on the headphones when she had got settled. The network chatter gave her some idea of what it had been like for her husband Chris who had learned to fly the very latest and fastest of the helicopter series. The pilot, Bill Dunham, gave her the highlights of the cities and towns they were passing, Linda noticing the fairy type lights far below her. Within a few hours they were landing at Stanstead airport ready for the next stage of her flight to Singapore, the Lion City. She kissed both pilots goodbye, her perfume lingered around the naval officers who grinned at each other as she climbed aboard a small buggy her luggage safely stowed, as the driver made his way to the airports passenger terminal/reception hall.

Roger Lane watched the little buggy as it receded into the distance and turning to Bill he said matter of factly, "Bill I don't think I can get into the cockpit just yet."

Bill observed with a smile, "Are you bragging or complaining?" both grinning, they entered the little *Sea Scout* cockpit and were ready to fly the lonely route back.

On November 8th 1960, John F Kennedy was elected President of the United States of America, the youngest man ever to be elected to this high office. The Yang Di Pertuan Mohammed Ali Daressalam 111, Sultan of Brunei Darussalam (Borneo) read all about this election with keen interest. The sultan had been invited by Her Majesty Queen Elizabeth II to attend the Christmas dinner at Buckingham palace in London. So he thought, *Whilst I am over in England maybe I should travel to America and meet this rather intriguing person and also congratulate him on his election.*

In due time, the messages had gone back and forward to America and the end result was yes the president would be very pleased to welcome him to the White House.

After a very glamorous and glitzy banquet with diamonds and every conceivable jewel being worn not only by the queen but also some pretty expensive emeralds and rubies worn by the sultan's sultana who really took the breath away.

He not only met the queen and the rest of the royal family but also had meaningful discussions with the foreign office and the heads of the military forces in England. This would be of great importance in the years to come.

He finally bade his farewells and flew off to the United States of America; here he was met by the president himself and whisked off (after appearing to a larger TV audience across the entire networks) to the White House where senior members of the John F Kennedy clan and the advisers had been assembled to see this sultan from the jungle continent, 'Borneo'.

The following night, a huge banquet was given in the sultan's honour; his beautiful wife the sultana capturing many of the hearts and minds with her impeccable manners and poise.

John F took him everywhere explaining the intricacies of governing such a powerful nation as the USA. He took him to the Pentagon which is a massive construction of offices, boardrooms, command centres, something akin to a large town or even a city. It was here he learned of the first ever 'Internet' which coupled all the computers in a link throughout the entire building. He was intrigued by this new system of connection.

Several days later, he was in the Oval Office with the president when he was talking about aircraft, the president being an ex-naval officer pricked his ears up.

"So you're talking about a personal private jet aircraft suitable for landing on your type of landing strips in your country and the undeveloped countries around your part of the world. Am I right?"

"That is quite correct mister President."

"Hey Bob! Can you get the chief aircraft designer at Boeing to give me a call, maybe get him over here for a bit of a pow wow?"

The next day in one of the offices, the chief designer from Boeing Mr Josef Franks; after introducing himself to the president and the sultan, quickly getting down to business by presenting various designs that were not in production as yet. "Now, tell me sir, what exactly were you looking for? What size, how many passengers, what distance you want to travel?"

"Well, I need to have a plane preferably jet propulsion, carrying some vital stores to our regions; also I need to have at least four separate bedrooms with bathroom facilities, seating for about thirty passengers, one pilot, maybe co-pilot or navigator, two air hostesses something along those lines would do nicely."

"Well, I will show you some artists' impressions of our finished planes and here are some detailed plans that will be in production very soon. I think that this model here will be exactly what you are looking for. It's a Boeing 720B powered by four Pratt & Whitney turbofan engines, it's a short to medium range aircraft and can use the short runways, it has a top speed of 621MPH, however it usually cruises at 564MPH, it is fuel efficient; we can custom furnish the interior to any standard."

The sultan eyed the drawings and plans, looking up at Mr Franks he said, "I will take some advice from my people in Brunei and will be in touch with you and your company very soon with all our requirements we shall need in our aircraft."

"You have not asked me the price of this aircraft, sir?"

"The price is not important only the quality is what we prefer."

Josef Franks closed his portfolio and just said, "We will await your drawings and instructions sir!" Two years had passed since that meeting in America with Josef Franks.

Whilst Linda was boarding her flight on the Vickers VC10 at Stansted Airport north of London; the rescue team with the wounded marines was boarding their chopper on the deck of HMS Bulwark; accompanied by Bungy Williams (who had wangled this trip out of the Surgeon Lt). The surgeon had also recommended that the QARNNS Nurse should also be in charge of the wounded men. This was due to her capability and knowledge of these kinds of wounds.

At Kuching Airport stood the Boeing 720B, the pride and joy of Mohammed Ali Daressalam 3rd Sultan of Brunei. It had been delivered last year with much pomp and circumstance. This was something to behold in aircraft design. It was gold in colour a thin red and green line strip along its fuselage, on the tail in red was the sultan's Royal Cypher or Motif. Truly she shone.

The Wessex helicopter landed near the Boeing and the job of getting the team on board began.

They all became aware of the Boeing jet plane and in unison said, "WOW!" as they gazed in awe at this magnificent aircraft. How they knew is a mystery but the media was there, flashbulbs popping off as the party moved to the bottom of the stairway leading to the planes cabin entrance door. The pilot was English and his co-pilot was Asian; both held out their hands in welcome and the very pretty Asian air hostesses clasped their hands together and bowed politely, "Welcome aboard, sirs!" they both said at the same time.

Slowly and carefully they stretchered the 3 wounded marines, Lt Chris Davenport was first, he was placed in a very palatial bedroom with an ante room at the side for his nurse, there also was full bathroom suite exquisitely furnished in gold black and green. It was the same for all three wounded men. There was also a neat bar and lounge with seating in the aircraft for about 30 people. Most were of the reclining design full overstuffed leather chairs.

Jack and Mac turned to Tom and said, "What do you reckon Tom?"

Tom on looking around the aircraft just replied, "I think we're in the wrong business." Gil just smiled quietly, nodding in agreement.

Mac said, "You've heard of the *Golden rivet!* aboard HM Ships. Haven't you? Well this airplane has a golden shithouse and not just one either, golden bowls, golden taps, the whole Kip and Kaboodle, is solid gold, wait till I tell me ma in Ireland, she'll never believe me though!"

The wounded were placed in very comfortable beds attended not only by the nurse but also with the Asian air hostesses who wore what you could only describe as the Malay *Sarong kebaya.* The long skirt was in pale silk green jade, the blouse was in black red interwoven with gold, a high collar like the Chinese Cheongsam. Their jet black hair tied back into a beautiful bun and held with a solid gold comb, gold, sapphire and diamond rings adorned their fingers. Olive skin with large brown eyes and red ruby lips gazed out in a radiance of beauty. The scent of a delicate perfume pervaded, embracing the marines' senses.

It had been cold wet and cloudy day at Stansted as Linda was seated in the rear of the plane with all kinds of naval, army, and air force officers with a smattering of British consular officials. She had been placed near a window portal which she rather liked and could see, she hoped, what lands lay ahead. Take-off was signified as the jet engines roared into life, the VC10 virtually standing on its tail in the shortest take-off ever for a passenger jet of this size.

The Vickers VC10 kept climbing until she broke through the thick cloud mass finally coming into brilliant sunshine, Linda gave a little sigh and lay back just to gaze out and see what a difference the sun makes. The pilot came over the internal flight sound system and introduced himself and after he pointed out, "We are now passing over Paris, France, later we will be travelling over the Swiss/Italian Alps, we hope you have a pleasant journey; we will stop for refuelling at Kuwait."

The plane started climbing high over the Alps; as Linda looked down, she could see these magnificent mountains like black iron and capped with the whitest of snow on the peaks.

"Beautiful sight, don't you think?" A young Naval Officer remarked, who was sitting in the seat next to her.

"It's very beautiful I haven't seen anything quite like it before," Linda answered. There was bit of a pregnant silence as they both glanced at each other. Linda demurely cast a glance at him as both their eyes met.

Clearing his throat and a little bit shyly he said, "I believe I've seen you before with your father, Rear Admiral Henry Cunningham at one of our Naval Parades in Plymouth, of course you would not have seen me, I was in the centre rank. However, he was a great orator, his speeches were understandable, forthright and motivational to us younger officers setting out on our own careers. Of course most of us young men immediately fell in love with you."

Linda laughed self-consciously and immediately felt at ease with the young naval officer.

***

On board the sultan's plane, the marines had taken over guard duties on their patients; being with them merely as a precaution as they had a vested interest in their safety.

They were nearing the straits of Malacca and soon they would be landing at the RAF Base Changi in Singapore. It had been an interesting flight very fast, smooth and quiet. The ambience within the plane was exquisite. As the plane banked several times, they could make out the lights of Singapore as they circled to affect a good landing.

It was the ideal airbase, reasonably close to the British Military Hospital (BMH). Even as they were landing, two military ambulances with motorcycle escorts were waiting to whisk the wounded marines into hospital. They would be able to get the finest hospital treatment from a variety of handpicked surgeons from all three services.

Tom on landing safely, turned to Jack and said, "You go with Gil in the ambulance with Dave, Mac and I will travel with the two officers, just to make sure everything's kosher, okay?"

***

The VC10 with Linda aboard was now nearing Kuwait in the Middle East for a scheduled refuelling stopover. They were to land at a military airfield as the Kuwaiti Airport was either too far behind building schedule or not staffed properly yet. The military one was used mainly by the British and its allied personnel, to say the least it was very Spartan in its amenities. The VC10 made a perfect landing and taxied to a concrete apron near the administration buildings. The captain then spoke about the length of time that they would be refuelling and for the cleaning and fumigation of the plane, which he said would probably take a couple of hours.

The passengers mainly service men and with a good sprinkling of wives and babies stood and began the slow journey to the exit doors. Last were the passengers in the rear tailplane area, but as officers will be what they are reputed to be, ushered Linda to the front of their queue.

Linda turned to the young naval officer saying, “I’m sorry but I don’t know your name.”

“Paul Cavendish. I’m sorry. I thought I told you.”

Linda smiled and said, “Maybe you did, I’m so overwrought these past few weeks, I really must pull myself together.” She had told him about Chris Davenport and his miraculous rescue by the Marines of 40 Commando RM.

Paul put his arm on her shoulder in a gentle understanding gesture. A little tiny tremor coursed through her at that moment of contact, it was quite unexpected and she was in some perplexity as to its origin, however she knew it was very pleasant.

The steps had been rolled into place and all of the passengers were streaming down rather woodenly as one does when you have been sitting for many hours. Linda was next and Paul just held her hand for safety so that she wouldn’t trip, Linda blushed a little but Paul did not see her face. Reaching the bottom of the steps, he continued holding her hand and guiding her to the administration block. She just glanced upwards and was astounded at the night sky. She stopped in her tracks looking in wonder at the heavenly formations of stars. On a background of royal blue were all the stars of the universe, as though she was walking on a space ship, all around her was this absolutely magnificent planetarium. Paul also gazed up with equal wonder at the night sky. His left arm curled around her waist which was so soft and pleasing, she gazed up at him and just rested her head on his shoulder, he was quite a good-looking man, slim, standing about six feet 3 inches, dark haired, clean cut lines to his face. *Hmm,* she thought, *he is very nice indeed.*

Holding hands now they walked in the fine sand around the buildings, the sand had taken on the appearance of snow! The hills beyond were dark and rather forbidding to look at but the air was balmy having a nice smell of musk which seemed to them both as being rather exotic. They had wandered a fair distance from the admin blocks; still lost in their own dream world. Paul turned to Linda and pointed towards what the British termed a wog shop.

"Let's see if we can buy a coffee in there, or even tea if you prefer." Linda smiled and nodded as they entered the native Arab shop. The door had a little bell attached to it and jingled as they entered. A small Arab boy appeared smiling broadly his white teeth filled his mouth and at once the atmosphere became nice and friendly. There was small table and a wooden form on both sides was the only seating arrangement. "Salaam Allah Kum," the boy spoke to Paul.

"Allah Kum Salaam," Paul responded. Holding up two fingers Paul asked the boy for two coffees adding "InshaAllah" to which the boy only grinned and darted into the labyrinth of covered passages and partially furnished rooms. The shop sold about everything known to man, it was dimly lit and the brass ornaments rotated on their strings, had a transfixing quality about them. After a few minutes, the boy came back, this time his slightly older sister came with him holding a silver tray on which two glass cups were resting. She was about 14 years old and smiled at the two westerners shyly, her head covered in a pink chiffon scarf. The boy who they had met would be about 11 or maybe 12 years old. Linda stood up and politely asked if they had a toilet and by sign language the message was received with giggles from the young girl.

Partitioned only by an aged curtain was the toilet which was of course Asian with a ceramic hole and footpads to put one's feet, easily marked. "Ah well, when in Rome," Linda murmured.

Paul was talking to the boy who understood a little English, he passed him the money for the coffee and also whispered to him if they had a rear room that if he wanted to, he could use. His sister Jasmine and an elder brother, Mustapha lived in the shop, his sister and the boy Ahmed slept in the same room. The boy grinned understanding the tall Englishman very well, he was well versed in the erotic behaviour of his friends and family members.

Paul grinned as Linda came back to rejoin him, "How did you go on?" he grinned knowingly at her. She rolled her eyes and made a mock agonising look at him.

Paul always carried a very small and compact leather-bound hip flask which contained, as usual, rum. He proffered it to Linda to blend it into her coffee which was very black and quite strong to taste. She said to Paul, “Is this Pussers Rum?”

“Of course, it is nothing but the best and brewed and bottled in the British Virgin Islands in the Caribbean.” He winked at her as he filled her glass tumbler. Rum is best drunk in a tropical or hot climate as it brings out the bouquet of the spirit and feels and tastes so much better. It was no surprise then that he gently took her hand and with the boy’s guidance was led to an inner room where he gave the boy some more money; after giving him a very nice clean bath towel he left grinning.

Paul looked at Linda and began kissing her eyes, lips, the nape of her neck and the hollow space along her collarbone. She was very receptive and eager, her breathing became irregular and the lust for more was dominant. Paul unzipped her black filigree patterned dress which he lowered over her shoulders to slide floating down to the floor.

Paul was now kissing Linda’s breasts and sucking gently on her protruding large nipples even when at rest they were still large and erect.

two white people as Paul slid off Linda's black lace panties and rolled down her black stockings, the suspender belt coming off too. Paul looked at the mass of black hair that hid the most succulent essence of all women, her pink moist interior. Paul took off his white shirt and black trousers, Linda helping him to release his pride of manhood; it was throbbing and mightily erect. Linda stroked it with great affection and gently pulled him towards her mouth as she slid her tongue in and around the exposed pink moist head; she had slowly eased his foreskin down, her tongue licking his penis rapidly.

Paul just lay her down onto the bath towel on the bed; his penis dripping now was gently eased into her vagina and so the rhythmic lovemaking began, slowly at first then as the minutes ticked by the more powerful strokes by Paul and Linda would get to a final climax of passionate lovemaking. Linda had not had a baby before, so would this be the father of her first baby? She was now thrusting her body and her passion at the large member entering and giving her soaring climaxes, she was now actually shagging him, her vagina sucking at his penis, her breath and moans became more passionate with each thrust. Her vagina was awash with semen and was trickling down her ivory legs which she had spread wide, now she slipped her long legs over his shoulders for maximum penetration, she wanted it all inside her now as much as he could give her.

***

***

Linda was in her element now gasping, moaning as she thrust her hips and vagina at Paul. It lasted for a full thirty thrilling-tumultuous-throbbing minutes, until gasping for breath having ejaculated inside Linda. At that moment, she felt a strong stream of hot semen bursting into her like a bursting star shell. It felt good and he sank by her side, both breathing heavily in a very satisfied way. She stroked his hair and brought his head and his lips to her breasts, soothing yet passionate.

After a few minutes, knowing that they would have to be at the aircraft in about thirty minutes or less, they both struggled to their feet feeling faint and spent. Paul observing Linda's aesthetically, beautiful figure, it was perfect and he thought that Chris Davenport was a very lucky man to have found and married this goddess of love. She moved around with an air of innocence and grace, not at all conscious of being naked. She was picking up her suspender belt and her black stockings, her well rounded hips and buttocks were visible as she was bending down, her breasts jiggling and swaying. Paul had recovered and had got a big hard on and just could not resist the tempting vision in front of him. He placed his hands on her hips, she wasn't expecting it but he thrust his penis gently between her cheeks of her bottom (glutinous maximus) and inserted it into her anus which at first resisted then slowly opened up to receive his pulsating cock. Slowly, she came erect and felt his neck and slowly bent down again wiggling and gyrating to encourage him to ejaculate once more before it was their time to stop. Standing erect slowly and still moving her hips in a circular gyration. She did this several times and soon Paul ejaculated inside her, he holding onto her breasts in a gentle and loving way.

***

From their peephole behind the curtains, Ahmed and Jasmine, his sister, had seen this entire exhibition of true lovemaking and accordingly had learned white men's form of lovemaking. They were erotically moved and inspired. Ahmed's dick was as hard as a chocolate frog, his sister still gently pulling his foreskin back and forwards, she had used some coconut oil to rub on her hands to make the masturbation really good and smoothe. Jasmine now knew what to do when her elder brother Mustapha eventually came home. He often came home and woke her up to give her some money and also to sodomise her, it was part of their culture, he had said once.

***

Paul and Linda had dressed hurriedly, having glanced at his Rolex watch he was sure they would be the last to get aboard for their next stage of flight to Singapore. On her way out of the gift shop, she had seen a small gold crescent moon with a small diamond set in platinum; the diamond sparkled as it dangled from the base of the crescent, she bought it with a few pounds to remind her of the night she spent with Paul. Sure enough as they came in sight of the VC10, the air hostesses were anxiously waiting at the doorway. The airport staff was to remove the stairs tapping their feet in anticipation of the plane leaving on time. Paul and Linda were now running and waving frantically.

With smiles from everyone as they mounted the stairs, Linda was first to board as she was on a window seat. They both looked a little dishevelled and flustered. Something like Hugh Grant, after he had been caught in an embarrassing situation with Divine Brown. But they both looked happy, which was the main thing. The air hostesses checking every seat to make sure everyone was aboard, spoke to Linda and Paul, "Hope you both had a pleasant stopover."

One of the colonels leaned over to Paul and said, "It is a beautiful night, don't you think."

Paul looked a little dazed and just replied with a smile, "Oh, absolutely sir, perfect night." To which the colonel gave a sidelong look to his fellow high ranking officers. All smiled, they had noticed Linda's naked ivory legs as she had entered and very much approved of them.

Linda just smiled shyly at the generals' interest in her.

At last they were on the final leg of the flight, dinner or evening meal was being served and both ate with relish, not realising they were that hungry. After the meal and a small bottle of wine were consumed, Paul and Linda were at peace with the world and fell asleep when the lights in the cabin had been dimmed down.

***

The surgeons had started all three operations on the marines who had just come in from Borneo. Chris was the most serious and had just not fully regained consciousness floating in and out of his delirium. The QARNN nurse was the equivalent of a nursing officer and had got more experience in the operating theatre than most of the nurses in BMH. She had organised all the equipment and sterilisation of every instrument the surgeons would need in the intricate procedures, especially with the operation on Lt Davenport, which had been X-rayed and examined thoroughly. The surgeons agreed that they would have to amputate the Lt's leg beneath the knee, it was too far damaged and what's more, gangrene was setting in. If they didn't amputate, he would surely die. The operations began.

***

The search and rescue team, Tom, Gil, Jack and Mac had been allocated a room in the Sergeants Mess (Huh!) at the direction of the CO. Colonel Briggs within Royal Naval Air Station Sembawang (RNAS) Far East Amphibious Land forces (FAREALF), the home base of 42 Commando RM. They also had a Land Rover and driver at their disposal.

"Grab that driver, we're going to 'slops' to get some new OGs then to the Chinese tailor's for a bit of cut and sew. That should make 'em a lot smarter eh? Seeing as we're in the Sergeants Mess we don't want that Provost Sergeant Gordon Norton giving us a hard time, do we?"

They all grinned at Tom's outburst.

***

Aboard the VC10 night had passed and given way to a beautiful tropical day, they had passed over the south China seas and were flying at some speed down towards the Straits of Malacca. A light continental breakfast was being served.

The captain spoke through the intercom and just advised them, that in just over an hour and a half they would be landing at Payer Leba Airport Singapore and to get all their personal belongings together, he also advised them about the temperature in Singapore. "We hope you enjoyed your flight."

Right on time, the VC10 made a perfect landing and taxied to the administration terminal buildings. There is a certain amount of joy and expectancy when one arrives at their final destination, a feeling of perhaps relief and the joy and of the prospect of their loved ones waiting to welcome them at the other ends of the earth. So it was on this day.

Linda strolled effortlessly along the long concourse that leads to the customs and baggage collection carousel. After collection of her overnight bag, she said goodbye to Paul kissing him lightly on the cheek, he gave her his personal monogrammed card, a final squeeze of her hand and he strode off. Linda noticed a prominent notice board being held high by a Royal Marine driver. She made her way towards him, "Hi, I'm Mrs Davenport; are you the driver of Admiral Mark Donovan?"

"Yes! This way, ma'am." Taking her luggage, he escorted her to the Naval C in C's far eastern command, staff car.

Outside the terminal sat a navy blue Rolls Royce parked in a 'No Waiting' area. He opened the rear door for her. He, being a typical Royal Marine, noticed she was very appealing, her legs parting slightly showing her inside thighs as she sat down in the hand stitched leather upholstery, he whistled through his teeth silently as he closed the rear door.

"The RAFFLES Hotel ma'am? That was on your itinerary?"

"Yes please driver! Er! What is your name? I can't keep calling you driver, can I?"

"My name is Watson, ma'am!" he replied.

"How long do I have the car for?" she asked.

"Well, we are usually based in Hong Kong but the Admiral had to come here to Singapore for his annual inspection which should last for about 2 months, he's got all the ships including the Carriers, submarines, not to forget the Fleet Air Arm and the base installations, quite a big job really, so I guess you will have me on and off, depending on the Admirals workload and commitments." The drive through the streets of the 1960's Singapore was hair raising, to say the least, the entire vehicle on the narrow streets and roads honked their horns constantly especially the black Mercedes diesel pirate taxis. Trishaws weaved in and out of the alleyways, market traders shrieking out in some Chinese high-pitched language, symbols clashing, Asian music emanating from some coffee (Kedai Koppee) shop. Linda was astounded at this hubbub of peasant society going about their business incessantly clamouring for attention and the Wang (Money) it would bring them.

The Rolls eventually pulled into the driveway of the Raffles to the covered portico and was immediately met by a smartly dressed Chinese in black trousers and a white military style jacket topped off with a Malay Topi or songkeok.

The Raffles Hotel in Singapore means 'Lion City' (named after Sir Stamford Raffles who created the busy port)

"Selamat pagi mem! Welcome to the Raffles Hotel." Watson opened the door, her long legs stretched out first and Watson took her hand to guide her out.

"Tell me Watson, can you take me to a milliner or local dress shop? I haven't brought much clothing with me."

"No need to worry about that ma'am, staying here at the Raffles, we'll just phone the concierge when we get to the room and they will send out for a tailor or dress maker who will have whatever you wish made up within the hour." The call went out.

At reception, the same friendly atmosphere pervaded the key to the suite was handed over and they both proceeded to the top floor where the scenery was most beautiful.

"Help yourself to whatever is available, and I will have a shower. I feel absolutely grubby, pour me a Brandy and soda," with that, as she was passing him. "Be a darling and unzip my dress at the back will you, Watson."

She headed for the bathroom dropping her dress off as she went through the doorway, stripping off the clothes she had worn for the last twenty-four hours, it felt good when she sank into the large spa bath which she had generously laced with the perfumed liquid soaps and oils the hotel provided.

Watson had switched on the radio and was listening to a popular Chinese song by Tsai Chin called the 'Second Spring', the westerners had nicknamed it the 'Ding Dong Song', it was an enchanting song and filtered through to the bathroom where Linda reclined in a sea of bubbles, very relaxed and quite liking the melody floating through. It gavc it a nice relaxed setting to a somewhat exhilarating and passionate adventure.

Wrapping herself in a huge white bath towel with a similar smaller towel around her head, she came out from the bathroom and sipping the brandy, eyed Watson.

"Tell me, Watson, do you know how to give massages."

"Yes, ma'am. I often have to be a second for the corps boxers, the soccer players and the rugby teams all at some time need their bruises attended to."

"Well, I'm not exactly a boxer but I would appreciate a complete massage after my exhausting trip."

"Very good ma'am, come over here and leave everything to me."

Gently he relieved her of her bath towel as she lay face down on a special divan that was near the window so that a nice cool breeze would permeate the warm air. Watson had nice strong hands which he first of all coated with delicate massaging oil. Starting at the nape of her neck which is where some tension pains usually occur, working ever outwards with firm strokes and the use of his palms kneading the soft pliable white fleshy skin, she was enjoying this as it was totally relaxing and eased her pain somewhat. Working his magic all the way down to her buttocks, legs and ankles where he massaged her toes and feet.

"Could I ask you to turn over, ma'am?"

"Call me Linda", she said rather throatily. For Watson this would be the best part. He'd had a hard on for some time now as he caressed her neck, shoulders and down to her large beautiful breasts and pink nipples which now were going erect and stiffer; she thrilled to this man's touch and she could sense that he was totally aroused at the prospect of this exotic experience. He noticed she had two small bruises near the top of her thighs going down to her pelvis region. He remarked on this and she just said, "I must have bumped against something in the aircraft." Watson just grinned as he continued his way down past her navel and then between her legs and thighs, he also probed two fingers into her vagina and began to manipulate her and reaching her clitoris, she gave several sighs of satisfaction, "What are we going to do about you, eh Watson?"

"I have a little suggestion to make, er… Linda. I am going to shave all this pubic hair you have down here."

"Why?" she asked.

"Well, out here in the far east, it gets very sticky and humid if you follow what I mean and the fact you have all this bushy hair down there will, of course, maybe cause you some discomfort and at times embarrassment; do you follow me?"

"Well, yes I do understand what you're driving at, let's do it!" He sauntered off into the bedroom and came back with scissors, shaving gel and a ladies shaver. Starting with the scissors, he carefully cut off the majority of black curly hair, applying the gel, he started shaving with great care and interest as he uncovered the beautiful lips of her vagina, finally it was done, and it was what the marines called a 'Skinny Minnie!' She pulled him gently towards her, opening his trousers to reveal a throbbing erect penis. She motioned for him to take off his uniform and then pulled his face down to her sweet and luscious vagina. His tongue darting in, his lips kissing her outer succulent lips, he opened her up, it was pink and fleshy like a passion fruit, inviting and sexual, finally finding her clitoris and licking her out.

She brought his face up to hers, kissing him with much passion; reaching down for his dick, she inserted it into her moist vagina and started to shag him with tremendous vigour, each thrust was sucking his dick to maximum, he had never ever had this encounter with any woman and was just thoroughly lost in a climax of glory with her. She had made him her slave for all time and he would remember her well, in his twilight years. Linda was always a free spirit ever since her first passionate affair with Tom Martial when he had been the first to take her virginity, it was the start of relationships that after waiting for Tom to return to her, she pined for him for a long time, but he did not return. She had other relationships with other marines and various men but none seemed to measure up except Chris Davenport, who was quite handsome and very fit. He's perfect! She thought. They eventually married in a fairy tale setting, no expense being spared for his lovely daughter Linda, by her father Rear Admiral Henry Cunningham. Married in the prettiest Devon village in an Old Saxon Church dating back many centuries.

It was a new feeling having all the hair shaved off from her vagina and really was most passionate with Watson who was enjoying every pulsating moment of this new encounter with such a beautiful lady as Linda; still thrusting his member into her as far in as he could get. She knew exactly what to do next, draping her long ivory legs over his shoulders gasping for air as he got the maximum depth within her, she was ecstatic with the continuous climaxes she was having. It felt good, very good she kissed him passionately wishing it would never end, but it did, in a final ejaculation bursting and gushing inside her, they relaxed panting and spent.

He did take her to the shower and soaped her all over to relax her from the cares of the world.

***

The operations at BMH had been finished after a gruelling eight hours, they had been placed in separate rooms and were still unconscious, breathing was normal and all were linked up with the monitoring tubes to the vital organs machines, dials, devices. Lt Davenport was being drip fed as he had been the worst case of dehydration. He was still unconscious but stable now.

Dave Younger's wife, Jean, was at his bedside and would remain there until he woke up.

***

The 'Boys' were having a lunchtime, Tiger beer in the Sergeants Mess at RNAS Sembawang much to the chagrin of the Senior NCOs of 42 Commando RM who took umbrage at their presence; however, they tactfully refrained from any verbal expressions seeing as how it was the CO's order. "Tell me Mac, how is it that you get along very well with the Provost/Sergeant Gordon Norton?" Tom asked.

"Well, it's like this; I think he likes Irishmen!" Little Mac replied grinning.

"Bulldust," said Jack, "go on tell us more and stop lying."

"Well, it's like this; I knew him when he was a marine, he was an Assault Engineer like me for nine years and then he swopped branches wanting to add his experiences on to the young recruits going through training, so he became a Drill Instructor."

"Hmm! He seems to have been quite successful; good on him!" said Jack.

Tom went to the bar, "Here sticks! When and if you receive a phone call from BMH on the marines' condition, get on the blower and let me know, the driver has an FFR in his vehicle; here's the call sign, Okay?"

The Bartender nodded, "Right Tom, will do."

"Get that driver, we're going into Nee Soon for a beer!" They all trooped off when the Land Rover arrived outside the mess. Tall lean and mean! (Except for McH who was always grinning and smoking), they all looked great in their freshly Chinese tailored OGs. They all said goodbye to Bungy as he was ordered to report to the Naval Dockyard near Sembawang. Bungy was a bit crestfallen as he just said, "I will miss you guys; maybe catch up with you later?" The Land Rover dropped him off at the gates and with a forlorn wave he turned and left to report to the main gate sentry.

***

Linda came out from the shower dressed in a white bathrobe still with her white towel turban atop her head. "Watson, do you know the telephone number of BMH?"

"Of course, er… Linda, I'll slip down to the car and fish out my log and be back in a jiffy."

Linda continued filing her nails. There was knocking at the door. "Come in!" Linda said. The door opened and a rather beautiful Chinese girl entered carrying a large portfolio case with her.

She was dressed in a green embroidered cheongsam with a high mandarin collar, the dress was slit on both sides showing her beautiful shapely legs; high heeled shoes completed the outfit.

"I am dress maker you sent for, ma'am. My name is Jenny. I am here to measure and make you dress."

Linda smiled at this rather pretty girl. "Well, you are a lovely girl and if you make a dress that makes me half as pretty as you, it will be beautiful." The girl blushed slightly. Linda took off her robe as the girl found her tape measure. Linda was totally naked and the girl gave a short gasp as she began to measure her tall ivory customer. Linda stood about five feet 9 inches, the girl was about five feet two inches and was struggling with height and some embarrassment. The tape measure slipping when she began to measure Linda's breasts, running her delicate fingers over her breasts and pausing over them in order to adjust the falling tape measure. Linda shivered with pleasure as it certainly did tickle. The girl noticed the involuntary passion of this fine looking English woman. The girl made rough sketches and all measurements were recorded onto the design she was making. Noting down her shoe sizes too. She had never seen anything this perfect before in her life, with a gleam in her eyes she thought; just maybe they could be friends?

The girl showed her a few designs from which Linda made her selection. The first was a black wrap around skirt when worn would be similar to a reverse tulip open at the front only when walking or sitting, hem length to fall below the knee, the separate top would be a white linen jacket with slightly padded shoulders, medium lapels, the jacket drawn together with pearl coloured buttons, curved at the bottom of the jacket. Three pearl coloured buttons on each of the cuffs. A very light weight black full brimmed hat, with dark blue veil, black high heeled strap shoes. She also chose an after five apparel (cocktail dress) in green and black, low neck line. She also ordered a black cheongsam with gold and red embroidery, with the usual split up each side of the skirt.

The girl had finished her business with Linda and had packed her drawings away in her large portfolio case, "I will return with just one dress ma'am in maybe two or three hours if that will please you?"

"Of course Jenny do not worry unduly, I know it will not be easy, I would also like to have my dress dry clean returned when you do." Linda gave her a friendly hug; the girl kissed her on her neck as she couldn't reach any higher, her slim centre finger accidentally or on purpose found its way into the now smooth tempting vagina. Linda was perplexed and a little shocked, maybe it's an eastern custom she thought and just smiled down at the beautiful Chinese girl. However, she was not displeased at the contact.

Shortly after the girl had left, Watson came in with his clipboard and brief. "I telephoned the BMH from the Rolls and found out that all three are out of surgery and have been placed in their respective recovery rooms. Lt Davenport has had his left leg amputated below the knee (Linda gave a gasp and started to cry) he is in a very serious condition, the QARNNS senior nurse is constantly at his side, her name incidentally is Amelia."

Linda continued to sob, repeating over and over, "My poor Christopher, my poor lovely boy!"

"You'll have to pull yourself together, you can't let him see you've been crying it will only upset him too much, I have been in contact with the Admiral and I have to report back to him soonest. However, when you wish to go to BMH later today, call me on this number and I will be here as soon as I can; okay Linda?"

She nodded and just said, "I will have to wait for my dress anyway, which should be in about three hours or so." Watson left to be at the Admiral's appointments.

Linda poured herself a stiff brandy trying to console herself, after a few more she began to feel a little happier and began painting her toenails and finger nails the colour of pink pearls. She also carefully applied her makeup, adding black eyelashes for maximum effect. That made her feel a little happier, knowing that soon, this afternoon she would be seeing her darling husband and she decided she would look her best. She remarked to herself, “I’m feeling quite tipsy but what the hell!”

The radio was still playing softly as she strolled around the room with her brandy held in stylishly long painted fingers, she swished her brandy around in the glass looking out on the balcony at the port of Singapore which she knew a little of its history when Sir Stamford Raffles had founded this island, when only a few Chinese fishermen, a handful of local Malays and maybe one or two Tamils had been occupying this island. It was also rumoured that Tigers roamed free and some actually swam the Straits dividing the Island from Malaya. It was also rumoured that a tiger had actually been found under one of the dining tables in the hotel? Well, the only memory of that was the name given to the lager brewed by a Dutch company who had appropriately named it ‘Tiger Beer’.

Linda was roused out of her reverie by a knock on the door. “Come in,” Linda called. On seeing the Chinese girl, she exclaimed, “Gosh that was quick.” She had not realised that it had been almost three hours since she had seen the lady tailor.

“I make for you very special, I very quick! We will try first fitting but should be, okay-lah.” She held out the dress she had made and also her black dress she wanted dry cleaned. “All okay now, ma’am.” Linda walked or floated over to the girl, eyeing with much appreciation the style and quality of her new outfit.

The brandy was having an effect on Linda; as she saw the beauty of the dress, she started to cry uncontrollably. Alcohol either makes you very happy and carefree or it can be a mighty depressant. Linda dropped to the lounge for support.

Jenny came up to her and said, “What is matter with mem’saab, you crying, why?”

Linda leant against her and told her about her husband Christopher and how they had to amputate one of his legs. Jenny lovingly stroked her face and neck just gently kissing her on her tear stained cheeks, she held her for a little while her sobbing was from the heart, and she was shuddering, so Jenny began to ease her tension in the nape of her neck and shoulders massaging with her lightest of touches. Linda was grateful of her loving and caring nature and didn’t resist rather she quite liked the young Chinese. Murmuring words of comfort, Jenny began opening Linda’s robe and lightly running her fingers over her breasts and now enlarged nipples, slowly they were both getting to know the love and the needs of themselves. Jenny undid her cheongsam and dropped it to the floor; she did not wear any underwear except for a very skimpy thong which separated her buttocks and from the observer there was no tell-tale wrinkles in her dress. She lowered her petit breasts onto Linda's thighs, which she opened with deft tender urgings. She was now kneeling in front of Linda; looking up at her, she placed her well-developed lips around the edges of Linda's vagina, opening them up to reveal a beautiful pink interior with the clitoris edging out for immediate attention. Jenny had a rather long tongue which at first was not noticeable, but now she probed the luscious vagina with passion involuntarily making Linda climax. With her finger, she gently inserted it gradually into Linda's anus to find that delicate spot where she could keep Linda coming until she gasped for no more, but at the moment it was too nice to stop, just wasn't the time. Jenny reached down and took off her very flimsy thong from between her legs to reveal a small penis complete with two small balls. Jenny took Linda's hand and led it down to her penis, Linda was quite shocked, but as she looked at it she thought what a little beauty how cute; this as she began rolling down the foreskin and feeling her balls, Jenny was very delighted at her new found friend's acceptance of her. It grew very stiff at Linda's touch, Jenny inserted it into Linda's wet, moist, vagina and within the hour they were both spent, saturated in semen. Jenny was born with two sexual organs: one male, one female.

"I'm famished," Linda declared, "I haven't eaten since very early morning, we'll have a shower but first I must order some lunch for us." She phoned the concierge on reception and ordered a dressed fisherman's basket for two, a bottle of Sauvignon Blanc and two small bowls of Egg FooYung Noodles. That done, they both went into the bathroom soaping each other all over, finally putting the shower on cold to really freshen them up. Shivering slightly, they towelled one another, laughing and the tears forgotten for now.

Lunch was delivered by a smiling Chinese waiter on a trolley, he noticed that they were very friendly together and wearing just bathrobes which were slightly open to the tops of their legs, he also knew what Jenny was but just smiled secretly as he went out. They both ate with absolute relish sampling the different varieties of fish, oysters, king prawns, lobster, cray fish tails and legs, crab claws which they snapped open with special tool like pliers, eating like two urchins, washing it down with glasses of the white wine. Grinning at each other as they allowed the wine and fleshy fish ooze out of their mouths to be gently wiped away from their delicate lips in a mock showing off.

They lay in each corner of the settee twirling their glass of wine like the very rich, with bellies nice and rounded with the superb lunch.

Linda wandered over to the telephone and asked for an outside number, then she dialled Watson to collect them in an hour or so. He did tell her that he would also be bringing the Admiral as he wished to meet the daughter of Sir Henry Cunningham to pay his respects. Watson also mentioned the fact that the Admiral had alerted the newspaper and the media to attend at the BMH for some much needed publicity, of the search and rescue mission, also the fact that Linda Davenport, the wife of the pilot, had journeyed from England to be at his side.

Jenny did a fantastic makeup job on Linda's face, she looked a picture with just a tiny black pencil line to accentuate her eyes which although not Asian just gave a hint of the orient.

They both got dressed with Jenny persuading Linda not to wear bra or panties that indeed she would look quite fantastic without and really didn't need any cups or bra as she had perfectly shaped breasts which held up on their own. Linda had to admit it felt quite risqué.

The phone rang, the concierge informed them that their Rolls had arrived.

Linda took Jenny's arm and said, "Will you come with me, I need a bit of support."

"Of course, it will be my pleasure ma'am." Linda had got her beautiful new outfit on, which fitted perfectly. On her lapel, she pinned a brooch that Chris had given her which was the Royal Marine Corps crest in sapphires, emeralds and diamonds set in gold. Jenny's eyes lit up with delight. She un-wrapped a package she had brought along and presented a very eye-catching black and white evening bag made from snake skin, simple yet effective for her new outfit. Linda packed all that she brought along in her overnight bag, Jenny took charge of it and together they took the elevator to the reception area. "Jenny, tell the reception staff I am checking out, thank them for their hospitality."

Standing there with his driver Watson, was the C in C Admiral Mark Donovan in full dress uniform waiting to escort them to the hospital. Linda walked towards them, she really was very beautiful to behold, tall elegant and sophisticated, this of course was not lost on either man's face, in fact the admiral's face lit up when he saw her walking towards them.

***

"Better get yourselves out here at the double, the Admiral's on his way to the hospital and we have to be there pronto!" The land Rover driver had got a message from 42 Commando RM to be there ASAP. "The media will out in force so tidy yourselves up, let's go!"

The mad dash to BMH began with horns tooting from all vehicles there was louder blasts from the Land Rover as they ploughed their way through the dense thronging horn tooting Chinese drivers; however, when they saw a Land Rover in their rear view mirror bearing down on them in a tail gating manner they soon got out of the way.

***

"So you are Henry Cunningham's daughter, he often talked about you when we served together during the war; you were quite the apple of his eye, now I see why." They both smiled at this recollection.

The Rolls arrived first, stately and regally, Admiral's flag fluttering in the breeze, the Land Rover tearing up the driveway to the hospital like the devil on their shoulders, screeching to a halt as the rear door of the Rolls was opened. Linda came out first, head bent down as she negotiated the door way, showing the beginnings of her large cleavage. The photographers snapping away incessantly as she stepped down, her dress had caught on the car door handle, she paused knowing that all her legs were on view, the photographers caught all the splendour of her naked ivory legs right up to her thighs, the Admiral was in the background exiting the same door, grinning, he gently freed Linda's skirt with some amusement.

The marines dressed in their tailored OGs with small RMs on their epaulettes, 40 Cdo lanyards on their left shoulder and their Green Berets with stay bright cap badges. They really did look 'Rough and Tough'. Approaching the Admiral they all halted in line abreast and saluted, "Sir! We are the Search and Rescue team reporting!"

The Admiral walked over to the group and began chatting with them about the way in which they had been sent out and the conditions they had encountered in Sarawak. He shook them all by hand and declared he was well pleased with the overall outcome of it all. "I have no doubt that there will be full report on my desk very soon, when I will make some recommendations."

The moment not being lost on the media and photographers who were flashing away merrily.

Linda walked over to Tom and whispered in his ear, "Thank you Tom, I am forever grateful."

She smiled demurely and secretively as she said it; looking at him with much pleasure. *SNAP!* She was caught in the act and it would be front page news in the UK, also in the Straits Times.

The hospital beds had been placed on a wide veranda which overlooked a really lush tropical garden. Lt Waters, Marine Dave Younger had recovered consciousness but Lt Davenport was still in a coma like state. After the photographic session, he would immediately be taken back to his hospital room for intensive care. They all trooped onto the veranda to take up positions for the photo shoot. Linda on seeing her Chris was overcome with grief and ran to his side holding him in her arms and crying uncontrollably, everyone standing back understanding her feelings exactly. The Admiral was the first to hold her in his arms and commiserate with her promising that everything would be done to bring Chris back to as full a life and good health, "You have my word on that, Linda." She nodded meekly and dabbed at her eyes looking once more at her husband, Chris, whom she remembered as being a very handsome young marine officer.

The QARRNS nurse, Amelia, took charge of the group saying, "Lt Davenport is in a very critical condition, I am now going to take him back to his room, he needs medical attention immediately, YOU! Pointing to the biggest marine, take hold of this bed and haul him back to his room, Follow me!" With that, she scattered the group not caring about authority or Admirals; she was a no nonsense nurse in charge and she cared.

The press photographers were snapping away happily at every conceivable opportunity, missing nothing. These pictures would be front page news throughout the world.

McH was on the fringes of the group and so was Jenny who he took an instant shine to as they were of the same height each one, very lightweight.

***

The following day on the front pages of the British newspapers: *Daily Express, Daily Mail, Daily Mirror,* Even the *Times*. In the USA: *Los Angeles Tribune, Washington Post, New York Times*. In Germany: *Der Spiegel Berliner, Wolfgang Deutschland*. In Italy: *IL DolcaVita Italia*. In France: *Legion La François*. In Australia: the *Sydney Morning Herald*. In Malaya/Singapore: the *Straits Times*.

The photo showed Linda emerging from the Admiral's Rolls Royce bending slightly forward to show much of her cleavage, her skirt parted all the way up to very nearly her 'Nether Regions'. Her long ivory shapely legs on full view. The only caption they could think of was "WOW." Page three showed the other photographs of the group which included the search and rescue team with the Admiral comforting Linda as she looked down at her husband Lt Christopher Davenport. There was also a rear view of the QARNNS nurse, Amelia, which showed a very shapely behind and hips as she bent to push the bed back into the private room.

The reporters had done a good write up of the team's success in graphic detail; however, they concentrated on Linda's story and the fact she had travelled half way 'round the world to be at her husband's side and where did she come from; what was her hometown? She just answered Plymouth England; they were quite surprised when the Admiral said he knew her father, Sir Henry Cunningham KCB, DSC. Linda would be front page news for a long time, her former anonymity was gone.

***

In London at British Admiralty House, Sir Henry Cunningham was enjoying his first cup of coffee when his personal Assistant PO Angela Ransome (WRENS) who had brought the newspaper in for his perusal, she glanced at him with that secret smile as he looked up at her.

Puzzled at her unusual gaiety at that time in the morning, he unfolded the paper to see his daughter Linda splashed over the front page. "My God, they've got my daughter nearly in the nude." He again glanced at his attractive assistant who politely, still grinning, closed the door quietly behind her. He was on the phone immediately with his wife, Mabel, in Plymouth, "Have you read the papers this morning, darling?" Tearfully, his wife replied that she had and was shocked at the nearly nude pictures of their darling daughter. Sir Henry replaced the telephone on its cradle, sat back pondering his next move. He needn't have worried, all of his officers, both young and old, wanted to shake his hand and congratulate him on having such a beautiful daughter as Linda. The marines throughout the corps had her as their No 1 pinup girl which appeared 'Inside' their lockers.

Sir Henry minding his own business as usual; strode into the officers' mess for lunch, as he got right in the middle of the dining area, all the officers stood up clapping and cheering him as if he was a great super athlete. Sir Henry although a trifle embarrassed rather liked this show of 'solidarity'. In the words of Ken Dodd he said to himself, "I feel quite chuffed!"

Later on he did telephone his wife and related what had happened to him at the Admiralty House at lunchtime, also later that officers were more convivial to him than was usual.

Mable although still not having got over the initial shock took some delight in what Henry told her.

Chapter 15
Straits View, Johore Bahru

Customs Barrier at Johore Bahru – Malaysia

Linda had spent the night at Chris's bedside; the nurses had provided a reclining leather lounge chair and a suitable blanket for when it got cooler in the night. The nurse Amelia visited them often in the course of the night. Amelia had also supplied Linda with a nightdress as she felt a bit overdressed and conspicuous in her cute new outfit. Linda could see that Chris was being well cared for; she really appreciated the heavy schedule that the nurse was putting in. Linda slept fitfully that night, waking only when Chris might need her or the nurse, but he never woke up completely, Linda worried for him, what if he never wakes up? She cast it from her mind as soon as she had thought it, he must get better. Towards morning, she began to talk to him even though he may or may not be able to hear her. She recalled when she first met him and the many places they had visited together, the romantic moonlight strolls, the gay parties at his and her parent's country retreats, their romantic and expensive wedding, the best man's rather risqué comments about their relationship and what he wished for them in the future. Their commission in the West Indies in the Caribbean as the personal helicopter pilot to her Majestie's Governor General, and as his Aide de Comp.

"I'm here Chris; I am here with you," she said as she kissed his hands with loving care and affection, tears welling up in her eyes. Nurse Amelia had listened to her reminiscing and felt some inner deeper empathy; Linda was not to know she had been overheard, she had been lost in her own thoughts.

Linda could hear the lively crickets and sequoias beating their wings in great numbers, the cry of the peacocks as they strolled freely around the hospital grounds, their tail feathers splayed out majestically. Nurse Amelia came in and taking Linda by the hand she led her to the nurses' quarters advising her to get showered and changed and altogether get freshened up for she was going to telephone the Admiral's Office for his instructions on what would be best for Linda's wellbeing.

"The Admiral is sending his driver over to collect you in about an hour, he has booked you in to the Straits View Hotel in Johore Baru, and it's much nearer for the Naval Dockyard which is just over the causeway and is a much more direct route to here at BMH." Nurse Amelia then retreated to her duties with the three marines.

Linda got dressed hurriedly and sped off to see her dear Chris; who was still in an unconscious state. "Darling, darling, darling," she quietly mouthed, "I have to leave you soon but I will be back very shortly, I love you Chris!" kissing his face and hands, she left reluctantly.

"Morning, Watson."

"Morning, Ma'am," as Watson opened the rear door for her. They glided along effortlessly, Linda peering out of the window taking in the early morning Chinese traders jostling their way through to open stalls at the side of nearly every road and the cacophony of noises they all made, it was quite different to her life back in England.

The Rolls Royce entered the entrance to the customs and excise barriers, which immediately opened to allow them a free gateway to the mainland of Malaysia. The border guards saluting them as they went through unchallenged. This was in a time of comparative peace and security.

The Straits View Hotel aptly named as it did overlook the Straits separating Malaya from Singapore, a causeway spanned the distance from mainland to island authorities.

Two Malay girls dressed in their sarong kebaya, they were barefoot, greeted Linda as she stepped out of the Rolls, she being very careful this time that she didn't catch her dress on the door handles. "Selamat pagi, mem," they both chorused.

Linda smiled and responded, "Samar Samar! Terima Kesah!"

They led her into a breathtaking Arabesque, Islamic inspired reception hall, cool, inviting and so oriental. Italian veined marble columns held up this massive structure, the floor also was polished marble. Large ceiling fans quietly turning causing little trickles of air and light to pervade this welcoming area. Watson carrying her light luggage glanced around to he was also taking in the scenery and thought, *Way hei man! A bit different to Durham this,* but he didn't say a word, just gazed in some awe. They were conveyed to their room which was rather like a suite, the white colonial plantation shutters were open, which gave a panoramic view of the Straits and beyond that the open sea. It quite took Linda's breath away. The telephone rang, it was the Admiral, "Trust you find your room to your liking."

"Very much, sir," she breathed down the phone in reply.

The Admiral gave a little chuckle and told her, "I am also sending over two of the group that rescued Lt Davenport, this is for your overall protection; Martial and French, expect them very soon. I will inform your father Henry Cunningham, well good luck Linda, hope your husband gets better soon. I have left word at the hospital for absolute medical care. And, keep in touch!" Watson returned to the Naval Dockyard for the Admiral's use.

***

Orders had been received at the Adjutants and Movements Office at 42 Commando. The adjutant was handed a movement's document that instructed that Martial and French were to be moved to the Straits View Hotel (he looked with some malice at this order, sneering), he perused the rest of the names on the list. Warden; to go on a Junior Command course in two days' time at Nee Soon Garrison. McHenry; to return to Sarawak by RAF Hastings ASAP, for special assignment in Brunei, for the sultan, Mohammed Ali Daressalam 3rd. The Adjutant threw down the papers onto his desk in some disgust, feeling a little jealous of 'these people'.

“Colour Sergeant! My office now!” Separated by a thin lattice and plaster partition, the Colour Sergeant of Movements entered and received a thorough briefing on the orders just received.

The Colour Sergeant who was of the same ‘ilk’ as the adjutant, lost no time, he immediately telephoned the Provost Sergeant and together they both ascended the sergeants’ mess steps and sought the sergeants’ mess steward. “Where are those reprobates from 40 Cdo?”

“Last time, I saw them Colour, they were in the swimming pool doing some fitness training they said!”

Grunting under his breath, he made for the swimming pool, his overstuffed stomach paunch getting the better of him. “All right you men get out of the pool, here are your orders!” As they gathered around him and the Provost Sergeant he felt a little bit intimidated. Here were four young men, one standing about five feet five inches, the other was six feet, the next stood at six feet two inches and the last one stood at six feet five inches, all in tip top physical condition not an inch of fat, very broad and very muscular, at this stage, he altered his attitude of belligerence and delivered a more controlled version of the orders. After the Colour Sergeant had left the Provost Sergeant, Gordon Norton, shook their hands and congratulated them on a fine rescue mission in Sarawak Borneo. He took McH aside and put his arm around his shoulders wishing him all the luck in the world on his special mission with the Sultan. He also said to Gil, “I will probably see you on your junior command course, however good luck, Warden!”

The telephone rang in Linda’s suite, it had been ringing quite a lot since she had arrived; most of it was to do with the world wide newspaper articles, some being very invasive in their comments however some were quite genuine in their offers of working in the fashion industry.

Jenny came on the phone, “Missy Linda I wish to come and see you, very important. I get your address and phone number from Nurse Amelia at BMH.”

Linda replied, “Why yes, of course, I’d love to see you.” She hung up, “Now I wonder what that was all about, maybe it’s about my dresses. Ah well, we’ll soon know.”

An hour later, Jenny arrived there was a knocking on the door. “Come in,” Linda responded. Jenny was little flushed with some kind of excitement also due no doubt to the hot humid temperature. “Sit down, here’s some ice water, have a drink first, and then tell me what’s on your mind.”

"Well Mem, two days from now, I been invited to attend, big fashion parade in Oriental Hotel on west coast, Singapore, will you please be my model in clothes, have made for you?"

"Well, I don't know I have never modelled before and amongst the Chinese girls I'd stand out like a sore thumb."

"Yes, yes, you quite right that is what I thought. Please mem you model for me?"

"Well, all right if you think it's a good idea just for you okay!"

"Many rich Chinese from all over Asia will come to view all collections of dresses, Korea, China, Hawaii, all over South East Asia, Malaysia. It is very big you like very much."

There was a heavy knock at the door so Linda went over to see who it could be; frowning she opened the door, the frown evaporated when she saw who it was and flung her arms around Tom and then Jack. She was a bit breathless and excited at the same time. "I didn't expect to see either of you again so soon; what are you doing here?"

Tom responded with a mock US salute and just said, "Just following orders, ma'am," grinning from ear to ear. He entered the suite and saw Jenny, "I hope we're not interrupting anything, Linda."

"Well, not exactly. We were just discussing a special fashion parade in two days' time, Jenny has been lucky enough to be selected to show her dress collections." Jenny was impressed with both marines as she eyed them up and down. *Hmmm*, she thought *what if they could model with Linda in the finale they would be outstanding.*

"I have good idea for you, will you accompany Linda in the fashion parade in the finale, I make good clothes for you like James Bond in movies."

Tom and Jack looked at each other and laughed out loud. "Well, we'll have to get permission first through the Admiral; Linda that would be better if you asked him?"

Tom quietly informed Linda, "We are in the hotel room opposite yours; this is for your protection; if anything goes awry, press this gadget and it will ring our pager."

"Before I go, I take measurements for your suits." Jenny by drawing two simple figures and then began by fitting the figures in as she measured, shoe sizes also, the last measurement was the inside leg, she knelt down before each marine and gently pushed the tape measure up into the 'V' of the upper leg and groin area. Both marines looked a little embarrassed except Jenny who quite liked the experience. "Which side you dress on?"

Both replied simultaneously, "Left."

Jenny replied smiling, "You both big boys!" She turned to Linda, "You look after big boys until I telephone you and I give more details and maybe send you, Silver Service Taxi."

There was another knock on the door; "Come in," Linda called out. The marines separated to each side of the door. The two Malay girls who had welcomed them to the hotel glided in with two enormous trays of local fruits the likes of which Linda had not seen before, such as kiwi passion fruit, spiky rambutangs, lychees, kumquat, tamarind, loquat, green figs and, of course, the usual well-known fruits: dates, coconut, banana, pineapple, mandarins, cherries, grapes white and red. All set in a silver tray beautifully arranged. Around the perimeter were various cheeses and biscuits. Jenny took a small bunch of grapes and held it teasingly above her mouth, smiling at the boys.

Linda and the 'Boys' didn't need much encouragement as the Malay girls withdrew.

Marines are always hungry and together with Linda and Jenny they left a jagged hole in the 'Fruits and Cheeses'.

Their tummies filled, Linda ushered them out saying she had to have a shower and a sleep as she had not got much sleep last night being at Chris's bedside. She said to Tom, "Call me at 3pm, I need to go to the market place in the town to buy a pair of jeans and a blouse as I haven't anything suitable at the moment to wear; we'll go in the Land Rover, okay?" she smiled and closed the door but didn't lock it, Tom made a mental note of that.

"Well, we've got a few hours to kill, what do you reckon Tom?"

"I think we ought to have a shit, shower, shave and shampoo! Also we'll get some dhobying done, we've have everything we need in here, so let's do it!" First the Aussie calf-length, black leather boots, shone up brilliantly. Then off with all the olive greens; all went in for the wash…

Showered and rested on the large queen sized beds, Tom phoned reception for a phone call at 1430 hrs.

Ring, ring, ring, ring, Tom and Jack woke up like a startled chuck, shaking their heads wondering where the hell they were. "Shit I was dreaming I was back in the bloody swamp."

Jack muttered, "Me too, except I was hanging on a branch on the edge of a cliff, yelling, 'God help ME!' Then a voice said, 'Do you believe in me?' I said, 'YESSSS!' Then he said, 'Let go of the branch'. After a few seconds, I then said, 'Anyone else up there?' Then, fortunately, the phone rang; it was just a terrible dream. Thank God!"

Tom and Jack had dried their OGs then pressed and ironed them. Tom looked at his G10 Omega watch; it was just on one minute to 3 pm. He was still in the hotel's bathrobe, so he motioned to Jack he was going to see Linda and give her a shake. Jack nodded grinning.

Tom padded over the hallway and slipped soundlessly through the door. Linda was in the nude under the bed sheets lightly snoring, he kissed her cheeks, nose and finally her lips, she woke dewy-eyed and smiled at Tom. Dropping his bathrobe, he climbed in beside her and ran his tongue around her nipples which having been aroused rose erect. There was no attempt at foreplay, this was what they both wanted. *What all men want!* she thought; her legs opened willingly and his erect penis was inside her throbbing as he worked it slowly at first, then with a more insistent pace. Linda was a woman that no one would forget; she was so alive and groaning with utter abandonment enjoying every second, her long nails snaking their way over his broad back and shoulders, incredibly sexually stimulating as he drove his member deeper into her. Drenched in sweat and semen, they both staggered to the oriental inspired bathroom.

Showered, dried and sitting comfortably in one of the French inspired armchairs, Tom reminded Linda to telephone the Admiral for his endorsement and permission for all three of them to attend the Fashion parade at the Orient Hotel Tomorrow night. Linda nodded and began dialling. "C in C's office of Admiral Mark Donovan," said a young navy lieutenant. "Who do you wish to speak to; can I be of any assistance?"

"Yes! This is Linda Davenport, I would like to speak to the Admiral direct?"

"Hold the line; one moment please!" the lieutenant responded.

"Mark Donovan here! Linda, how nice to hear from you; how can I be of assistance to you?"

Linda began explaining the special invitation to appear as a model in the acclaimed Southeast Asia fashion parade and gala to be held at the oriental Hotel at 7pm tomorrow night. Her voice was very articulated and had a resonance of a sexy nature, she really attracted men of all ages, the Admiral was no exception. She also wished to take her two body guards with her too.

She went on to mention that a great number of influential Chinese business men and millionaires would be present including the Prime Minister of Singapore, Lee Kwan Yew, maybe also soon to be President; Tunkhu Abdul Rahman, Malaysian Leader. "I would also say that you would be an honoured guest, also to escort me."

"Hmmmm! I'll get back to you on that, maybe revise my schedule, I don't see any reason why we should not attend excellent opportunity for cementing good relationships in the South East Asia and pacific theatre. My Aide-de-Comp will contact you later. Will speak to you later."

Tom had slipped out to his room and got dressed in their freshly pressed olive greens, boots, web belts, light blue lanyards, small RM's Green Beret complete with stay bright cap badge; however, Jack preferred his highly polished brass cap badge with the king's crown; atop was the lion!

Linda had got dressed in her black dress she had had dry cleaned, complete with her broad brimmed black hat; she looked absolutely gorgeous and the 'Boys' thought so too.

The Land Rover screeched to a halt, they had found the Johore Market place, complete with 'Sweet water canal' running along the side for the open waters. They sold everything here, everything live and absolutely fresh. The babble of Malay, Chinese, Tamil, Indian was lost on the English, but friendly smiles as they perambulated around to find a pair of light jeans and a blouse or two, also Linda needed a pair of soft sandals for everyday use. Actually, Linda was causing a bit of a stir in the hearts of many of the men, who were whispering and pointing in her direction. The streets surrounding the market were also filled with every known merchandise grain, sacks of delicious smelling spices, flour, and salt, sugar brown and white.

For instance, at the market you had to point to a chicken that you wanted to buy which was alive and crowing for your consumption later in the day. "Come back, missy, in one hour, will be ready for you!" Wow! One felt like a murderer, especially western women.

Linda finally found a dress shop and ducked her head to get into the shaded shop. She was welcomed by two sisters whose skin was jet black; they were a cross between a Malay Mother and a Black Tamil father, he was her second husband. The girls looked in wonder at Linda, their perfect white teeth and the surrounds to their dark brown eyes lit up their faces. Linda was impressed with them.

Explaining in broken English what she wanted to buy. They brought many pairs of jeans which they said was very light and easy to wear. They also brought out heaps of blouses in multi coloured printed Batik material, very cool, very beautiful.

Linda bought two pairs of jeans, three blouses, a pair of soft native leather sandals and a large brimmed panama hat which is normally worn by men, but it suited her. She asked the girls where to change, so they pointed to the back of the shop which in truth was a bit untidy and ancient; however, when she came out, she still looked ravishing. The clothes she had worn and the clothes she bought were packed into a large brown carrier bag. The Malay girls after being paid were very excited and friendly; Linda had obviously over paid them but what the hell, money talks eh? Putting their hands together as she was leaving and smiling broadly and waving goodbye saying, "Terima Kesah Mem."

"Terima Kesah Banyak."

Linda paused at a door further down the roadway, looking up at the Malay sign; she asked Tom and Jack what it meant. "Kedai Koppee," they both said.

"Coffee shop!" Linda brightened up. "Well, let's go in and have one."

Jack turned to Tom and just shrugged, "Why not."

They were served a soup like coffee in a large glass with handles by Enche (Mr) SAID; the coffee tasted okay but was very sweet to the western palate.

Linda outlined what she wanted to do for the rest of the day, "We have to go back to the hotel, see if there are any messages, then I must go to BMH. I will have to stay with Chris for at least four hours in case there is any chance of him coming out of his coma." Tom and Jack nodded in agreement to her wishes.

Arriving at reception, Linda inquired, "Any messages for me, Mrs Davenport?"

The concierge looked in the pigeon holes, "Yes ma'am, there is just one!"

Linda ripped open the letter and beaming with delight she said to Tom and Jack, "It's on for tomorrow night, we're going to the Oriental with the Admiral, he will be escorting me and you two will be in front with the Land Rover in convoy!" she hugged them both to her and still smiling just said, "We must go over to BMH, meet in twenty minutes here in the reception area!" In the suite Linda phoned Jenny and told her the news that the Admiral was coming to the fashion show and to make the necessary arrangements for his invitation and seat. Jenny was ecstatic with excitement; she had instructed the dress makers at her shop to make extra outfits for Linda and the 'Boys' as she called them. It would be dreams come true for Jenny.

The Land Rover sped through the highways and the byways towards their goal of BMH so that Linda could see her beloved Christopher to find out if he had come out of his coma. Jack was driving and although he was a good driver, many times Linda had her heart beating wildly but she did not utter a word of caution or fear. Tom and Jack were joshing each other about their driving skills, but they were nothing compared to the Singapore kamikaze drivers they were amongst, all vehicles honking their horns endlessly as they behaved like weaver birds in and out very nearly colliding with each other's vehicles on the roads, it was doubtful whether any of them had ever passed a driving test.

Presently they arrived in the comparative calm of the hospital grounds; Linda breathed a sigh of relief as the hospital hove into view.

"I don't know! You two must be the worst drivers in Singapore!" she was smiling as she was ticking them off. Tom and Jack just grinning.

"What do you mean, that was a good drive, you should see us when we really try, but we didn't want to scare you!"

Linda sought out the QARNNS nurse, Amelia, at reception and had her paged. "I just can't go barging in there, I need Amelia's advice," Linda whispered to Tom. They both nodded solemnly.

Presently Amelia came along smiling at Linda and Tom detected a private look she gave Jack.

In a covert or private eye contact. Tom mused: I think she fancies him! Well, he thought, what hot bloodied female wouldn't; he was a very big dependable sort of man and a damned fine marine; he would do well in the corps.

The nurse led them to Chris's private room where he had been in a coma for the last few days.

Typical street scene in the 1960s' era

Linda stayed with Chris holding his hand and talking to him as if he could hear what she was saying.

Tom felt a bit awkward and said to Linda, "Be a few minutes; I'll see how Dave's getting along."

***

Jack and the nurse, Amelia, were having a cup of tea and reminiscing about life back home in England. "Whereabouts in UK are you from?" Jack asked.

"Chatham in Kent, my father was a Royal Marine in the Second World War, he was a sergeant major in 48 Commando, and one of the conflicts he was engaged in was at Walcheren."

"You sound like you've had a good education."

"Yes! Daddy used to say knowledge is power, so Mummy had me educated at Chatham Grammar School for girls, very strict but excellent teachers. Daddy wanted me to join the WRENS; however, my interest was in the medical profession so that's why I preferred the Queen Alexandria's."

Amelia was a little amused at his turn of phraseology, smiling she said, "Where are you from Jack?"

"Well, I'll tell ya! I'm from Northampton."

"And what kind of work did you do there?"

"Well, after I left college, I started work on the squire's estate. I was a good shot and could set many traps for rabbits and Ares."

"Sounds interesting; however, I can't see you being a manservant or a gilly for the local squire; sounds more like a poacher to me," she said smiling with a twinkle in her eye.

"Come on, it's getting late and I usually have a swim at this time in the remedial pool, have you got any swimming trunks with you?"

"We always have our boxer shorts on, noice and cumfurtable under these OG's." Amelia came out of the changing rooms tucking her hair under her swimming cap, glancing up she wasn't expecting to see such a powerful man as Jack, quiet, confident, fair-haired with steady blue eyes; gazed at her in her backless swimming costume sweeping down to just above her well-shaped and rounded buttocks.

They both entered the water at the same time; both were strong swimmers and soon were competing in a race up and down the length of the pool.

Laughing and out of breath, they hauled themselves out of the water. "We must keep in touch Jack, leave your address with me and we can write to each other, OK?" Jack just nodded, smiling.

***

Back on board HMS Bulwark, the grisly task of removing the corpses had been done several days ago, were put in body bags and stored in the cold room. The 'chippy' had made the wooden boxes lining them with a hessian based material which was lightly tarred on one side and having an aluminium backing on the reverse side, similar to preservation of ammunitions.

This consignment was awaiting a suitable flight of the RAF to convey them to Singapore for autopsy examinations.

***

Linda had been at Chris's bedside for many, many, hours, and was beginning to feel absolutely weary. Chris was still in a coma, the nurse, Amelia, had looked in several times to check his pulse, heartbeat and to change the bottles and sachets of solutions that were keeping him fed and alive. Jack and Tom were outside the room in comfortable armchairs but even so they too were beginning to feel the strain of the waiting and inactive.

Nurse Amelia shook Linda awake as she had just dozed off for the umpteenth time, "I think you had better go back to the hotel and get some sleep, you look all in my dear!"

Linda's eyes filled up with tears, she just nodded, making her way unsteadily to the door for Tom and Jack to drive her back in the wee hours of the morn, it was about 0300 hrs and as you may know that is when most humans are at their lowest ebb.

Thankfully, they climbed aboard the Land Rover; Tom was driving this time, "I just wanted to get there in one piece if you don't mind!" he said to no one in particular. Jack cheesed down.

They were making better time at this time of night; however, they still had to watch out for the black Mercedes pirate taxis hurtling down the highways. "Hey up," Jack said. "Why don't we drop in on Bugis street for a Tiger Beer?"

"Sounds good to me, how about you Linda, want to see how the other half live?"

"If you think we must, but I am feeling very tired," Tom said

"What did she say?" Jack said,

"She said okay!" *Liar, liar, bums on fire!* Tom thought.

They parked up and found a suitable table in the Bugis street open vendors market, it was a hive of activity, the smell of cooking was everywhere on the humid air. The clientele was mainly servicemen, navy, army, some RAF, majority were Royal Marines from 42 Commando RM. All were 'Shiters' having been in the Britannia Club all night until they got thrown out by the Red Caps. A lot of them knew Tom and Jack and made a bee line for them when they sat down. "Jack, Tom how's it grow-in?" It was Arthur Ainsworth, Eric 'Punchy' Walker, with his sparring partner Willie Tervitt, George Gallagher, Tom Magee. They had in tow an American marine and the biggest American matelot they had ever seen standing about seven feet two inches. Also in the group was an SBS marine sgt. Everyone offering to buy them drinks which they politely accepted. Sitting down and back slapping Tom and Jack, they finally focused their boozy eyes on Linda.

"Well, wot have we got here, Tom. Where'd ya find this lovely, bootiful thing?"

"She's the wife of the Chopper pilot we rescued in Sarawak the other week. Name is Lt Chris Davenport."

"Oh yeah! We heard about that. Well, strike me purple. I'om glad to meet your acquaintance Mrs!" They all beat a path and started kissing her hand.

"My you're all real gentlemen!"

With that they gave her a toast with their cans of Tiger held in the air, "To the Real Marines! And Miss Linda," some of the lager beer finding its way down their throats.

Bugis Street in the 1960s

Every one of the group insisted on buying them drinks, Linda was never nervous but felt at one with them all, she was after all, a free spirit and could handle men of any age. She did feel more alive and happy after her vigil at Chris's bedside, she was glad they had called in to this open market and as Tom said, "The other half of mankind."

She did, however, turn to Tom and said, "There are a lot of pretty Chinese girls here!"

One of the group; George Gallagher, had overheard Linda's comment about the Chinese 'Girls'. He quietly said to Linda, "These pretty things are not girls, they're 'Kyeteyes' males dressed up as females!"

"Oh I didn't know that, they're so pretty." Down at the end of the street was a Chinese stage which was lit with kerosene lamps with stainless steel reflectors fitted to the base. Clashing of symbols and shrill throaty songs were emanating from this arena; string like instruments, like a cat being strangled was also adding to the clamour of this special national heritage play from a bygone Era. Most were men all painted up, playing female roles?

Linda had never seen anything like it before and was fascinated by the whole spectacle of Bugis street. Tom and Jack ordered from one of the stall holders, kebabs in satays sauce with small bowls of noodles for the entire group around them.

As dawn started to break, Tom Linda and Jack said their goodbyes, Linda hugging them all in turn they mounted the Land

Rover and sped off down the narrow streets and alleyways, chickens squawking that were getting out of their way. It was a great night, Linda thought as she mused over what had just happened, with a deep sigh, she fell asleep in a careering Land Rover bound for the Straits View Hotel in Johore, Malaya.

She was hardly aware of getting to the hotel and being undressed and put to bed by her two guardians, she passed blissfully into a deep sleep, filled with sounds of heavenly music.

It was a little after 1200 hrs when Tom and Jack woke to the sounds of an incoming chopper, both jerked up but realised it was the large overhead fans in the room beating the humid air around that abounds in Malaya.

"Better wake up, Linda, Tom. We have to be on our way about 1630 hrs."

Tom padded off on his errand, "Wakey, wakey rise and shine come on mateys you've had your time, stop sleeping, stop sleeping." Linda wondered what the hell was going on, but saw Tom smiling at her and just grinned back at him, thrusting off the coverlet as she rose.

"I'm going to ring down for some lunch and have it delivered via room service, I'm going to keep it simple and order nasi goreng and prawn cutlets, is that okay with you Linda?"

"I really don't know, I've never had that dish before, but go ahead anyway."

"It's just fried rice with certain very small vegetables cooked in naturally brewed soy sauce, quite nice really, trust me!"

"I will; thousands wouldn't," she laughed as she said it.

***

At exactly 1630 hrs, the phone in Linda's room rang, "Hello. Your car is here with velly important gentlemen; he is in foyer now. Please come now, Miss Linda."

The Rolls was waiting in the shaded portico area in front of the hotel and Admiral Mark Donovan stood in the foyer area, resplendent in tropical whites with the golden epaulettes and the 'scrambled egg' on his peek cap. He smiled when he saw Linda offering his arm for her to take, "I want you to meet my Aide-de-Comp." The young Lieutenant had his back to them and was just admiring the view of the straits. "This is Lt Paul Cavendish," Linda immediately recognised him and flung her arms around his neck.

"Paul… well, I never! Fancy meeting you again." Tom and Jack had just come on the scene and just winked at one another.

"Well, I gather you know my young lieutenant," smiling, the Admiral led her to the car. Watson was there, opening the rear door, and he too was smiling.

Polite banter between all three with the Land Rover leading the way through the maze of Singapore traffic; Tom and Jack had plotted the course they were now navigating.

Soon, they were in what amounted to a holiday style town and on a marine parade with sea and sand set in a rather nice tropical setting. They drove up the long drive to the Oriental Hotel which had recently had an expensive refurbishment, all were impressed as they approached the covered portico leading onto a vast foyer or in this case a reception hall. This hotel was very much in the Chinese style but lavishly decorated and again the use of marble floors was most evident, indoor palms and plants decorated in the discreet alcoves. The use of gold and red; which were two of their favourite colours of the Chinese, particularly the Red. On seeing the Rolls entering the entrance, Jenny rushed down the wide staircase to greet them all. Putting her hands together and bowing slightly she said, "Welcome, I so glad you could come; we have very special night here, all most welcome, officers very smart too." Winking at Linda as she took her arm as she whispered, "You will steal show here; I make very special dresses for you!" Turning back to the group which now included Tom and Jack Jenny said, "I get young Chinese boy to show you to bar, please wait here. Mr Tom, Mr Jack you come with me we get good clothes for you in show."

The Admiral, his aide and his chauffer Watson; standing quite tall were being warmly welcomed by prominent Chinese business men, most of whom were millionaires. They were honestly interested in the presence of the Commander in Chief of South East Asia command. The music drifted through the entire building and was mainly Chinese but was suitably arranged not to be too quirky, rather more melodious for western ears. They all retreated to the bar which was doing excellent business; waiters were scurrying around with trays of wines and champagne, it seemed like a scene out of one of the Hollywood classic films of the 1940s. Watson had been observing the guests who he mentally made a note of, being part of his job he thought. He particularly focused his attention on a male who he recognised. He went over putting out his hand in friendship. "Vernon Cock?"

"Well, blow me down, it's Spot Watson, what are you doing here?"

"I might ask you the same question," Spot replied. Vernon was dressed in a white sharkskin evening jacket, black trousers and shoes, a red cummerbund was around his waist, a black handkerchief in his breast pocket and single small red rose in his lapel buttonhole. "Very smart, Vernon. Come over to meet the Admiral."

"Sir! This is Marine Vernon Cock. At present, he's in 42 Commando RM."

"Well, we are glad to meet anyone from the navy's soldiers, aren't we Cavendish?"

"Very much, sir, and may I say how splendid you look, Marine Cock."

"Tell me, what brings you here on this particular night?" The Admiral was curious to know.

"Well, I have become friends with a Chinese family and in particular one of his daughters, they're business people, so they invited me here tonight." He was also carrying a very small expensive jewellery case.

"Tell me, and I know it's none of my business, but what is inside that case?"

"Well sir, it's a gift for my friend's daughter which I will present to her tonight as a special token of our friendship." Vernon opened the velvet bound case and showed a beautiful small and dainty diamond which sparkled in a bed of blue velvet, a tiny silver chain of exceptional quality completed the necklace, the diamond being held in a platinum setting, it was small and very delicate, dainty.

"Hmmm, interesting. I do hope you have a very pleasant night; it was a pleasure meeting you," the Admiral smiled kindly and shook the marine's hand.

A small Chinese boy led them to their respective seats in a large Auditorium which tonight was opened to the sky. The stars were in great numbers, the balmy air floated with the scent of joss sticks and light scented perfumes. It was a glorious setting and soon all the fashions of the east would be on display. The crowd was excited and eager to see everything. The buyers held their clip boards ready to write and note every fashion that maybe they would order. There was also a smattering of buyers from USA, Australia, New Zealand, South Africa and South America and one from Gt Britain. The head of the Singapore fashion world appeared on stage to welcome everyone to the first ever fashion parade to be held in Singapore. He asked for the Commander in Chief of the Royal Navy Far eastern Command to join him on stage. The Admiral obligingly made his way to the raised dais and shook hands with the Chinese millionaire who had organised this rather splendid and glamorous event.

"Sir! Would you be so kind enough to announce the opening of our fashion show tonight."

The Admiral responded looking around at the gathered faces in the audience, he decided on a very diplomatic course of action. Standing tall in his immaculate officers' white tropical suit with the gold epaulettes and laurel wreaths on his peaked cap he turned to the Chinese MC and said, "Mr Wang Lung, I am very honoured to be asked to open this magnificent show; however, I feel that this honour should be bestowed on the President elect of Singapore Mr Lee Kuan Yew!" The place went wild with this act of diplomacy, clapping not only for Lee Kuan Yew but also the humility of the great Admiral himself. On reaching the dais a broadly smiling Lee Kuan Yew shook the Admirals hand and declared in both Chinese and then in English how proud he was to open this inaugural Singapore fashion event.

The models were heralded by traditional Chinese fanfare music as they entered wearing many varied costumes and flowing robes all exceptionally decorated with floral or dragon motifs. The audience responded with a huge applause as the models paraded up and down the raised aisle. The Chinese models very small and dainty with extravagant makeup which emphasised their oval-shaped eyes to perfection, their pale skin flawless, their generous lips in a bright red, orange, peachy, raspberry, the eyebrows in various shades of blue and green which sparkled in the floodlit areas. Flashing bulbs of the media cameras not to mention the TV moguls on their special equipped positions both above and below; capturing all the colour and splendour of this oriental fashion show. The day clothes, the sport and leisure clothes, the after five apparel and cocktail dresses, evening dresses fashionable and or slinky, the nightwear and also the lingerie, which got a special excitement from the male Chinese businessmen. Beautiful silks and satin materials, some inspired by the Vietnamese mode of dress long silk trousers overlaid with a long sweeping split sided dresses all in various shades, hues and colours. The mood had now been changed to a more western style of music. On a big screen in the background they had projected Tom Jones singing *What's New Pussycat!* There was even a South American combo that had come over with the business elements and would be playing later to add to the glamour of the occasion.

The Admiral and his Aide De Comp, Paul Cavendish, were thoroughly enjoying this rather unique spectacle, especially with a never ending supply of pink gins. He had, of course, been to fashion parades in London and Paris but this was quite different being oriental.

This next segment was devoted to the designers from Hong Kong who also had a flair for very elegant and fashionable designs; Tsai Chin sang her latest song *Second Spring* as they paraded their very latest fashions.

There was a bit of a lull to the proceedings at this point, as the audience wondered what was coming on next. On the big screen appeared a youthful Cliff Richard singing his current hit record of *Living Doll,* finally Linda stepped from behind the elegant curtains on to the aisle and pandemonium erupted as they all recognised from the newspapers who she was, in the dress which had made her famous, especially with those long ivory legs being exposed as she stepped purposefully and may I say provocatively along the catwalk. She wore the black tulip wrap around skirt, the white linen long sleeved coat, cut fairly low, the black full brimmed hat and blue veil, black high heeled shoes. She turned and smiled at everyone, her face was so beautifully made up, and her voluptuous lips moistened a rich ruby red. Thunderous clapping ensued as she deliberately bowed which showed off her cleavage to great advantage. Striding off very elegantly with a great deal of poise, she had won every man's heart.

Next were the Chinese models; all were dressed in various colours of jade green, sapphire, pale gold, aqua marine, light blue, red, they were modelling the latest and most elegant cheongsam.

The slit up each side of the dress showed to the world perfectly formed long slender legs. Then on came Linda, she was also dressed in a black cheongsam with Chinese motifs in gold, red and green, high Mandarin collars on all dresses. She stood out from all models due to height and English beauty; her thighs were on view as she stepped provocatively along the catwalk. Her breasts unfettered, jiggled and bounced as she strode amongst the dainty Chinese models. The assembled audience were spellbound not a sound; all were just captivated by this succession of beautiful works of art. As the procession reached the culmination of the parade, the audience erupted in a spectacular appreciation of what they had just seen; the cameramen and their crews capturing every moment of this show.

Next was the day wear which had a lot of trouser suits which also were in various colours; of particular interest were the flared bottoms of the white trousers with beautiful arrays of batik blouses. The after five apparel and cocktail dresses were shown in all the colours of the rainbow, very sexy and appealing to most men. Linda was wearing a black cocktail dress which was split into four parts on the skirt and was slightly weighted on the hemline. It wasn't apparent when she walked, just the odd time when she turned around, her legs came into view. The South American combo had taken up their positions and was joyously beating out one of their exciting rhythmic Latin American dance tunes. All were dressed in huge sombreros red neckerchiefs and puffy white shirts tied in the waist and completed with red cummerbunds, black flared gouache trousers complete with silver buttons down each leg. Cuban heeled boots completed the outfit. The Chinese models were captivated with this intoxicating rhythm and beat and were actually dancing along the catwalk. Also Linda, who had been in the Caribbean with Chris on his last commission as the Aide De Comp and chopper pilot to the governor, had learned many of the Latin American dances on her frequent visits to Havana, Mexico and Cuba. The band played on whilst the band leader called out to Linda, "Meez Linda which dance you prefer?"

Linda replied in a nice clear voice, "The tango!"

The band leader's face cracked into a huge smile as he announced to his band, "The tango for Meez Linda!"

She looked around I must have a partner for this she thought, her eyes fell on Paul Cavendish who was sitting very close by. She beckoned to him and said, "Paul come up here and dance with me!" Paul rose and joined her on stage; a very tall athletic handsome young naval officer, irresistible to most women and what was more, he could dance! They both stood together as the crowd took in this gorgeous looking couple as the band struck up with the most sensuous Latin American dance known to man.

They went all out together on this dance, the movements were erotic to the eye; as one marine was fond of saying, "Dancing is the vertical expression of the horizontal position." To all and sundry and the cameramen with their TV cameras whirring and recording every movement; they had to agree, as Linda twirled and embraced her partner in the various expressions of the tango, her skirt rose in the four positions showing all her legs up to the upper thighs, she looked and felt 'magnifico'. Again, her breasts were brilliantly loose and captured all men's attention as they wobbled to the rhythm of the tango. Not only has the body to give off dramatic effects but also the facial expressions are vital with this erotic South American dance. Certainly, both Linda and Paul were well suited to this erotism.

Although it had not been scheduled; all guests were enthralled with the show and spectacle they were witnessing and as the dance came to a tumultuous end with a passionate kiss, the place erupted with pent up emotion and passion as they clapped and whistled as the pair, arm in arm walked down the catwalk with a certain panache at their whirlwind dance.

After a brief interval, it was the array of evening dresses to be displayed. All, in beautiful colours, long sexy, and slinky, off the shoulder and on. The Chinese models wore mostly Asian designs which always suited the Oriental girls, they swayed down the catwalk smiling at the guests, buyers, newsmen and reporters; truly this was a most magical night of nights.

Finally, Linda came on in a golden evening dress, low cut which showed her milky white breasts off to great advantage; her hair had been swept back into a French pleat, held in place with a diamond studded comb. Around her neck she wore a ruby and diamond necklace set in gold and on the back pierced in a platinum setting. Her earrings also were in rubies surrounded by tiny diamonds. Her fingers had her engagement ring and her wedding ring which sparkled in the bright lights of the show. Tom and Jack stood slightly to her rear each in black trousers wearing Cuban high heeled black elastic gusset boots. Their shirts were white and the design dating back to the 18th century open to the sternum with fluffy sleeves and wearing black diamond studded cuff links. They each carried their evening jackets over their shoulder in an attitude of nonchalance and defiance. So as to be eye-catching, one was powder blue and the other jacket was white magnolia. Eyes were slightly made up just a little darker so that it emphasized their individual eye colouring. Linda coolly strode down the catwalk with Tom and Jack three paces behind, as they reached the end Tom and Jack fastened their press studs on their shirts digging out a neat clip on bow tie in black and with a flourish put their evening jackets on. They were good looking, lean and mean and glared at the assembled audience with a bold aggressive look. The women stood up and clapped and screamed as the trio made their way to the models' exit, suddenly the air was filled with flowers thrown by all the females in the audience; Jack and Tom stooped down and picked a red rose up and both stuck it into the buttonhole in their lapels. Tom stooped again picking up an orchid which he presented to Linda who was grinning from ear to ear as the thunderous ovation continued. Jenny appeared with her Asian models who had taken part in the show. All lined up on the catwalk and together they made a bow to all the assembled audience. Jenny especially turned to Linda and knelt on her knees and lightly kissed her hand in tribute for her absolutely excellent contribution to the fledgling fashion industry in Singapore.

The entire group of models and their designers assembled on the catwalk to tumultuous applause from those who had travelled many hundreds and sometimes thousands of miles to attend this glorious evening of fashion.

Afterwards in the great hall, which was superbly decorated with the most excellent array of tropical plants; in the four corners stood four bars each to the taste of the various nationalities attending, however the best attended was the scotch whiskey bar. Linda had changed into her tulip style dress, in the white linen jacket she had fastened her bejewelled Royal Marine brooch which absolutely glittered in the special lighting system in this hotel of the orient. The 'Boys' too had changed back into their OGs. Waiters floated around despatching their trays of wine and ice water. In the middle of the floor stood the Admiral, his Aide de Comp, Paul Cavendish, Linda with Tom and Jack on each side of her, chatting pleasantly with one another and the Chinese millionaires who were interested in the presence of Commander in Chief, Mark Donovan. The Admiral had wasted no time in talking with both the incoming Malay Prime Minister, Tunku Abdul Rahman and his counterpart the soon to be prime minister of Singapore Lee Kuan Yew, it was an agreeable moment to get together informally, which the Admiral readily took advantage of.

Linda was, of course, the centre of attraction, her charm, her poise and the fact that she was a very beautiful woman. Her eyes strayed over the shoulder of the Admiral at a bit of a commotion in the guests, who were parting to allow a tall lean figure of a Royal Marine who was obviously intending to talk to the Admiral. The marine was dressed in KD, white belt, puttees, highly polished SV boots, white lanyard (42 Cdo RM) swagger cane under his left armpit, Green Beret with stay bright cap badge; in his left hand he had a brown envelope.

In a fairly audible voice he said, "Excuse me, sir!" he continued as the Admiral turned to face him, "I am Marine Pearson, Guard orderly at 42 Commando; I have AN IMPORTANT message for you!" With that he took the envelope out of his left hand and gave to the Admiral.

Whilst the Admiral was reading the message, Tom and Jack closed in on Pearson, "Pete! How're you getting along? Haven't seen you in yonks."

"Good to see you both. What're you both doing here?"

Grinning, they both answered quietly, "Well, it's a long story, but we're doing a bit of modelling, but don't tell the boys or we're fucked!"

Pete just cheesed down, "It's a deal, trust me!"

"That's wot we wus afraid of," said Jack.

The Admiral had read the message, turning to Linda he said, "It's not all bad news, mainly it's for you! To inform you from the doctors at BMH that in all probability your husband Lt Davenport, may be coming out of his coma and that you should waste no time in getting over there to be at his bedside for when he eventually surfaces; maybe tonight or early tomorrow morning." She stared at the message and tears began to fill her eyes as she fought to regain her composure. The message, she passed to Tom who on reading it was galvanized into action.

"Right Jack, we take Linda and I'M DRIVING, we need to get there quickly and in one piece, let's go Linda!"

"I'll LEAD THE WAY, I KNOW A GOOD ROUTE," Pete said. With that, they all saluted and left the building.

In convoy they sped through the various lanes and roads, most drivers getting out of the way as Tom kept flashing and honking as they sped through streets that should have been deserted at that time of night. Nearing the entrance, Pete pulled over to let them through, flashing his lights twice to wish them well.

They were met at the entrance by Nurse Amelia who quickly talked to Linda in giving her the absolute news and truth of Chris's condition. Speedily, they sped to his bedside, where Linda took his hand and began talking to him in soothing tones.

Two doctors, one from the army and the other was from the navy, who were examining, came in on their routine patients' visit, looking at the array of dials which each had a specific piece of information about Lt Davenport's improving condition; they smiled at Linda and introduced who they were and just exactly what and when her husband might likely come out of his coma. This information calmed Linda as she was truly upset to see her once fit and strong husband in his present condition. Tom and Jack stayed in the background of the hospital room like ancient sentinels guarding and waiting for the first signs of recovery by Lt Davenport, who they had miraculously rescued from a certain death in that hideous environment in the depths of the Borneo jungle and its many swamps. Nurse Amelia, the QARNNS nurse, was always at the patient's bedside; although, when she saw Jack, she really just wanted to escape the rigid codes she was ruled by and wanted to talk freely with Jack whom she had taken a fancy to. She whispered in his ear, "Follow me, we must talk and have a cup of tea in the common room."

***

Aboard the BOAC Comet MK4, sporting the latest engine configuration of 4 Rolls Royce Avon MK524 Turbojets, it would cruise at 520MPH at 42,000ft operating range would be 3,225 miles. The comet had been diverted to Singapore from Japan. It was late taking off from Payer Leba Airport with the entire media newspaper and cameramen who had covered the inaugural fashion parade and they had some very good stories and films they would release to the fashion press and glossy women's magazines. Steven Geddings, freelance journalist, was busily typing out his report, in business class, on his portable Olivetti typewriter. Not only was he reporting about the fashion show but also he had researched into the real story of why Linda was out here and her husband's rescue by a specialist group of Royal Marines; Linda's mercy dash to support her injured husband Lt Chris Davenport. It was making for a very enthralling story. Steven would project her into a very different world to what she had known, although at the time he wasn't aware of this rocket to fame and fortune. He had masses of photos and film taken by his best friend and companion Luke Steinberg.

It was a comparatively quiet and relaxing flight stopping in the Middle East at Abu Dhabi and also at Malta for refuelling before landing in London. Steven Geddings read his report and was well pleased, let's hope his editors would agree. He yawned and grinning went to sleep.

***

With doctors at his side and Linda holding his hand gently, he gradually came out of his long coma as if through a mist, the pain in his lower left leg was very great and his face twisted a little in agony, but above all this he was immensely overjoyed to see the face of his beautiful wife smiling down on him as he grappled to retain consciousness, she was indeed very dear to him and he had longed for months to see her; his eyes filled with tears and so did Linda's. He was alive and that is all that mattered to them both.

The doctors were checking him out as the QARNNS Nurse Amelia entered the private room; she had looked after him all this time and was immensely relieved and overjoyed to see him return, and although she knew he would never be the same as before; yet there was a flicker and a spark that was starting to glow. She administered his life giving drugs through the established canulars and the plastic tubing. This would give him some relief from the pain in his amputated leg. Tom was also present and saw all this with some increasing admiration for this handsome young chopper pilot who had won the heart of his long lost teenage love, Linda. However he prided himself that he had carried out her heart rendering appeal; for Tom to find him for her, and this he had done; not alone but with certain handpicked Marines he knew he could rely on; the full nine yards. (27 ft of live ammo!)

Tom and Jack left and made their way to the Land Rover which was FFR fitted and so made their reports to the operations group in both 42 Commando RM and also to the rear echelon of 40 Commando RM, who would transmit the good news of Lt Chris Davenport's recovery in BMH Singapore. They also contacted the Admiral (C-in-C Far Eastern Command RN) with the good news; the Admiral was delighted and asked that his best wishes be passed on to Linda.

Tom and Jack stayed by the Land Rover knowing full well that the military machine would crank up; as the news circulated throughout the upper levels of command. Tom took out one of his long slim panatelas and lit up with a certain amount of nostalgia looking back over the months and also with a certain amount of pride not only in his own endeavours but also those of his closest companions and oppos.

Jack was also in a reflective mood and paced the gravel crunching it as he strode aimlessly; his only consolation was in the hard graft of getting Chris Davenport back in relative safety. He eyed his friend Tom and both knew what was on each other's mind. He occasionally glanced at the night sky which was graced with all the stars of the universe and in some way this helped him to see the greater role of man for the future.

The radio in the Land Rover crackled into life, Tom donned the headphones and took hold of the mike, "Hello this is 42 Bravo 4, how do you read me over?"

"This is Sierra, Romeo and Tango receiving you loud and clear!"

"These are your orders. You are to report for duty at 0800 hrs at 42 Commando Guardroom. Where you will receive further orders."

"Sierra, Romeo, Tango. Message received and understood. Out to you 42 bravo 4."

"We'd better say good bye to Dave and Lt Waters, Linda, maybe Chris if he's conscious." Tom eyed Jack and whispered and winked. "Not to mention Nurse Amelia, hey Jack?" Both were grinning and entered the BMH Hospital building with a brighter mood.

First call was on Lt Waters, but at this late hour he was peacefully asleep, so they just left a note on their personal logbook, saying they were reporting back for duty and wished him a safe and speedy recovery. They both signed it and quietly left the room. Next was to call on Dave Younger, they were not surprised to see his wife Jean still keeping watch on him, she had been dozing in a rather well upholstered armchair and woke as soon as they entered the room. She smiled at both Tom and Jack, rising and embracing them in a form of love and gratitude for Dave's safe return, although she always understood the risks that all marines take on active duty. She looked after Dave and was always at his side a very loving and caring, almost matronly type of girl. They whispered their goodbyes and looked at Dave's progress to see if he was healing nicely, he was always a very handsome lad and came from the same hometown as Jack. 'Norfhamptun' as Jack would say.

Next, of course, was to Linda and her husband, Chris, she was just dozing but came out of her sleepy state the minute they entered the room. "We have to go, Linda. We're ordered back first thing in the morning so we will have to say goodbye for now." She embraced them, both her full lips brushing their cheeks and then their mouths in a sensuous manner. Tom felt aroused just by her doing that. Reluctantly, they parted and on reaching the corridor that led them to the foyer they by chance bumped into Nurse Amelia coming out of the nurses' quarters, Jack was quite delighted to see her and so was she. He took the chance and drew her aside whilst Tom walked on hoping to leave them alone for once. Jack scribbled his regimental no and his military address on his logbook and gave it to

Amelia; she embraced him and gave him a lingering kiss, looking up at him with tears in her eyes. Jack said, “Listen, wots your uvver name?”

She just simply said, “It’s Brooklyn.”

“Well, from now on I’ll call you Lyn so’s you know whose contacting you; okay?” she nodded in a silent sorrowful manner. He took one last look at her and his usual gruff voice said, “I’ll see ya later; my promise!” But orders are to be obeyed and reluctantly they both withdrew to the Land Rover and the journey to The Straits View Hotel to pack and maybe snatch a few hours’ sleep before checking out early morning.

***

At 0530 hrs, the shrill ringing of the telephone in the bedroom of the Straits View Hotel startled Tom and Jack awake. They heard the Asian voice on the line, informing them of their breakfast through their early morning call, “We hope you had velly good sleep, Tuan. Now, time for wakey wakey. Good breakfast for two in dining loom, you like velly much. We see you in thirty minutes, yes?” Tom noisily replaced the phone.

“Shit, shower, shave and shampoo; let’s go!” Tom growled.

It was indeed a great breakfast, English, of course, or it could have been Irish or it might have been Australian. Tom and Jack got stuck into it enjoying it as if it were their last meal. Tom finished and strolled out onto the veranda to take in the sight of the Straits and of course to enjoy his favourite smoke of a slim panatela. Jack joined him breathing in the fresh salty air.

Dressed in tailored, pressed, olive greens, SV boots, puttees and wearing their treasured Green Berets, the tall, broad-shouldered marines paid up and left the Straits View Hotel making sure they had a receipt chit for the paymaster who would no doubt ‘have to pay them’, Tom and Jack grinned at this mental picture.

The Land Rover sped effortlessly through the relative quiet town of Johore Bahru stopping at the Customs barrier were they had to produce the necessary papers to exit Malaysia. “Salamat pagi,” Tom roared out above the constant stream of traffic and honking horns on every vehicle.

“Samma, samma,” the young officer replied and with a huge grin waved them through, it is not a long journey from Johore to the Royal Naval air station at Sembawang, especially if you go through the HMS Dockyard, passed Aggie Weston’s which the naval families use and for a refreshing swim in the large pool, followed by a cooling Tiger Beer. Stopping at the guard room, then through the main gates and onto the Sembawang road to the entrance of Far East Asia Amphibious Land Forces (FARELF).

Tom gunned the Land Rover a little faster causing a bit of a dust cloud behind them, Tom and Jack just grinning at the possible commotion to the guard commander who would be wondering what was happening at this time in the morning. They screeched to a halt at the Barrier Pole in a cloud of dust and the smell of burnt tyres, "Hey Lance Cpl, we're reporting as ordered, what's the drill."

"I don't believe it, It's Tom Martial and Jack French, how're you doing, not seen you for yonks." They of course recognised the Provost lance CPL, "Johnny Colclough! Well you're a sight for sore eyes, how long you been in 42?"

"Been out about a month or so. Did ya bring Mouse out with you?"

"Clare! Naw, she'll be out in another month; had to straighten all our packing and personal stuff out first then I have to get a suitable house to rent, but we'll get it sorted."

***

The BOAC Comet MK4 arriving from Singapore landed perfectly on the tarmac in London very early morning and taxied onto the debarkation ramparts. Smiling air hostesses at the exits made for a speedy controlled exit by all the weary but excited news media men and women who were eager to reach their editors in the offices dotted in and around London. Steven Geddings with his faithful companion and cameraman, Luke Steinberg, were one of the first off the plane and made for the usual customs excise and immigration control officers, eager to show their passes and were cleared in record time. They grabbed the first taxi on the rank giving out the Fleet Street address to the driver. They both knew that what they had would be on the TV and newspapers very soon, of which they were quite excited about.

Two hours later, after absolutely taking out all the stops and may I say with frantic efforts on all personnel in the offices of the major TV Stations, both in UK, US, CANADA, Australia and New Zealand the early morning news broadcasters had their story of the recent inaugural fashion parade in Singapore; together with the new British discovery of Linda Davenport in a new role as the outstanding novice fashion model and as an 'analogue' or to put it simply as a follow up to her mercy dash to her husband's side after Lt Chris Davenport's miraculous rescue by an elite team of Royal Marine Commandoes from 40 Cdo RM operating in the depths of the Borneo jungle. It made a very welcome change amidst all the stories of turmoil in the world and not to forget the political disasters both at home and abroad. It raised the public's morale to see one of their very own English beauties with her raven black hair, green eyes, and a body of sensuous delight, dancing with a young naval officer whose appearance was very much like the description of the commander in Ian Fleming's book of James Bond, tall athletic and extremely handsome figure of a man. The two marines also in the background tall with rugged good looks complimented the whole show, not to mention the exquisite dresses of the cute and dainty Asian and Chinese girls almost like dolls but enchanting. The newspaper had hit the pavements and stalls on the front page was Linda strikingly beautiful in the arms of Lt Paul Cavendish in tropical whites dancing the sensuous Latin tangos her beauty with those ivory white legs wrapped around the Lieutenant was electric. She appealed to men of all ages and although married she was not owned by anyone but was a true free spirit.

***

"And now the good news!" As the newsreader on the BBC solemnly announced, however, halfway through the news reel/flash he was grinning quite broadly as he saw the most beautiful girl he had seen since Bridget Bardot the sex kitten and her pouting lips. Linda Davenport dancing in the exotic island of Singapore; with all the trappings and aroma of the Far East.

Admiral Sir Henry Cunningham's wife, Mabel, was in the conservatory at the rear of the fine old English manor house. Her au-per maid Kristina from Norway was just setting out her ladyship's breakfast as Mabel began sipping her Indian tea. The Elizabethan manor house was indeed a beautiful edifice of black and white wattle and daub, with the main supporting stonework in solid sandstone. There was a fairly long drive up to the massive oak doors which were iron studded; a small grill was affixed to one of the doors for observation from within. After entering the great hall, which was also in black and white tiles, straight ahead was a magnificent broad staircase sweeping up to a companionway which led to the bedrooms and study areas. On either side, at the foot of this magnificent staircase were two mannequins dressed in the

Royal Marines blues no 2 and pith helmets of the RM Corps of drums, complete of course with dress cords Royal Assembly, the old style rope tightened, wooden side drums emblazoned with the royal cypher.

Kristina had brought in the usual amount of newspapers which Lady Cunningham regularly perused whilst she had her continental style breakfast. She opened the first page of the *Daily Mail* and their again was her daughter Linda splashed in large print and dancing with one of her husband's royal naval lieutenants. She let out a cry of anguish and Kristina knew why as she had already seen the newspapers and the TV commentary with the exceptional story and coverage of 'Scene Singapora'. Just then the old style 1890s' telephone rang, which also tended to unnerve her. It was her husband Sir Henry and she sobbed as she spoke of her daughter again being in the news half naked as she was apt to say, "Now calm down my dear, I'm sure it will all turn out for the better. We've just got to weather the storm, pull yourself together; I will try and see you at the weekend. Chin up old girl. Bye for now!"

***

It was late afternoon as the RAF Hastings took off from Changi Airport with Tom and Jack bound for Kuching Sarawak in Borneo. The intelligence section of 42 Commando RM had briefed them on what to expect after their arrival back to 40 Commando's HQ. The Hastings was a very versatile aircraft and was used primarily for delivering much-needed stores and equipment; however, it could and did carry quite a lot of RAF or army personnel. The aircraft was very suitable for airfields with very short runways; hence it was used to good effect in Jungle clad areas. As with all military aircraft, it was very noisy and soon Tom and Jack dropped off to sleep and must have dozed off for the entire trip. On approach to Kuching, they were rudely awakened by one of the RAF air despatch handlers. Jack stood up and gave him a mouthful but due to the noise the Air dispatcher had his headphones on and did not get the full drift of Jack's outburst; however, he backed off when Jack grabbed his tunic and gave him a fierce stare; as he let go, Jack pushed him backwards, he stumbled and luckily Tom caught him before he hit the decking, "Now then flyboy, try and keep your balance and don't try to manhandle any of us marines or you'll be in deep shit, SAVVY?"

White faced, he got out of the way in double quick time. Tom and Jack grinned at each other, picked up their backpacks and made for the exit as the plane had made a first class landing at Kuching.

Looking around it was very late afternoon but on the concrete helipad stood an Army Westland Scout AH.1 helicopter, which rightly they assumed was for them. The pilot acknowledging them with a wave of his arms in the gesture of 'close up on my position'.

"We should just about make Brigade HQ before nightfall; sit in the rear I prefer the load evenly matched," The Army Air Corps pilot smiled at the two burly marines. "ROGER THAT!" Jack and Tom spoke as one, both grinning at the 'Pongo Pilot', however they had seen these army pilots in action and were suitably impressed with their flying abilities.

In a few years to come, the scout would be replaced with the Westland Wasp mainly for the Royal Navy. The scout was fitted with skis or skids, this one also had small fat wheels on either side for any suitable landing zone or pad. The turbines were winding up to fever pitch as the pilot rolled her forward head down and finally to lift off, skimming over the green mass of the Sarawak jungles and the brown attap houses.

Offshore, HMS Bulwark was slowly cruising and awaiting any orders that she may receive. Just going through the normal ship's routine with the helicopters and marine personnel practising ship to shore drills.

HMS Bulwark

Royal Marines forming up in their 'Sticks' preparing to board the Westland Whirlwinds; somewhere in the South China Sea. The whirlwinds were reliable but could only take about five fully equipped marines they would be replaced by the Westland Wessex helicopters although they kept some whirlwinds for lighter loads. Note the MT section vehicles on the rear end (Aft) of the LPH. HMS Bulwark R08. Formerly, she was an aircraft carrier but was converted to the amphibious role in about 1958-59. Her sister ship was HMS Albion.

Just before last light, the scout landed at Brigade HQ, where they reported to the duty officer.

RSM Chisel was also in attendance, rising from his desk in a most belligerent and threatening manner, "Well, well, well! So you've decided to return to the pointed end have you?"

"Well, it's like this, sir!"

"Shut up! Did I give you permission to speak, eh?"

"No, sir."

"Well then, in a few minutes you will be seeing the CO. In the meantime, I'm going to give you a piece of my mind. How dare you behave in such a priggish manner in Singapore? I've had no end of reports of your behaviour, not to mention you two in a ladies' fashion parade. What are you, a couple of PUFFS? We do expect some sort of decorum from our Royal Marines and the honour of the Corps! Have you got that?"

"Yes sir! Absolutely sir!" both answered as one.

"Right get yourselves squared off, when I open that door to the CO's office, I will give the order to march in, you will halt facing the CO at least three paces before his desk, is that clear?"

"Yes, sir! As crystal."

Lt Colonel Robert Loden sat at his desk surrounded by detailed maps of every part of North Borneo. He eyed the two tall, well-built marines with some kind of great interest.

"All right RSM that will be all for now."

"Sir?"

"I'm going to speak to them privately RSM."

"Very good, sir."

"Okay stand at ease, draw those two chairs up, what I have to say is first of all, well done on the search and rescue mission of Lt Davenport and thank goodness no one was killed in our unit. Secondly, I congratulate you on your behaviour in Singapore and yes even the worldwide publicity it generated. The RSM and I have slightly different views on that side of things but I am assured by the lords of the Admiralty that they found it both interesting and amusing. Now then; we do have a problem with Marine McHenry."

"What kind of problem, sir?"

"You are aware he went to the assistance of the Sultan of Brunei at his majesties' request."

"Well, yes sir, we thought he'd got a square number there, sir."

"Well, he's been snatched and taken over the border into north eastern Kalimantan at this place called Gorantan. Come over here to this map as you can see there are two Buatans, the first one is the one we are interested in, according to our mole there McHenry is being held in a fairly solid looking police station just inside the Indonesian border. You thought that where you had been to rescue Lt Davenport was dense bush country? Well this is worse there are no real settlements here as far as we know it's really bad bush. Look at it all over here it's just dense thick jungle for hundreds of miles, that's why I've selected you two to get out there and rescue McHenry. He will in all probability have been interrogated to their extreme methods. Tomorrow at first light you must be ready to move out. We will transport you by helicopter as far as possible but you will have to slog it out until you get to this position overlooking the police station north of Gorantan. Travel at night."

"Excuse me sir, we cannot do that in the jungle, you cannot see your own hand in front of you; it's just absolute blackness."

"We have thought about that angle and have received a new gadget for you, it's experimental and is meant for the chopper pilots in Viet-Nam; however, we have procured them for this mission. They are 'night vision goggles'. After you leave this O group, you will go to see the QM and take whatever you will need for this mission. You will need to travel as light as possible but take some PE, cortex and detonators. If you can't use it maybe McHenry would be able to?"

"How many in our group sir?"

"There will be three others going with you, Jin Tin who went with you last time and of course you will need an SBA, Bungy Williams, also we are sending you with a signaller, name of McPherson, do you know him French?"

Jack said, "Well, if it's the same marine, he may be the one in my squad. He's a good quiet and reliable marine. After passing out as Kings Squad, he was specially selected for a signaller's course, so he could be the one I knew."

"Very good! So that will be all for now; however, I must say that I have received good reports from the C-in-C Far East command

Admiral Mark Donovan who was very impressed with your conduct and also from Lord Davenport who incidentally is the father of Lt Davenport, did you know that?"

"No sir! We weren't privy to that information."

"All I can say is good luck and god speed."

After leaving the CO's office, they called into the QM's store to get kitted out with latest weapons of their choice including browning sidearm's with thigh holsters, grenades which had to be primed with the usual detonators making sure the pins were well and truly splayed and secured. Jack chose a Bren LMG which had recently been modified to accept the 7.62 rounds same as the SLR. Tom chose the latter so that ammo would not pose a problem out in the field. The QM, Fred Hayhurst advised them on certain nutritional and medical packs for their benefit in a hostile environment, to which they certainly would rely on heavily in extreme conditions. The ration packs were the Asian variety, with rice and curry powder also had powdered coffee, these were in resealable plastic bags. The latest insect repellents and cam cream which would make life a little easier to bear. Camouflaged face veils and bush hats.

"Don't forget your safety razor blades and morphine capsules." The QM had tried to think of everything and with a flourish produced very small tins of Tiger Balm which contained many soothing qualities against the ever present mosquitoes and sand fly's. Also he had acquired a resealable plastic pouch of tobacco the cigarette papers plus matches. The SLR had been fitted with a scope and a silencer by the Unit Armourer, which looked like a good piece of kit; this would enable either one of them to take out any nosy sentry silently. Jack also acquired from the Ammo Storeman a box of 7.62 Tracers. This time they selected the Bergen rucksack which held more and was really very comfortable with its steel frame and padding. They packed a WW2 44 pattern backpack for Jin Tin and incorporated in it everything they thought he would need on this particularly difficult mission. The QM produced the latest binoculars from the Swiss, very small, very light and with tremendous magnification. Also a very small 35mm camera that fit in the palm of your hand.

Amidst all this concentration and quietness came loud noises ascending the outside verandah and heavy footsteps complete with a familiar Yorkie accent, you've guessed it; none other than Bungy Williams the SBA, accompanying him; although more refined and polite was the Signaller McPherson. Jack immediately recognised him as one of his squad mates and held out his hand in greeting, "Haven't seen you since squad training. How's it going, Mac?"

"Not bad, Jack, but I preferred the comforts of Pompey rather than out in this hellhole." McPherson was a quietly spoken, well-educated Scot from I think he said Perth.

"Right you two over here and start selecting your equipment for this rescue operation, you Williams! Keep the noise down."

"All right Q. Keep your hair on, only just got here," and with a wink and a grin at Tom and Jack, padded over to the section which was earmarked for the use of the SBA. He took particular note of what he had been supplied with, nodding and making notes as he packed it into his backpack, which was slightly larger than the 44 pattern backpack; on the side of it was fitted a sheath for his native parang which he found advantageous in thick jungle bush, just had to reach behind him to access the finely balanced Iban blade. He had purchased the backpack as well as four string hammocks very light and super strong from Arab Street when he was in Singapore at only a few dollars and was quite proud of his find and purchase. "Here, Q! Can I have this shiny black Browning?"

"As long as you sign for it my lad; and we want you to return it to the store!"

"Roger that, Q!" he said, grinning and carefully running his hand over it lovingly, to him it was an attractive prize.

"Don't forget the Ammunition Williams, it's over there, just take what you think you'll need, remember the weight." Bungy tossed a string hammock to each member of the team grinning as he did so.

The QM; had been in Korea and had served with 41 (ind) Commando RM; his branch was in heavy weapons; however, what he didn't know about modern firearms wasn't worth knowing. He had also come into contact with the US Marines and had firsthand knowledge of which weapons to take on an expedition like this one. He advised McPherson to select one of his latest acquisitions from the US Marine Corps who were now serving and using this sub machine gun in Viet-Nam the Colt Commando known as the XM177E2 5.56mm, which was good choice, very light and good for close quarter battle in the ULU. Remembering that, he had a very bulky and heavy Radio transmitter. Which if they got into serious trouble he would have the ability to contact the nearest artillery battery or the fleet air arm for support and fighter cover? Food, water and ammo top priority. All of them carefully weighed up what was to be carried and chose as wisely as possible which items they would need most and most importantly be able to carry it in dense Jungle Bush.

After a shower and a good night's sleep, they were whisked away in a Wessex Whirlwind helicopter at first light bound for Brunei where they would refuel for the next leg into unknown territory and a lot of hard graft, but they knew it was for McHenry and that spurred them on. There were now five of them, Jin Tin had also made an appearance and was warmly greeted by Tom, Jack and Bungy; Tom handing over the 44 Pattern backpack to Jin Tin; however, McPherson who had not met him before just shook his hand and said, "Hello." The open doorway was indeed most gratifying not only in a visual sense but for the relative coolness of the air passing through it. The acknowledgements of the Stick leader to the pilot had been through the usual headphones to make sure all was secured and ready for this fairly long journey to Brunei.

The headphones crackled into life after about an hour into the journey, "Pilot to Stick Leader, we're being diverted from Brunei to HMS Eagle, she has just arrived from her station in the South China Seas and we shall be able to land on her for our refuelling, which needless to say is more convenient as well as more secure. Please pass this info on to your group; over!"

Tom answered, "Stick Leader; all understood. Out!" Tom wrote the message down from his message pad in his map pocket and handed it around to the rest of the group. The noise in the helicopter cabin prohibited any vocal messages. They were now circling the majestic Aircraft Carrier HMS Eagle and what a sight she was; very impressive in her proportions and her bow just cutting effortlessly through the green and white foaming sea. Then they were swooping down on her from the rear and feeling the roller coaster style of ride as she slackened and gained speed and height adjustments to finally landing with a kind of sigh as the pilot cut down her engines, the naval deck hands rushed in and immediately took charge of both the helicopter and the marines aboard her, hooked her up to the refuelling point for the avgas she desperately needed.

The marines gathered up their stuff and were led across the steel deck and down the central lift well to descend to the main hangar and the various companionways to the Royal Marines detachment quarters and mess deck. Although the ships naval and fleet air arm officers and sailors were expecting the marines from 40 Commando RM they really were quite taken aback by their appearance and especially by the Iban tracker Jin Tin who was in his customary native rig. The Chief Petty Officer checking their weapons as each marine proved his weapon, “Right lads welcome aboard, follow this leading seaman here to the marine detachments mess deck and well, you should just be in time for a tot and a bite of lunch; however, get a No 8 shirt for your wild friend here, you simply can’t go in the dining mess deck without a shirt eh?”

Jack standing quite tall, grinning rasped out, “Oh absolutely, Chief! Wouldn’t dream of it; we’ll get him fixed up.”

It was a tight squeeze to get through the twisting companionways and hatches, sweating profusely due to the humidity and the strain, they were greeted by the all the lads in the RM ships detachment amid cheers and a glass tumbler of grog was handed to each man including Jin Tin who was beaming all over his little brown oval face. Bungy raised his glass and made the customary ‘Cheers opps, first today! Down the hatch’, but he didn’t; instead, he cradled it like a baby and just sipped it to enjoy it in the best naval tradition. A few of the marines knew Tom and Jack from earlier years and much banter and lamp swinging, back slapping went on. Jock King was one who knew them both well; he was a talented boxer and often gave exhibition bouts at the various sports events in the corps. After a brief spell with the lads, it was time to make for the galley. But first it was important to lock away their weapons which was duly carried out and locked securely; no disrespects but it was not a time for accidental discharges at this stage. On entering the main galley everyone stood up and cheered the group who they totally respected having heard from their officers as to what kind of marines they were and what a successful search and rescue operation they had done previously in rescuing Lt Chris Davenport; however, they knew nothing of their latest operation into enemy territory. The Chief Petty Officer Chef beckoned them in a loud voice, “Those marines there, come to the front of the queue!”

Tom and Jack looked at one another and winked. “Blimey,” Jack said quietly. “Must be having a good day!”

After the ‘Tot’ everything the galley staff had prepared tasted great as it gave the ships company an appetite. So the team dug into it with some gusto as it would be the last civilised meal they would get for some time, even Jin Tin looked happy hoving into the large steaks.

The two marines working in the ‘grease pit’ came out after the group had finished their meal and collected their metal trays, wishing them good hunting and, “Gawd bless ya.”

As they stood up to leave, the entire sailors and marines in the galley stood up and led by the marine detachment began to sing *Sarie Marie*, “We’re a bunch of bastards, bastards are we, born in a whorehouse, shit on pissed on, fucked all over the universe, and we’d rather fuck than fight for liberty!” Everyone burst into laughter and clapped as the group made its way out; back to the RM Detachments Mess Deck to collect their weapons and head for the main hangar to await their call upward and onward.

They lined out on the flight deck at 45° to the nose of the helicopter and waited for the thumbs up from the chopper pilot. Heavily laden, they spaced out to give enough time for the marine in front to load his gear. Tom was last in to take the seat nearest the pilot and so he would be the link between pilot and passengers. “Stick Leader to pilot; all secure and ready for take-off; over!”

“Roger Stick Leader; message understood; OUT!” They rose at an angle nose first, gaining height and speed as she sped for an unknown landing in dense jungle, maybe they couldn’t land as the jungle in this area in the 1960s was dense and formidable. It might be a case of roping down; however, they had to take in the fact that their equipment could be a problem. The marines had often practised these roping down techniques but today was a different story as they had heavy equipment which of course would have either tethered to their legs or let down first to the ground. However, the marines relied on the pilot’s judgement in these cases, he would find a suitable LZ if at all possible; he was after all a marine pilot and of course would fully comprehend the situation.

The whirlwind headed straight out to sea instead of overland, she headed due north; all of the time on a circuitous route to avoid and confuse enemy detection of their eventual destination. His co-pilot and navigator reached a given point on their estimated map and compass bearings; then she banked and turned due south to eventually reach the coast to fly along the Malaysian/Kalimantan border. The chopper pilot flew in a zig-zag pattern to confuse any notion of his destination, finally flying as low as he could afford over the swirling jungle canopy below. The co-pilot/navigator had found a suitable LZ by the side of a wide river that in all possibility should lead the rescue party to Buatan. He came in low just missing by inches the large rain forest trees which stood about 80-100ft. From above the opening in the trees looked like a black sink hole but the navigator had noticed a rippling shine on the water as the sunlight just penetrated the leafy foliage. The chopper eased its way under huge rain forest trees gliding in a very spacious area which some eons ago had been an idyllic location for the Iban or Dyak tribes. Finally with a surge of arresting power, he landed in a clearing with giant swathes of air engulfing the surrounding lush vegetation. "Pilot to stick leader, get your men off the chopper as quickly as you can, good hunting and good luck!"

"Stick Leader to pilot; message understood, register this position we may need to be picked up at this location. Code word: ***BULLDOG!*** Watch my signal on debussing!"

Jin Tin was the first out and made sure that the LZ was safe underfoot, he nodded to Tom and Jack and promptly took cover in the lush ULU. The marines adopted the drill they had been taught being careful of anything and everything that might be harmful peripheral vision highly important, all equipment unloaded and safe. Tom knelt at 45° to the nose of the aircraft and gave the thumbs up to the chopper pilot. The helicopter lifted vertically and then turned 180° heading off in the direction which he had arrived; the downdraught was quite tremendous has she headed out through the narrow gap which she had entered by.

The vacuum left by the chopper was an unnerving silence, until the jungle sounds took over. The tree monkey's whooping the sounds reverberating again and again as each group informed the other of possible danger, like an alarm system. Butterflies were dancing through the shafts of sunlight, the tree frogs were croaking and the sequoias' constant vibrating wings, added to the cacophony of sound all around them. The team observed them, taking in every detail, finally Bungy Williams let out a big fart which all got some amusement from. "Gawd Almighty, wot we got 'ere, eh?" Bungy was eyeing the immense trees and the foliage which closed in on all sides in various shades of dull green, but there was some weird feeling about this clearing. "You bloody roughie-toughies, don't half pick some weird places; looks like the land of the never, never! Bloody hell!" Tom put his index finger to his mouth in a gesture for silence from Bungy. Tom and Jack and the rest surveyed the LZ. The giant buttressed rain forest trees standing majestically like the inside of a cathedral their foliage spreading like a canopy over the area. The river flowed silently to their left, the ground seemed firm but lacked serious vegetation which seemed strange but yet served a useful purpose of habitation and yet there was none. The entire group stared around quite fascinated and transfixed by this strange and weird place, but yet it would be indelibly, irreversibly burned in their memory. It was a most compelling place. Jin Tin came out from the dark fern lined foliage and was very upset; his eyes stood out like organ stops as he surveyed the area. His attention was riveted on a petrified tree which stood in the centre of the clearing; nothing grew for about 5 metres around its base. The tree itself had two branches reaching up about 25ft with what looked like fingers spread out from its branch. The base was blackened as though it had been in a fire but had survived; a hole was in the hump between the outstretched arms like a death stroke.

Jin Tin Just said, "Bomah! This place, very bad; evil."

Finally, Tom Broke the silence with a simple sentence, "We must make camp before darkness sets in," pointing his arm to the right where he rightfully assumed the high ground would be. Jack nodded in agreement, striding over to the tree to get a better look he touched the tree which seemed like very hard wood or stone even.

Jin Tin spun around and said to Jack, "NO touch!" Out of the hole appeared a black and yellow snake which struck Jack on his hand as quick as a flash Jack recoiled in pain and surprise. Jin Tin sprang in and with lightning speed severed its head; it lay on the ground wriggling in the throes of death. Jin Tin grabbed Jacks arm and cut a thin slit along the bitten area, bent down and sucked the blood and poison from the flesh wound, spitting it out as he went. Bungy also moved in to help with special anti-venom serum injections and bandages.

Jin Tin just said, "We should go! Tuan." All saddled up and Tom leading the way started hacking their way through the tangled foliage. Tom and Jack hoped the ulu would thin out at the top of this hill. By the time they got to the top of the hill, the sweat was pouring out of every pore. It was indeed much thinner at the top and the group lost no time in selecting their campsite, it was getting late in the afternoon and soon it would be pitch black. Lashing their parachute cords to suitable young trees and securing their ponchos over the ridge of cord and securely pegged out. Jack chose a young straight sapling for his ridge. Ground cleared, perimeter vine out, all round their bivvies. Brew was on the go and a sentry always on, fully equipped and ready. McPherson chose a very tall young sapling bending it down he attached his antennae to it, and let go, which soared into the uppermost canopy, this would give him greater access to the airwaves and messages he was about to send out.

Tom and Jack spread out the waterproof map, orientated it to the ground features and took compass bearings. They discussed at length how long it would take for them to traverse this section of the jungle and especially when they would enter the Kalimantan border which would be dangerous.

Jin Tin arrived and began helping them with information he had so far gleaned, "We reach here, there is plenty of bamboo, we make raft and we travel as fast as we can down river, better by river, maybe we can go by night too, what you think Tuan?" Jin Tin looked pleased with himself, as Tom, Jack and the team listened in and assimilated this latest information.

"Sounds good to me," growled Jack, Tom nodded still thinking about any other course of action.

Bungy thrust a mug of tea into Tom's hand, "Here; better have a cuppa char!"

Jin Tin had brought back a big fish from the river and he gutted and beheaded it and cut it into steaks giving each member a good-sized fresh piece of fish. It was out with their one and only mess tin and into the hot margarine which fried the fish rather well, adding the salt and pepper to taste as well as a little curry powder. That's the way to cook fish straight from the water and into the pan.

The watch roster was made out, weapons cleaned and oiled, in the night they would use their toggle ropes for wakeup call and communication. However they would also test out the night vision goggles which the QM had supplied.

Tom remembering what he said before: "One capful per night!" Tom visited each one of his group and carefully poured a capful of Pussers Rum for their consumption, it would be a tonic to warm their inner being. Bungy especially savouring the smell first of all, then imbibed it rather than just drinking it. With a blissful look in his eyes he said, "That's a good drop-O-Nelsons blood."

****

Outside BMH Singapore, the ambulances had arrived as the doctors, nurses and staff gathered outside as they waved good bye to their brave patients. Linda came out first with her husband Lt Chris Davenport who had recovered reasonably well but was still very weak. Linda had secured a flight back home to Plymouth, England, where she knew he would probably get better and be amongst family members which was very important at this stage.

Lt Waters was being transferred to the Cameroon highlands in the north of Malaya in an Officers' Rehabilitation Centre, which was thought to be a far healthier climate and much cooler with less humidity, ideal for the patient's recovery.

Marine Dave Younger was being released to the care of his wife Jean in Serangoon Gardens where she was quite capable of nursing him back to full health and fitness. She was perfect for this role the doctors had thought. However, the naval doctors would be able to visit him periodically to check his progress. The doctors thought that it would take at least six weeks before his wounds would heal and be fully consolidated.

Both ambulances had Land Rover escorts manned by Royal Marine Police and set off for Paya Leba Airport which was for Linda with Lt Davenport. Lt Waters for the domestic flight and Lt Davenport for the international flight to London. The other ambulance took Marine Young and his wife to Serangoon Gardens. The Admiral Mark Donovan had arrived at the airport to wish them both a safe journey. Linda during the course of the conversations with the Admiral; who they had got to know very well, handed him a note to contact her father in London to say they were on their way home and as a postscript please have my winter coat delivered to the London airport on arrival by courier; she was surprised to see so many reporters and photographers, questions and light bulbs were flashing as the party reached the foot of the airplane steps; a final wave from Linda to the delight of the photographers as she boarded the flight to London and eventually home to Plymouth with her wounded husband Chris. But she would not be expecting the reception or the clamour she would get when she arrived at London Airport!

***

Jack spent a somewhat unpleasant and painful night with the snake bite and his hand had swollen and was throbbing. Bungy had visited him using the new night vision goggles that he found were a useful bit of kit; however, he got spooked a few times with the nocturnal animals' eyes peering down at him from various directions and heights. Bungy used an ampoule of morphine to combat the pain in Jack's hand and arm. Bungy had to admit Jack was one real 'Roughie-Toughie Marine'.

The night wore on and soon it was time to 'Stand To' at first light; each marine covering his arc of fire. The night sounds giving way to the cacophony of the monkeys, bullfrogs and saccades.

The everlasting cacophony of insects and the buzzing of the mossies and flying beetle creatures. Jack was put on guard whilst the rest of the team prepared a brew and breakfast. Tom prepared enough for himself and for Jack knowing he would be impaired with his swollen hand and arm.

They inspected their weapons and gave the working parts a light oiling. The camp was then dismantled and packed away no trace of it should remain; soon the jungle would reclaim it.

A fresh coating of insect repellent and cam cream diagonally applied would help camouflage their Caucasian faces. Tom made sure everyone took their paladin and energy tablets, it was going to be a long day. Jin Tin had gone on ahead to recce the proposed route to the bamboo cluster section, where they would cut and bind them together to make a very stable and buoyant raft. The trip down to the water's edge was not as exhausting as the uphill struggle. They made good progress to the RV of Jin Tin's choice he even had some lengths of bamboo cut and a heap of vines ready to start lashing the raft together. The trick to lashing bamboo together is to use small sticks as spacers along the length and between every branch of bamboo; this will allow the vines and lashings to pass between and over the next section of the raft, also to lash cross members to hold the whole raft together. It took the group most of the morning of arduous work to get a raft about 20ft long and 4ft wide which would float and accommodate the five men of the rescue team and their equipment which would have to lashed and securely fixed to the raft. There were four cross members, number one and three were slightly longer on each side, this would allow two uprights on each side rising at an angle of 45° standing about 4*ft* high, these in turn were joined at the top with another cross member securely lashed. Down the centre was a single bamboo member that held all the uprights together. At least they would have something to secure their Bergens and kit to.

Finally, they stood back to admire their handiwork, wiping their faces with their sweat rags, Jin Tin grinning pleased with his western comrades. Tom, Jack, Bungy and Mac also well pleased with their hard graft.

Tom ordered, "Okay let's give it the float test! Keep hold of the for'ard and aft lines, we don't want it drifting off at this stage, eh!" Heaving and straining they slid it down the bank into the brownish slow moving river, which would take them across the border into Kalimantan territory and dangerous enemy outposts.

"Let's see what we got for lunch, eh?" Bungy was reeling off the contents of each can. "We could have meat stew, or frankfurters in some kind of brine, or chicken supreme! With rice flavoured, curry powder and a few raisins."

Jin Tin butted in, “Or I will go and kill an iguana and cook it in bamboo, velly nice and tasty!” Bungy pulled a face of distaste. Tom and Jack informed Bungy that the iguana tasted a bit like chicken, but Bungy was not at all convinced.

“You bootnecks will eat anything; I’ve got my serious doubts about you lads.” Silently, Jin Tin slipped back into the bush and was immediately swallowed up in its cavernous lush green interior, it would be a while thought Tom and Jack as they watched Bungy’s face; a curious mixture of curiosity and maybe a tinge of revulsion at the thought of eating a large pre-historic lizard; out here in the depths of hell. Jack set about gathering enough dry wood, which in the jungle is not an easy task as most of the time the air and trees are saturated with moisture and the frequent downpours of monsoon rains. They were not idle as each man prepared his selection of kit availability during the push by river toward their destination and recovery of McHenry whom they hoped would be in good shape and also be able to use the PE they had brought along. McHenry would be in his element blowing up his jailers and the prison he had been incarcerated in; for what to him would seem like months. Tom remembered his infectious smile at times of great stress and discomfort. They had been mates and ‘oppos’ for a long time, serving in various commando units; he was a marine you could totally rely on.

***

The VC 10 from Singapore came gliding down gracefully as Linda got a tinge of excitement at seeing the familiar sights of London flashing past as the aircraft made a perfect descent. The speed at high altitude is not evident until the plane is very near the airstrip and then the speed is quite electrifying going at great speed before the pilot starts his braking procedures, then it’s evident. The wheels touched down with a slight bump, the air flaps (elevators) thrust into the right position for air braking and the final taxiing to the airport terminal building. With a sigh Linda unbuckled her seat belt leaning over to see how her husband Chris was faring.

He was still sedated and sleeping peacefully, the female flight attendant smilingly approached and quite casually, in a quiet tone, informed Linda that the captain had been radioed that the press had been waiting for Linda and were in a state of jostling fever; in order to get as close to Linda and her wounded marine husband as possible. The stewardess also said that a special courier was waiting to come aboard to deliver her package off. Linda seemed a bit bewildered at the amount of commotion she was causing but smiled a little self-consciously. The stewardess also said it would be better if Linda and Chris got off last, this would give the other passengers a better chance of exiting the plane. Linda and Chris were of course in the first class part of the VC10 it had more space and with Chris needing medical attention it was the only place for him. The weary passengers one by one collecting their hand luggage from the overhead lockers and slowly making their way outside to friends and relatives confused with the amount of the media attention but happy to see their loved ones home safe and sound at last. The courier was in conversation with the female attendant who was pointing him in Linda's direction, his eyes lit up when he saw Linda, handing her the rather bulky package she had ordered from her father before she left Singapore. The courier, young and very smart in his motorcycle suit, took all of the detail in as he appreciatively admired Linda's features and aquamarine Chinese cheongsam dress which was high collared but the lower half was split up to the thighs on both sides. "Charming," he muttered as he handed the package over savouring every minute. Linda smiled at him and handed him a crisp five pound note. He self-consciously took it; with one last appreciative glance and was gone through the door. Linda unpacked her winter coat which was her favourite; it was a black diamante mink coat with matching mink hat. All the female flight attendants gazed at her from afar, were thrilled but also a trifle envious of her. The Royal Naval ambulance was waiting, two strapping SBA's entered the cabin and gently lifted Lt Davenport onto a special stretcher which they wheeled out into the melee of photographers waiting in the passenger arrivals lounge, Linda walked alongside of her husband holding his hand gently more for reassurance than anything. Chris looked at her rather confused at what was happening to them. Flashbulbs going off as Linda was being snapped left and right with Chris in the background, the TV stations were filming her every move, she looked 'Essence' as the marines would describe her. The RN ambulance took them both to Brize Norton where they were met by a Royal Naval helicopter which flew them down to RNH Plymouth, where they had a special ward for amputees.

***

Jin Tin had returned with the kill he had promised, it was very nicely parcelled in banana leaves tied with raffia dried grass. He had gutted the iguana and prepared it for cooking in the bamboo poles, knocking out the sections which joined the bamboo together except the last base section, cutting them into lengths of about 3ft. The meat of the iguana he pushed down the barrels of the bamboo and filled it with water sealing off the top end with clay, this would seal the bamboo and create a kind of pressure cooker inside the bamboo. Jack and Tom quickly made an open fire on which they laid the lengths of bamboo cooking poles.

It would take an hour or maybe two depending on the process going on in the pressure poles and the aroma of cooking. Jin Tin was expert in this method of cooking so the boys left it up to his expertise. Tom had used his water bag and strained it through the canvas sock and used purifying tablets to get enough water from the river to replenish all bottles and for cooking.

McPherson the signaller had reported to Brigade HQ giving them a sitrep of their progress thus far. He was very quick as he didn't want any enemy radio operators tracking his position.

He packed his precious radio and earphones away and enclosed it all in a waterproof bag for the river trip later, and maybe into nightfall; checking his weapon and availability of the ammo pouches. He made himself a good strong mug of coffee as the Asian packs had this in re-seal small plastic bags; a new additional commodity in the 1960s. He thought, *Well I don't know what the Iguana will taste like, but it smells okay.*

"Looking at the map, how far do you think it is Jack?" Tom asked.

"It's a bloody long way; I would guess about at least 100 miles downriver."

Tom scratched his chin. "Well it won't be so bad going downriver but I'm just wondering about getting back to this position, assuming of course that we are successful in rescuing McH."

"Hmmm yes! I was thinking about that!"

Jin Tin was squatting by their side listening to their conversation. "I know of a plan! To get back here! You have ringgit; money? What we do, I go see river traders, I make deal with them, you see; they travel very far from this side of border to Kalimantan to trade, I make good deal!" Jin Tin's dark eyes lit up; smiling much to himself he stood up very pleased with his solution.

Jin Tin moved off to attend to his cooking whilst Tom, Jack, Bungy and McPherson busied themselves with their own preparations and just mulling over what Jin Tin had said. After a while Jack said, "Sounds good to me, Tom!"

Mess tins were placed out and Jin Tin speared a good amount of meat from the bamboo pole into each mess tin, true to his word it was cooked and gingerly Bungy tasted it first, his face altered from scowl to pleasant as he hungrily wolfed it down. "I have to admit, I wus wrong, it's not too bad at all; wait till I tell 'em in Wombwell Yorkshire when I get home; that's if I ever get out of this hellhole!"

They all grinned at Bungy's remarks in his northern accent as each one had total recall of where their hometown was; each one in his own quiet way wished they were home too. Tom sipped his hot mug of coffee, still looking intently at the map spread out, mentally taking in the terrain and contours of the large jungle area's they were about to cover. He lit one of his panatelas and in a thoughtful mood planned what to expect on this downriver journey.

Finally, Tom broke the silence, "Okay, let's get this show on the road, came out! Lash up and stow, sling your night vision goggles around your neck we're going to need them soon!" as he glanced upward. "Wipe out any trace of this camp! Load your gear; make sure it's secure on the raft."

"Bungy take a look at Jack's hand and if necessary give him a pain killing shot!"

"Check weapons, load, safety catches on! Okay Bungy lead off, Mac you're next, Jack bring up the rear; make last check, in our area. Collect the bamboo paddles and rudder; move out!"

Gingerly one by one, they stepped aboard the raft which at first seemed unstable but it kept righting itself as the weight shifted along its length and breadth. Finally all were aboard; Jin Tin being the last one to cast off and leap aboard as the steady current floated them out onto the river, which seemed quite broad except for the overhanging branches of the bushy trees and the submerged logs which sometimes posed a threat to navigation, so they kept in the middle of the river but always on the lookout for native craft which they could hear, the shrill sound of the outboard motors giving the team fair warning of their approach.

Thcy all began to paddle slowly with their rough bamboo paddles, Jin Tin was at the stern end steering the unwieldy craft as he knew more about this part of the world than any of the group.

It was getting very late in the afternoon and soon the light would close down, in the jungle would be total blackness but here on the river might just be possible to keep going, especially with their new toy the night goggles, which they would presently have to wear. Jin

Tin was doing an excellent job of navigating; but even he was thinking they may have to tie up somewhere and be able to hide the raft from curious eyes on the river. After a good four hours of toil and sweat; Jin Tin pointed to a perfect spot on the riverbank. They had donned their night goggles and could make out low overhanging bushy branches that swept into the river and would thus conceal their raft they could clamber ashore for a well-earned rest and tomorrow at first light they would be able to continue in better light.

Taking their equipment ashore, they slung their string hammocks and overhead cover up quick smart and settled down for a most uncomfortable night's sleep or rather they just dozed, they were attacked by everything that could fly and bite, but having taken notice of QMS Hayhurst they had powerful insect repellents (which could take the paint off cars) together with the Tiger Balm which kind of, froze the nerve endings on their face. Paludrine was essential to take.

The night sounds gave way to the day sounds of the monkeys and the croaking of the tree frogs, saccades; far off you could hear the barking belching of one of their primeval apes.

The marines quickly stowed their gear away, except for the hexamine stoves on which to have a refreshing mug of tea, also they threw a handful of vitamins and multivitamins the QMS had advised them to take; they would need the extra energy for THIS trip. A slight mist pervaded the banks of the river; soon it would be time to get those tired aching limbs back in action getting as much mileage as they could in daylight hours. Tom just grinned at Bungy who was finding this kind of life not to his liking, muttering and farting as he went through his daily routine. But first he tended to Jack's hand and gave him another painkiller.

"They hand will be reet in a few days Jack," Bungy promised.

So! The sodden group left the Mozzie ridden bank and trooped aboard the raft ready for another grueller. Lashed up and stowed, they paddled two on each side of the raft, soon their aches and pains dispersed and with rhythmic strokes were making good progress, their olive greens completely saturated in sweat with the 90° humidity in the air. They took cover twice in the low hanging bushes along the river as and when they heard the sounds of an outboard motor. Their progress, however, was better than bush bashing it through the dense jungle ulu. Tom called for a halt after they heard again the outboards shrill screaming after the long prop shaft bounced over the numerous logs floating in the river. They had been paddling for five hours now time for a break, so pulling well into the sides again for cover; they gratefully strode ashore for a brew and some scran. It was now nearing midday and getting hotter especially out of the cover of the dense jungle canopy. As soon as they entered the cover of the rain forest trees it seemed very much cooler, Tom Jack and the team set to and made a beautiful mug of tea, pouring from the aluminium mug to the plastic one so they could drink it without taking the skin off their lips. Soon they each had a mess tin full of stew mixed in with the rice and stirring nice and gently until it seemed edible, scoffed it down, followed down with the sweet mug of tea.

"Tom look up," Jack said quietly pointing to the jungle foliage, there standing on the branches were two orange coloured orang-u-tangs, one being the male was quite big and very strong he was bending a thick branch, as thick as your wrist; one can only imagine he being seven times stronger than any human. The other was obviously female as she had a tiny baby with her that was very light in colour, they were just curious of what was beneath them, not scared or frightened in the least, just gazing down at the team in an animal look of fascination. Tom moved slowly and located his miniature 35mm camera and taking aim took a good photo of them from various angles. Presently, they grunted and moved off swinging lazily through the upper reaches of the jungle canopy.

Jack grinning tossed a remark to Bungy, "You won't get many of them in Wombwell eh Bungy?"

"I don't know about that; maybe on a Saturday night after a good session on the bevy!" All the team grinned, it was time to go.

"Okay get your gear together. Bury the gash; leave nothing, check weapons; let's move out," Tom intoned with a rasp in his voice.

Having a rest and some nosh, gave the team a bit more impetus, especially the mug of sweet tea. They set to with a will now and pushed just that little bit harder, for soon they would be in 'Bandit country', where all their training would come into focus, their sixth senses would be on high alert. Jin Tin steered very well with his homemade tiller and rudder avoiding many floating logs and debris that was always a threat to them. On and on they pushed always with the one purpose in mind, the rescue of their friend and 'oppo' McH. They just hoped he was in good shape and could travel. Knowing McH as they did, he would have found a way to survive any kind of punishment or torture.

It was late afternoon and already the shadows were lengthening soon it would be very dark.

The night vision goggles would be a boon to seeing in the blackness of the tropical night.

They pushed on now in darkness, shapes looming larger as they paddled down the river which was getting a little faster, that helped them a lot. In unison, they paddled ever onward each stroke they thought was getting them nearer to Gorantan and the prison. One of the reasons, Jack thought would be the river was being joined by several tributary's pouring off the high ground to his left. He could hear the gurgle and splash of water; probably over a waterfall as it joined the main river. The night vision goggles gave a weird green glow but they were essential to the team as they were able to see their way ahead in complete darkness. On and on they paddled, sweat pouring out of every pour, just another ten or fifteen miles would be the goal. Jack reasoned they had travelled about 80 miles along this river; soon they would have to leave it and proceed through the virgin Jungle to their destination at Gorantan. Tom and Jack knew that they would make better time through the Ulu if they took the high ground which was sparser than the valley floors; where a great deal of leaf foliage enriched the smaller bushier trees and shrubs.

It was now 0200 hrs; Tom and Jack reasoned that they should leave the luxury of the river travel and advance down the spine of the continent to reach their goal, but first they would rest up, have a much deserved sleep and in the morning freshen up, have a good nosh-up so they would be strong enough to beat their way through the Ulu.

They swung into an overhanging bushy area, which successfully hid the raft from view. Gingerly, they scrambled ashore trying to find a firm footing in the ooze, sometimes sinking up to the crutch, which was unpleasant to say the least. It is not an easy thing to make camp in these conditions; they managed to climb higher, and somehow they were able to find suitable young trees and made their 'Bashers' up quickly slinging their string hammocks to the young sapling trees, which would keep them off the ground, you never knew what would be crawling through at this time and place. Watches would be kept but each Marine would probably snatch a few hours' sleep. "*Remember only one capful per night,*" Tom remembered the QM's words with a warm, secret, cheerful, nostalgia.

The dawn chorus woke everyone from their reverie, with heads shaking to clear the sleep-laden brain; each marine unpacked his gear and began preparing for his 'Nosh'. With bleary eyes, mouths yawning and Bungy, muttering and farting, so began another day in their young lives. Jin Tin had made himself comfortable in the higher branches of a rainforest tree, on seeing everyone was going about their daily tasks he slid down and wandered into the centre of the group and began his own preparations for breakfast.

Having got his mug on the hexamine stove, Jack strode over to his Bergen and extracted the team's one and only entrenching tool. "Well, I'm orf for my morning, George; look after my brew whilst I'm gone." Tom meanwhile was observing both the map which was spread out on the ground and the surrounding features. He took compass bearings, away from the weaponry as it tended to give a false reading due to the metal content.

Tom thought that this would be the hardest part of the trip, unless they could find an old animal track that would lead them in the general direction of Gorantan. Sometimes the jungle has some big surprises; a cautious and investigative approach will require a great deal of patience especially when everyone is dog tired of the continuing, repetitive slog.

Slowly and methodically, they went through their daily routine, Tom on looking around his group decided that all would have shower in the waterfall which was cascading down close by.

They all looked like they needed freshening up and certainly a refreshing cold shower would be a tonic for what lay ahead. Tom strode around to each of them and told them what he wanted them to do, "Go in, two at a time; take your weapons with you, and stay alert."

"Roger that Tom!" each one commented.

Finally, it was Tom and Jack's turn, stripping off they were a fine example of manhood. Tom tall and darkly handsome. Jack fair haired and standing very tall both well-muscled and absolutely fit. The water came gushing down in a fine white current of never ending pure water. It was quite exhilarating and made you feel much more alive and completely refreshed.

Jin Tin was passing close by seeing if there were any fish in the shallows to catch. On glancing at Tom and Jack his eyes bulged out like organ stops. Gesticulating and pointing at both Jack and Tom he just was astounded and burbled out, "Apa Itu! Sangat Besar!"

Jack just grinned at him and said, "'Ere what's the matter with you Jin Tin, doesn't yours shrink and shrivel when you're having a cold shower."

The remainder of the team just grinned; Bungy muttered, "I wish mine would shrivel to that size!"

The preparations for the big push were completed, cammed out they hauled on their packs and saddled up, and Tom today, was the point man (leading scout). The first part of the journey was an uphill struggle against the dense undergrowth, however soon they were nearing the spine of the country and the jungle was more navigable. Tom took many compass bearings to ensure they were on track for Gorantan in Kalimantan.

Old decaying Jungle trail, forgotten in time

Presently, they came on to an old jungle trail that had not been used for years but was still a very good pathway to the crest of the high plateau they were seeking and indeed it was a godsend for their long journey south. Presumably it had been abandoned to the quicker river routes which would suit traders far better than slogging it through the dense jungle with heavy loads. They were making very good progress due to this old trail. Tom and Jack reckoned they would reach the outskirts of Gorantan before nightfall. Although still observant, they cast caution to the wind in favour of speed. They reached the spine of the country; here it was not as dense but much clearer, through the immense trees they caught the occasional sight of the great river down below. McPherson carrying the heavy signals equipment was having a rough time, but he never complained, just happier that they had found a good track and were making good progress, as always everyone was sweating neaters.

About midday, Tom signalled a halt as they had been travelling about five and a half hours and just needed a rest and a mug of tea. Surprising what a nice brew will do for the human body, it tends to revive the spirits a little, must be the English tradition of the welcome cup of tea. They spread out in a wide circle each covering his opposite numbers back as they prepared their nosh and tea; offloading their heavy packs as they stretched their limbs to get some feeling back into cramped muscles, looking after one another like a well-trained band of meerkats.

"'Ere where's that entrenchin tool you were usin Jack? Have to keep me bowels movin; must be those senopods they keep shovin in the tea!" Bungy was grinning all the while conveying these pearls of wisdom.

"After you with the tool," they all chorused!

"Watch out for the shit beetles!"

"And the snakes!" Bungy was now a bit alarmed at the word snakes!

"Aw fuckit. I gotta go!" Everyone was cheesed down as Bungy staggered off into the ulu clutching his entrenching tool and native parang, toilet paper poking out of his bush hat.

All too soon the rest period was up and soon they would haul their packs and equipment once more onto a seemingly never ending trail in pursuit of their 'oppo' McHenry held captive in some hell hole of a prison in bandit country. Tom gathered his team together to give them as much information as he could on the track they were advancing on and the likely approaches they would have to make to recce the area once in they were in striking distance and were able to view the terrain more closely.

"Saddle up, check you equipment and weapons, leave nothing!" Tom led off, followed at safe distances by the rest of the team.

They journeyed on, each man with his own thoughts and instant memories of life back home or their loved ones patiently waiting for their safe return to the world.

***

The Royal Navy helicopter came in gracefully throttling back as the pilot negotiated the landing on the football field at Stonehouse Barracks very near the Longroom, overlooking the estuary to Plymouth sound and Drake Island. It was quite blustery and cold and Linda was quite grateful for the warmth of her black diamante mink coat and matching fur hat. A Royal Marine driver and ambulance was parked nearby. How the press had got to know where the helicopter was going to land is a complete mystery, however, thinking back they did have scanners which could pick up any free to air conversations, so maybe they did and had. Linda was being snapped at every move she made and it indeed was a scoop for any news or cameraman to sell it or to get it to his editor, as she and Lt Davenport were the flavour of the month. Their photographs and newsreel would go worldwide especially to the free world like America, Australia, New Zealand, Canada, South Africa and Europe, especially France where they had an eye for absolute beautiful women and Linda was all of that. Plymouth was overjoyed with one of their own making the headlines, such a wonderful heroic story as well; of the rescue of this handsome young pilot Lt Chris Davenport, he had gained popularity as well as sympathy from the general public, as an amputee; whose family tree and his ancestral home spanned many centuries in Devon. Lord Davenport and his wife, Caroline, were also there to see their son, Christopher, and Linda. It was quite an emotional reunion for them when they saw their son being carried out from the helicopter with Linda at his side, the newsmen were taking all the pictures they could, the TV camera crews having a field day as the family drew together in warm embraces; Chris Davenport was a little ashen but struggled to smile for his mom and dad. Slowly, they negotiated the stretcher through the thronging Newsmen and positioned him comfortably in the waiting Royal Marine ambulance, Linda elected to travel with Chris, whilst Lord and Lady Davenport retired to their Rolls Royce following closely behind the RM ambulance to RNH Stonehouse Hospital.

Lady Mabel Cunningham had opted to meet her daughter, Linda, at the hospital; she really did not want to be caught up in the frenzy of the newspaper and cameramen with their flashing bulbs and sometimes with ribald comments to all and sundry, not her scene she thought. Her chauffer drove her there in the brand new Bentley continental. She was shown into a private reception area where they would be able to meet and talk in perfect comfort, which Lady Cunningham desperately needed for her daughter's return from the Far East. They would have much to talk about; she was also distressed at Chris's physical condition and wished to see him with Linda at his side.

***

Chapter 16
Gorantan, Kalimantan

The rescue team with great caution, had reached the outer fringes of the jungle, before them lay the gradual descent from the high ridges they had travelled on, to what appeared a well cleared green agricultural district. They shuck off their heavy packs with a sigh of relief. It was getting dark now and soon they would be in total blackness as the night swiftly descended upon them. Tom and Jack eyed the area with their small binoculars before it became too dark. Jack also collected suitable grasses and supple branches for camouflage, which when attached to their uniforms and equipment would be very useful for concealment.

Jin Tin squeezed himself between them and whispered, "I musti pergi ker Rumah besar!"

"What did he say?" Bungy asked.

"I think he said he wants to take a walk and recce the police station down there!" Tom whispered.

"That's not a bad idea," Jack replied. "He'll quite easily pass as a local or maybe a trader from Brunei."

"Here give me one of your arrows, Jin Tin? What we'll do is just write a brief note to McH to let him know we're here; just very short and sweet."

"Use the blowpipe Jin Tin!"

Jack wrote; "Tom-n-Jack. R ere. B reddi. 2 nite." Taking a well-chewed piece of chewing gum Jack stuck the paper onto the arrow shaft, smoothing it gently to enable a good flight.

Before he left Tom produced a wad of local currency (ringgit… dollars). Handing it over to Jin Tin whose face lit up to see so much dosh, he would have to be very careful in his negotiations with the river traders tonight, he reasoned.

Jin Tin grinned at them as he set off in the gathering gloom of the late afternoon, time for a cold snack before the evening's active measures. It would be the frankfurters tonight, and a mars bar from the 'Nutty pack' also they took the energy, health and the Paludrine tablets; the QM had advised them to take, it would need all their energy levels to do this rescue of their oppo McHenry. They geared themselves up with everything they would need in this midnight attack making sure the weapons were in pristine condition ready for any action they were likely to encounter. Tom made his way over to McPherson's position (SIG's) and suggested that he should contact Brigade HQ to inform them of their present location on a fast zipcode. Having thought about everything, they all took off their GP boots and socks, changing them after first massaging in some foot and body powder (Foo Foo). One thing in their favour was the element of surprise, which Tom considered crucial for their complete success. As far as he was aware, they had not been seen or their presence being observed or compromised in their journey thus far. After darkness descended on them, they donned the night vision goggles observing the time and frequency of the guards watch roster on the twin towers guarding the entrance to the prison. Principally, it was a police station but had been heavily fortified recently.

Jin Tin made good speed down the cleared grassy slope and nonchalantly made his way towards the big house as he had described it. Passing close by the gates, he was challenged to move on and away from the open iron gates which were quite solid in their construction. Jin Tin was able to see inside and in the centre of the prison grounds stood a bamboo cage on raised wooden pillars, he could also see a blood soaked figure inside and judged it to be a white man. There were no other prisoners. He would wait until dark and return with his message in the blowpipe, first though, he would go to the river and the makeshift docks and negotiate with the traders for the 'Teams' escape in one of the bigger river craft that plied between Brunei and Gorantan. This might take several hours of bartering with these wiley Chinese traders.

The river traders had sold all their merchandise and were squatting down with a bowl of rice and smoking their favourite weed in their pipes they were in a pleasant state of mind as Jin Tin squatted down in their largest of the river craft which had as a bonus, a cover which extended all the way over the boat, it also had a good outboard engine of great horsepower he would be happy if they agreed to his terms of payment. So! The haggling began and took as Jin Tin suspected two hours of bartering for the right price. He didn't mention they were marines or what they were doing here in Gorantan, or that they were heavily armed, that might have really made a big difference in price. The river traders assumed they were Ibans or just members of his kampong (native longhouse or village). Jin Tin was pleased with himself that he too could be as wiley as they were. He bade them farewell and retired to the vicinity of the police station to wait his chance at a good shot with the blowpipe and the secret message. The area inside the prison walls was lit by kerosene lamps, so he was able to see reasonably well the layout of the interior yard. He was in his native outfit as usual and merged well into the surroundings being dark skinned and a very skilful Iban warrior, he observed the guards on the twin towers and waited for a time when they would be ready for their reliefs to take over. Sure enough, they were changing and chatting together, and Jin Tin took careful aim and sent his arrow through the iron gates to land with a slight thud in the back of the bamboo cage not far from the figure lying prostrate on a rough bamboo and rope native bed. As with all prisoners, they develop an animal type of instinct for unusual noises, McH was no exception he had been brutally beaten recently and always was aware of what next they would be meting out to him. He felt a sudden waft of air along with a faint hiss passing close by his head together with a small dull thud in one of the bamboo bars. With bleary and bloodshot eyes he looked in the direction of the disturbance, he could make out a small thin arrow with a white piece of paper in the shaft. Gingerly and shakily, he twisted around to prise the arrow from the bamboo bars. He had to read it several times due to the dimness, to really believe that his friends and oppos were close by and not only that, they would rescue him, there was no doubt in his mind that they would do so as promised. This gave him so much hope that slowly he started to feel much better; he grinned painfully, the energy slowly returned to his aching bruised body, there is nothing more invigorating and refreshing than hope itself.

Having completed his tasks, Jin Tin returned to the group following his footsteps of the upturned leaves which had a light green phosphorous fluorescent underside, which was plainly visible in the darkness. He quickly relayed in broken English and some well-known Malay words and with gestures conveyed the events which had happened to him down below near the prison and the subsequent bartering with the river Traders. Tom and Jack grinned, clapping him good-naturedly on the back for his efforts with the important message to McH and the river traders. They would rest for a few hours until midnight. In the cleared areas it is possible to see reasonably well; tonight they would have some decent light from a half moon.

Tom glanced at his G10 Omega watch, it was just past midnight, time to go! The whispered message “Saddle up” came through from Tom along the line as they struggled to their feet. The packs were swung onto their aching shoulders, however McPherson's was a lot heavier and required the assistance of Bungy Williams who was the nearest to him. Jin Tin had dropped down from his tree and would lead out to the police station located far below.

The leafy camouflage was added to tunics, the face cream streaked carefully across in a diagonal pattern, weapons were checked, safety catches applied, magazines within easy accessible reach, Tom attached the silencer onto the end of his rifle making sure it was thoroughly fixed into position, nothing was out to dangle or tinkle. "Let's go!" came the whispered command. "Keep a safe distance apart," rippled down *the thin green line.* As the shadowy figures moved cautiously out from the jungle canopy and into a rather pale green and dark world.

Steady progress was maintained; however, everyone was attuned to their environment and peripheral vision was very important each taking in all the details of their surroundings for possible traps or difficult terrain, as well as places of defence and cover if they came under fire from the police station or wandering patrols of the Kalimantan Army. Never underrate the enemy was a well-known phrase of the Royal Marines training cadres. Stealth tonight would be paramount in each marine's mind.

Jin Tin was out in front carrying a rather long sapling pole, must have measured about 16 feet or slightly more, his skin being dark brown he melted effortlessly with the darkness, just the brightness of his eyes and his white teeth when he grinned gave him away. The team had approached to within 100 yards of the police station; there were lights on the twin watchtower

Positions which would help the team as the defenders would have their night site impeded due to the reflected glare. Tom, Jack and the team fanned out keeping well into the darkened areas whilst Tom indicated he would take out the guards and also the lights. He flipped the night vision goggles up setting his scope to the correct distance, making sure by traversing from left to right that he would be able to knock both guards out simultaneously within seconds. He breathed deeply and exhaled slowly; taking careful, aim he gently squeezed the trigger, one shot then quickly traversing the next shot, both shots just made a low coughing sound as the bullets left the barrel and found their targets. Both were headshots and the guards slumped down without a sound, next was the lights, as Jin Tin sprang forward using the sapling as a pole vaulter would; straight over the Iron gates, landing on the soft ground like an agile monkey. He made his way straight for the bamboo cage where McH was held captive and with deft swings of his parang he cut out chain and lock, he swung open the door gesturing for McHenry to follow him, but McH was not in good condition and so Jin Tin helped him along as best he could.

Leaving Jack with the Bren, Tom made for the iron gates and shrugged out of his Bergen and quickly found his readymade PE and detonator which he attached to the gate locks, lighting it he quickly found a safe place at the side of the watchtower as the gates and locks exploded outwards. Running forward, he just caught McH as he was stumbling along with Jin Tin who was finding it difficult to support him. Tom tossed him over his shoulder and made a 'B line' for the gates and he never stopped until he felt safer then he could let him down for a quick examination and a much needed drink of water. Jin Tin had caught up with Tom; pointing out the direction of the river and the waiting boat traders.

Jack signalled to Bungy and McPherson to head off to catch up with Tom and Jin Tin, he would cover for them with the LMG (Bren Gun) Bungy would be better with the medical bag than here with the possibility of getting hit.

As the police station had been compromised in an attack, the remaining guards fully armed streamed out of their quarters to defend and ward off any attackers. They were met by accurate fire from Jack's LMG, as with the traditional well aimed three taps on each target he dispatched many of them; before they realised their vulnerability and took cover. Jack tossed a few grenades in well placed areas in the yard and took off in a rearguard action pacing it out in order to eventually rejoin the main group.

He did stop a few times acting as rear-end Charlie, with well-aimed shots he dispatched a few more. Taking the initiative he shrugged off his Bergen and found the two green trip wire posts which were already prepared with the trip wire, pacing it out he ran across the narrow pathway that led from the police station to the river driving the posts into the ground and deftly and with some trepidation carefully attached the mills bomb (36 grenade) to the trip wire. There were now some serious ordnance incoming, whizzing very close to him as he dived for cover near his Bergen and the all important Bren gun. He quickly fired quick double taps from left to right, rolled over with his Bergen to a new position and fired a few more rapid shots off, he could now hear and discern there was a vehicle starting up in the compound and he hoped it would be only a soft skinned vehicle rather than an armoured personnel carrier, he reasoned it would be the former, in which case he might just stand a chance of some serious damage to it.

McHenry was still across Tom's shoulders; luckily McH was only slightly built which helped a lot in the fireman's lift position. They were legging it as fast as they could knowing Jack would hold them off as long as possible.

Jin Tin was first aboard the river craft jumping aboard and frightening the shit out of the wiley Chinese traders, who had been catching a few hours' sleep before they were due to leave for home in Brunei. Heavily laden Tom carried a barely conscious McH aboard the rickety gangplank; needless to say the Chinese were suddenly overwhelmed with burly Marines carrying heavy weapons. Gently, Tom lowered him onto the nearest native cot and signalled Bungy to look after him. McPherson was also instructed to set up the radio and signal Brigade HQ to give them the latest SITREP and to standby for further messages.

Tom took off to join Jack who had been hard pressed with the volume now of 'incoming' ordnance zapping past him, he had been lucky so far but knew that if Tom didn't get back soon he would be in deep SHIT. He had used his ammunition wisely and only on targets he thought were definite; using the three taps routine instead of blasting away, which is generally what happens in a panic stricken environment.

Tom had made it back to Jack's defensive position, panting with the exertion and effort, however he quickly got the SLR and using the scopes night vision capability, picked off a couple of the guards who were pursuing them. Jack turned round and grinned at Tom with his thumb in the air, mouthing the words "Good shooting". Tom jerked his thumb back so that he would cover Jack's tactical withdrawal to the river craft. Jack nodded and with a final good burst of rapid fire took off on the perilous road to the river. After zigzagging for about a hundred yards, he threw himself down to take up another defensive position to cover Tom's withdrawal, the whining of the rounds spitting along his track. All were sweating profusely; the night air was heavy with moisture, like a wet blanket around them. *Might rain,* Jack thought that would either hinder or help them, the Chinese have a saying 'Ying-Yang' which translates to 'Catastrophe or Opportunity' which would it be for them this night!

Jack had perhaps used half of his magazines but he still had the full bandoliers in his Bergen, he would at a lull in the battle, have to fill the spent magazines. But for now, he still had three full magazines of 7.62 ammo which was very hard hitting round, that would be able to go through at least three men if they were grouped one behind the other, certainly would knock their socks off Jack mused. The four-wheel drive vehicles were coming at them down the track rocking a bit crazily as they came down and hit the ruts, suddenly there was a mighty explosion as the vehicles hit the trip wires blowing the driver out as the vehicle sped out of control and rolled over with the occupants trapped beneath it.

Tom took the opportunity to leg it back to Jack's position as Jack laid down covering fire for Tom. It was hairy to say the least but Jack was a PW and knew all the possible 'wrinkles' on board the river craft all was pandemonium the Chinese traders were very upset and kept up an incessant chatter, cursing and gesticulating at the newcomers, until Bungy stood over them pointing his browning automatic at their heads in a fierce manner, with bared teeth he said, "Shut the fuck up! You savvy eh!" He had no intention of using the browning but it had the calming effect he wanted, as he bent to attend to the wounds the Chokies had inflicted on their 'oppo' McHenry. Jin Tin grinned at the Chinese traders and spoke to them in Malay urging them to prepare for cast off and the river trip. They were scared; as well they might be of repercussions and possible death at the hands of their Kalimantan Army commanders both now and in the future. They could hear the noise of the battle that Tom and Jack were involved in and shuddered at the prospect that they too would be embroiled in. Trembling, they went about their business of getting ready for a very fast getaway.

McPherson lost no time in getting his radio transmitter signals unit set up, donning the headgear; he quietly talked into the mouthpiece articulating his words clearly and with pauses.

"Hello Sunray; this is Romeo, Papa, Tango, how do you read me over?"

"Hello Romeo, Papa, Tango, we read you loud and clear; over!"

"Sitrep! Hostage rescued, we are under fire, will need assistance on my code word!"

"Sunray here, message understood, will await your code word and signal over."

"Romeo Papa Tango over and out!"

McPherson closed his set down and doffed his head phones, carefully straddling them around the transmitter. Grabbing his fighting order and the new Colt Commander .5.56 XM177E2 sub machine gun. He spoke to Bungy on his way out, "Won't be long; just going to try out me new gun!" grinning at Bungy as he leapt onto the flimsy jetty; on his way to join Tom and Jack in their desperate fire-fight.

That left just Jin Tin and Bungy aboard the traders craft who were very disturbed and uncomfortable with their new occupants, however they just didn't like the odds of an Iban head-hunter and a mad Yorkshire man with a loaded browning automatic; pointing it erratically at them as he tried to attend to the wounded marine.

All marines are trained first and foremost as riflemen, light machine and sub machine guns rocket launchers, inerga grenades and occasionally with sidearms. This time, however, McPherson had never fired this particular weapon, he had made himself aware of the various functions on the light sub machine gun so that he knew the basics. Weaving his way through the bushes and the incoming ordnance, he finally managed to catch up with Jack and Tom, flinging himself flat alongside Jack. Tom just grinned and said, "What took you so long Mac?"

He ignored them and flicked the safety catch off and squeezed the trigger nice and gently taking aim at an exposed head on the upturned vehicle, the SMG had a good feel to it and he noticed the head was in a bloody mess as the 5.56 rounds tour through the guards' skull. "You surprise me Mac!" muttered Jack.

"Well, you should know I'm not just a pretty face. Remember in training?" Jack nodded in agreement McPherson was a high scorer on the range and indeed had got his Marksman's badge (crossed rifles) and wore it with pride on his sleeve.

"Well let's get this show on the road, we advance to contact and engage them, pepper potting forward, each covering the forward Marine as he gets underway; okay?"

"Roger THAT!" they all spoke in unison. Tom being the first to go forward against the enemy. Jack and Mac gave covering fire as he advanced in quick darting movements, shooting at definite targets as he went and changing magazines on the run. He hardly noticed the heavy weight of the Bergen the adrenalin rush was taking over his discomfort. He flung himself down in a comparative safe spot and taking careful aim, he unleashed a powerful three tap shot in an arching stream from left to right taking out vital targets as he shot. The idea occurred to him that the petrol tank on the overturned vehicle would probably be the best option and so taking careful aim with the scope, he fired several rounds hoping to ignite the fuel and really give ’em a roasting. “Jack! Use the tracers!” The flash and enormous roar of flames shot into the air blowing fragments of metal which came crashing down around the enemy positions and indeed shocked the shit out of Jack, Mac and Tom.

Taking the initiative Tom with weapon in the air ran forward and dispatched any remaining guards that were still alive and breathing.

Looking back Tom gestured to Jack and Mac with the jungle sign of turnabout and so they ran as quickly as possible towards the River craft and maybe their chance of getting out of here alive.

Their lungs were seemingly on fire as they ran panting down the narrow paths and towards some sort of safety.

Bungy saw them first and poking his browning automatic at the Chinese helmsman, he gestured to them to get the craft ready for a quick getaway. In the minds of the Chinese, they didn’t need much persuading and soon the twin outboards were roaring into life as they waited what seemed like an eternity for the three marines to reach the boats.

They flung off the ropes to the jetty and leapt aboard, “Jack you’re on the stern with the Bren cover our arses if they appear.”

“Roger that!” roared Jack. Tom went to examine McH, having a word with Bungy at the same time.

The twin outboards roared into life as the Chinese traders not wishing to stay around any longer gunned the motors leaving a terrific wave to the rear of them, which slapped the bank and sent the other boats rocking, which upset the sleepy occupants who came out to see what the commotion was all about, they however quickly pulled their heads in; not wishing to be any part of this conflict.

The Chinese traders were expert at navigating these often log strewn waters and even in the half light they were very switched on to the rivers constant changing moods and currents.

Macpherson donned his head phones and amidst all the chaos around him, contacted brigade HQ in a calm controlled voice procedure he gave their ‘Sitrep’ and map references and location.

Tom reasoned it would not be long before the word reached a rear echelon of the Kalimantan Army who would certainly be in hot pursuit of these seasoned marine forces and their clandestine, dangerous rescue operation in Indonesian territory.

The river craft was settling down to a steady pace; dawn was breaking and getting lighter the mist hung on the river and it gave a surreal quality to the environment they were travelling in.

The constant day noises of the insects, birds, the whistling whooping of the monkeys added to the general background atmosphere of the Borneo jungle. Nevertheless, the rescue team were on the constant watch for any sign of pursuit, which Tom thought would not be far away.

As it is the usual drill for the marines, they were checking and re-loading their magazines making sure that all were adequately filled and the working parts oiled for immediate action.

Jin Tin was at the forward end and stood on the prow like a ships figurehead, giving the Chinese helmsman warning of any logs or debris in their path.

Faintly they could hear the chopping sound of a helicopter as it beat its way through the air following the river as it twisted and turned on its way to the coast, which also divided and made its way to the state of Brunei and for them to their start point and pick-up area.

Tom listened and waited; so did the rest of the team for a time when they knew they would have to take cover in the overhanging branches and bushes along the rivers banks. Jack had spotted a good hiding area, it was black inside were hardly any light could penetrate; the branches were high enough for the craft to enter and was ideal for their purpose. Jack signalled the Chinese helmsman who readily saw the advantage of a great hideaway from the Chokie army chopper.

The suspense was electric as the chopper passed slowly past them and continued on its way searching the river for any sight of the river craft that had suddenly left the scene at Gorantan.

Tom had made up his mind and took his silenced SLR fitted with an excellent scope, he motioned to the team he was going off the craft and would return soon. Dropping over the side, he waded ashore in the swampy gooey mess reaching firm land with some struggle, carrying his rifle high in the air to avoid contamination and possible stoppages. He could see an opening higher up the bank and towards this he moved with some difficulty, the branches and the undergrowth was thick in this waterlogged area. Breathing heavy, he settled down to await any sign of the chopper as he knew it would return for a second recce of the river. He made sure his weapon was ready for action safety catch off and shrouded his face and shoulders with the large face veil for camouflage, high on the bank, and then he waited.

The unmistakeable sound of the chopper was again coming in his direction and soon would be in target range. He breathed deeply a few times, exhaling slowly, raising his rifle as the chopper came into view. First shot would be the pilot, second shot the radio/navigator, third shot if they had a waist gunner, final two shots would be the fuel tanks and the tail rotor.

The chopper nosed its way along, obviously they had some idea that the craft was in hiding and needed a closer look at a possible hiding place. What luck Tom Thought as he squeezed the trigger the navigator was on the left side and the pilot was on the right, the 7.62mm round passed through the head of the navigator and through the head of the pilot, two kills with one shot! The chopper was now bucking wildly so Tom rapidly shot off his other targets watching the helicopter going out of control and flames starting to billow out with black smoke trailing behind. The chopper in its death throes bucked and rolled down the river for a few hundred yards before it smashed into a tree and slowly slid down into the water gurgling as it submerged into the inky mess, with a final hiss, it was gone.

Jack and the team had heard the shots and seen the helicopter bucking and flashing past but were not privy to what had happened exactly, they were only glad that Tom had got rid of it and now they could continue on their journey and to what they hoped, safety.

Tom struggled back through the tangled undergrowth being careful not to get sucked into the messy ooze that surrounded the river craft, but with help from Jack and the team he scrambled aboard. "Okay, let's move out!" rasped Tom. He glared at the Chinese who got the message instantly. They were now slightly more afraid but aware of the dangerous men they had aboard.

The able bodied men of the team lent a hand to get out into midstream, and then it was up to the river traders to get the twin outboards bursting into life for what they hoped would be a trouble free run to their RV point with their RM chopper.

"Whilst you've been getting a sun tan I made you a cuppa cha!" Jack said with a note of respect in his voice.

"Cheers Jack!" rasped Tom. "Good on ya!"

"How's McH? He okay Bungy?"

"Well, he's as good as I can tell, he's bandaged, he's been given a strong painkiller injection, but we must get him as quickly as Christ will let us, to proper medical facilities aboard ship." Tom made his way to McHenry's side smiling down at his friend with all the care of a lifelong friendship, McH opened his eyes and with a smile on his bloodied face gripped Tom's hand and whispered, "I knew you would come back for me!" a tear in his eyes.

They were now making good progress; it was quite clear with not too many logs barring their way, the prop shafts had been elongated, so that if they did hit a log it would connect with the prop and not the propeller, therefore bouncing it over the obstacle in the river, a simple but effective method of protecting the aluminium drive propeller.

The marines kept watch on all sides with weapons at the ready just in case of any surprise attack from the banks of the river. The cover over the boat was very good as it tended to conceal the merchandise that was being carried. They had made good progress and had travelled they estimated some sixty miles from Gorantan, but they still had some way to go before they reached their destination and their airlift; code-named '*Bulldog!*'.

Bungy handed around some nutty bars he had been secretly conserving for just the right moment, even the Chinese looked happy when he offered them a mars bar.

Jin Tin was fishing with a line fixed to a sapling pole he had brought aboard, called 'Trolling' in the western world and indeed he was having a measure of success with a good catch at his feet in a native wicker basket, the fish still alive flapping around, he looked happy with his lot. Jack heard it first, a faint sound but quite a heavy throb, he put up his hand to alert the team to listen, and pointing in the direction they had come. "I think we've got company boys!"

"Okay, stand to!" Tom growled at the team. "Keep your eyes peeled!" The tension grew as they waited, each one with his own thoughts and desires for a good life and getting home.

There was flat decking on the rear end of the boat so Jack and Tom adopted the lying position Jack with the bipod firmly lashed to the Gunwales in order to get as firm a mounting as possible for accuracy of fire. Tom peered through the powerful scope and was the first to see the Kalimantan Navy vessel that was pursuing them.

It was new class of assault craft for patrolling rivers and estuary, powered by water jet induction which means that it had no propeller and could easily out race any native craft that existed in northern Borneo, or indeed in Southeast Asia, the Indonesians had introduced this type of craft in the past 3 months, so Tom and the team were in deep shit.

It was coming at them at great rate of knots the jet of water from the aft end giving away the knowledge it was a jet propelled boat and was also heavily armed with .50 calibre weapon mounted up on the roof of the reinforced coxswain's cabin. The boat was corkscrewing along the river so as to give a difficult target to aim at. Too far away just yet, we have to get it somewhere in our range of fire, thought Tom.

Jack turned to Tom and with a wink said, “Do ya, a swop Tom? Can’t let you have all the fun eh?” Tom grinned and handed Jack the Special SLR he had nursed for what seemed like days.

Jack looked through the scope and made a few minor adjustments.

Tom gladly took over the Bren and settled down for what would be a fight to the death of them or us, he thought, checking that all was ready to ‘Rock ’n’ roll’.

Jack had noticed through the scope that the bridge with the .50 Cal atop was reinforced with at least 25mm (1 inch) of Dur-aluminium or one of the aluminium alloys, especially light but armoured.

The jet craft was about 700 yards away and the .50 cal HM gun started spewing out bullets towards them, most Jack reasoned were going about 6 feet above their heads and were very inaccurate as the craft was swerving to either side of the river so as to avoid any would be fire from the river craft they were pursuing.

Jack looked through the scope breathed deeply then exhaled slowly, following the antics of the jet craft until he squeezed the trigger as the machine gunners head was just a graticule left to dead centre of the cross wires. There was no wind so the tracer which Jack had inserted sped through the 600 yards finding its target, as the gunner’s head blew apart. The next target would be the coxswain or the driver of the boat, Jack also taking this Chokie out in the same manner. Tom gave them long bursts from the Bren gun raking the side as low as possible trying to sink the jet boat; however it may have been laminated with some new bulletproof material that could resist certain calibre’s of ordnance.

The Chinese were by now very frightened as the deadly interaction of fire built up around them. They also were incredulous of the marksmanship of these heavily built marines who had raided the fortified police station rescuing their comrade and virtually destroying what was obviously a large group of well-armed guards.

Tom was joined by McPherson the signaller on the aft end, “What signal do you want me to send?” Tom replied.

“Inform them we are under attack, give our location, ask for Sky hawk back-up. SCRAMBLE. ASAP.”

McPherson nodded and crawled back under the tarp to make his call.

The call was received on board HMS Eagle, the klaxon being sounded throughout the ship as the fleet air arm pilots were galvanized into action as were their ground and maintenance crews in the hangers below decks.

Two sky hawks were quickly dispatched roaring down the flight deck with the ease and skill of seasoned pilots as they curved onwards and upwards with absolute grace, the flight deck crews watching them go in pride and admiration.

The destination and global position was transferred to them via their intercom in their helmets.

So the stage was set for them to help out a tiny rescue team in enemy held territory fighting for their lives in a muddy river they had never seen or even heard of. But now they would find them and quickly too. At over six hundred miles, an hour they were in the vicinity of the fleeing river craft and they could quite clearly see the jet boat careering very fast after the covered merchant vessels river craft. The sky hawks passed over the traders' boat and let loose with 20mm cannon striking the jet boat amidships, the second sky hawk also took the same course and with its twin cannons obliterated the jet boat in a tremendous roar and flash as the fuel was ignited and blew it into a thousand pieces.

Down below in the Traders boat just before the action started Tom and Jack and the rest of the

Crew didn't hear the sky hawks at all, but they ducked down as a great shadow passed over them, seconds later they hear the massive roar of the jet engines as the aircraft flew towards the jet boat, watching the shells hit the jet boat as if in slow motion seeing how the 20mm shells tore into the boat amidships as it was turning, the second air craft completely pulverised it, as it blew into a thousand pieces before their eyes. The sky hawks wheeled around making a second run over the heads of the river craft and its precious inhabitants, passing low, they could see the pilot as he saluted the marines, the shock waves from the jets making little waves and rivulets as he passed over, the second one also following close by.

The river had widened at this juncture, allowing the pilots to do a victory roll then swooping high into the air and as they separated to left and to right climbing steeply for their flight back to HMS Eagle.

The Chinese shaking their heads in disbelief: that this kind of warfare was happening right before their eyes.

Tom, Jack and the rest of the team breathed a sigh of relief at this latest turn of events, Bungy letting go a massive fart as he grinned at his fellow mates. "That's a relief!" he muttered.

They all grinned at one another. "He's always full of shit," Tom joked.

Turning to the Chinese Coxswain, Jack bellowed, "Okay Lee Kuan Yeeee, let's get the hell outa of here and fast. You SAVVY eh?" The little Chinese was nervous and disorientated but he recovered quickly and gunned the motors for more speed, they hadn't far to go now.

They settled down to a more even pace and soon the miles were swallowed up, the oppressive heat was building up, however the movement through the water brought a kind of cold clammy feel to their sweat drenched bodies. Tom lit up a slender panatela cigar; the aroma drifting around had a kind of calming effect. He could see the Chinese were grinning and gesticulating to Tom for a 'Freebie'. Tom thought what the hell, my gesture at international goodwill and friendship. He handed them a cigar each and watched as they lit up with pleasure written all over their faces. The chirping of the cicada's and the whooping of the monkey's added to the native ambience of the Borneo jungle.

Two hours later, they were in the vicinity of their pickup point and Tom crawled over to McPherson, making sure his friend McHenry was comfortable and still under sedation, he felt a lot of love for this happy go lucky Irishman, who it was a pleasure to be in his company.

Turning to McPherson, Tom said, "Send the code word ***'Bulldog'*** to HMS Eagle, we will be there very soon, Okay Mac?"

"Sure Tom! WILCO." McPherson had left his radio transmitter on; so now he pressed his mouth into the rubber mouthpiece and sent the message: ***"Bulldog, Bulldog, Bulldog!"***

Jin Tin was on the prow looking for the exact location they had first arrived in, seemed like a week ago, they were all dog tired red eyed, unshaven, sweat soaked and suffering from BO.

Jin Tin was now gesticulating to the Chinese helmsman to turn into a rather black looking hole which on entering was rather lofty with huge cavernous rain forest trees heavily buttressed on four sides, tendrils of some parasite growing leafy and dark green, foreboding, but still had that aura of evil, the hairs on the back of their necks stood up as if a sixth sense warned of some oppressive danger lurking.

The Chinese felt it too and were gazing around in total awe, their eyes stood out like organ stops. “Okay, let’s get unloaded and get ashore!” bellowed Jack.

“We haven’t got all day the chopper will be here soon, chop, chop, Lackey! Lackey!”

Tom just grinned, “Well, you heard the man get on wiv it!” Tom gently took hold of what passed for a rough litter that had held the frail body of McHenry during this tumultuous river journey, which had been successful so far. “Jack! Get the other end, will you?”

Jin Tin talked to the river traders and with a smile handed them his catch the fish he had caught during their epic journey. The traders were delighted as the fish were very big and a comparative delicacy for the Chinese. Even the heads they used for fish head soup with local spices.

Bungy was kneeling beside McHenry taking his temperature and heart beats and generally making sure he was as comfortable as possible, occasionally McH opened his eyes for a few seconds, just gave a week smile at Tom and the boys and fell back into his coma.

McPherson was on his transmitter and talking to the incoming Chopper pilot giving him the rather secluded pickup point that was first used for their insertion a few days ago. “Use the PE, make a fire and throw some wet wood and grass on it, he should see the smoke rising through the trees,” Jack ordered. Sure enough, the PE blazed rapidly until the wet soggy wood hit it and then the black smoke spiralled up and beyond the canopy, as a marker of their position.

“When you hear the chopper throw out an orange smoke canister, so the pilot has a definite sighting!” Tom added, with a throaty intonation in his voice. Taking off his Bergen and stretching his aching limbs, Tom glanced around him, feeling that they should recompense the river traders for what they had just gone through, better go and offer them a great deal more money.

Tom gestured to Jack to follow him back to the Chinese traders on the river craft.

Smiling at the Chinese, he shook their hands and said, “We thank you very much for your help!” he pointed around at his group, “Terima Kaseh Banyak!” this he hoped would be understood by the Chinese as they had lived out here all their lives and must have picked up the local lingo.

They in turn bowed and smiled in understanding. Turning to Jack, Tom quietly said to Jack, “Take out your stash and give half of it to me!” Jack turned his back to the Chinese and took out his bundle of local dollars (ringgit) which both he and Tom had kept dry in a sealable plastic bag, carefully he halved it, as did Tom with his stash. Both turned towards the Chinese and with as gracious as possible gesture gave the large bundle of money over to what they knew as being the Headman of the Traders. "Kung hoi Fat Choy!" Tom and Jack said laughing together. That was the only Chinese they knew other than the more vulgar words to Mama Sans for their younger female siblings affections.

The traders were very excited and went round hugging one another brandishing the large bundle like some kind of trophy, but really joyous, thanking the marines in very long and eloquent Chinese good wishes.

With a wave, the river traders left for their homeland, the Marines also smiling and waving them as they pulled out into the brown broad swollen river, back to their families and the stories they would tell their children for a very long time.

The sound of the chopper brought fresh hope and a surge of energy to the fatigued marines.

The orange coloured canister was flung out and the chopper duly appeared in amongst the cavernous interior, landing gently with a sigh as it touched down, all were loaded aboard.

McHenry was loaded first and gently lashed down by Bungy and Tom, Jack was last to board as he looked around the site to see that nothing was left to indicate that they had been there.

Lifting gently, the chopper did an 180° turn with nose slightly down she cruised out of the cavernous LZ. Tom donned the earphones. "Stick leader to pilot, can you land at Brunei Airport and drop off Jin Tin our Iban tracker?"

"Affirmative Stick leader, WILCO."

The breeze coming through the open door was refreshing, soon they were heading back to the Ship, passing over what looked like lush green ulu but the team knew it differently from ground level, always enchanting but at the same time hard graft with blood sweat and tears.

At last, a welcome sight HMS Eagle stood majestically at sea as the Wessex helicopter gently swooped down to her steel decks, landing perfectly and with a sigh shut down her motors, the blades slowly revolving, coming to rest so that her precious human cargo could be unloaded.

The captain and the flight deck officers peering curiously through the wrap around windows in the control tower, as the sick bay staff arrived to take charge of the wounded and badly beaten

Marine McHenry. Slowly and carefully, Tom, Jack and the rest of team Bungy Williams McPherson, declined any assistance but used the stretcher that they had brought and carried him to the lift well. Here they gave him over to the sick bay staff (SBA's) who would take good care of their beloved friend and oppo, McH.

Only here were they ushered away as the medical officer and his SBA's got on with the task of bringing McH back to good health.

Jack, out of the corner of his eye caught sight of a nurse, which he thought that's strange never seen a female aboard this carrier. He turned around to see Amelia Brooklyn smiling at him,

"Lyn," he shouted as he made his way over to her, his *fragrance* hitting her nostrils as she cautiously embraced him, unshaven, sweat covered with remains of the ulu still hanging from him and the Bren gun slung over his shoulder like a toy, but they both were all smiles and indeed glad to see each other again. "I'll talk to you later," she quietly said. She left to accompany McH to sick bay and surgery; she cast a shy look at Jack as she disappeared along the passage and companionways.

They stood there in the hangar looking around and taking off their gear and weapons. The master-at-arms appeared and in a loud commanding voice gave his instructions as to what he had organised for the rescue team.

"All weapons will be cleaned, thoroughly, oiled and put away in this cabin in a LOCKER we have specially prepared for you. This locker will be locked! There are also some bunk beds we have installed they should be quite comfortable; as I have one me-self. Meals will be at the regular time. All jungle bunny garments will be sent in a bag to the Chinese laundry who will then launder it for you! You lucky people eh? ALL webbing will be scrubbed as new so as any creepy crawlies will be annihilated, and get *yourselves* scrubbed down and shaved, SAVVY? Right! Get on wiv it ven; eh?"

Turning back, with a wink he said, "Well done lads!"

"I fought for a minute he was goin to charge us wiv somefink," muttered Bungy.

The lads just roared with laughter as they got on with unloading, unpacking and stripping down to bare essentials. "'Ere I hope your girlfrend don't come back when we is starkers, eh Jack?"

"Well, she'll certainly have something to remember?" Tom gestured with a grin.

With a will they took on cleaning their weapons first, all working parts laid out on a plastic tarp, the 'Jolly Jacks' appearing cautiously to observe the thoroughness of their cleaning and indeed noticing all the bright parts of the various weapons. As instructed, it was first of all inspected by the ships detachment 'Joey' Officer, all clean all passed and locked in the locker inside the cabin which had been specially erected for them in the 'Aircraft Hangar'.

The webbing was scrubbed clean and hung on the hooks which generally held the ropes and tackle of the fleet air arm engineers, mechanics, air frame fitters and the ammo party.

With towels draped around them they toddled off down the first ladder to the nearest bathroom for a much needed scrub-up.

All doors (or hatches) are heavy and also they are securely lockable and watertight for obvious reasons; inside there were rows and rows of stainless steel sinks and mirrors for the necessary 'scrape'. Along the back bulkheads and along the side were shower stalls, and to these they inserted their tired grimy bodies as the warm beautiful clean water cascaded over their tormented bodies, everyone had a grin on his face with such luxury.

Chapter 17
Plymouth, Devon, England

Linda had been very busy both in her little antique shop and what with visiting her beloved husband Chris in Stonehouse Hospital and indeed by being interviewed and photographed for various highly paid TV commercials; she really had no real downtime to relax in. BUT! She liked it! And the pure novelty of being recognised wherever she went was a new and thrilling experience.

The phone rang in the evening in her bedroom over the shop. She really wondered who could be ringing this late at night.

"Hello."

"This is Huw Haafter calling from the United States of America, just thought I'd make first base with you and make you an offer you can't refuse. Whad'ya say, if I book you on United American Airlines and ya come over here to see me in Los Angeles? For a photo shoot! I guarantee you won't be disappointed in my offer, whad'ya say gal?"

Linda was rocked back on her heels so to speak, "Well, I don't know really, I do have a lot of engagements, and also I've got to see to my husband, Chris, who is recovering from an amputation of his leg just under the knee. I really don't know what to say at the moment, naturally I am very interested as I have heard such lot about you and all those bunny girls you have in your Hollywood mansion…" she trailed off not knowing what else to say. (There was a brief silence.)

"This is the deal: you and your husband, Chris, will fly over together, I will get him the finest medical care that is available in America, he also will be fitted when he has recovered enough, with the latest prosthetic limb, I guarantee they are good, whad'ya say Linda?"

She thought that one out for a few seconds and replied, "Well, Huw how can I refuse, it's a deal! Arrange it and let me know the date and thank you very much for your truly wonderful offer; goodbye Huw!" She put down the phone and collapsed on the overstuffed bed, her head in the clouds.

A few days later at her shop on Union Street (Unionstrasse) Plymouth, a motorcyclist courier arrived in the doorway, handing over a fairly bulky package, which he asked her to sign for.

Excitedly, she tore open the package and was amazed that Huw had sent her $5,000 in cash and two airplane tickets for her and her husband Chris to fly to Los Angeles in America.

"WOW!" she exclaimed "What a GUY, 'EH! Doesn't do things by halves. Better see if we can get Chris ready and start packing."

There would be a lot of hurdles and protocol involved with moving Chris from medical facilities in England to transporting him by special ambulance and then a special compartment in the American aircraft. These things she would have to do and with the help of her father all would be accomplished, especially the new prosthetic limb that Huw had promised.

She lifted the phone and dialled her father in Admiralty House London. Angela Ransome answered, "Hello Admiralty House here; how can I help you?"

Linda replied, "Hello Angela, this is Linda speaking, could I have a word with my father Henry Cunningham?"

"Most certainly Linda; I'll put you through."

"Sir Henry, your daughter is on the phone." There was slight pause and a click and Linda began unfolding her story and request to her father, who listened with a great deal of interest and concern for his beautiful daughter who needed his help.

The doctors the nursing staff (QARNNS) lined up outside RNH Stonehouse Hospital, the nurses dressed in their navy blue capes as Chris was taken out to start his journey across the Atlantic to the new world where they hoped he would be fitted out with the very latest prosthetic limb. The nurses wore big smiles to wish him bon voyage and kissed him lightly as he passed by each of them.

The ambulance and the Bentley drove to the helicopter landing zone which was selected because of its size; known locally as the 'Brickfields' primarily used for school/RN/RM sporting events. Lady Cunningham, with tears in her eyes, gave Linda a blue velvet case. "These were your grandmother's special jewels, and they mean a lot to the family, my darling." She hugged her daughter that only a mother's passion could bestow.

They had placed Chris into a special wheelchair; two muscular marines from Support Company, 43 Commando. RM lifted him easily into the navy blue RN helicopter, leaping carefully aboard to secure Chris to the bulkhead just below the pilot's compartment. Chris had a smile on his face as he was once again flying, not piloting but still it gave him a surge and a thrill to be airborne. The marines touched his shoulder as they left with a wink they had gone.

He watched them as they lithely jumped onto the grass pitch, remembering his youth, which seemed so far away now.

Linda crushed into the side of him, her perfume and her closeness was intoxicatingly provocative and he remembered the softness of her satin smooth body, her long legs wrapped around him in the many passionate sexual love affairs they had ultimately enjoyed together, and he would never, never, give her up, no matter what.

The long rotors began their sweep as the avgas engines started to whine and eventually with supreme power she lifted off, with head slightly down she headed off for London Airport for the flight to Los Angeles via New York. Lady Cunningham waving them goodbye as she tearfully wept at the hope of (a) a safe journey and (b) the prospect for her son-in-law to get the finest medical treatment known to man and also hopefully a new prosthetic limb so that he could walk once more, with her beautiful daughter Linda.

At London airport, they were met by a military ambulance and driven the short distance to the overseas terminal, thence to the waiting throng of people awaiting their turn to board the United American Airlines plane. However, the officers in charge of the plane had been forewarned that Lt Chris Davenport and his wife, Linda, would be high priority passengers, so the throng parted as two burly security guards whisked them through to be accommodated in the first class part of the aircraft. He was treated like a major celebrity especially by the very attractive American stewardesses; Linda kept a watchful eye on them but gave way to the natural fondness that the stewardesses imparted on this handsome marine officer.

It was a pleasant journey and time seemed to pass incredibly quickly, as always the stewardesses very busy, but always having time and patience with all the passengers and especially with Chris and his charming wife, Linda. The American accent of the mid-west and the rather more accentuated well-educated English accent of Linda turned heads as they discussed all manner of personal and private experiences. Linda also mentioned her trip to Singapore, which the stewardesses were familiar with, having landed and stayed there on their regular flight routes.

With hugs and kisses to all the flight attendants, Linda and Chris left the ambience of the airplane and with a wheel chair provided by the airline they made their way to customs for their checkout procedure. It was arranged that they would board another flight tomorrow morning for their onward flight to Los Angeles. The customs officials couldn't have been more nice and welcomed them as if they were their own kinfolk, they especially joshed Lt Chris Davenport and gushed over Linda with eyes sparkling in the lights of the airport. Actually, Linda got a little flushed with all this attention and a faint blush rose in her cheeks, to which the rather tall young handsome customs officials got a bang out of; winking at one another they opened the way to the outside departure hall and lounge watching her every move as she elegantly strode to the rotating carousel for her baggage.

She needn't have worried about it, as a young smart chauffer appeared, saluted her and introduced himself with a Texas drawl, "Ma'am, I'm your driver and my name is Ross! I've been instructed to look after ya'all so just follow me to the front door where the Chrysler Continental will be our transportation to the Noo York Waldorf Astoria. Could you identify your luggage ma'am?"

As they drove through the streets of New York, Linda was awe struck with the towering masses of buildings, she really had no idea how magnificent they actually were, having only seen photographs of them in the glossy magazines, but to see them up close and the clamour on the streets, the endless amounts of people; well she was dumb struck. Chris too was very quiet and seemed lost in his own world; Linda snuggled up to him and whispered something in his ear which seemed to brighten him up considerably.

The big Chrysler Continental pulled up to the forecourt of the Hotel, the smart well dressed doorman in dark green with gold buttons opened the rear doors for Linda who gracefully exited the car with just a peek at her long ivory legs, "Welcome ma'am to the Waldorf Astoria. Allow me to help your wounded friend; I'll get a wheelchair for him, ma'am."

"Thank you! That would be very kind of you," as she looked him over with those startlingly green eyes of hers.

He saluted and left for the doorway and signalled a bellhop to his side, whispered in his ear and turned again to help with the unloading of her cases, the chauffer also being of great assistance to Linda and Chris.

She entered a great reception hall, the floor of imported black and white veined marble shone like jewelled stars in the sky, the huge towering marble columns of Greco Romanesque design reminded her of the 1930s such attention to detail of the mahogany panelling and finally the reception desk itself, a specimen of man's ultimate design of pure opulence in craftsmanship.

She took control of the wheelchair herself and approached the reception staff.

"Welcome to the Waldorf ma'am, I assume you are the Hon Linda Davenport from England together with your husband Christopher Davenport," smiling, he cocked his head slightly for her answer.

"Yes! Quite right, it's a pleasure to be here in this rather lavish hotel," she smiled back at him with a smile that seemed to light up the place, white even teeth, white surrounds to her beautiful green eyes, certainly very desirable thought the mature desk clerk, as he bent to check her in, ringing a small bell for one of the bellhops to attend Linda's luggage which was being transported in a very ornate baggage trolley.

Turning to the bellhop, he just said, "Room 739. Hope you have a pleasant stay, ma'am."

The elevator quickly sped them upwards, complete of course, with elevator music softly played

The view was just fantastic of the New York skyscrapers and the Hudson River and Bay. One of the queens was heading out to sea, sounding her horn as she left with streamers and the gay pennants floating after her.

A South American maid entered the suite and smiling at Linda she just said, "These came for you senora, they are very beautiful, Quey Lynda!"

Linda bent down to smell the lovely bouquet of flowers and smiled at the dark-skinned maid as she turned to leave. She read the note attached it was from Huw, "Welcome to the USA looking forward to meeting you tomorrow Love Huw!"

Just then the phone rang, "Hello."

"I guess it's you, Linda? Don't worry about anything, every courtesy is being accorded to you and Chris; hope the journey didn't tire you out too much!"

"On the contrary, we quite enjoyed the trip and everyone was absolutely super, couldn't have wished for a nicer group of people."

"That's swell! So, until tomorrow then, Linda. Bye for now." The phone clicked off and Linda mused about tomorrow.

The chauffer Ross had brought up the luggage and was busy unpacking just enough 'stuff' that Chris and Linda would need for tonight; for it was assumed to be a suitable dress code in the hotel's rather exclusive restaurant. As for tomorrow they would have to be off fairly early for their flight to Los Angeles, so they would need travelling clothes. Ross the chauffer said as he was leaving, "If you need me ma'am, I am in the adjoining room; just use the 'bleeper' I have given you, just press once, thank you ma'am." He closed the massive doors with a bow.

Linda kneeling at Chris's wheelchair and as always was chatting to him about what they would be doing tomorrow and how exciting to be in America, Chris was just smiling and watching her facial expressions with a degree of love they had both become aware of, he didn't say much as Linda made up for his lack of conversation, I suppose that is why he found her both attractive as well as a good conversationalist. He remembered that in the officers' mess they were always surrounded by young and the mature Royal Marine Officers from 2nd lieutenants to lt colonels and sometimes on rare occasions Generals. She was captivatingly beautiful with a good acumen for business. Chris just held her hand and gazed in her eyes, *I am a lucky man,* he thought.

Still talking, she wheeled him into the enormous bathroom with all the trimmings of a parisienne *la salles de bains les toilet!* Linda looked around wide-eyed and so did Chris who was grinning from ear to ear, "We're in heaven!"

With that, she slowly undressed in front of him twirling her lingerie around her fingers and looking directly at him with a huge smile on her face. "Ah, you're so right, mon cherie!" she declared as she then started to disrobe him, carefully, slowly, to avoid any hurt to him.

***

She looked at herself in the very gold ornate mirror which actually seemed to fill the room.

"Now what should I wear with this gorgeous black dress, Chris?" He eyed her as she opened the blue velvet case her mother had given her. In it was just three pieces of jewellery. There was a genuine natural pearl necklace from around about the 1920s. A diamond brooch that split into two, to make earrings; together with a neat not ostentatious necklace made around the same period. The diamonds shone in the huge overhead chandelier as she looked at them to choose which! The triple string Pearl necklace or the diamonds?

Chris solved it and just said, "The diamonds go well with your black dress, wear those." *He was right*, she thought, *exactly right.*

Ross the chauffer had chosen well for Chris, he had laid out his Officer Mess dress, which looked really great against Linda's captivating beauty of black; ivory white skin and glittering diamonds.

She took hold of the wheelchair handles and led off to the elevator and swung into the hotel's restaurant which occupied the very top floor. It was surely the most breathtaking restaurant she had ever seen. Huge expansive floor to ceiling windows looked out onto the New York skyline, twinkling lights of the buildings and beyond lay the Hudson River and Bay, plying to and fro were the big liners and the little tug boats and river craft going about their business even as the night wore on. She thought, *I'm in the city that never sleeps!*

A waiter approached them smiling and beckoning said, "This way Ma'am we have a reserve table for you and your husband."

Chris looked rather resplendent in his Marine officers mess dress, black trousers with the thin red line down; although of course the other was tucked into the wheelchair seating. The bolero style jacket was red with very dark navy blue lapel facings, his one and only miniature medal proudly on display, above it were his gold wings which signified he was a marine pilot, he looked quite dashing with his blond close cropped hair, military style.

She perused the menu proffered to her as the waiter offered her and Chris the customary wine taste for their approval.

There was a band playing quite the right kind of music which captivated both Chris and Linda in the background with the white tuxedo coated band leader, conducting the orchestra, playing the 'Moonlight Serenade' very apt, very melodious and very nostalgic for both of them.

Watching them from across the room was a United States Marine General who unusual as it were was dining alone as he was on his way to London the next day. He was in his dress blues and must have been in the marines for quite some time as he had rows and rows of medal ribbons on his chest. He watched them in very close scrutiny observing all the little details that only can be made after a rather intensive life in the marine corps.

He beckoned the nearest waiter, "Say, would you mind approaching that British couple over there and ask them if I may join them for dinner; here take my card and present it to them, will ya?"

"Of course, sir." The waiter reached their table and presented the card and pointed to the General's table.

The General waved and smiled in their direction. The waiter reported back to the general that indeed they would be delighted if he joined them.

After the customary introductions and handshakes, General Beydler was curious about Chris's missing lower leg, "Say what happened to your leg, Lootenant?" Chris didn't answer for a moment as he was thinking how best to answer whilst at the same time raising his soup spoon to taste the delights of roast garlic and tomato soup which smelled really good.

"I was to deliver some officers from the tri services into fairly dense terrain in the jungles of Sarawak, Borneo in Southeast Asia. I was piloting the new Lynx helicopter which was fairly new to the fleet air arm and indeed also to the Royal Marines."

(Chris paused here for effect and another spoonful of delicious garlic/tomato soup), the General interjected at this pause and said, "Say! I heard of that chopper! They said it can fly upside down, is that true?"

"Well, as I was carrying some high ranking officers, I really didn't try that stunt!"

The General laughed at this remark, "Go on, Lootenant, tell me more!"

"Well, the next thing I heard as we topped over a rather large feature was whoosh and a deafening explosion on my tail rotor, which of course sent the chopper into fits and swirls of ever decreasing spirals until finally we splashed down into rather unpleasant ooze which quickly enveloped the aircraft and we sank slowly into a greenish hell. My navigator and co-pilot was badly sliced through the head and looking at him I knew he was dead. So I unbuckled and groped around the side of the aircraft, but it had landed on the left side (port side) where the door was, I could not open it as it was in the slime of the swamp and I just had to get topside to get some air. I was experiencing some excruciating pain in my lower leg and really I just could not help my comrades at all, more's the pity.

"The Kalimantan Army were quickly on the scene and took me into captivity until I was rescued by a group of Royal Marine Commandos who had been specially selected to find and rescue me; in may I say very trying and exhausting conditions out there."

It was also the first time Linda had heard this side of the story and it filled her with some pride as she had also been a party to this selection of the 'Special Group'.

"Goddamnit, if you all had been in the US Marines every goddamn one of you would've got the silver star at least!"

"Mighty brave boys, I can tell you."

Linda smiled at him as he made these outbursts and just kept tasting her soup, being mindful of not getting any down between her curvaceous ivory breasts. The General turned his attention to Linda wanting to get to know who this beautiful young lady was. "Say, I seem to remember seeing your face somewhere, but for the life of me I cannot remember."

Linda replied, "Maybe it was in the *New York Times* recently."

"Hell yeah! That's where I've seen you in Singapore and then again in London, Yeah, that's it for sure. So why are you and your husband here in the USA?"

"There are two reasons why we're here one is for Chris to get a prosthetic limb; we've been told that they produce the finest in the world, due to the demand from your own veteran community, wounded and loss of limbs from the Viet-Nam conflict."

The General looked concerned and a little pleased that she should know so much about their advances in that particular field and yes he thought she's right they have got them much better than at any time in history.

"And the second reason?" he asked.

Linda blushed a little and smiled at him as she replied, "Well, I'm here to do a photo shoot in Los Angeles with Huw Haafter at his mansion."

The General sat back in his chair and surveyed the pair of them, who looked to all the world such innocent, decent people.

"Well, if I was you I'd certainly keep an eye on him he's one tough hombre! An he always gits what he wants!" the General warned.

"I'll certainly remember what you say, General!" Linda replied.

They didn't speak for a while as they were into the main course and it was just too delicious to talk, but instead just the occasional glance and a smile from all parties.

"Say, would you mind if I get a photograph of all three of us, my wife would be delighted to see ya all? By the way I'm flying off to London tomorrah, gotta have a talk with some top brass in your government hierarchy, maybe I could post the photo's off to your parents, if that's okay with you both?" The General grinning at them, how could they refuse?

"Of course, General, we would be delighted," Linda answered for them both.

The photographer was duly summoned and the group was taken very professionally and when they later saw the pictures the General was ecstatic with them. "Gee whizz, we sure do look swell!" turning to the photographer, he said, "Say buddy, can we order six prints of that photograph?"

"Certainly sir!" The General took a large swig of his imported wine and was a very happy man to have met such a nice couple as the Davenports.

The dessert arrived which was also delicious; no words were spoken as they consumed it with absolute pleasure.

The General leaned back in his carver chair raising his glass just beamed and said, "Here's to you Linda and to you young lieutenant. Hope you have a very happy time in the USA and for the rest of your life may it be fruitful and kind to you both!"

They all raised their glasses and drank to the toast. Tapping his finger on the table for emphasis he said, "I fly out to London tomorrah, so if you give me an address I can post them to, I will certainly get em off pronto!"

Linda wrote out her father's contact address in London, as that is where the General would be landing on arrival in England. She handed him the slip of Waldorf Astoria notepaper with the London address on complete with telephone number.

A puzzled look crossed his face as he read the notepaper, "Goddamnit, you mean your father is Sir Henry Cunningham and he is one of the lords of the Admiralty?" He looked at Linda and then at Chris. "Waal, I'll be blowed! I sure will look him up and tell him what a great daughter and son-in-law he has. I'm much obliged; wait till I tell my wife, Martha, she'll be tickled pink." With that, he pulled out a big cigar, lit it and sat back comfortably with self a contented grin.

Chapter 18
HMS Bulwark, on Station
Southeast Asia

There was a gentle knocking on the cabin door that sufficed for the accommodation for the 'Rescue Team' housed in the aircraft hangar. "YEAH come in!" roared Jack. The gentle knocking persisted. Jack roused himself and wrenched open the door. He was about to get physically inclined; however, standing there in her nurse's whites was Amelia Brooklyn looking very clean, wholesome and dare I say delectable! "Lynn!" Jack burst out, "How nice to see you, won't you come in?"

"Er…no thanks Jack, is there somewhere we can talk?"

Jack quickly donned his shirt and led her away to the Aft Gun Sponson. The sun was going down in the west. "What a beautiful sunset," she remarked, looking up at Jack with an admiring look of love and tenderness in her eyes. There were marines and a couple of sailors on the Sponson; however, one by one they quietly left to give them a bit of privacy. Her lips were red and full bodied; her blue eyes were clear and her perfume invaded his senses. "I might not see you for a while, Jack. I'm flying out tomorrow with McHenry to BMH Singapore, so I just thought I would see you to say goodbye."

Jack's big hands took hold of her, gently pulling her towards him and kissed her long and passionately.

"Lynn, I will miss you very much. We will keep in touch and someday soon we will be together."

Lynn was a bit breathless and just kissed him back with equal passion. "Sooner rather than later, Jack!" she chided him with a smile.

Hand-in-hand, Jack escorted her back to the Sick Bay, to say a final farewell, embracing her gently as she turned to go.

Jack returned to the cabin in the hangar, smelling of 'Roses' and looking a little flushed and sheepish. He lay down on his bunk clasping his hands behind his head, just stared into space and said nothing. The boys noticed his mood and started joshing and chipping him.

"Hey up, Jack, is she the one eh? She's a real cracker that one, there's not many in a pack like that, eh boys?" They were all grinning at Jack's embarrassment.

"Why don't you all just zip up?"

Jack grumbled. Later, after they had their 'Ki' (Hot Cocoa) and buttered roll; last pipe was sounded and Jack and the boys drifted off into their own Dreamland.

At 0600 hrs Jack, Tom and the boys were rudely awakened with the early morning 'Pipe' on the Ships radio system, followed by an equally rude on duty 'killick' (Leading Seamen) in the 'watchroom' "Wakey, wakey, rise and shine, hands off cocks and on with socks, wakey wakey, you've had your time, now let me have mine!"

Like robots, the boys rose in unison wrapped their towels around them grabbed their shaving gear in the green wallet and just mechanically made their way to the heads and shower stalls.

***

Later on that day the Master-at-Arms appeared in the doorway of the cabin. The boys stood up and waited for whatever was going to be passing through those bad and broken teeth of his.

"All of the Rescue Team are to be deployed to Brigade HQ on the mainland; the CO. Colonel Loden wishes to speak to you for your further orders. Is that CLEAR?"

They all replied in unison, "Yes sir, very good sir!"

"Just one question," asked Jack, "WOT toime are we heading orf?"

The Master-at-Arms closed in on Jack, tapping his heavy ebony cane of office on Jack's muscular chest. He looked up at Jack and said "Get your gear together and when I say GO! YOU GO, is that CLEAR?"

"Yes sir! Absolutely sir! Like crystal!"

He looked around the cabin and left with a warning, "Get this cabin cleaned out thoroughly, UNDERSTOOD?"

"YES SIR, ABSOLUTELY, SIR!"

The team lined up on the steel flight deck, crouched down as a 'stick', waiting for the pilot to give the thumbs up for entry into the Wessex helicopter. Their newly pressed tailored jungle greens, fighting order, green berets, (except for Bungy who had his navy blue beret on with his navy brass badge), gleaming weapons and their Bergens at the carry.

"Okay let's move out!" growled Tom; as he bent low to avoid any possible contact with the rotor blades. In file they clambered aboard the chopper, Tom donned the earphones and reported to the pilot that the 'stick' was aboard and ready for lift-off.

Each member of the team had his own thoughts and reminisces of his life and his ambitions, some for promotion and others just to get home to girl friends or relatives that gave them much happiness, however they still kept an eye out for where they were heading for and took in all the strange sights of this tropical land. They were travelling over a great green sea and then they saw the beaches, the palm trees swaying in the breeze, little children running on the beach and waving at the British helicopter as if it was a very strange looking contraption from a different world. Then they were flashing swiftly past small townships and then it was all jungle clad as far as the eye could see, interspersed with large kampongs on the rivers edges.

"Pilot to stick leader, we will be landing in approximately five minutes; do you read me over?"

"Stick leader to pilot; message understood over and out!"

Tom stuck five fingers in the air to his team, which everyone understood. They started getting their gear within easy reach.

The first port of call was to the QM's Basha where they were required to surrender their weapons and any other ordnance that they possessed. QMS Fred Hayhurst was delighted to see them. "Back again boys, glad you made it!" he said with a grin. "Where are we off to this time?"

"Dunno Q, we just go where we 'is' ordered," Jack whimsically replied.

They stood on the same wooden decking, looking at the same wooden building they had done, seemed like months ago, being inspected by the same domineering RSM Chisel. "Well, well, well! What do we have the pleasure of this time?" he said with a grin. His steely gaze missed nothing, but this time he did not say anything cryptic or derogatory. He just stroked his moustache and perambulated up and down the platform, never taking his eyes of any one of them for very long, finally with a ramrod posture he ordered, "ATTEN-SHUN! Right turn, quick march, left wheel (into the CO's office they marched). HALT! Right turn; salute."

"Thank you RSM, stand the men at ease."

"STAND AT EASE!"

The CO spoke, “Behind you are some chairs, bring them nearer to my desk so we can talk, I want you to stay RSM and I’ve also asked my clerk and our intelligence Officer Major Tapling in; so we can have all the information of your recent Rescue Mission; it’s intended to be an in depth de-brief, so that we are all aware of all the activities on your part.”

There then followed a long two hour de-brief on each marine’s movements, each giving exactly what they had done and the sequence of events. It was all recorded by the CO. Also Major Tapling and the HQ Company Clerk. Later all the information would be analysed and compiled into a very detailed account of their rescue mission.

The CO looked quite pleased with all the information which he would have to submit to his higher commanders and generals. Rising from his chair he said, “Thank you gentlemen for your patience and input. However, here is the comparative good news! For the rescue team. Jin Tin, your Iban tracker has sent an invitation to attend his wedding which will take place tomorrow. I have no doubt it will be one you will never forget!” he grinned broadly as he said this.

“I am sending you with an armed platoon which will be led by Sgt Cliffold, the LMG group led by Cpl Lawson. Just remember you’re British; and may you have a good time.”

The RSM marched them out again.

“Phew that was some hard yakka! You roughie toughies are something else! Give us a smoke Tom, I need a burn to calm me down,” Bungy grumbled on.

“What are going to take for a wedding present?” asked Jack. “How about a bag of golf clubs,” grinned Bungy, wheezing as he said it.

Tom turned to Jack, “Listen, we’ve still got a bundle of notes that we kept back from our last rescue mission; you give him what you have left and I’ll give him mine; okay?”

Jack’s face brightened. “Yeah! Good idea, Tom.”

“Problem solved,” Tom replied.

“How about some Chinese five star brandy! And some nutty for the kids too, eh…” Bungy chipped in.

“Good idea!” everyone chorused.

***

The next day, dawn saw them on the river, in two heavy duty rubber Gemini's heading towards Jin Tin's Longhouse which lay right on the river, there was a fairly long wooden jetty that looked like it had been there a hundred years or more; however it could still bear their weight as they came alongside, to offload and disembark.

Once ashore, the LC Coxswains waved farewell and left in a roaring broadside sweeping curve and headed back to base camp.

Hefting their Bergens and weapons, they headed up the jetty to be met at the end by the older headman and his equally old wife who must have been at least sixty plus years old. Little half naked, cute children, some with runny noses ran amongst the marines laughing and tugging at them for anything that was free. (Known as Buckshee in England.) The old headman welcomed them in his native tongue; with huge smiles all round, they were led up by the old couple up a fairly hefty tree trunk, at the top of which was a carved head of one of their gods or a talisman. The old man reverently clasped his hands together bowed and touched the head as he passed onto the raised decking of the Longhouse. Not wishing to upset anyone, all the marines did the same. Being an old sweat, Sgt Clifford in his Cornish drawl ordered the marines to make sure their safety catches were on and then line up down the far end of the Longhouse, whilst he surveyed the amenities and the defensive positions if needed. "Okay, lay your gear down just relax for the time being, keep a close watch on your weapons, one man to be on guard at intervals around the clock. Mind your head on the heads (ancient skulls of past enemies)." These hung down in baskets near the edge of the decking.

As this was a wedding day, all kinds of food had been placed out on the spotlessly clean close woven reed mats. Everyone was smiling in welcoming the marines, shy glances and giggles coming from various groups of them. They were dressed in their finest sarongs; the breasts were left bare with just a tiny native necklace around the upper breasts.

Below to the right of the Longhouse; smoke was rising from what appeared at first to be a pile of banana leaves. A young boy of about 11years old started to speak to the marines in English, to which the marines warmed to him as he was able to explain what was going on and what was being said and prepared for the wedding of Jin Tin and his bride who he said would not arrive until later in the day when everything was perfect and ready for all guests. They asked the boy about the smoke rising from the leaves, he laughed and said that it was the Iban way of cooking one of their delicacies, ‘a pig’. Apparently, very early morning the men would light a big fire, when it got very hot with all woods red hot then they chose a time to put flat smooth rocks on the burning embers then either cut the pig up or gut it and lower it onto the flat stones covering it with larger woods and also the banana leaves this would cover and hold the heat in, cooking it like a pressure cooker style and be very tasty from special herbs which had been added to it.

In the longhouse were many quite spacious apartments where each family lived, the whole ‘kampong’ was one big family group. The longhouse might cover about two or three hundred yards and were built on sturdy hard wood stilts, this kept them above any water level in the monsoon season. Of course there were bigger Longhouses as each group started to increase.

In a small recess; there stood brass gongs each size from small to large thus giving a different sound. The gongs had a raised inverted cup in the centre this presumably for a more shrill sound, at these sort of gatherings they were played rather robustly and with great effect on the crowds of families.

The half-naked little children looked wide-eyed at the marines sitting close up to them and to the marines looked very cute and appealing. Jan Slade fished into his pouch and brought out his 24 hour pack nutty bag. The cry went up from the kids as he dished out, mars bars, Rowntrees’ fruit gums, Wrigleys’ chewing gum and chocolate blocks. Of course all the marines had a pack of these but would spread it out over the time they were there in the Longhouse.

The SBA Bungy Williams was as always very busy with minor cuts bruises and stomach upsets. But there was one that was more serious than he could handle.

Bungy decided he had to get McPherson over to his makeshift RAP and see ‘IF’ Mac could signal for a chopper to take this woman and her little child who was in a critical condition and needed surgery in a hospital, the child was in an unconscious condition and looked very poorly, the little child really needed more professional care.

“Ere Mac! Can you get on the blower and ask for a Casevac medicare flight at our location?”

“Sure Bungy, I’ll send the request out to Brigade HQ. Be back in a sec to confirm your request.”

Twenty five minutes later they heard the sound of the helicopter which was where it got its name from chopping its way through the air, finally landing with its skids balancing on the edge of the wooden jetty, two marines had gone down to the jetty to guide the chopper in and help with the precarious embarkation of the woman and child. Bungy had also decided to send one other woman and he sick child as he couldn't figure out what had gone wrong with her newborn baby, which had an odd odour emanating from its breath.

The chopper balancing precariously on just one skid waited and was successful in embarking the two women and their babies, and with a wave and thumbs up from the two marines gradually lifted off carefully and flew to the nearest hospital for much needed treatment.

Bungy got to the end of the waiting queue and arose saying, "I need a fag and a drink of somefink!"

"TEA OKAY BUNGY!" the marines chorused.

"'Ere I fought we had some coffee in these Asian packs, don't we?"

Jan Slade dug into his pack and found the re sealable plastic bag of coffee wandered over to the young Iban girls who were boiling the water, proffering the mug and with some sign language they poured some hot water into the mug, retracing his steps to put the tube of condensed milk and a couple of spoonfuls of sugar, "Here ya go bungy a nice cuppa coffey, what else do ya want?"

Bungy sidled over to Tom and Jack's position, Tom was having a nice cup of tea and one of his slim panatelas, "'Ere Tom can ya spare wun fer me?"

Tom just smiled dug into his breast pocket where he kept one or two slim cigars in a special plastic cigar container, handing bungy the cigar he said, "I suppose you want ignition too eh?"

Sgt Cliffold approached Bungy, "Here! You'd better have a tot of rum in your coffee Eh? Put hair on your chest!"

"Cheers Sarge. Didn't know you cared!"

Bungy grinned as he walked away, mumbling, "Bloody roughie toughies."

Bungy wandered out onto the rear decking and contentedly puffed away on his freebie!"

Time went by fairly quickly, the young Iban girls inviting the 'Boys' to eat some of their prepared delicacies. Which they did try out; finding the taste quite different to normal English, European food. Meanwhile, Bungy on the rear decking noticed a Quarter Deck bronze cannon.

The sound of a native style conch shell sounded and the brass gongs began to be beaten with really resonant tones, it was to alert the kampong to the arrival by boat of the bride-to-be.

The two marines had stayed at the end of the Jetty style wharf in order to assist with the docking of this specially painted and prepared wedding vessel.

The bride was quite young and very beautifully and exquisitely made up; her younger sisters were her assistants or bridesmaids; they too were very young and very attractive.

Now, I am going to try and remember the Iban names for what she wore; as it has been a very long time ago. She wore; starting from her headdress: A Sugu Tinggi (High headgear) Rawaii Tinggi (high corset with rattan coils with small brass rings). Kain Patating (Sarong or petticoat with small bells on the bottom). She also had Antin Perak (Silver stud earrings).

The younger Iban men came out onto the jetty to escort her and her accompanying family ‘party’ in welcome to their Longhouse. They wore the Baju Gagong (Tough animal skin shirt) and their Sirat (Leather loincloth) they also had a type of lightly feathered headdress. In their hands were ceremonial staffs, which had a square solid hardwood cage; inside of which was also an ironbark (*Belian*) square block about 2in or 50mm in length and about 1in or 25mm square they were a loose fitting and able to move up and down in the cage.

These were being banged onto the boards and made a clacking noise and apparently were to drive all the evil spirits away from their longhouse.

The-bride-to-be moved with an easy grace in bare feet and with head bent shyly traversed the length of the jetty mounting the simple tree pole that afforded the only entrance to the Longhouse, presumably this pole could be jettisoned should they be attacked.

The agility of the young was most apparent from a lifetime of physical tasks that purified the body and strengthened it. The headman, Jin Tin’s father, met the bride and made her very welcome, in a semi serious manner but nonetheless sincere and friendly as if welcoming another daughter. After the welcome, she was led away to an apartment (*bilek*) that would be suitable for the finishing touches to her attire and makeup, also I suppose where she could have a drink of some refreshing liquid or maybe just ice cold water. The marines stood at the back of the wedding throng but saw everything that was happening; being head and shoulders above anyone there. The little children had taken to adopting the tall Marines looking up at them with wide-eyed curiosity and holding their hands.

Finally, the moment had arrived as Jin Tin appeared looking rather resplendent in his traditional Iban costume 'Ngepan' and Labang Packau (headgear) He stood facing his father and waited for his 'bride-to-be', to follow him. She came out with her little sisters; the gongs were being sounded, something like the Nepalese chimes. Then it was quiet as the ceremony then took place. The marines hoisted the little children onto their shoulders so that they could have a bird's eye view of what was happening, their little heads nearly touching the cross beams, but they were very happy with joy.

Whilst all of this was going on the young men and the elders were going in a very great circle around the Longhouse and still using their ceremonial staffs were 'clacking' along to ward off evil spirits.

After what seemed like a lifetime, the ceremony was over and the bridegroom and his bride were free to enter their new apartment specially built in the Longhouse.

However, knowing that the marines were their honoured guests; Jin Tin brought over his bride to meet with them. Jin Tin spoke their names to his bride who looked very shy but offered her hand in friendship. Jin Tin got to Tom and Jack who were smiling broadly at Jin Tin. Jack just stretched out and hugged him, the look of surprise on Jin Tin's face was unforgettable, letting him go, Jack gave him his *present* of the wad of money left over from their last mission.

Tom was next, big, broad and very handsome Tom looked at the bride with some interest and she caught his gaze and flashed him a bright smile and looked away rather shyly. Tom hugged Jin Tin as well and thanked him saying in Malay, "Terimah Kaseh Jin Tin!" Tom also gave him his wad of money, this would certainly cement good relationships all round.

The festivities were about to begin, each marine was given a cupful of 'Arac or Tuac' which was very strong alcoholic rice wine, but the marines did not know how strong this was, however as time passed by they did get to know!! Out came the Chinese 'Five Star Brandy'.

And that was dished out to all who wanted to partake of it. Jan Luscombe remarked as imbibed it, to Tom, "Don't light up when you're drinking this stuff Tom! It's lethal!" Tom just grinned but decided to take his advice.

Good humour and friendship was the order of the day, the girls passing by bare breasted with bamboo trays of their special dishes encouraging the marines to be tempted to eat all they could. All the time the Iban men were still chanting and clacking with their iron wood ceremonial staffs nonstop, like a rhythmic sound a sort of background cacophony.

The afternoon passed into evening, all the area was cleared, Jin Tin had departed with his bride, and so the dancing by the girls began, joined by now the marines who were rather ‘Shiters’ having consumed the necessary quantity of rice wine and Chinese five star brandy.

But they danced around rather clumsily but getting a good response from the children who roared with laughter at their befuddled attempts at dancing in bare feet.

The dancing stopped for a little breather; Marine Gregg standing on the decking at the entrance to the Longhouse, dressed only in a pair of beach shorts or trunks got everyone’s attention, by raising his arms and bending of one knee in the stance of a judo expert. (He had been attending the Singapore judo club.) He was going to demonstrate ALL the movements in the warm-up to a judo international match. His motions and summersaults with both hands then one hand, then no hands, were phenomenal his facial expressions was also evident, he was one of those boys that had very clean cut features. The gongs had been brought into play as he went about the tremendously powerful physical display; this lasted for a full twenty minutes, after which he was bathed in sweat, which glistened off his lightly tanned body. The small Iban boys and the gathered families, gave him a resounding round of applause, it truly was a magnificent display of physical fitness, prowess and skill.

Even Sgt Cliffold had tried to relax, and had joined in the bare foot dancing but he did feel awkward and danced like Capt Bligh, (of the Bounty fame) but he had a smile on his face which was rare for him.

The evening wore on and little by little the Marines were left on the reed decking, talking in groups, smoking and drinking whatever they thought was alcoholic.

Sgt Cliffold spoke seriously to everyone to make sure they looked after their weapons, to which Jan Luscombe laughed. “Pay attention, Luscombe, I’m not talking about your private parts, just listen up, EH?”

He detailed off Cpl Lawson and his LMG section to go forward to the Longhouse entrance; he would go to the rear decking where he had a good observation, the rest he just positioned in a fairly tight group to the centre of the Longhouse. “You know the routine fellas, fasten your slings to your wrists, that way you won’t lose it, eh?”

It was good day, the wedding was very colourful and the ambience was great, the welcome was second to none, friendships had been made with the Ibans, who no doubt would talk about it for a long time. Tom lit a cigar sat back on his Bergen and with a cup of coffee, thought about Linda, her image appearing in his mind's eye, her black hair and green eyes, he remembered her so well.

Tom must have dozed off; he felt a tugging at his sleeve and a little voice saying quietly as in a whisper in his ear, "Wake up tuan, wake up!"

The decking was dimly lit as everyone had gone to their apartments to sleep. A little boy who had spoken to them in English was looking intently at him as he gradually regained his consciousness.

"What is it?" he asked the boy.

The boy just grinned. "You please come with me, tuan." (Sir.)

He led him to one of the apartments, opening the door just wide enough to enter, a young woman had prepared a special drink of green tea which smelled very aromatic, she gestured for him to take it and drink it. She was still dressed in her sarong and as was the custom, bare breasted. Her skin was a lot lighter than most of the Ibans, her breasts were firm and thrust their way forward, the nipples very large and protruding, the aureole around it was also abundant. Tom remembered her from earlier when he had been surveying all the females in the Longhouse nothing missed Tom's scrutiny.

The boy spoke quietly, "She; her name is Pannggaan, lost her husband in battle six months ago, she want you to stay with her, it is permissible. She can select who she wants; you like, tuan?" The boy looked at him in a kind of pleading manner. Tom took a while looking from the boy then back at the woman who was quite desirable and clearly smitten with Tom's good looks. His mind was made up and he nodded to the boy and smiled at the Woman Pannggaan. Her face and her eyes lit up and she smiled showing her beautiful white teeth and full, darkly coloured lips.

The young boy headed for his cot and pulled the shabby curtains closed, the accommodation was dimly lit, casting flickering shadows across her face and her pale coloured breasts and skin. Tom was certainly getting aroused and just slowly took her sarong away to reveal her undulating tummy her slender waist and lightly tanned thighs, her legs had a nice shape and sheen like a gentle glow of healthy skin. He unbuttoned his olive green shirt revealing his muscular chest with just enough hair on the pectorals, and let it fall to the floor, he unbuckled the tabs at each side of his waistband, she had gone to her knees and was slowly unbuttoning his trousers, and they fell away to the floor as his member sprang out erect and throbbing. She looked up at him, the dim light catching a sparkle from her eyes. Gently, she took hold of his member and still looking at him slid back his foreskin revealing the pink moist head, slowly and deliberately she slid her lips down trying to get as much into her mouth as possible, her tongue played over the end of his member tantalizingly, erotic and beautiful. He gently stroked her hair and moved her head slightly from side to side, giving the oral more sensitivity and producing an intimate sucking noise, she let go for a minute and licked the end of his member, whilst still looking at him in an affectionate way. He led her to the raised platform bed and laid her down gently, it was a fairly hard bed not having the luxury of any spring interior. Her legs, she spread enticingly, Tom sucked her brown nipples which stood out provocatively long, his member finding its own way into the moist lips of her vagina. Slowly, he began his penetration of her; she was very uninhibited and started to moan with the sheer ecstasy of her joy in the joining of them both in this exotic sexual intercourse.

***

Chapter 19
Waldorf Astoria

General Beydler met up with Linda and Chris the next day in the lobby of the Waldorf Hotel, purely by chance, as they were all going to catch their flights, Linda and Chris to Los Angeles on a domestic and the General to London at the international terminal. The General was dressed in a very smart dark blue business suit sporting a homburg and to complete his purely British look he had bought an umbrella which he raised in the air on catching sight of them, grinning from ear to ear as he greeted them. He raised his homburg to Linda and just said,

"Mighty glad to see you this morning, whad'ya think of this umbrella, just thought I oughta be prepared for your English weather!"

"My, my, General you certainly do look rather smart and dare I say 'spiffing'. What do you think Chris?"

Chris with a grin on his face just said, "Yes, quite different!"

Linda countered, "When you do get a chance to see my parents give them our love, tell them we are being well looked after and are happy."

"I sure will and I'm mighty glad to have met your acquaintance, hope you find everything to your satisfaction in Los Angeles, good luck with the photo shoot! Lootenant I sure hope the prosthetic limb is a great success, so I'll bid ya'll good bye!" with that he kissed Linda's hand and went out for his waiting yellow cab.

The enigmatic chauffer, ex-US Marine, Ross, had helped with their packing and in general had made it very easy and simple for Linda as she wasn't a particularly tidy person when it came to stowing things away neatly.

Having completed the register signing at the hotel desk, the chauffer led them to the waiting Lincoln continental for their journey to the Airport JFK, for their last leg of the journey to Los Angeles.

After take-off they both marvelled at the New York Skyline as the plane tipped and levelled and tipped again for the passengers to see the giant skyscrapers and indeed the extent of the Grand Central Park in the centre of a bustling city that never sleeps.

They kept climbing to the normal cruising height of about 35,000 feet, the clouds were below them like candy floss, although travelling at somewhere in the 580 miles per hour bracket it just seemed like they were just drifting along at a leisurely pace. Familiar names kept popping into their heads as they journeyed west. Philadelphia, Baltimore, Washington DC, Then the vast states, and towns like Illinois, Missouri, Kansas, Tennessee, Arkansas, Oklahoma, then the majestic Rocky Mountains, with the Grand Canyon, Utah, then California, finally landing in a perfect touchdown at Los Angeles. All this Linda shared with Chris and he seemed lifted in spirits as she spoke lovingly to him about these places she had only heard of in the movies.

The United American Airlines stewards and stewardesses had looked after them very well and in a way they were both sad to leave them, just before they were due to depart one of the senior stewardesses, blonde hair, blue eyes a very wide smile with perfect teeth, approached Linda, and said quite excitedly, “Huw Haafter has contacted us and just said you will be picked up by his chauffer in the departure lounge!” Linda just smiled and nodded and held out her hand to say goodbye. However, the excitement of seeing Los Angeles and indeed the prospect of what lay before them compensated for their temporary loss.

They were escorted by one of the stewards who had got Chris on his wheelchair and taken to the VIP lounge. Linda looked down through the enormous plate glass windows onto the departure terminal hall and she was astounded at the mixture of people and races all excitedly milling to and fro to their various destinations and flights. It seemed to Linda that indeed this could well be termed the ‘Melting pot of the world’.

A tall, rather tough looking man approached them, dressed in a western style cream shirt, well embroidered, with tan trousers, cowboy boots with Cuban heels and sporting a real western Texas style wide brimmed hat, he had a tied pony tail dangling out of the rear of the ten gallon hat.

“Howdy ma’am, I’m here to take ya’all to see Mr Haafter, I was told to look for the most beautiful girl in the world so I guess that must be you!” he smiled one of his most friendly smiles. He glanced down at Chris in the wheelchair, “I also heard a lot about you Lootenant, mighty glad to make your acquaintance sir! My name’s Hank,” he shook Chris’s hand.

With that he just said, “Follow me, folks.” As he pushed the wheelchair, he gave out the luggage numbers to a waiting Negro porter and just said, “Collect their baggage and deliver it to the Cadillac outside, pronto!”

“Are you the chauffer we were told to expect?” Linda enquired.

“Well ma’am, I’m kinda of chauffer and also I’ve been with Huw for a very long time and I’m kinda of his ‘gofer’!”

He smiled at her at her perplexed expression. “Don’t you worry, ma’am. We’ll take good care of you!”

They left the airport terminal for the waiting Cadillac which was an open tourer (drophead) probably dating from 1958 but in an absolute pristine condition, long sleek and typically Hollywood style, white with red leather interior.

As they drove along through Los Angeles, Hank would point out the various places of interest, Sunset Boulevard, sunset strip, muscle beach where all the great and famous bodybuilders trained, getting a good suntan as they were training. Up through Mulholland drive and up into the millionaires paradise in Beverley Hills and then higher.

Huw Haafter’s mansion was absolutely astounding in both size and grandeur, no expense spared in its construction. Linda and Chris gazed at it in amazement. The Cadillac drove up the long driveway, coming to rest at the open porte-cochere`re or Portico.

Huw Haafter was on the steps along with some of his devoted staff and his glamorous house pets. Chris was astounded at their beauty, as they surrounded him twittering and giggling.

“Welcome to Los Angeles and welcome to the ‘House of Dreams’. It’s very good to meet you Linda! And the brave lootenant, welcome, welcome my dear friends!” Huw was, as always dressed in his robe, as casual as you would expect him to be, gushing with pride and happiness at seeing them both. “Let me show you around the place it has a few surprises believe me!”

Linda was intrigued at this casual remark.

Huw turned to Hank and just said, “Hank take their luggage up to no 10.” Huw smiled as he said this. They mounted the steps and entered a great open foyer, the floor of which was imported Italian veined marble; two staircases led up on either side to an upper floor, richly decorated in carved mahogany, a touch here and there of solid gold fittings and balustrade.

Linda wheeled Chris into the hall and he too was quite aghast at the design and attention to detail of the construction of such a residence, he just thought it’s the best money can buy.

The glamour girls still giggling and flirting with Chris led them into the main lounge room which was high lofted, an enormous, spectacular stone fireplace reached up into the vaulted ceiling, made from American redwood spliced with pine.

Huw had summoned all of his staff and introduced them individually to Linda and Chris.

Everyone beaming with delight at meeting these two English guests, who had overnight become world celebrities. Huw also introduced his photographic team, who he explained to Chris and Linda that they would be seeing a lot of them tomorrow in the studios for the extensive photo shoots, which would also be done on some outside locations.

Huw turned to Chris and with genuine affection and concern said, "Tomorrow Lootenant we are going to take you to the 'Rosemary Meadow Medical Facility Clinic', where you will be well looked after and when they feel that your wounds are fully consolidated, so they can get to work and make sure you've got the finest prosthetic limb possible, hey! You'll be able to walk again and maybe run, they're that good! Many of our Viet-Nam vets swear by them!"

"In the meantime folks, take the lift to your floor and freshen up for Lunch which will be at 1230, listen for the gong!"

Chapter 20
Kampong – Lillico

It was getting light; Tom had been awakened by the cocks crowing and knew instinctively he must leave his treasured Iban woman for the decking outside her apartment. Dressing in his OGs, he gently bent down and kissed her tenderly as she awoke from her sleep, dewy-eyed and smelling of a native musk perfume, she smiled as she remembered her night of nights with this handsome, strong, marine, she would have tales to tell or maybe just to remember. Her arms reached out to him as he bade her a silent farewell, "Goodbye my flower of the East!" he said quietly.

Then he was gone; through the rough wooden door picking his way gingerly over the feet of his Platoon, but not missed by the ever watchful eye of Sergeant Cliffold who it seemed only slept with one eye open. He smiled to himself and thought the 'Lucky Bastard'.

The cocks and hens below were now in full throttle and together with the snorting and grunting of the pigs foraging for any scraps of food thrown down on them from above became quite a farmyard affair. Slowly, the kampong became alive and the young bare breasted girls appeared from their various apartments to get on with the daily preparations and the chanting of the young men was again in full swing as the wedding was still an ongoing celebration.

Food (*Makan*) was no problem as the villagers had got it all worked out. Down below was a fire and on the fire suspended a giant *Wok or Pot* and I do mean giant, spanning about 3ft in diameter and made of thick steel or might be cast iron. In this wok went nearly everything of an edible nature; meat, pork, vegetables, egg foo yung noodles, as well as spices and at the last minute dozens of eggs all beaten in vast bowls, the whole kip and kaboodle was spun round rapidly by one of the Iban cooks, who had started early morning and was sweating profusely but happily stirring his pot for everyone the smell was really appetising the marines losing no time in fishing out their MESS tins and mugs queuing up behind the other villagers and the invited wedding guests.

Standing on the decking overlooking the mass of bodies below him he addressed the marines in his usual Cornish drawl, "Now listen up you fella's after you've got your scran down and had your Nutty bars, I want you saddled up and ready to move out by 0900 hrs, that clear?"

All just grinned and chorused, "Yes Sergeant, absolutely; 0900 hrs! Roger that!"

"'Ere doesn't he ever shut up!" Bungy murmured to Jack and Tom. They just slapped him on the back, and said that's Mr Ed, he's just going through the routine he always dun!"

Soon, it was time to move out fully booted and spurred as the saying goes. Tom sought out *Jin Tin* which was not easy as he would be in the bridal apartment that he had had built for him and his lovely bride, but he engaged the boy who he knew, that was the son of Pannggaan. Jin Tin appeared grinning from ear to ear, "Yes Tuan Tom, you wish to speak with me?"

Tom put his arm around his shoulders and hugged him in close friendship, "Listen! Look after Pannggaan for me will you Jin Tin?"

He looked up at Tom and with a serious look on his face he said, "I will Tuan Tom." The whole kampong lined up on the verandas and the open windows to wave the marines off with cheerful grins from everyone and in particular Tom sought a glimpse of Pannggaan who was leaning out of her window, her pale skin in contrast to the rest of the villagers, her upthrust perfect bare breasts was a very great treat for Tom as the platoon made its way out along one of the trails leading to the border, where their patrol would begin and last for at least seven days and as usual totally in the dense jungles of Borneo. The wedding celebration would go on for another three days and three nights.

***

Chapter 21
Hollywood Hills

The alfresco lunch was set up near the large ornate gardens and blue shimmering pool, all of his 'Pets' wore their different coloured bikinis of red, gold, green and pale blue. It was like a scene from a movie set, except this was for real, Huw Haafter surveyed his new kingdom and indeed was a very satisfied man with his accomplishments although initially it hadn't been easy for him with the vast criticism from the established press, due to its semi erotism of his models and pictures, but now he had made the grade and was a very fortunate man.

He gave Hank his bodyguard and right hand man the signal for sounding the gong for lunch, which could be heard in all parts of the grand house.

Linda and Chris had settled into their palatial room and had dressed in suitable attire for this luncheon. Chris sat in his wheelchair looking every bit the handsome young marine officer.

The lift or elevator was a copy of one that Huw had seen in Paris, France, which fitted in with all of his luxury fittings and grand designs.

All heads turned as Linda and Chris entered the covered patio area where a grand spread of all types of foods, were decorously laid out. Linda had a black Chinese dressing gown embroidered with large dragons, Chinese scenes and mythological characters all in gold, red, green and deep blues. The glamorous girls gathered around Linda and Chris admiring the rather beautiful Chinese style kimono touching the motifs and with exclamations of admiration. Chris was in the middle of all this admiring the curvaceous curves of the different races on view as they wobbled like a jelly on a plate, he had a permanent grin on his face, rather like a nervous disorder he just couldn't help it, a little twitch started in his left eye and the surging in his wedding tackle was rising uncontrollably.

Huw came amongst the penthouse pets and selected a girl on each arm and with a grin shouted, "Okay gang let's eat!" with that they all made for the heavily laden tables of every kind of sea food and fruits. The latest recording of the Beach Boys was playing in the background, a few of the pets had decided to float decorously in the large extensive horizon pool as it seemed to go on forever and cascade down into the valley below where all of Los Angeles was a mirage.

Huw sat with Linda and Chris chatting amiably all the time, but also extracting very subtly the background information he sought from them both. "Tomorrow we start on the photo shoot Linda; and for you my boy. Hank and myself and your good lady will take you to the Rosemary Fields Clinic, a medical facility, for your new prosthetic limb. Now there is no need to worry you will receive the best possible treatment known to man, I guarantee it!" he smiled, showing rows of perfect white teeth.

He turned to Hank and in his own inimitable style he said, "Hank can you bring the coach around after lunch, I'd just like to show everyone the sights of Los Angeles and particularly to our English friends, I'm, sure they will appreciate some good old American scenery."

"Sure, boss. My pleasure," Hank replied.

Chris didn't say much but he was certainly very happy in the present surroundings he just kept smiling as first one, then another, of the most beautiful girls in world came up to him to ask where was his home town and how long had he been in the Royal Marines and "Gee we have marines too, right here in San Diego and also in Quantico!"

Chris just smiled and said, "Yes, I know, we have regular contacts with them and sometimes we have joint exercises in the jungles of Asia, we also met up with the first batch of US Marines heading for Viet-Nam. In actual fact one of the Pilots aboard the USS Kittyhawk, a Lt/Colonel Mike Beaurhanse extracted my Lynx helicopter from its watery grave in Borneo, thereby saving a lot of expense to the British Government and indeed I was truly grateful he had rescued it!"

Wide-eyed, they all looked at him with greater interest and trust. One or two of the girls blurted out, "Say; where is Borneo Lootenant?" Chris looks a bit amused at their Naivety and just looked around at their inquisitive beautiful faces.

He spied Hank in the background, waving his arms and calling out, "Hank can I have a minute over here please!"

"Yeah Lootenant what's your pleasure?"

"Do you have a world globe anywhere in the house?"

"Sure have! Lootenant; you want me to bring it to ya?"

"That would be fine Hank, thank you!"

Hank brought the globe in on a trolley it was so big. The girls clustered around Chris and the enormous revolving technicolour globe. Chris then pointed out where they were situated at the moment then slowly revolved the planet describing each major land mass and ocean as he slowly made his way to the other side of the world to where they never knew of the presence of the Asian world or indeed of its inhabitants. They were in awe of Chris as he described the people and their customs, it was when he came to describe the head hunters of Borneo that they gave out gasps of unbelief and wanted to know more about his duties in Borneo.

Turning around they asked Linda, Miss Linda did you go to BORNEO? "No my darlings I only went to Singapore near Malaya. It's called Lion City and was founded by an Englishman called Stamford Raffles as a free port which in time became a British Colony."

"Say, you two guys have travelled a lot and know lottsa things," one of the taller girls exclaimed.

Linda replied, "Well, I assume because we just travel in different circles than you do; and I'm quite sure you will know more about your part of the world than we do, maybe we'll get to know more about your history too."

The girls looked a little sheepish as not one of them had done any serious reading, content just to be photographic models and make hay whilst the sun shines. However, there was a serious glint in the tall girl's eyes as she took all of the well-educated English beauty's comments and grammar in to heart.

Huw had been listening to all of this geographical data and their explanations of peoples and their customs and beliefs of each and every country and island that was crossed in their circumnavigation of the beautiful globe he had had in his possession for a very long time but never really had taken much interest in it until now, with the absorbing observations and knowledge of these two British new found friends. Huw looked up at the blue, blue sky in deep contemplation and resolved that he would like to read more and do some serious research that surely would enrich his life; for he thought "Knowledge is like power. Isn't it?"

A new awareness came into Huw's mind that indeed this young English couple, especially Linda, who was both beautiful and had an amazing knowledge of the finer things in life of both nationally and internationally deeply entrenched knowledge, which he found excited him and was of exquisite value. The ambience around the pool with the their new found friends was electric and thrilling all at the same time, Linda wasted no time in searching out each and every one of their backgrounds and asking pretty ordinary questions whilst at the same time she looked into their eyes which she always assumed were the windows of the soul. The girls were impressed with them both and indeed at one stage they were utterly surrounded with laughing, giggling, noisy, long legged beauties. A gong was sounded and Huw Haafter stood and informed the girls that the bus would arrive very soon and to get a wrap for the sightseeing tour of Los Angeles. The girls all were giggling, as the bus rounded the corner of the house and stood majestically in the driveway, and what a bus it was the very latest in streamlined design built by Bentley in Crewe, England, not their usual product but they had respected the demands of Huw and built a handmade modern sleek bus. Leather hand stitched seats, panoramic windows double glazed, neat tables for the cocktail cut glasses all were made at Waterford in Ireland, no expense was spared in this lavish new bus, and of course powered by one of Bentley's most robust diesel engines. Chris was lifted into the bus on his wheelchair then all the girls chattering and laughing boarded having found their wraps to cover their modesty a little, and so their tour of Loss Angeles started with prominent features pointed out by the tall Texan Hank no doubt with much gusto and the pride of a truly dyed in the wool American.

***

It was night time in the Kuwaiti Desert a lone figure was leading a white camel on which was riding another figure dressed in her burqa to protect her against the extreme cold of the night desert winds. Beneath the burqa she was adorned in a royal blue kaftan with long white linen pants, her boots were meant for riding and had a fairly high heel to fit into the camel's stirrups they were of the finest Moroccan brown soft leather. Her right leg was curled around what the Europeans would call the pommel; her left hand gripped this leather covered phalanx symbol as they swayed and rolled like a ship in an undulating motion at sea.

The kaftan was embroidered with gold emblems of their tribe and faith, her head was covered in a shemagh or shlemiel of the most exquisite design with solid gold coins and pierced filigree ornamentation hanging loosely past her ears, her face was beautifully made up in the arabesque style, her skin was like very fine ivory alabaster plaster smooth and sensuous; heavy black makeup around her eyes and ruby red lips which were full and provocative.

The sand of the desert at night resembles white snow, the sky above is a rich indigo blue colour, and the stars are so bright your eyes are drawn compellingly upwards to see the majesty of creation; it's as if you are travelling through space on a magic carpet, they are so real you can almost seem to touch them, the moon acting as a luminary by night.

The young girl's name was Jasmine and her brother Mustapha was leading the camel into Kuwait, he had finally found a deserving rich man to give his sister away to in a solemn marriage that he had promised his young sister he would find for her. Jasmine was not at all afraid anymore of what lay ahead in her marriage to a much older man, she was confident of the woman's role in a marriage that had to be arranged, she had learnt a lot from the English woman she had witnessed in their lovemaking and she had decided she would become the most desirable of all of the older man's concubines or wives, she was young eager and very beautiful, she would rise to be the best of his household, not by sly methods but purely and simply by love of everyone she would encounter in this strange new adventure. She would copy the English woman's art of pure sexual enjoyment and the power of love she had witnessed her exercising over the rather good-looking tall Englishman, Paul. She decided that she and her ageing husband would have a son and he would be the most handsome of the household and one day would be head of the family she was going to join, in marriage. She also had the dream of her son becoming very rich, well loved by all of his contemporises and subordinates, that he would one day would lead, into a better future for all of the Arab world.

Epilogue

Linda became a very successful photographic model and was snapped up by MGM in Hollywood starring in many espionage and undercover spy films which were located in Prague and Warsaw, filmed in black and white to give the story all the authenticity of the real world behind the Iron Curtain.

Lt Chris Davenport was fitted with the latest prosthetic limb and had to get used to walking and manoeuvrings that would be required. He was not discharged from the Royal Marine Corps but kept on to train other young officers to be the best combat pilots in the world. The stipulation was that if he could pass the fitness programme every year including the assault course with his prosthesis limb, then he would continue his service career; however, he had to go back every two years to have a new prosthetic limb fitted. Eventually, they became so advanced and sophisticated in their development that one could hardly tell he had a false limb at all as they were to become fitted with a computer which could discern what movements he wished to perform, including waterproofing and swimming. Chris was steadily promoted to the rank of major and he truly was a great inspiration to all of his officers and marines alike.

Tom, Jack, McHenry, Young and Bungy Williams the Naval SBA, continued their service in South East Asia and returned home to England in time for the corps tercentenary of 1964. This celebrated 300 years of service as marine corps since 1664.

The Royal Review was conducted at Buckingham Palace and the Queen inspected all ranks of the serving and indeed the preserved marines from their various RMA Branches. They were dressed in ceremonial dress blues, lovats and combat dress. Amongst them stood Marines Tom Martial, Jack Trench, McHenry, Dave Younger and SBA Bungy Williams newly promoted to Petty Officer, sporting now a fully grown beard, which looked a lot better than the stubble he had on in Borneo. A special couple had been flown in aboard an RAF family flight from Kuching, Sarawak in Borneo and that was Jin Tin and his pretty wife, dressed in a very resplendent Iban ceremonial dress, complete with a short version of the Parang or it could have been the Malay Kris. After the official inspection by the Queen, the Commandant General pointed out the marines who had taken part in a daring rescue of a downed helicopter pilot in Borneo.

The Queen spoke to each of them and with a lt col carrying an official tray which contained the MM for Marine Tom Martial, MM for Marine Jack Trench, and mentioned in despatches for Marine McHenry and Marine Young also for Petty Officer Williams the QGM. The Queen with the help of the Commandant General pinned these medals on the marines' very proud chests. The Queen also spoke to Jin Tin and his wife and he was awarded the MSM for his role and tracking skills in the rescue operation. It was deemed a very important exercise in international public relations with winning hearts and minds. Jin Tin had never seen anything like this spectacle in all of his life and would be the topic of conversation in his Longhouse for years to come.

RM19461 Marine Johnny Lees got married the previous year in August 1963 to Phyllis Wigston formerly from Belfast Northern Ireland in a whirlwind romance and travelled extensively in the Corps, serving in 42, 43, 45, 43, 40 Commandos in the Royal Marines.

But that's another story.

Linda gave birth a few years later to twins, the girl had blonde hair and the boy had black hair.

Tom was tragically killed in Malaya in 1968, the marines of 'S' Company last saw him waving from the Bell 47 helicopter; strapped to the side basket as he was being air lifted to the Military Hospital in Kuala Lumpur. Unfortunately, he died of his wounds, leaving behind a very beautiful wife named Judith. He lies in the Roman Catholic Churchyard at Crown Hill in Plymouth, Devon, England.

Jack French later married Lynn whom he met a year or two later in Devon. She had decided to become a veterinarian. Jack rose through the ranks serving in Northern Ireland as an RSM, later he was promoted to LIEUTENANT. RM.

"Per mare per Terram."

Plymouth Hoe, Devon.

The Royal Marines on Parade on the HOE at Plymouth in Devon England in 1964 to celebrate the Corps Tercentenary, 1664–1964.